BLACKLEG BATTLEGROUND

Lightnings danced and crashed and their thunder was like cannonfire.

From the lead wagon, Darby Curtis kept his eyes on the climbing ground ahead and to the east. At first, as a sheeting rain began to fall, he saw nothing. Then there was a hint of motion in the haze and he focused there. He felt his scalp drawing tight below his hatband.

On the rise beyond the wagons lance tips sprouted, then roached headdresses with eagle feathers whipping in the wind. In an instant the prairie was alive with mounted warriors descending on the wagon train at a dead run. Darby clutched his rifle.

"Blacklegs!" he yelled.

And dove into the cluttered wagon box . . .

THE
SUNDOWN
BREED

BY DAN PARKINSON

ZEBRA BOOKS
KENSINGTON PUBLISHING CORP.

ZEBRA BOOKS

are published by

Kensington Publishing Corp.
475 Park Avenue South
New York, NY 10016

First printing: July 1986

Printed in the United States of America

For Virginia, James, Jeffrey and Catherine

—All in different ways adventurers, each in all ways the best of the Sundown Breed.

PART I
The Venturists

I

The old frame saddle was wide and lumpy. Its leather was stained and cracked. It squeaked with each movement of the huge mule carrying it, adding notes to the clatter and clank of the pack train. Darby Curtis swung a long leg over the bracing, shifting from sidesaddle to straddle, easing the soreness of his rump.

The tall mule, John Adams, ambling along an uphill trail carrying Darby's hundred and eighty pounds and an equal weight of possibles and tack, turned lazy ears at the motion, then ignored him. He moved as though he carried no burden at all. Delicate hooves selected easy footing on a path that was no more than an old trace through the redlands. John Adams stood nineteen hands at the withers and was barrel-broad, long-limbed and graceful. Alert long ears tested the wind. Intelligent large eyes studied the trail and the wild land around it. The mule knew more about terrain and travel than his rider did, and Darby was content to let him call the shots.

Flanking him on the right was Hildegarde, her bell clanking steadily as she walked.

Hildegarde was as big as John Adams, and her load—like those packed aboard the eleven mules following them—would have exhausted a saddle horse in a very few miles. Yet, like her brother, Hildegarde moved with grace and a steadfast purpose that devoured miles each day without falter or balk.

Of all the mules, Hildegarde was the steadiest—a natural leader, though she lacked the smooth gait of John Adams.

9

So Darby rode John Adams beside Hildegarde, and Hildegarde led the train.

The rest of the mules were unbridled. So long as Darby had Hildegarde, he had them all. They followed her because they chose to, and each of them carried a pair of great packs that one day soon would be money in Darby's pocket.

Where the trail was narrow the mules moved single-file, a string of tall animals dwarfed by huge packs, strung out over a hundred yards. There were Madison and Hamilton, Fanny May and Lucifer, Monroe, Washington and Beelzebub, Jefferson, Longhandle, and Sam and Bernice bringing up the rear. Even the smallest of them, the short-hocked Sam, stood a full six feet high at the withers and was broad and powerful as a dray horse, though more slender of hip and leg. Their inquisitive, sensitive eyes studied the unfamiliar terrain as they moved, and long ears swiveled to study each sound on the wind.

This was new country to them, though Darby had studied the map. From Arrow Bend to the new settlement at Vernon was roughly three hundred miles. Chance Curtis had said it should take him twenty days. Darby figured to make it in fifteen.

Here was a region of hills and breaks, where trails were old and seldom used and wound between steep bluffs and brushy canyons with the cunning of the animals that had first made them. The vegetation was scrub, thick in some sheltered places, sparse where the sun and wind could work. The soil was hard and red, laden with shards of blood-red stone and chips of clay. It crackled and crunched beneath the delicate hooves of the mules, and a thin red fog of dust hung in the air where they had passed. Nettles clustered on open hillsides, standing above the gray-green grass, and clumps of scrub oak stood in the valleys. Field birds warbled in the thickets hiding from the mid-day sun. A single dark hawk circled above, distant but far nearer than the cottonball clouds that lazed beyond, islands in a turquoise sea of sky.

Puckering dry lips, Darby Curtis whistled a few notes of

10

"The Bonny Blue Flag," and John Adams's ears turned toward him in curiosity. To his right, Hildegarde snorted. Darby turned in the frame saddle and looked back. The trace was wider here, and the mules had closed up. Four or five mules back, Lucifer did a little dance and launched a friendly kick at Madison. Madison dodged nimbly, then arched his neck to nip Lucifer on the rump with strong teeth. Darby grunted. A man who didn't know mules would think those two hated each other. The fact was, though, that Lucifer and Madison usually were partners in crime. What mischief one of them couldn't think up, the other usually could.

Far back of the train, riding easy on his line-back dun horse, Vincent Copple waved as Darby turned around. Even at this distance, Darby could see the flash of the black man's teeth, the glint of sunlight on the big buffalo rifle he carried. In this year of 1865, with the war in the east so newly resolved and the whole country unsettled, a man carrying valuables went armed. And he brought along his friends. Vince Copple was a quiet man, reserved and shy in the way of one who has once been a slave. But he had eyes that could see and the sense to know what he was seeing, and Darby knew for a fact he could hit what he aimed at with that big old gun.

Though not as tall as Darby's lanky six-foot-two, Vince Copple was bigger, more than two hundred pounds of shy smile and rippling muscle wrapped in skin so deeply brown as to be almost black.

Chance Curtis, Darby's father, had found Vince hiding in a thicket ten years earlier. Chance had been on his way west with a brace of vicious jackass studs and a dozen or so huge draft mares of the breed called Oldenburg. He had the notion he could make do in the mule breeding business and was on his way to try. But his help had gone off and left him and he had problems. So he fed the frightened Negro, gave him a coil of good rope and a stout club and put him in charge of the jackasses. "Keep 'em moving along," he told Vincent. "Don't let 'em kill you—which they will if they get the chance—and don't let 'em kill each other. And keep 'em away from those mares. They ain't up to that kind of thing 'til we get home and I nail up a plank for 'em to stand on."

Far from the plantations of the east—and from the war when it later came—Vince Copple could have gone his way once the herd was delivered to Curtis's spread in the Smoky Hill territory. But he had stayed. And the mules they traveled with now were the offspring of those same great mares and those two mean jacks.

Darby Curtis had been no more than fifteen at the time, but neither he nor his mother had been especially surprised when Chance Curtis—gone east to buy equipment to start a steam mill—had returned instead with giant mares, a pair of jacks and a black man. Such was not unusual behavior for Chance Curtis.

Hildegarde snorted again, her ears turning forward. Darby swung around. A horseman had appeared atop a rise ahead, and now came toward them at a run. Darby waved, then twitched the reins and John Adams increased his pace to a steady trot.

Trinidad Salazar bent low over the extended neck of his favorite mustard pony and rode as though the devil were on his tail. With each long pace of the racing pony he dusted its rump with his wide hat. *"Moros!"* he shouted. *"Los Indios! Veinte! Treinta! Alla!"*

Indians! Darby drew one of the pair of repeating rifles strapped to John Adams's saddle frame. At the Spaniard's approach, the lead mules halted, those behind closed up and Vince Copple spurred forward.

Salazar skidded his pony into a rump-down stop and waved his hat. *"Vagabundos! Veinte o más! Allá!"* Excitement flashed in his dark eyes. He pointed toward the crest. *"Los Moros desplazados! Bandidos Indios! Carretas con buyes trabajas y muchos Moros! Mira . . . allá!"*

John Adams's head was high, inquisitive ears cocked ahead. He snorted and Hildegarde answered with a loud bray that brought the other mules crowding in, a tight cluster of large, bright-eyed animals dwarfed beneath high packs.

Now there was frenzy atop the climbing rise. Tall slab-side wagons crested there drawn by four pairs of oxen. The wagons were linked tongue-to-tail, three of them in tandem. A dark-haired man rode the high box of the lead wagon. He ducked as an arrow flicked past him. He shouted and flailed his animals with words and oiled reins. The oxen loped down the trail, a pace akin to racing for them but still slow, still methodical. A thrown bright lance caromed off the lead wagon's fore corner. The cursing driver ducked out of sight in the deep boot, then came up feeding paper loads into an old carbine.

A shotgun's roar echoed. A gray-bearded rider on a dancing roan charged down on a knot of painted warriors, firing as he came. They scattered and he raced through, swinging his spent weapon. An arrow whisked past his face.

"Blacklegs!" Darby Curtis shouted. He raised his rifle and fired, heeling John Adams at the same time, tugging rein as he lowered his gun. The saddled mule and Hildegarde considered the situation, then decided to agree with him.

With a lunge, John Adams veered aside, off the trail.

A low bluff stood there, ninety yards away, and the mules strung out toward it, Hildegarde on her rein now taking the lead. Trinidad Salazar and Vincent Copple hung back, letting the last mule pass before they swung in on the flanks, defending.

Up a grass slope through scattered brush the mules trotted, Madison breaking into a lope to skirt a stand of salt cedar before rejoining the train. The Indians had seen them, and a dozen or more broke off from harrying the wagons to gallop across toward them, lances high, bows strung and arrows nocked. Two of them carried rifles. As one brought his to his shoulder Trini Salazar drew a long pistol and made a sweeping charge, shouting in Spanish as he emptied the revolver among them. No Indians fell, but it stopped them. They spread, broke into ones and twos and scattered both ways into the brush. The ox wagons had turned now, making for the same bluff, following the mule train, and the man on the roan raced around the long rig,

13

two revolvers blazing, driving warriors back. Up on the tall box the dark-haired man had set his gun aside and was crouched, whipping the reins, urging the oxen on.

Three mounted warriors bolted from a thicket and ran toward the wagons, trying to cut them off, turn them back. With a fresh pistol from his saddle holsters Trini Salazar stood in the stirrups and let his mustard pony run, belly down, directly at the three. *"Arriba! Andale, Andale!"* The gun roared, almost a continuous thunder as he veered past the warriors so close that the leader's horse reared and plunged, throwing its rider into a cedar clump.

The mules had reached the bluff. For a moment Vince Copple was beside Darby. His eyes were wide. "If that Spaniard could hit anything he'd be a marvel to see."

A feathered lance drooped from the pommel of the mustard pony's saddle, flopping crazily as he ran. Caught between charging braves, Salazar ducked low over his saddlehorn and ran, making for the bluff. Atop John Adams, Darby swung his rifle, sighted and took one of the Indians off his horse. The other swerved away.

For once in his life, Darby thought, the Spaniard had not exaggerated. More than twenty Indians, he had said. At a glance, Darby decided the count was nearer to forty.

The tall wagons were coming up the slope, their driver ducking as Indians rode by on either side, loosing arrows. Then a lance took his off lead ox in the neck and the animal sagged in its traces, bringing the assemblage to a tangled, shuddering stop. They were eighty yards away. Darby heard the delighted yipping of Blacklegs as bright-painted warriors circled beyond, assembling for a rush. He picked one out, held a bead on his wishbone and fired. The Indian flipped over his mount's rump and was gone.

From the flank of the huddled mule herd Vince Copple leveled his big rifle methodically and blew a howling warrior into some better world, then worked his action and aimed again to cover the shouting man who had leaped from the lead wagon and was running upslope toward them.

Trini Salazar had his pony under control now, just to one side of the driver's path. A feathered warrior broke from the ring, heeling his horse and drawing his bow. Salazar wrenched the flopping lance loose from his pommel, turned it and hurled it at the warrior. Bright feathers rippled in the sunlight. *"Viva Aragón!"* he shouted. *"Muerte a los Moros!"* The shaft thudded into a bullhide shield, almost knocking the warrior from his mount.

"Whoof!" Copple exclaimed. "That Spaniard's a spear-chunker!"

The running driver reached the mules and dodged behind John Adams. "Holy Mother!" he panted, then glared up at Darby. "You might have come out after me. You need an invitation or what?"

Darby bristled, opened his mouth, then closed it again. "You're welcome," he growled. "What are you doin' out here?"

"How should I know?" the man snapped, pressing a load into a battle-worn carbine. "It's Mr. Poole's rig. I just drive."

"What I want to know," Darby pressed, "is what you're hauling. What is it those Blacklegs want?"

"Not a thing in those wagons but saltpeter. What are you carrying?"

"Trade goods." Darby snapped a shot at a cluster of braves heading their way, waving lances. His eyes narrowed as he glanced toward the crest of the trail, several hundred yards away. Three mounted Indians sat their horses there, silhouetted against the sky. One was a tall, feathered warrior who held a crook lance and a dark, circular shield. Darby squinted. "Bird," he said, and pointed. "That's Bird out there."

The man glanced up at him, then away. "Saints preserve," he rasped. "The yokel knows these heathen by their names."

The bearded man on the roan had disappeared beyond the trail. Now he came again, lunging up from a cedar clump directly behind a pair of mounted warriors. The roan lunged, plowing between the two, shoving their horses aside. As he went through the man drew up his legs and kicked violently to both sides. Heavy boots caught one mount on a shoulder, the other on a cheek, jarring them. They shied, tried to turn and went down in a tangle of mounts and riders.

Trini Salazar, wild with battle frenzy, was ringed by three warriors, closing on him. The bearded rider charged through the fray, shouldering one Indian from his horse, swinging his gun to club another. Grasping the halter of the mustard pony, he pulled it to a run, the raging Spaniard shouting from its back. In a moment they were among the mules. The bearded man swung down and dodged a furious kick by Trini. "Howdy," he nodded at Darby. "My name is Poole. My partner there is Billy Sipe."

"Darby Curtis," Darby told him. "Yonder is Vince Copple and that catamount you brought in is Trini Salazar. He's a Spaniard. Trini!" he roared at the wild-eyed Mediterranean raging atop the mustard pony, "Get down and shut up!"

"Mister Chance used to throw him in the stock tank when he got like that," Vince Copple advised.

In the field, Blackleg warriors swarmed over the abandoned wagons, then paused, confused. They ripped tarps and dug in the grayish substance they found there, looking at it, tasting it. Darby wondered what they had expected to find. They gathered there, then turned toward the mule herd and the sheltered men.

"I didn't figure they'd be interested in saltpeter," Poole said. " 'Course, there wasn't any chance to explain to them that that's all I'm carryin'."

"So now they're thinking about my mules and packs. Criminy!" Darby snapped another shot to keep the Blacklegs at a distance. An arcing arrow breathed past him.

"You get down off that mule, you'd be less of a target," Poole suggested. "Lordy, I never seen mules the size of these."

Darby tossed Hildegarde's lead to Vince Copple. "Keep her tight," he said. "You see that crest up there, where the three Blacklegs are? Will your rifle reach out to there?"

"I 'spect," Copple raised a brow, looking up at him. "You want me to try?"

16

"No, just keep your eyes up there. I'm going to dicker."

Ringing them against the bluff, most of the Blacklegs had dismounted now and were disappearing into the brush.

Darby glanced at Poole. "Mr. Poole, why don't you and your partner go drop the packs off some of those mules, would you? Especially that one . . ." he pointed to Madison, "and that big dark one back there. Careful with him, though. He'll cave in your slats if you give him a chance." He winked at Vince Copple. "You know what to do."

He fired one more shot for effect, then dropped the rifle into its sheath and pulled out his other one, fully loaded. Turning on the frame saddle he unbuckled John Adams's packstrap and let the twin light packs drop to the ground. Then he touched heels to the big mule, guiding its head to the right. In a moment he was gone, through screening brush.

II

Keeping an eye on the glimpses of Kiowas out in the brush, the men unpacked all of the mules except Hildegarde. Vince Copple handed her reins to Trini. Madison, head-up, watched the movements in the brush curiously. Copple patted him, then slapped him on the rump. With a snort, Madison jumped, then cocked his ears, shook his head and ambled into the open. The others followed, ears up and eyes alert, fanning out as they went. Packs and trapping had been removed. Therefore it was time to graze.

Lucifer, tall and dark, raised his head to study a repeated surreptitious movement beyond a low bank of flood-carved clay. The movement came again. Lucifer's head went high in curiosity. Then he curled his lip, lowered his ears and moved that way, creeping with huge stealth.

The Indians were closing in under cover. Edwin Poole scratched his head and wrinkled his brow as he watched the eleven tall mules wander out toward their crescent line.

On a high place the man called Bird sat his horse and watched the scene below. He was tall, muscular and copperdark. Raven hair was pulled into a high roach that sported three eagle feathers. The crook lance he held was long and stout, trimmed its full length with beaver fur and bright feathers. A circular black shield dangled from its thongs at his left shoulder.

The two with him were lesser warriors of the Blackleg Society, young men still being indoctrinated into the ways of manhood. Now and then Bird spoke to them, pointing out placements and movements on the field below between trail and bluff.

Now he raised himself on his flat saddle, shielding his eyes to see better. Between the Blackleg warriors creeping up on the defense cluster and the defenders themselves, the area was full of the large, odd horses he had seen earlier. Unburdened by either pack or harness, the big animals were spreading out, grazing quietly, stopping to stare •curiously at the warriors in the brush. Bird was puzzled. It was not like the white men to sacrifice their stock.

He started to say something to the two attending him, then froze as rock crunched softly behind him and the unmistakable double click of a rifle action being cocked brought his head up.

A deep voice, oddly familiar, addressed him in slurred, halting Kiowa. "Bird, it would be a good idea if you would call off your warriors and tell them to leave my animals alone."

Bird turned slowly, and found himself looking at the curious, extended nose of a mount much larger than his own. The head was that of a horse, yet ugly. It reminded him of the little horses he had seen *Mejicanos* use to carry great loads in the lands of Comanche and Jicarilla. Atop the tall animal a large, young white man looked down at him, pale eyes shaded by a wide hat. The repeating rifle he held was trained on Bird and did not waver. The man did not even glance at the two braves, who had spun around at the sound and now backed their horses away a few steps. He gazed steadily at Bird.

Bird slapped his reins and drew them, turning his horse to face the newcomer. "You know my name."

"The name of Bird is known," the white-eyes answered, his Kiowa halting but correct. He selected the form of the word "name" which meant great respect, and spoke without irony. "I have known Bird for a long time. You once called me by a name, also, when I was a very young boy. I was honored that Bird would speak to me. There was peace then. Why do the Blackleg men make war now?"

"I do not know you, white man." Bird held his gaze, studying him. "It is not the Blackleg men who make war.

19

We have heard from the roving people that white men come to take our lands. In the wagons, they said, are powder and guns for the hunters. They will bring the soldiers and kill our people. We take the powder and guns. Then the soldiers will not come."

Darby puzzled over the response. Where had the Blacklegs gotten an idea like that? He knew of no soldiers, except the few at the forts. And there were hunters, but not many.

"The wagons carry only cave lime. The Blackleg men have seen that. And some have died. It would be the best thing now if Bird and his warriors would go in peace. Leave my friends and my animals alone."

Bird scowled at him. "The ugly horses carry large packs. Maybe that is where the guns and powder are."

"Those packs are mine. They carry trade goods for the people who make corn on the river. You have seen that we are bound for there."

Bird drew himself straight in his saddle, ignoring the rifle trained on him. "If we take the ugly horses and the packs, then we can see for ourselves what they hold."

"Some warriors have died today. If you do not go, there will be more."

Bird was aware of the young braves flanking him. They were waiting. This man was one and they were three. With a quick motion of his hand he turned the hooked lance so that its needle point was toward the white man's chest. "Then maybe today is a good day to die."

Darby tensed, but his rifle didn't waver. "I know you, Bird. By the name of your father, who was called Buffalo Rattle, I tell you that what I say is true. Buffalo Rattle would have believed the son of Chance Curtis."

The warrior's eyes widened. Behind him the pair of braves looked at each other in puzzlement.

"Name yourself," Bird demanded.

Darby grinned. "You once called me O'gatedota. That was a long time ago. Will you call off the Blackleg men now, respected one?"

Bird studied him, dark eyes narrowing in recognition. Then he nodded. "You have grown tall, wild one. And if I do not? Would you kill Bird?"

There was no hesitation in Darby's response. "I would. I think we would both die, then."

Their eyes locked for a moment more, then Bird shrugged and lowered his lance. He turned to look down at the field off the trail, where Blackleg warriors crept toward the wandering, fanning mules as the two trading parties crouched below the bluff. "It is too late. Stalking Horse leads those warriors. When they take the ugly horses, they will be theirs. Stalking Horse wants them."

"Is Stalking Horse a chief? Does he not obey Bird?"

The Indian looked back at him. "Stalking Horse is a young man. It is a time of young men. When Bird goes to sit in council with Hawk That Hunts Walking, Stalking Horse will lead the Blackleg men. He has been chosen. Today he follows Bird to battle. But he does not follow Bird in battle. Today the Blackleg men have painted themselves to take the white man's goods. That is what Stalking Horse will do. If we see tomorrow, then we will do something else."

It was the logic of Kiowa society, and Darby shook his head, remembering. There would be no getting around it. "Then maybe more will die today. Without my animals, the Blackleg men will take nothing."

"But see," Bird pointed. "Your ugly horses are free. The warriors have only to take them now. It is nothing."

"You don't know about my *horses*," Darby muttered in English. Then he lowered his rifle, raised a hand palm-out to the warrior chief and tugged John Adams's reins. "Bird has spoken with me and I am honored. I think it would be the best thing now if Bird would stay up here, out of the way. When tomorrow's task is decided, the Blackleg men will need Bird to lead them."

Cautiously he backed the mule away. The young braves held their bows with arrows nocked, but made no move to stop him. Bird gazed at him across the edge of his black shield. The paint on his face was vivid, the tall roach of hair with its three feathers a savage contrast to the dull reds and greens of the hills beyond. Without changing expression the warrior set his hook lance in the ground then raised his hand, two fingers spread in a vee. He touched them below his eyes and drew them downward, breaking and smearing the lines of paint on his cheeks. "For today, the names of our fathers are enough, O'gatedota. For today, Bird will do as you say. If tomorrow comes, that will be another day."

Darby paused. "Who told Bird the white soldiers will come?"

"The roving people. You call them Pawnee. They say the white man's war has ended in the east. Now the soldiers will have nothing to do. White hunters come now, kill too many buffalo. I have seen this. Now we must fight, O'gatedota. The white soldiers will come and we will have to fight."

Darby frowned. "Do you believe that?"

"Hawk That Hunts Walking believes. The Kiowa people have had a message from the Great Father, saying we should come to council. Hawk That Hunts Walking thinks it would be better to stay away and wait to see what happens."

"Where will the council be?"

Bird grinned at him then. "Near the place where Bird gave you a name, wild one. The place called Willow Ford on the Smoky Hill River."

"It is a long time since the people of Hawk That Hunts Walking have hunted on the Smoky Hill."

"It is a long time," Bird nodded. "Some, like Cloud and White Bear, believe that the Kiowa and the white man can live in peace. Hawk That Hunts Walking is not so sure."

"Does Hawk That Hunts Walking want war?"

"No more than any man does. Yet, he says, it seems as though the white man wants nothing else. I do not know. Bird has known peace with Chance Curtis and other white men. But they did not bring the blue soldiers. The Pawnee say there are some who will."

"This is a big land, Bird. There is enough room for everyone."

Bird shook his head then, his feathers tossing in the

sunlight. "The land is only as big as the paths of the buffalo. Our people must go where they go. Without them we would starve."

At the suggestion of Darby's rein the big mule turned away and trotted off the trail, down an incline and out of sight. Bird and the two braves turned again to watch the drama below, where the men of the Blackleg Society now were closing in on their prey.

The mules were in motion.

Lucifer, tall, dark and intent, extended his head, nose low, and tried to make himself invisible as he crept silently through low brush, disappearing into a shallow wash where he had seen stealthy movement. His tail twitched with glee and his eyes were alight as he went.

The other mules ambled on, spreading in a fan of grazing, resting giants as they moved outward from the bluff. Trini Salazar kept firm grip on Hildegarde's rein, glanced with interest toward the top of the crest where Darby Curtis had joined the three Indians, then devoted his attention to the field before him. The mules were moving along, approaching the ring of stubble brush where he knew hostiles lurked.

Vince Copple ignored the mules. Not for a moment did his eyes leave the crest where Darby and the feathered warrior faced each other. His rifle was at his shoulder, ready to fire. Poole and Billy Sipe looked from one to the other of them, then at each other, and Poole shrugged. Whatever was going to happen, he estimated, was fixing to.

It came without warning. One moment there was silence, then a shriek of pain and an Indian buck sailed, tumbling through the air, from the wash where Lucifer had disappeared. His scream was drowned by a harsh, staccato braying, and Lucifer burst from the scrub greenery. His ears were back, his mouth open and his eyes aflame with high good humor as a raced in search of more sport.

Madison, meanwhile, thrust his head over a screen of sage and nuzzled the painted savage crouching there. The Indian looked up, jumped, tripped and fell, losing his balance and his weapons in the same motion. Madison snorted, stepped over the sage and extended a large, dainty hoof to pin the warrior to the ground. When the warrior squawled and kicked, trying to break loose, Madison rolled him over onto his stomach, pinned him again and nuzzled him, curious about the harsh Indian smells of smoke, sweat and animal grease paint. After a moment he began chewing on the man's hair.

Pandemonium erupted. Hamilton felt himself gripped from both sides, hard fingers burrowing into his short mane, and raised his gentle head to find Indians clinging to him, trying to subdue him as though he were a horse. He tolerated the treatment for a moment, then shook them off with a swing of his head, and gently kicked the one coming at him from behind.

Monroe had wandered into a massing party. Suddenly there were Indians all over him. Having no better idea at the moment, he sat down. Nearby, Beelzebub was bucking and snorting, dancing in circles, flinging warriors in all directions. The placid Jefferson snorted in surprise when first one Indian and then another sprang aboard him, straddling him, drumming him with their heels. He glanced around reproachfully, then ambled across the few intervening feet to nudge a few savages off the unyielding back of Monroe.

Stern-minded Bernice watched the excitable Fanny May playing tag with several warriors, chasing them in a circle while Sam willingly dashed about before them, keeping them from escape, then Bernice bucked a warrior from her own back, bit another on the ear and returned to the bluff. Once there, she turned her back on the whole embarrassing scene.

Washington and Hamilton, noticing that Monroe had addressed his problem by balking and sitting down, did likewise. From a distance the three, sitting in a circle with enraged savages clinging to them, dancing around them and bouncing off them, seemed to be discussing matters of state.

At the bluff, Poole stood with his mouth hanging open, then closed it long enough to mutter, "Well, I never . . ."

Thirty yards away a savage who had been sent tumbling by Lucifer came to his feet, drew a knife and went for the throat of Monroe. Poole's shotgun roared and the Indian was thrown backward to land in a bloody heap.

Two braves broke around the mule defense, heading for the bluff. The nearest was a young, feathered warrior who straightened to throw a lance, then crouched and headed straight for Hildegarde. The second followed, loosing an arrow at the men and reaching for another. The arrow bedded itself in the flesh of Billy Sipe's leg. With a curse Sipe drew a fresh revolver from beneath his coat and dropped the Indian, firing round after round into him as he fell. The lead warrior dodged aside, disappeared behind a salt cedar stand and reappeared at another point, still homing on Hildegarde. He was twenty feet from the bell mare when Vince Copple appeared from behind her, reins in one hand, his big rifle in the other. The rifle thundered and earth erupted beneath the warrior's feet. Then the muzzle came up.

The Indian dove to one side, rolling as he hit the ground, and Trini Salazar emptied a pistol at him, its slugs ripping sod all around the tumbling form. *"Mátenlo!"* the Spaniard shrieked, and broke from his shelter to go to the attack. Copple shook his hand, then swung his rifle to whack the Spaniard across the belly. Salazar doubled and went to his knees.

"Crazy," Copple said to himself. "Plain crazy." When he brought his rifle to bear forward again, the young warrior was gone.

Salazar held his aching belly and shouted rapid Spanish at the black man. Copple gazed down at him and shook his head slowly. "I never seen a man act like you do. Never in my whole life. Why don't you get up and see if you can help that gentleman over there. He has an arrow stuck in his leg. You see?"

He had no more time then to sort out the Spaniard. Most of the Indians had fallen back from the mules, surprised and frustrated. But one, a brave looking for glory, still stalked among them, and the object of his attention was

Lucifer. The brave raised a lance and Lucifer backed away, seeing real danger. Copple raised his rifle again and fired. The brave dropped like a stone.

Darby Curtis burst from the canyon thickets then, astride John Adams, and shouted at the Indians in rapid Kiowa. Some of them turned to look at Bird, still on the distant rise. He raised a hand, then lowered it and turned away.

By last light of evening the five built a fire and roasted cuts of Poole's dead ox. There had been a time of truce, while the Kiowa gathered their casualties and the traders gathered Darby's mules. Now the Blacklegs were gone. Darby didn't think they would come back.

Billy Sipe was nursing a punctured leg, and Vince Copple had an arrow crease on his shoulder.

"The trick is the bell mare," Darby told Poole as they chewed on tough ox and knots of the terrible Spanish bread which Trini Salazar had managed to concoct. "As long as I have Hildegarde, and she has her bell, the other mules won't go far."

"Indians ain't dumb," Poole allowed. "Next time they might have it figured how to get mules."

"It's a big country. Not much chance of runnin' into the same bunch twice, the way they move around."

"But you knew the chief of this bunch."

"A long time ago. I grew up around Kiowas up on the plains. Bird was a big warrior, even then. I remembered him. Never thought I'd see him down here. But then, they move around a lot."

Poole got out a pipe, filled and lit it. He looked around in the dusk. The mules grazed contentedly nearby, the horses not far away, all hobbled, and Poole's oxen clustered apart, dim-witted and ignored by the other stock. "You said you was going down to Vernon."

"Yeah. Then back up to Arrow Bend to cash in. Then I guess I'll head back to the Smoky Hill. You see, I made a deal to buy these mules. I saved up to pay money down, and I'm paying them off with these trips. I think this trip will square me. Then I can go into business on my own. I'm buyin' from my Pa. He charges ten per cent interest on the loan."

"Billy and me, we're bound to Fort Smith with that saltpeter. Only seven bulls left, but I guess they can get us there. You know, I never seen mules as big as them of yours. Do you suppose they could haul wagons?"

"They can do anything they set their minds to." Darby carved another chunk of ox. "Their mothers were Oldenburg mares. Biggest horses you ever saw. My Pa had to stand those little jackasses on a plank to breed them. But it was worth the trouble. There aren't any better mules anywhere. He started with a herd of Oldenburgs and two jacks and so far he's bred out forty-four of these big critters. Plumb wore out those two jackasses, but they died with big smiles on their faces."

Vincent Copple snorted. The dark-haired wagon driver, Sipe, his leg salved and bound, stared sourly across the fire. Except for complaints about his leg, complaints about the food and complaints about the west in general, he had remained aloof from conversation. Now he took a sip of coffee, made a face, spat it out on the ground and got to his feet, wincing as he did so. "I tried mules on dray one time. Beat 'em half to death and they still wouldn't work. I wouldn't give a nickel for all the mules in creation." With that he turned, shook his head and hobbled off toward the wagons.

"Nice fella," Darby muttered. "Is he always like that?"

Poole shrugged. "He's from New York City. He doesn't like it out here."

"Then why doesn't he go back?"

"He never said," Poole said. "And I never asked."

At his words, Trini Salazar had turned sharply. Now he glanced toward the wagons where Sipe had gone, then back at Poole. "*Por Dios!* New York Ceety?" His dark eyes flashed. He launched into a diatribe in clipped Spanish and Darby raised a hand.

"Damn it, Trini, why don't you learn English?"

27

Salazar blinked, started over. "*Perdóneme. Para mañana* I, Trinidad Salazar, go New York Ceety. Miguel Jesus Montoya *esta . . . ah . . . esta en* New York Ceety. *Hijo de perra . . . el es . . . ah . . . ai, si!* He is sonamabitch, Miguel Jesus Montoya. I go New York Ceety. Fin' heem, *verdad.* I keel heem! Sonamabitch." He turned away, brooding.

After a brief silence Poole looked at Darby. "What's that all about?"

Darby shook his head. "I haven't the slightest notion. He gets like that sometimes. Good with mules, though."

"Mister Chance found him down in Texas, afoot an' lost 'way out on Llano," Vince Copple told Poole. "It was while Darby here was away. There was some Comanche after him an' he was about half dead. Mister Chance brought him home."

"That's my father," Darby said. "Chance Curtis. I borrowed Trini from him."

Poole was gazing thoughtfully into the fire. "You got any definite plans for after you pay off on the mules?"

"Yeah. I plan to make money."

"Sort of my notion, too. Darby, I'm sittin' here and I'm lookin' at your mules and my wagons, and I'm thinkin' we might want to meet up someplace right soon and talk."

With first light they went their separate ways after scouting the land together. The Kiowa had gone. With gear assembled and loads slung the mule train headed southwest, the oxwagons east.

When they both were distant and receding, brush parted on a hillside and a Kiowa warrior stepped silently onto the trail, leading his pony. For a time he stood, gazing southwest, his chiseled face unpainted and set in lines that were hard and speculative. Stalking Horse accepted with stolid grace the defeat of the Blackleg men the day before. The wagons had not held the rifles and powder they had thought, and he was sure the ugly horses carried no such goods. They were going the wrong way to be bringing

28

supplies to the hide-hunters.

The medicine of the white traders had been strong. Tall Elk was dead. Two Snake and Calling Dog were dead. Others were injured. Stalking Horse accepted these things. When the Blackleg men painted themselves for raiding, or for war, they were ready to die.

Yet he was puzzled. Somehow his brothers had not taken a single one of the ugly horses, though they had tried. There, he felt, lay the medicine of the traders.

Through the night he had lain silently and watched. He had noticed the brass bell on the ugly-horse mare. And he saw that mare take the lead when they moved out.

Stalking Horse did not follow where Bird and the Blackleg men had gone. Instead, now, he swung to the back of his pony and set his path eastward, toward the new day's sun.

Thus Stalking Horse did not see that day the line of wagons that came from the south, heading for a rendezvous on the Kansas Plains.

But Bird saw them and the Blackleg men, unpainted now, watched for hours as the little train made its way northward toward the high lands where the western herds would graze in the fall. The wagons were ringed by armed men, and scouts rode ahead and to the sides. Among them were Pawnee and renegade Osage. A dread came upon Bird as he watched. After a time the Blackleg men turned away and put heels to their horses. Bird dipped the hooked lance toward the distant valley where the Far Grass People were camped. The wagons they had attacked were the wrong wagons. These he saw now, he knew, were the ones the roving Pawnee had talked about. Yet these were too well guarded, too strong to attack.

It was time to go back to Hawk That Hunts Walking, to tell him of these things. It was time for council. Bird would say what he had seen. Then Twenty Buffalo and Turns The Wind would add their wisdom, and others would speak. And Hawk That Hunts Walking would listen to it all, and finally he would say what they must do.

For the Far Grass People buffalo were life. Once there

had been so many buffalo that none who could hunt ever went hungry. But the words of the roving Pawnee were ominous. They spoke of white men who would wipe out herds, and of soldiers who would help them. They spoke of war, of starvation and death.

Bird turned his black shield to deflect the wind. Even on this bright day it had an edge of cold about it.

III

The long trestle crossing at Westport was under repair. It had been built in wartime, to move troops and munitions across the river. Now it was being shored up, retimbered and buffered for heavier commercial use. New iron rails on fresh ties sang as a big, new locomotive puffed its way across, slowing for the turn across the river. More than thirty pullmans, boxcars and flatcars followed, clicking rhythmically over the tie-ends as shoring crews paused below to watch their progress.

The train was creeping by the time it left the trestle, its piercing whistle signaling the approach to little Flint Station beyond the curving cutout grade.

Steam erupted and the whistle sounded a long blast as the locomotive eased past the station docks, bringing its passenger cars to a halt at the plank aprons.

The cars were full. The crowds disembarking included soldiers, tradesmen, families with their eyes to the west, politicians and businessmen, people traveling a short way and people traveling far. A decade before, this river and this place had been the gateway to the frontier. Now the frontier began to fade, its line grew indistinct and it pressed westward as the end of war released pressures of expansion held bottled by emergency for five years.

Rain that was hardly more than summer mist glistened on iron boilers, wood shingles and the silks and tight felts of headgear. One of those who stepped from the passenger cars was a tall man, broad of shoulder and thick-bodied, his full sideburns streaked with gray. His attire was conservative, his manner retiring. Only his size and the assured, reserved manner of him might have caught the attention of anyone who did not know him. He stood on the platform and glanced around him with dark eyes that missed nothing. Then a ghost of a smile appeared and he nodded and stepped forward, holding out a hand. "Ah, sir, it is a pleasure to see you again. How many years has it been?"

The man who came toward him was nearly as tall, but thinner, a man whose gray hair spoke of middle years but whose movements were lithe and controlled—the easy motion of the master fencer, grace at rest concealing power and the capacity to use it in an instant. His smile was a wide, sardonic grin beneath cool gray eyes that said only what they intended to say. He took the big man's hand firmly. "Far too many, Mr. Bliss. A lifetime, it seems, though only a wartime in fact. I trust your journey was pleasant."

Bliss glanced at the puffing locomotive. "As much so as the times in which we live can afford, sir. I have covered in three days the distance the General's old phaeton might have made in a week with fresh teams twice a day. And yet—I suppose it is advancing age—I think I would trade the mechanical lurch and jostle of these things for the comfortable sway of a good coach and a spirited team. You're looking fit, sir. A bit snowy about the ears, perhaps, but otherwise unchanged."

"I was in Hampstead when your message came. A small business there to attend to. But I finished it and came along." They walked together toward a wide building that housed both a depot and a travelers' inn. "I was intrigued, of course. You said you wired on behalf of the General."

Bliss looked around. The crowds were dispersing. "That is correct. He still, now and then, takes an interest in things."

"I am not surprised," the lean man nodded. "He will make a show of retirement, tend his stables in Delaware and all. But he will stay in touch."

"The war was hard on him, sir. It tore at his heart. And then when Mr. Johnson decided against his reappointment

. . . yes, I know he is past seventy, and the president saw it as a kindness . . ."

"I am sure he did. Like honorable pasturage for a splendid old stallion. Mr. Johnson is a politician. He wouldn't understand."

"No, sir. Very few would understand. The new director, though, I believe he does. A good man. Two days in office and he sent a messenger and a coach. I was there when the old man came. The new director was quite sincere. He said he could untangle the webs that would be spun, but he needed help with some that had already been."

"Appropriate," the gray man said, approving.

In the inn they found a quiet booth and Bliss ordered tea. "Do you have Canton?" he asked the waiter. "If not, a good pekoe blend might do." When the man had gone he winked at the man sitting across from him. "In honor of the General. Do you mind?"

"I'd have it no other way."

"The General also, were he here, would skirt for a time about his subject before coming to it."

"That is his way. But not yours, Mr. Bliss."

"No. Not mine. Very well. As I recall, the General has never requested a service of you without first granting one in exchange?"

The lean man smiled and nodded. "An affectation of his. Such has seldom been required."

"Of course. Still, he prefers to maintain it. Tell me, do you still seek the men who killed Merritt Fields? It has been several years now."

The man's face held almost no expression now, only a slight, serene smile that pulled at the corners of his mouth. Yet there was expression there. It was in the eyes . . . cold gray eyes that suddenly burned with embers from an icy hell. Bliss shivered and looked away. It came to him again that, through all the years he had known this man, still he had never—never quite—known him. And he never would. He had come close only once, the day he had watched a hawk in stoop. In some places, those few who knew him had a name for him, a name somehow more suited than the

33

name that was his. In their whispers they spoke of him and called him nemesis.

"The time doesn't matter," the man said softly. "There were five of them. I found only two. But to seek, one must have a direction. No, I do not seek. I only wait."

"I see. The General thought you might be interested. He offers you the name of one of the three remaining. The name is Poling. Mercer Poling. I have a packet for you that contains all we know." He drew a thin envelope from his coat and passed it across. "It is yours."

"Thank you, Mr. Bliss." The hint of hellfire in the gray eyes had receded. The face was serene. "And how may I be of service to the General?"

"As usual," Bliss said, "by doing what you choose to do . . . his way. Ah, here is our tea."

The waiter came and went. When they were alone again Bliss poured. "I suppose you are familiar with the incident at Sand Creek the past fall. The Indian prisoners who were massacred by those volunteers."

"Under Chivington. Yes."

"And that there has been considerable unrest among the plains tribes since then."

"Not without reason, in some cases."

"Assuredly. Some of the victims have deserved to be victims. Still, there are white people out there who are trying to live in peace . . . some of them have done so for a very long time, until now. The high plains are a time bomb now, sir. The Indians have been savagely attacked, and they retaliate. At the same time the border has collapsed and settlers are pressing into those lands in large numbers. And now the war between the states has ended." He gazed at the lean man, savoring a bleak irony. "Isn't it remarkable that the end of a war should bring about violence, just as the beginning of one does."

"It will bring more than that, Mr. Bliss." The man's expression was unreadable.

"Yes. Most likely. There are the soldiers."

"New recruits with service time to be utilized . . . somehow . . . and officers who have tasted glory and now

34

seek more."

"Essentially, yes," Bliss nodded. "There will be ambitions to be watched. Colonels who wish to be generals, generals who wish to be president . . . men ready for war and suddenly plunged into peace . . ."

"And the new director has ample resources to follow each career. What service can an aging amateur perform, Mr. Bliss?"

The big man grinned. Many were the professionals who had encountered this amateur in the years since the collapse of the Boston Combine. And of them all, it was the amateur who survived. "Those are the big fish, sir. The General has taken an interest in littler fish of late. There is to be an attempt at negotiation with the Plains tribes. There is a man named James Chrisman who feels he can avert further disasters. He intends to speak with the chiefs of the Kiowa nation, then with the other tribes. Something of an idealist, but not a bad sort, really. He feels that if the Kiowa can be reached, then possibly there might be an accord with the Arapahoe, and through them the Cheyenne and Comanche."

"An idealist." The lean man gazed at him. "Yet, aren't we all, in our ways?"

"He is being duped, sir. There are other interests involved, who see wide lands for the taking and will stop at nothing."

"There are always those."

"One of them is your Mr. Poling."

"Ah."

"And that, unfortunately, is about all we know."

"The General would like me to take a hand."

"Yes, sir. Take a hand as you see fit, of course. Except the General would consider it a favor if in doing so you might give Mr. Chrisman some advantage in his cause. Peace with the Kiowa may be a slim hope, after Sand Creek, but it may at this moment be the best hope we have."

The lean man sipped his tea. "Not Canton," he said. "Not even pekoe. But the thought is there. You

35

mentioned soldiers."

"A major, to be precise. Brevet colonel until recent months, now stepped back to his permanent rank. Something of a showman in his way, flashy and all, but by and large a cypher. Yet for some reason he now commands a full squadron detached from Fort Leavenworth. Nothing so very unusual there, except that some strings were pulled to bring that about. They were pulled by Mr. Poling and associates of his."

"The associates?"

"You have the information there, sir. An odd mixture of buffalo hunters, railroad speculators and some whose enterprises are unclear. I am afraid that is all we have."

"The General's interests have broadened these days."

"Possibly a result of retirement, sir. I can assure you, though, his eyes have not dimmed a whit."

"It is a long time since I last visited the Kansas territories, Mr. Bliss."

IV

At the town of Willow Ford sturdy buildings clustered along a pair of dogleg streets, a haven of firm-rooted stability in what only a few years before had been wilderness. First there had been a settler here, then others followed, and even before these lands beyond the defunct "permanent frontier" were patented, a town had arisen at the westward edge of settled lands. Beyond lay a narrow region of rolling hills and narrow, wooded valleys where a few hardy souls now sought homesites—and where a handful, widely scattered—had secured legal claims based on squatters' rights going back a generation. Settlement beyond Willow Ford had become "legal" only a year ago, the land consigned through patent agents who made their own rules and fees. But those who were already there were recognized and legalized. They were a fact of life and their lands were conveyed directly, over the protests of the patent agents.

Among these, the *fait accompli* settlers, were the Wilsons, the Pecks and the Untermeiers, who had jumped the frontier because of the war back east, and old Chance Curtis who had been there a long time when the rest arrived.

So the town of Willow Ford was a frontier, between the settled territory to the east and the contested strip just west where immigrants paid the price of patent or moved on—or sometimes disappeared if a better price was offered.

The strip extended maybe forty miles, its boundaries imprecise. And beyond it the land was vast and open, empty rolling plains whose status was simply that there were Kiowa there.

South of the Curtis place, in the patented strip, a man so weathered he seemed old climbed from a six-foot hole to lean on his spade and shade his eyes. His woman came to stand by him and the children gathered close. Not half a mile away a long line of Indians plodded eastward, and the family marveled at the sight of them. They counted more than a hundred out there, braves with bright feathers riding painted ponies, horses pulling laden travois where women and children walked alongside, and in the lead a rank of brilliant-plumed warriors flanking four who were chiefs or medicine men.

"They have such colors," the woman said. "Like bright birds in a picture book."

Emmett came from the wagon with the old man's rifle, but the old man shook his head. "We'll not need that," he said. "They're peaceful, like the others that we saw. They see us here, but they mean us no harm and they know we mean them none."

"They're going to the town," Jim said. "A man came by with mules while I was out there setting stones. He said they're gathering there to talk about a treaty. He said the army's there, and people from back east who want to meet the Kiowa and talk peace."

"They look like knights of chivalry," Emily clasped her hands and her eyes were wide, seeing the distant warriors. Her mother smiled at her, a secret smile. Emily was of an age.

"I reckon they're just people," the old man said. "For all their heathen ways they may be much like us."

For a time they watched, as the Indians passed by toward the town of Willow Ford. Then the old man went back to his digging and the woman returned to the wagons and her fire.

Jim saw the riders coming as he worked to set a cairn. There were four riders, armed men all on dark horses, and they were at the wagons by the time he got there.

They were rough men, all wearing guns in holsters at

their belts, and they sat their horses and looked around, at the wagons, the hole the old man was digging, the lean-to made of elm boughs where they had spread their bedding.

"You mean to settle here?" one asked.

The old man leaned on his spade. "It's a fair place and no one's taken it. When we were in the town, we asked. They said most of this is unclaimed."

"There is a patent," the man said. "A land company holds it. It's consigned. You want to squat here you'll pay the fee."

"They didn't speak of fees or patents in the town," the old man said. Emmett moved to stand beside him, the rifle in his hand.

"They do now," the man said. "The land's consigned and Mr. Poling is the agent. This place here, the fee is five hundred dollars." He looked around again. "Then I'd say another hundred every year until the claim is satisfied. Place like this, that might take a while."

"We have no money to pay fees," the old man said. "We can farm and we can make do, and we can pay an honest sum for filing, but we can't pay what you say."

One of the other riders had set eyes on Emily. Emmett saw him grin and wet his lips. He twitched the rifle upward. The one in the lead saw the motion and turned to his companion. "Blue! None of that, you hear? At least not now."

Emmett steadied the rifle and now he held their eyes. "My Pa has said what we can do and what we can't. You had your leave to light down and visit friendly. Now it's passed. You can turn around and go."

Two of them thought about going for their guns then, but the leader stopped them with a wave. He saw how close to him the old man was with his spade, he saw Jim behind them with an ax in his big hands and he saw the level point of the long rifle.

"You'll have two days," he told the old man. "You can pay the fee or move on. When we come back there'll be no more talk."

When they were gone the old man walked to the hole in

the ground and looked down into it. "It might have made a good well," he said.

"We can stand," Emmett told him. "Those are boomers. We can make a claim with a land office, and they can't force us off."

"And whose blood would you have flow?" the old man asked. "Bullets and fire don't care who they get." He looked around him then, at his woman, his sons and his daughters. "We'll go back to the town. We can find work for a time. Then when we have a stake we'll look again. I guess it's best that way."

When the wagons were packed they would turn them east toward Willow Ford. Yet when the old man and his woman stood together in silence, gazing across the land, it was to the west they looked.

On a bright morning wagons rolled into town, buggies and carts were on the roads and Willow Ford bustled with activity. The homespun and calicos of settler dress mingled with the finery of visitors on the streets, and everywhere were the blue tunics and yellow stripes of soldiers. It was a time of festive awe, an occasion like few the little town had seen.

In a meadow east of town the tents and wagons, the canvassed barracks and grazing remounts of a squadron bivouac covered an area larger than the town itself. And north across the river, brilliant in the morning light, stood hundreds of teepees—tipis, according to Jean-Claude Rousseau, the French Canadian visiting reporter whose penchant was that every word except his own name should be reduced to its minimum number of letters. All across the far hillside spread the traveling lodges of the nomadic Kiowa.

The Great Father in Washington had sent word that the Kiowa and their chiefs were to assemble at this place so that his emissaries might speak with them. Though concerned about the numbers of soldiers accompanying the peace delegation, the Kiowa had come. Spotted Horse and his band arrived from the northwest. Antler and his Evening Wind people came in from the west. Medicine Wing and the silent Adago whose mother was Apache led Fire Dancer People from the great plains. Then Cloud, backed by the sturdy White Bear and his major chiefs Kicking Bird and Small Bull, arrived from the south, the red-painted warriors of the Horse Clan riding in the lead as befit the major tribe of all the Kiowa people. Several thousand Kiowa now were gathered across the river from Willow Ford and their cooking fires painted a haze against the sky.

It was a powderkeg, some said, casting dire glances to the north. Indians were unreliable, unpredictable. So, others agreed, was the army. An incident, the dour ones feared, could unleash havoc. And yet, those who knew them better pointed out the Kiowa had not made war on the white people. There had been encounters—small occasional problems widely scattered—but the Kiowa were at peace and stayed that way.

Of all the Kiowa villages, only the people of Hawk That Hunts Walking had not come to Willow Ford. No one knew where Hawk That Hunts Walking was this season, except that he was far to the west in the high plains . . . or else southwest where the Comanche hunted.

It was a disappointment to the assembled Kiowa that Hawk That Hunts Walking had not come to Willow Ford. Of all the societies of all the bands, the two most splendid were the respected Real Dogs and the fierce, mystical Blackleg men of Hawk That Hunts Walking's tribe. Had these been present, the Kiowa nation could have displayed its full pageantry to impress the representatives of the Great Father.

On a flat near the riverbank soldiers had assembled a meeting ground—tents for the dignitaries, tables and chairs for the officials from the Department of Interior, a parade ground for the First Squadron, detached from its regiment at Fort Leavenworth and now under the command of Major—recently Brevet Colonel—Alfred Grimes. The major's command was more than two hundred strong, consisting of three full-strength troops of horse cavalry and a howitzer platoon. Among his officers were two veteran captains and four first lieutenants, two of them in command of troops.

Fresh from the white men's wars in the east, the First Squadron had been redressed and was at full battalion strength. They had come west provisioned for permanent maneuvers in the Kiowa lands.

Farm wagons had been arriving at Willow Ford since daybreak, bringing produce and surplus grain to restock the stores depleted by the settlement's sudden population boom. The previous day, a three-wagon string of high-siders pulled by oxen had come in from Lawrence, piled high with milled goods and dry goods, which the several merchants of Willow Ford had bought as the parcels were unloaded. Edwin T. Poole had pocketed hard cash on the venture, and had subdued the grumbling of his driver, Billy Sipe, by paying him a share. It surprised Poole, as it always did, that Billy did not take his money into town. Instead, the easterner preferred to stay out with the wagons for a time and Poole had the impression he was leery of the soldiers.

Still, a man's business was his own business.

So Poole went to town. Pipe jutting from his whiskers, he strolled the streets and looked in the stores and was there when a top-hatted visitor said to another, "I just saw some of the biggest mules I ever saw. At least I think that's what they were." Poole went to look.

West of the town, still distant but coming at a good pace, packed giant mules trotted down a long grade toward him. A pair of rough men standing near shot glances at each other. "That's Curtis," one said, and Poole saw him finger his gun.

"Forget it, Winter," the other snapped. "Pasco said no trouble while Poling's here. Save it for another time."

"It'll keep," the one called Winter said. "It'll keep. Where'd Blue get off to?"

"He's sniffin' around some settler girl over at one of the stores. Same one he saw the other day out at that squatter

42

place. Shame they cleared out. We could have had some fun there."

They were gone then, and Edwin Poole puffed at his pipe and thought about what he had heard. Obviously, the soft-voiced one, the one called Winter, didn't care much for Darby Curtis. He shrugged. It was their business, not his. He went out to meet the mules. He would have Curtis's outfit camp next to his wagons.

Behind him three men had emerged from a store. Two were civilians, one an officer—a short, stocky man in spotless uniform and gleaming accoutrements with the insignia of a major of cavalry.

"Look out there, Colonel," one of the civilians pointed. "Those are traders, coming from the west. As Mr. Poling knows, there are no legitimate traders licensed to the west of here, yet they come and go as they please, probably trading with the heathen more than with honest, legal settlers. To my mind people like that are no better than renegades."

The other civilian nodded, hard eyes hooded in a lean, scarred face. "There are some difficulties so far in regulating the new patent lands. There are a few pre-emptive squatters that we can't touch, unfortunately, either through patent requirements or by licensing their trade. The law sometimes protects the lawless, I'm afraid."

The major glanced at him. "Mr. DeWitt used the term 'renegade,' Mr. Poling. Is that your concern, or is it that the people there before your patent don't have to pay your fees?"

"You misunderstand, sir." Poling's face was bland. "The people who were there before were never legally there at all. Only the patent—my patent—opened that strip to settlement."

"Do you suggest that is a matter for the army?"

"Not at all," Poling said smoothly. "No, it's a minor concern, really. The pre-emptive squatters are only a few, and I am quite capable of arranging . . ." he glanced across the street, where Winter and Tram were coming out of a store with Blue and Pasco, ". . . of arranging that there be

43

no more abuse of the patent from now on. No, the army's concern, I feel, will lie to the west of here where the lands are not yet patented. This Kiowa treaty exercise is foolishness. You will find, sir, that the Kiowa are not to be trusted. Any treaty they make they will break, and there will be a state of war. They will have to be dealt with, then.

"And of course," he added, "the officer who deals with them promptly and thoroughly when that occurs will have quite an accomplishment to his credit, won't he?"

"Not to mention influential friends," DeWitt chimed in.

Major Alfred Grimes did not respond. He only looked thoughtful.

In the press of crowds and traffic, none of them had noticed the tall, lithe man in casual traveling clothes and flat-crowned hat who stood nearby, at his ease, disinterestedly watching the town and its traffic. He was simply one of many new arrivals, seeing the sights and passing the time. Cold gray eyes under his hat brim seemed focused on nothing, and his attitude was serene and relaxed. But he had heard all that was said. For two days he had missed nothing of what was said or done by Mercer Poling. It was his business to miss nothing.

Darby Curtis saw Poole coming out to meet the mule train. He waved, then flicked the reins on John Adams and the big mule stepped up his pace. To his right, Hildegarde increased stride and pulled ahead, to the length of her lead. Darby chuckled. She was exercising her authority. Her bell clanked merrily.

Vince Copple loped his dun mount up beside him, staring off to the left where hundreds of tipis stood beyond the river. "Whoo! Did you ever see a sight like that?"

"Not near that many. Looks like the whole nation is here. Big doin's, Vince. Not every day a government commission comes to the Smoky Hill to meet with the Kiowa."

They descended the hill and approached the bustling little town. Darby frowned at sight of all the soldiers. It looked like half a regiment had descended on Willow Ford. "Hell of a lot of escort for a peace commission," he noted.

In the road ahead Poole waved his hat. "Halloo! Swing around to the south with those hay-burners. You can camp over there by us."

He urged John Adams to the right. The mule glanced at Hildegarde, who hadn't caught the signal and was trotting on, straight ahead, slightly in front of him. Darby called to her, "Gee, Hildegarde! Gee! Damn it, who's in charge here, anyway?"

Hildegarde turned elegant ears toward him and glanced back. Then she and John Adams decided to honor his request and swung right, off the track. The rest of the mules followed obediently—all but Madison, who decided to comply in his own way. He turned left, out of the train, and ambled through a stableyard between high fences, then nudged up the bar on the stable gate, pushed it open and walked through and into the wide door of a barn. Trini Salazar raced to catch him, shouting in rapid Spanish. Inside the dark barn the big mule glanced around, paused for a nibble at a feed bin, then heard Salazar coming behind him. He raised his head, brayed loudly and ran to the far barn door, which was ajar. He pushed through, veered to the right in the busy street and found himself blocked by an empty flatbed wagon.

Madison backed off several steps, bobbed his head enthusiastically, then broke into a full-stride run, directly toward the offending wagon. Horses reared, people shouted and faces turned his way. Seven strides and he had his speed. His head extended, ears back, he launched himself into a soaring leap and cleared the wagon. The heavy packs on his back flapped like swollen wings as he flew, landed, skidded to a halt and then walked sedately southward toward the bend in the street, heading back to where the others would be.

Behind him was a thunder of hooves, then a mustard pony sailed high to jump the same wagon, its rider waving his wide hat and shouting, *"Arriba! Arriba! Olé!"* With only a quick glance back, Madison went his way, ignoring the spectacle of the vividly-garbed Spaniard leaping wagons in the street.

Taking him for a runaway, a soldier darted from the side, reaching for his harness. Madison raised his head and the soldier raced harmlessly under his chin.

Salazar was beside him then, riding his short horse and shouting up at him, *"Estupido! Mula loco! Vamonos alla, hijo de burro! Loco! La mula más loco que doscientos caballos!"*

"Lord have mercy!" someone shouted. "What was that thing?"

"It looked like a mule," another offered.

"I never seen any mule that big. An' flyin'?"

"I believe that was what is called a pegasus," Edwin T. Poole explained to the fascinated crowd near him. "They're a Greek breed and extremely rare." When he had their full attention he lit his pipe and sauntered away.

Muscles rolled in Vince Copple's shoulders as he and Darby lifted a pack from Monroe's back and set it in a pile with the others. The campsite they had chosen was fifty yards from the standing wagons and ox pen that marked the Poole-Sipe camp. They unstrapped the second pack, set it down and turned Monroe over to Trini Salazar to be relieved of frame and halter, and fed.

Vince wiped sweat from his face. "I wonder how come they chose Willow Ford to have this powwow."

"Probably because it's here," Darby shrugged. "I doubt if half those people over there would have agreed to come to Fort Larned. They're afraid of the soldiers. So somebody figured that out and told somebody else to find a better place. And somebody said 'I know a place,' so this is the place."

"Sure. And since this place is the only place within a hundred miles of anyplace except this place, then this must be the place. Sometimes you sound just like your daddy."

"Works fine for us. We'll make two-three hundred off this ground meal. Good pay for a two-day haul."

"Wheat meal," Billy Sipe said, inspecting one of the big packs. "Where'd you bring it from?"

"From home," Darby pointed vaguely west. "My pa's place, two days upriver. He has a mill . . . among other things."

"I thought there wasn't anybody but Indians west of here. That's what some of the traders said."

"Those traders just got here. They don't know anything. We've been up there for better'n twenty-five years now. I was born there. So were all my kid brothers and sisters."

"Cheez!" Billy stared at him. "I didn't know people were actually *born* out here."

"Dar-bee!"

The men turned. Racing toward them, skirts raised above trim ankles, was a vision of well-molded blue gingham and wind-blown red hair. Bright teeth glistened between lips parted with laughter. "Darby Curtis! Where have you been?"

Billy Sipe gawked, thunderstruck. Darby and Vince pulled off their hats. Several of the mules turned curious heads toward her, and Lucifer extended his nose to judge her path, then swapped ends. She laughed, turned slightly to the right and swatted the dark mule resoundingly on his surprised rump. "Don't try that with me, you devil," she snapped. Then she was past the tall animals and collided with Darby Curtis, her arms around him. "Darby, wherever have you been all these months? I thought you might be dead!"

Darby caught his balance and returned her enthusiastic hug. "Melly Bright-eyes! Bless your heart! I knew there was some reason I wanted to hurry back to Willow Ford."

"Well, I can't say you hurried overmuch," she scolded. "For all we knew up here there might have been pieces of you decorating a half-dozen Comanche lodges by now. When did you get home?"

"About a week ago. Just in time to load up with millin's and high-tail down here for the big event. You suppose your daddy is in a buyin' mood? You better say howdy to Vince here so he can put his hat back on. And that over there, with his face hangin' out, that's Billy Sipe. Green from New York City. Billy, this is Melissa Muldoon. Her daddy

47

keeps store over there where the signal flags are."

Sipe stared at her, his eyes hungry. A calculating grin tugged at his lip. "How do you do, Miss Muldoon?"

Melly giggled and curtsied. "Quite well, thank you, Mr. Sipe. And Mr. Copple . . . so nice to see you again. Pa's buying meal, Darby. How much did you bring?"

"Twenty-five hundredweight. We loaded light. Will he go a dollar?"

"Six bits at the most. But he'll pay cash. Oh, Darby, I have missed you. Where have you been?"

"Far enough to make enough to buy thirteen mules free and clear—and the meal and packs to make a profit here. You tell your Pa I wont' go a cent less than eighty-five, and a dime for sacking. You haven't been spooning anybody since I left, have you, Melly?"

"Don't be ridiculous. Would I tell you if I had? What did you buy those mules for? They were already yours."

"No, they were my Pa's. I'm going on my own, and I won't go beholden. You better fetch your Pa after this meal. I won't lower the price if it gets rained on waitin' for him to pick it up. Eighty-five is rock bottom and he knows it."

"Eighty-five then, and you throw in the sacks. He was hitching his team when I left. I saw Madison in town so I knew you were here."

"I won't throw in the sacks for less than eighty-eight."

She regarded him intently for a moment, blue eyes calculating. "I thought I might fry some chickens this evening."

He surrendered. "Eighty-five it is."

"Done." She stepped to him, hugged him again and then smiled brightly at the others before hurrying away toward the little town. The men stood watching her. Billy still held his hat in his hands, rolling the brim with his fingers.

"Cheez," he muttered.

Trini Salazar had come from the feed bin, and his dark eyes lit as he watched the red-haired girl walking away, her stride strong and graceful, hair whipping in the wind. *"Ai,"* he pronounced. *"Que rosa. Que linda. Ai, palomita de mi* corazon!"

"You just left a hundred and twenty-five dollars layin' on the table," Vince Copple advised. "Maybe you ought to let somebody impartial do your dickerin' for you, Darby."

"Name me somebody impartial where Melly Muldoon is concerned."

V

"Far as I can see, the whole thing shapes up to be nothin' but trouble." Edwin T. Poole spat through his whiskers and refilled his pipe. "If what they've got in mind is a peace treaty, they brought in the wrong bunch to talk peace with Indians."

Poole and Darby stood beside a porch near the south end of Willow Ford. Everywhere were people, thronging the dogleg street of the place, going in and out of commercial buildings—people on foot, on horseback, driving teams. And among them everywhere were soldiers.

"Out there where those thickets stand," Poole pointed, "that's a hunter's camp. There's at least twenty men out there, come up from who knows where carryin' buffalo rifles and plenty of gear. Commercial hunters. Hide-hunters. They don't say much, kind of keep to themselves. Fellow named DeWitt is all that's been out to visit with 'em. But it's no secret what they're out here for. Give them some skinners and haulers and put them on a herd, and they'll drop twenty to thirty buffs a day per man. Hides'll bring a dollar apiece at railhead and they'll leave the meat to rot."

"There isn't any railhead," Darby pointed out. "The nearest track is a hundred miles from here."

"Less than that," Poole shook his head. "Sixty at most and they're layin' track every day. You see that bunch over there by the hotel? Railroad men and land speculators. Here to see what they can grab off the Indians. I don't like it much, Darby. Remember what that Blackleg told you, down there in the redlands? Durned if I don't think he had the right of it."

"What worries me is the soldiers," Darby said. "A troop would have been plenty of escort for a commission party. But there's a whole squadron here. They have security around their camp, but I saw it from the hill. They even have mountain howitzers."

"Well, one thing they're doin' that's good, they've got a cordon on the river. If there's as many trouble-makin' bucks in that Kiowa camp yonder as there are trouble-hungry jaspers over here, I'm damn glad they're keepin' the two sides separate."

"I heard Cloud is over there."

"That's what I hear. Talk is just about every branch of the Kiowa has come in . . . all except one. Somebody called the Kah-nahtenee. You know them?"

Darby had started to stroll toward the busier end of the street, toward the river. Now he stopped, frowning. "Yeah, and so do you, some of them. Those Blacklegs we tangled with, they were Kana'tenee. It means something like 'good grass far away,' or the Far Grass People. Their principal chief is Hawk That Hunts Walking. When I was a kid they were around here mostly, but they follow the big herds. Their main warrior clans are the Real Dogs and the Blacklegs. No surprise they didn't come. Bird said they wouldn't. They don't trust this setup at all."

"I thought Cloud was the main chief of the Kiowas."

"There isn't any such thing. Cloud's band is bigger than most, so he has a lot of respect. If the nation needs a leader a lot of them might choose Cloud. But not all of them. Those who don't choose to follow a chief . . . well, they just go their own way."

Around the bend in the settlement's street, the activity was more hurried, more dense. Darby and Poole stayed to one side as they walked, working their way through crowds and traffic.

"That Washington commissioner, name of Chrisman . . . he was talkin' on the street today. He says he means to have a treaty with the Kiowas that will let white men move

51

onto some lands out west of here."

Darby shook his head. "If he has a treaty, it will be with those Kiowa that agree to it. Anybody that isn't here or doesn't agree to it won't be bound by it."

"I took the notion he meant well."

"He might, at that. But what about the rest of them? When this Chrisman is gone, back east, what about the ones they leave out here? And why so many soldiers? You get the feeling somebody's politickin', Mr. Poole?"

If Poole had an answer to that, he didn't voice it. Just ahead was a space between buildings and two rough men came from there, thrusting an Indian between them. Each of them gripped one of the red man's arms and they twisted cruelly as they dragged him into the street. A thread of blood ran from the corner of his mouth, and one of his cheeks was puffed and swollen. The men glanced around and one—the man Poole had heard called Winter—shouted, "Poling! Mr. Poling! Here!"

The man who came toward them was lean and well-dressed. Quick dark eyes flanked a prominent nose in a face scarred by pox.

As he approached Winter said, "Look what we caught, Mr. Poling. Found him out behind your office, kind of hiding in that little alcove by the back door. He might have been tryin' to get in."

The Indian was a young man, his face contorted by pain and swelling bruises. He wore a simple buckskin shirt and leggings, his long hair was unbound except by a flannel band and he wore no ornamentation of any kind.

"Raise him up where I can see him," Poling said. The men turned the Indian's arms, twisting them up behind his back, arching him upright.

Poling stared at him, then glanced toward the river. "Is he one of them?"

"I don't know. Blue and me, we just caught him snoopin'."

"Winter asked him politely who he was," the other added. "He didn't tell us. We swatted him a little."

The two gunmen were grinning, enjoying the sport.

Darby started forward but Poole stopped him. "Better be a mite careful, Darby. Them's killin' men, I believe."

"I know who they are," Darby pulled away. "At least that one buzzard there, Winter. I busted him good one time when he got out of line. Turn loose."

A crowd was gathering and a pair of soldiers pushed through. "I'm Lieutenant Barnes," one said. "What's going on?"

Poling didn't look around. "My men caught this savage trying to get into my office. He may have slipped across the river. I want to know what he was after." He gripped a handful of the Indian's hair and twisted his head around, hard. "Who are you? What were you doing at my door?"

"Probably doesn't speak English," the lieutenant said. "Anybody here talk Indian?"

"I do, a little." Darby had pushed through to them. He fixed Poling with hard eyes. "Let go of his hair, Mister. You're humiliating him."

Winter grinned at him. "Back off, Curtis. He's ours and I'm gonna humiliate his arm right out of its socket if he doesn't talk to Mr. Poling."

Darby ignored him. "I said turn loose of his hair," he told Poling. "And call off these bloodsuckers before they hurt him."

"He's my prisoner," Poling snapped. "If you speak his language then you ask him what he was doing behind my office." The Indian tried to pull his head away from Poling's grip. Poling twisted his hair tighter and slapped him across the face. The Indian spat blood. Then, in a voice clipped and low with scorn, he spoke brief phrases and spat again.

Poling glanced at Darby. "What did he say?"

Darby had seen enough. "What I said," he growled, "was for you to turn loose of his hair." He grabbed Poling's arm, half-turning him. Hard fingers dug into the sensitive nerves of the man's elbow and he twisted, grating cartilage and bone. Poling's fingers sprang open, releasing the Indian's hair. His face went white and he drew a whistling breath of pain. Darby shoved him aside and he backed off,

53

a rage in his dark eyes, panting open-mouthed and cradling his violated arm.

"You bought it, squatter," the one called Blue snapped, releasing the Indian's arm to go for the revolver at his hip. He stopped, staring into the muzzle of Edwin T. Poole's shotgun.

With one arm free the Indian stabbed stiff fingers at Winter's eyes and spun loose from him. Before Winter could react the brave turned again, kicked him in the crotch, then dove through the gawking crowd and ran. The lieutenant drew his revolver, started to level it and Darby knocked it into the air. "You want to start a war?" he hissed. "Put that thing away."

Barnes frowned at him, then nodded and returned his gun to its holster. "You're right, of course. Private, go after that . . ." The private hurried away, but the Indian had disappeared. He had dodged between buildings and was gone.

Poling stood half-doubled over his injured arm, a hatred in his eyes. Winter rolled on the ground, retching, for this moment nowhere near the tough, fast-gun threat that was his reputation and his pride. Blue still stared into the muzzle of Edwin Poole's shotgun and into the mild blue eyes in the bearded face behind it. The private reappeared, shrugging and shaking his head.

Barnes shook his head, worried. "If he was one of those from across the river . . ." he turned to Darby. "Could you understand what he said?"

"He could have been Pawnee, I guess," Darby shook his head. "I don't speak much Pawnee."

"He wasn't a Kiowa, then? He wasn't one of those across the river?"

"No, I can tell you that for a fact, that he wasn't one of those across the river."

"Then maybe there's no harm done here. I hope not."

Darby glared at Poling and his gunmen, noting with a slight shock that the sheer rage in the land agent's eyes was like a physical force. He had never seen the like of it. "If some folks would learn to act like civilized people," he said, shaking his head, "they'd get along a lot better."

The words seemed to unfreeze Poling. With a snarl he slid his good hand into his coat and suddenly there was a man before him, a tall, casual-seeming man in traveling clothes and flat-crowned hat, and there was a slim revolver in his hand trained casually on Poling's brisket.

"The young man is right, Mr. Poling." His voice was low and mild. "And it would be a shame if you drew that gun. The time isn't right, you know. Not just yet."

Poling froze again. The gray eyes on him were as cold as winter ice and he felt there was something he should know, something he should remember . . . but could not.

Slowly then he turned away, and Blue and Winter followed him across the street. Darby glanced at the stranger, puzzled. The man only nodded and walked away.

With the excitement over, the crowds dispersed, and Darby strolled with Poole along the side street.

"That Poling, he's bad news," Darby said. "You see that look he got on his face there for a minute? I never. . . "

"I was busy watchin' his houn' dog at the time, but I reckon. You know, I got to thinkin' there, it might be nothin' would suit your Mr. Poling better than if there was some Indian trouble."

"I'm thinkin' the same thing."

"Was a good thing that buck they beat up was a Pawnee and not a Kiowa, wasn't it?"

"He was a Kiowa."

Poole stopped to stare at him. "You told that soldier he was a Pawnee, You said he wasn't one of them across the river."

"He isn't one of them. But he's a Kiowa. His name is Stalking Horse, and he's a Blackleg warrior. I just wish I knew what he's doing all the way up here."

"Blackleg? You mean he's one of them that attacked my wagons?"

"He led the attack."

"Then why in the name of the Almighty did you help him get loose?"

"Mr. Poole," Darby cocked a quizzical brow at the older

55

man, "you've been talking about you and me goin' into business . . . your wagons, my mules. How'd you like to try runnin' a freight line if the Blacklegs . . . and maybe the Real Dogs with them . . . was out for blood? Besides that, you have to understand about the Blacklegs. They're a weird bunch. Whatever they thought they were doin' that day we had to hold 'em off, this thing today is somethin' else entirely. It doesn't make any sense to hold grudges against Blacklegs. It just makes trouble, is all."

"Indians ain't that much different than anybody else."

"I'm not talking about Indians generally. I'm talking about Blacklegs. Even their own people don't spend much time tryin' to understand them."

"The other tribes, those over there, they don't have Blacklegs?"

"No. Oh, they have lots of other societies. But not Blacklegs. The Blackleg men are Kana'tenee, and that's all."

All seemed in order at their adjacent campsites. Billy Sipe sat atop Poole's lead wagon smearing salve on his healing arrow wound, and Trini Salazar slept on a mound of emptied packs, a fierce, innocent smile at his lips as he dreamed fierce, innocent Spanish dreams. The oxen were penned and hay-fed. The horses were picketed and the mules grazed in a meadow of grass and clover. Vince Copple saw them coming and walked out to meet them.

"All quiet here," he said. "Did you notice if there's a smithy down there in that town? We need a bell."

"A bell?"

"Hildegarde's gone and lost her bell. I can't find it anyplace."

Darby frowned. "How could she lose her bell?"

Copple shrugged. "Beats me. But she don't have it anymore. Seems like I remember her havin' it earlier, but it's gone now. We'll have to get another one made up."

"I got a haunch of antelope hangin' in the trail wagon," Poole told them. "Billy and me are gonna fry some up come evenin'. Why don't you fellers join us for supper?"

"Count me out," Darby told him seriously. "After I

56

change my shirt I have to go back to town and eat a hundred and twenty-five dollars worth of fried chicken."

Dawn was pale in the eastern sky and meadowlarks were tuning up when Darby Curtis returned to his camp. It had turned into a memorable evening. He had spent an hour in uncomfortable conversation with Patrick and Margaret Muldoon and several of their brood while Melissa and two of her sisters worked on supper. Then, at the long table that occupied most of one room of the Muldoon house, he had devoted two hours to devouring fried chicken, greens and pan bread, topped off with peaches, cream and honey. After that had come another hour of conversation with Patrick Muldoon, some of it increasingly pointed, while the women did the dishes.

Then, when Patrick Muldoon began to yawn, Darby had said his farewells. He had waited for a time in a willow grove while the night wore on and one by one the lamps went out in the Muldoon house. Then Melly had come, fresh and cologned and starry-eyed, and they had walked the quiet hills by moonlight.

What with first one thing and then another, Darby had not managed to get his sleep that night. He did not regret it in the slightest. He whistled as he poured water into a pan, heated it at a rekindled fire, washed and shaved. He was still whistling when the rest of them rolled out of their soogans and came searching for coffee.

"A toast," he said when their cups were filled and they had rubbed the sleep from their eyes. "To the High Plains Freight Company."

Vince Copple blinked at him. "Who's that?"

"That's us, gentlemen. We are the High Plains Freight Company. The six of us. All we have to do now is figure out the stock percentages."

Billy Sipe glanced around. "Six? I only count five."

"Well, the other one is sort of a silent partner. Matter of fact, he doesn't know he's a partner yet. But he will before the day's over."

"Who's that?" Poole asked.

"Name is Patrick Muldoon. He has a store in Willow Ford. Melly says he'll put up two hundred and fifty dollars, and I figure that entitles him to be a partner."

"And he doesn't know it, yet?" Vince Copple eyed him suspiciously. "I guess that's no surprise. But how'd you get Miss Melly to promise that much of her daddy's money?"

"I dickered hard."

In the little town below, dawn brought a frenzy of activity. Today the treaty talks would begin, and everyone—townsmen and visitors, soldiers and traders, manipulators and innocent bystanders—made ready for the big occasion.

Bugle calls and drill-field commands drifted on the morning breeze from the First Squadron's bivouac. From across the river, where a thousand Kiowa prepared for the day, there was a responding tattoo of drums and dew-claw rattles. Smokes of hundreds of morning fires stood tall and spindly above the Smoky Hill Valley, rising gray-white above hill-shadow where they took the sun like streamers of pink and gold.

The buffalo hunters were gone. Their campsite was vacant, their trail pointing west.

"Ain't no surprise," Poole suggested, a worried frown creasing his brow. "All the Kiowa gathered in here, never be a better time for them to head out there."

"Maybe they don't know Hawk That Hunts Walking is still out there someplace," Darby said.

"Maybe. Maybe they just don't care."

"Then they're crazy. How many of them did you say there are? Twenty or so? Those Blacklegs'll be on them like quills on a porky if they start messing with the herds."

Poole was studying the cavalry bivouac, a mile away and brilliant in the morning sun. "I don't know, Darby. Maybe them hunters knows somethin' we don't."

Billy Sipe drew the task of tending camp for the day. He sulked and complained, but was overruled.

"You tend the rank stock," Darby told him. "The mules will pretty much tend themselves. If you need to move them, all you have to do is get Hildegarde there to go where you want them. The rest will stay with her. Might be a good idea to hang a couple of pans on her halter until we get a bell made, but I think they'll stay together. Now, that big, dark one there, that's Lucifer. Don't get behind him. And the main thing is, keep Trini in camp." He pointed at the grinning Spaniard. "Even if you have to hog-tie him, I don't want him anywhere near those Indians."

When the camp was policed and the stock tended, Vince Copple started toward town with a list of supplies, harness, tackle, chain and rigging they would need to turn Poole's wagons and Darby's mules into a functioning jerk-line outfit. Among the required items was a bell. Edwin T. Poole set out to make the round of the area's business people. Somewhere here was a potential cargo that needed to be hauled someplace. Whatever it was, it would be the first venture of the High Plains Freight Company.

And Darby Curtis headed for the meeting ground by the river. He was worried about what was going on. He wanted to learn as much as he could.

He also wondered vaguely why Billy Sipe, who according to Poole had not wanted to go into town yesterday, was so all-fired anxious to get away from camp today.

In a little, shuttered office in Willow Ford, Mercer Poling frowned at the men around him. His arm still ached from the day before, and a nagging worry had kept him awake through most of the night. Something about the gray man who had pointed a gun at him, had seemed to be taunting him . . . he couldn't unravel it, but something was wrong.

"I want to clear all this away now," he told the men. "I shall stay here only through the treaty talks. There may be an opportunity there, as DeWitt says, but I doubt it. The interpreter thing is so vague as to be almost stupid. But since you insist, DeWitt, we shall see. At any rate, once the talks are done I shall return to Washington. I work far more

59

comfortably there. I am wasting time out here.

"We shall assume there will be a limited treaty, and that the commissioner will make no further demands. We shall assume also that, once the tribes are gone, Major Grimes and his squadron will be posted to Camp Jacob, to oversee the treaty lands.

"That is where you come in, DeWitt. You will apply promptly for the post of sutler, and I can assure you the major will approve your application. From that point, you will deal directly with Cully and you will stay in close contact with me.

"You, Pasco," he directed his gaze at the rough-dressed man who led his patent collectors, "continue as you are doing now. I want a precedent set that will apply to the new patents when I get them. No squatters. You set the fees, and make them high, and you enforce them."

"Me and the boys . . ." the man began.

"You will have Tram and Blue. Winter is coming to Washington with me. And by the way," Poling glanced at Winter, "where is Blue? He is supposed to be here."

"He went off studdin' after some squatter girl last night, Mr. Poling. You know how Blue is. I haven't seen him since."

"Well, find him. Then all of you join me at the treaty ground. And all of you, stay out of trouble. DeWitt, stay for a moment. The rest of you can leave."

When the gunmen were gone, Poling asked, "What did you find out?"

"The man's name is Kichener, sir. Ernest Kichener. He seems to be with the government—at least he has credentials of some sort—but nobody with the commission party seems to know anything about him. I don't think they even know him." He shrugged. "That's all I could get, Mr. Poling. There just isn't anything more."

Poling scowled, rubbing his sore arm. "And that Curtis? What about him?"

"Nobody, sir. He's a son of one of the old squatters in the strip—Chance Curtis, the first one there, from what Pasco tells me—he was gone for a while, maybe in the war, then came back and started mule-freighting out on the plains. He speaks Kiowa, grew up with them he says. Winter knows him. He says he's going to kill him when he gets the chance. I gather this Curtis may have whipped him one time, probably over something to do with the patent fees, and you know that isn't something Winter would ever forget. But Curtis is nobody."

"Very well. You tell Winter to leave him alone. He can have his sport some other time, when there is less at stake. I'll expect you at the grounds, then. Good morning."

For an hour or more, Winter searched the town for Blue. And when he did not find him in the town, he searched the nearby camps. There was no trace of him anymore. Somehow, Blue had simply vanished.

Finally Winter gave up. If Blue couldn't show up on time, that was Blue's lookout, not his.

VI

"Those are simple, primitive people over there, sir. Think of them as ignorant children, unschooled in the arts of civilization. Thus, in order to deal with them, one must first impress them. A certain amount of pageantry is wholesome, and should place them in the proper frame of mind to respond in a positive manner to your authority."

As he spoke, Major Alfred Grimes paced the length of the high-walled assembly tent. Its canvas was bright with morning sun, and Commissioner James Chrisman noticed again how splendid was the little major's own attire. Shadowless light glistened on the bright saber at his hip, the high polish on his boots, the insignia on cap and collar, the clustered medals on his breast.

Chrisman turned again to the open flaps of the tent. Beyond lay the freshly-dressed parade ground, conference tables set and ready at its far end where a brace of big cottonwood trees would provide shade. Beyond that was the shallow ford of the Smoky Hill River. Above its far bank the land swelled upward and away, and there stood the massed tall lodges of the Kiowa people. Behind the assembly tent soldiers had established a cordon, and people had begun to gather there to view the morning's events.

"It all sounds a bit pompous and gaudy, Major," Chrisman said. "I had envisioned a more simple meeting, I suppose. I had thought we might simply sit down with their leaders and see what we might iron out. Still, I imagine there is no harm in a little entertainment beforehand. I'm certain your cavalry—performing in close-order drill—can be quite colorful."

Grimes glanced around at him, frowning. "Colorful" was not the word he would have chosen. "Awesome" would have been better. How better to deal with a pathetic bunch of poor primitives—nothing more than squalid nomads at best—than to present to them the power and pageantry of crack cavalry drill? It should leave them so thunderstruck that the civilian commissioner could wrest from them any sort of accord he might want. Yet, he held his tongue.

"Just leave the ceremony to me, Mr. Commissioner," he said finally. "I think a simple squadron drill should leave them something to think about for a very long time."

"I suppose," Chrisman sighed. He shaded his eyes and squinted toward the river. "Ah, I see them. They're coming over. I should go out to meet them."

"With all respect, sir, I suggest you wait. Let them assemble first. Then you can make your entrance with proper dignity. I have assigned a unit to escort you and your party across the parade ground at the proper moment. Captain Michaels will advise you."

At the river, a line of Indians on foot waded across and reached the corner of the cleared area. Two of them were old men wrapped in robes. The rest were young braves who had yet to earn ornamentation.

The group paused there. Sleeping Fox, seventy years old and partially blind, motioned his grandson to join him. "Look now, Dark Wing. Tell me what you see."

The youngster took his time, looking around, taking in all the details. Then he said, "Grandfather, the soldiers have cleared a field here. Over there are tables and chairs, and across the wide field are all the people. I see white lodges, and many people. They are looking at us. Past the lodges are blue soldiers. Many of them. They are on their horses, and they stand in straight lines. Three groups, three lines each. What does it mean, grandfather? Will they make war on our people?"

Sleeping Fox lowered his head in thought. "Look at the field again, Dark Wing. Are there marks upon it?"

"Yes, Grandfather. There are sticks in the ground with

little flags on them."

The smile that crossed the old man's face was one of pure delight. "Dark Wing, go back to the village. Tell the chiefs there that we are to be entertained. Then they will know the proper courtesies."

At his side the ancient Many Moons shrugged within his robe. "You were right, Sleeping Fox. The white men are like children. It is not enough that we meet and talk. First they must show us their toys."

Soon there were more than seventy Indians on the treaty ground—old men, youngsters and several women. They crossed the river carrying various packs and bundles, and Sleeping Fox heard the words of the interpreter and instructed his people. Bundles were opened, and a half-circle of hide mats placed on the ground in front of the conference tables. Back rests were set on these, with blankets atop them. Women and children by the hundreds gathered on the far bank to watch.

A procession of mounted Kiowa formed below the lodges, and proceeded at stately pace down to the river, across the ford and up the bank to the cleared ground. Four groups of four brightly-garbed warriors came first, carrying plumed lances and painted shields. Following them were a dozen stern-faced men wearing feathers and robes. And behind these were four more fours of the warrior escort.

"We have just been impressed," Major Grimes remarked casually to Commissioner Chrisman. "Now let's do some impressing of our own." He drew his saber, raised it and brought it down in a flashing arc. From beyond the tents Troop B of the First Squadron came at a canter, sunlight flashing on metal, glinting on polished accessories and giving brilliance to the blue tunics and yellow-striped gray breeches of the mounted men. In tight synchronization they flowed onto the field, broke smartly left and right, did wheel-abouts in unison and formed a rule-straight rank facing the assembled Indians fifty yards away. Drummers beat a rolling tattoo.

"Very smart," Chrisman admitted. "Very nicely done."

Then from the flanks Troops A and C charged the field

in columns of three, hooves pounding and heads up, stirrup to stirrup and bit above gaiter. Bugles sounded in unison and the two troops wheeled past the ends of the motionless B Troop line to meet at center and pass through, seemingly brushing each other as the lines threaded by in dress. At a single bugle call the two full troops in full parade dress formed six abreast and saluted the treaty table. Then the entire assemblage paced forward, a square "C" of mounted cavalry, until its lead columns flanked the conference area and the assembled Indians.

The Indians watched without comment or gesture.

"That should do it," Grimes said. "Captain Michaels, escort please."

Flanked by an honor guard of cavalry, the treaty party walked across the field, through an opening in the center of the line of B Troop, and took their places at the table. Chrisman had the center chair, flanked by Major Grimes and L. W. Holmes on his right, and Commissioners Pro Tem John Bell and Franklin T. Price on his left. Despite his misgivings, Chrisman was impressed at the cavalry's spectacular overture to the talks.

"Ask their chiefs to be seated," he told the contract interpreter, "so that we may begin."

The man walked to the cluster of Indians, then returned, face ascowl. "Sir, the old man over there says he is very pleased to be so welcomed, but the chiefs aren't here yet. They are just coming now."

Grimes muttered an oath and they looked toward the river. From the lodges issued a long double column of mounted warriors, hundreds of them. The first ones were already across the river, the rear ones still pouring from the village. When all were across, they paused on the river-bank, then two groups of fifty or more warriors, all carrying plumed lances and wearing red and black paint, broke free and galloped in an arc, around behind the waiting cavalry, to take up positions behind each of the startled soldiers. Some of the cavalry mounts became skittish and Grimes shouted, "Captains! Have your men hold their ranks! Damn!" he breathed.

The next wave was a long, synchronous line of young braves on painted ponies, all heavily ornamented and splashed with brilliant colors. These lined out at a canter, around the flanks of C Troop and into the center of the military formation, where they turned sharply right and charged at a gallop, straight toward the lined troopers of B. At the last instant, the braves reined their mounts into skidding, turning halt, and then sat silently, their backs to the pale, stunned soldiers. As one, the braves drew out bows and an arrow each, notched their arrows and shot them into the ground before their mounts. While this was happening, two groups of warriors painted black from head to foot, wearing scarlet headdresses and riding horses with matching scarlet emblems painted on neck and haunch, circled the military formation and neatly boxed the two flank troops.

It had all happened in seconds. At the treaty table and beyond the cordon lines, stunned people watched, eyes wide, mouths hanging open. A husky brave in breechclout, moccasins and white-feathered roach sprinted across to stop before the treaty table and recite something in Kiowa. The scowling interpreter spat, then turned to Chrisman.

"He says he brings the welcome of the chiefs of five nations to the representatives of the Great Father. He says the chiefs come now to hear whether you have something to say."

Chrisman smiled thinly and leaned toward the flushed and furious Grimes. "Did you say something about pageantry, Major? Something to impress them, perhaps? Well, I am impressed."

The ceremonies done, a cluster of Kiowa in various garb rode into the conference area, flanked by stern, fully-armed warriors whose faces, shirts, legs and horses were painted in intricate designs made up of various shades of red.

"The Horse Clan," Darby Curtis muttered from the cordon line. Only once before had he seen the senior warriors of the Three Rivers people out in force and decked in their finery. It was a sight one did not forget.

At the perimeter of the conference circle the robed Kiowa

dismounted, handing their reins to flanking Horse Clan warriors, who took them aside, then spread to close the river end of the area, making a complete square of mounted men.

There were twelve chiefs. They strode to the conference table and each solemnly gave his name. The interpreter repeated the introductions and clerks wrote in their journals.

Spotted Horse and his subchiefs Thunder and Eagle Claw presented themselves. Then Antler of the Evening Wind People came with the medicine man Carries Water, followed by Medicine Wing and his son Deer, the sullen, dark Agado flanking them. Beaver Tail Man introduced himself. Then Cloud, Kicking Bird and Small Bull of the Three Rivers People.

Darby caught sight of the tall, muscular form of White Bear as well, but the man did not go to the table. White Bear was a warrior. He would let Cloud and Kicking Bird speak for him in conference.

"Our proud soldiers seem to have been neatly outclassed," a voice said at Darby's shoulder. "I wonder if it would be so in the field."

He turned. The man there was the one who had backed Poling down the day before, and now Darby had a better look at him. The man was tall, lithe and immaculately tailored. He might have been between forty and fifty years old—silver showed prominently at his temples, below the flat-crowned hat that shaded his eyes—but he had the physique of a younger man. Darby had a quick impression of a steel blade sheathed in quiet gray clothing.

"It might," he said. "I hope we never find out. I doubt if those dress-up soldiers know enough about the Kiowa to ever know what hit them if that happened."

"Don't let the spit and polish deceive you," the man said. "Most of those troopers are fresh from war and tough as nails."

"So is every Kiowa who ever raised a lance. Mister, those Indians are born seasoned. They have to be."

"You know them, then."

"I've known some. I grew up around them."

"And you speak their language."

Darby glanced at him. There was a hint of humor in the cold, gray eyes.

"How did you know that?"

"The same way I know that Pawnee yesterday wasn't a Pawnee. Since you understand the speech of these people, would you like to listen to the conference?" His hand on Darby's arm was gentle and friendly. Still Darby had the fleeting thought that it was just as well he wanted to go where the man suggested . . . that had he not wanted to, he might have gone anyway.

They passed through the cordon. A soldier who stepped forward to bar them backed off instantly at a glance from the stranger in the low-crowned hat, and they were well across the parade ground before Darby said, "My name is Curtis. Darby Curtis. And you?"

"Forgive me," the man responded. "My name is Ernest Kichener."

Near the conference tables a captain of escort stepped from his post to block their way. Kichener drew a small wallet from his coat, opened it and displayed it. The captain saluted him and returned to his position. They found a place to stand and listen, just behind the center table.

Chrisman was just completing his introductory remarks, extending the respect of the Great Father in Washington to the Kiowa people. The interpreter hesitated and spat before speaking. Darby wondered where they had come up with Kirby Quinn to interpet for them. Everybody knew about Quinn. The man was a liar and a cheat, and he hated Indians. Still, Quinn spoke the language.

"There has been war among the white people," Chrisman said. "But now the war is over. The path is clear toward peaceful growth of our nation."

"The white men have finished fighting among themselves," the interpreter, Quinn, said in Kiowa. "Now a new sun rises and the white nation seeks new paths."

Kichener muttered to Darby, "Listen closely. Tell me

what you hear."

"We come as friends among the Kiowa," Chrisman spoke. "Just as your people need open spaces and the buffalo, so do our people need room to grow."

Quinn hesitated a moment, scowling. Then he told the chiefs, "Now the white people are all friends again. The Kiowa have all the spaces where the buffalo are. The white people need these spaces."

Darby's eyes went wide. "That isn't what he said. That isn't right."

"What is he doing?" Kichener whispered.

"Hell, it sounds like he's declaring war. He's changing what the commissioner says, making it sound like the white people are ordering the Kiowa off the buffalo grounds."

At the whispers Quinn glanced around, his eyes mean.

"Do you think it is intentional?" Kichener asked.

"Those aren't the kinds of changes that would be accidental."

"Keep listening."

There were whispered remarks among the seated chiefs, then one rose to his feet and stepped forward a pace. He was a young man, not over thirty years, slim and whiplike, with intelligent eyes set in a face that was thoughtful and reflective.

"This one is called Kicking Bird," a clerk told Chrisman.

The Indian removed his ceremonial robe and draped it on his arm in sign of peace. When he spoke his words were slow and deliberate. "The Kiowa people are honored to hear words from the Great Father. We know the Great Father's white children have been at war. At times that war has spilled over its proper banks and we have seen it in our lands. We have stayed apart from it. It was not our war. We are glad the white people are at peace. But now we wonder whether they have had enough war, or whether they look for someone else to fight."

"He says the Kiowa are willing to talk with the Great Father's people," the interpreter said. "They have watched the white men fight each other and wanted no part of it.

They wonder who the white people will fight with next."

Darby gritted his teeth and whispered to Kichener.

Major Grimes leaned toward Chrisman. "Arrogance," he muttered. "It sounds as though he is threatening us."

"I can't understand why," Chrisman said. "I have expressed nothing but friendship to them."

Darby could contain himself no longer. "Not the way they heard it, Mister." At the conference table, men looked around at him, frowning at the interruption. Kirby Quinn spun around at the words, bristling. Hand at his sheathed knife, he shot Darby a murderous look.

"What did you mean by that, sir?" Chrisman asked him, stern eyes studying him.

"I mean that fellow isn't saying it right. He's twisting things around so it comes out different. Kicking Bird didn't make any threat. He spoke of respect and concern. That's all."

Major Grimes had turned to the escort. "Captain, who is this . . ."

"He's with me," Kichener said quietly. He displayed the little wallet, but only to Chrisman. "He is fluent in Kiowa."

"That isn't surprising," Grimes snapped. "I've heard about some of these westerners."

The Indians were whispering among themselves. Kicking Bird walked to the table and looked from the hired interpreter to Darby, then at Chrisman. He spoke in Kiowa and the interpreter responded in clipped tones, angry.

"He wants to know what the trouble is," Darby told Kichener. "Quinn there told him I was interfering with the meeting, trying to make trouble."

"Then maybe you should set him straight," Kichener suggested.

"I certainly will." Darby turned to Kicking Bird. "The words of the tall hat and of Kicking Bird . . ." he started, then stopped as the Indian turned away.

Kicking Bird gestured and a robed man got to his feet. With a start Darby saw that the man was bearded. He was white. He walked to the table and addressed Chrisman. "Sir, Chief Cloud was aware there might be difficulties with

70

the languages here, and he wanted no misunderstanding. My name is John Miles. At least, that was my name once. I am called Sha'ata'ee by these people." He glanced at the interpreter. "No harm is done. No one among the Kiowa would believe the words of 'Runs Backward' Quinn. They know him too well."

Darby stared in amazement. John Miles had once been an associate of Chance Curtis. But he had been dead for ten years, so far as anyone knew. Darby felt he was seeing a ghost.

The interpreter, Quinn, paled and shot a glance toward the cordon. Darby followed his glance. Among those there, he recognized Poling and the enforcers Pasco and Winter. There were others who appeared to be grouped with them.

"Did you vouch for this man, Major?" Chrisman pointed at Quinn.

Grimes shook his head. "I did not, sir. He was brought to me . . . by friends. I assumed . . ."

Chrisman looked away. "Possibly you assumed too much. Very well, we will both assume that a poor choice has been made. Mr. Quinn, you are relieved. Gentlemen," he glanced at the members of his party, seated to either side. "Mr. . . . ah . . . Miles has offered his services as interpreter. Shall we accept?"

"Who vouches for him?" Grimes glowered. "The man obviously lives among the Indians."

"John Miles was always good for his word," Darby told Kichener. "My Daddy knew him a long time ago. I thought he was dead."

"I vouch for Mr. Miles," Kichener told Chrisman. "I suggest you go on with your conference. I will be glad to discuss my credentials with you later, Mr. Commissioner."

With a thunderous look at Darby, Kirby Quinn stalked away toward the cordon. Glancing after him, Darby saw Edwin Poole gesturing at him from one side. The treaty seemed in good hands, and Kichener was no longer at his elbow, so Darby edged away and trotted to where Poole waited.

"Have you seen Billy?" Poole asked. "Or the Spaniard?

I got back to camp and there wasn't anybody there."

"I told Billy to stay there! And I told him to keep Trini there! The mules . . . are they? . . ."

"Oh, they're all right," Poole assured him. "There just wasn't anybody around so I thought I'd better check. I found Vince and sent him on out to stand guard."

Darby's face went bleak. "You better go on back and keep watch, Mr. Poole. I don't know about your greenhorn buddy, but if Trini Salazar is running loose with all these Indians around, we could have trouble."

Poole headed south toward the camp. After a moment's thought, Darby pushed through the crowds at the cordon and turned west, making for a rise beyond the stables from which he could scan the area.

From a distance Winter, watching, saw him go, and shouldered people aside as he dove into the crowd then came out again with Mercer Poling, followed by DeWitt and Kirby Quinn. Winter pointed. There was brief conversation, then Poling shrugged and turned away. DeWitt and Winter trailed after him.

"Runs Backward" Quinn stood alone then, with his back to the crowds and his hand at the long knife he wore. His eyes were hard and flat, his mouth drawn thin with hatred. He was remembering.

At first he hadn't recognized Darby Curtis. A lot of years had passed since that day when he had seen him last . . . that winter day at Purcell's Store on the Kaw.

Quinn and a partner he remembered only as Smith had traveled a long, hard way in miserable weather to bring furs to sell . . . all the way from the flint hills down into the frozen, timbered valley of the Kaw where there was a good cash market. On four gaunt pack horses they carried enough prime pelts to give them both a fair stake. Cold days and numbing nights it had cost them to come to Purcell's. Yet, it was necessary. They needed to sell their wares a long way from where they found them.

He and Smith had never counted their money. The pursuit they had feared on that hard journey had never been behind them. Somehow, they were ahead of them.

Nine hard-eyed Indian bucks, two marshals and a beanpole of a kid were waiting for them at Purcell's. The kid spoke Kiowa, and when Quinn and Smith were in the store and the door closed behind them he stepped forward and had one of the Indians make a mark on a piece of paper. Then he handed the paper to a marshal. "Look at their furs," he said. "This is Buffalo Rattle's mark. It's on the underside of every pelt in those packs. These men stole those furs from Buffalo Rattle and his people eight days ago on the Smoky Hill. We came to get them back."

Smith had gone crazy then. His bullet killed a Kiowa and a marshal's bullet killed him. But in the shooting, Quinn escaped and ran . . . and spent years on the run before it all blew over. The Kiowa on the Smoky Hill now were not the same Kiowa as then. Nobody remembered a trivial incident at Purcell's store.

But Quinn remembered. The kid had cost him his stake that day. And now today the same kid—grown up but still the same kid—had cost him good wages from the Indian Commissioner and an even better bonus from Cain DeWitt.

He saw Darby reach the rise beyond the stables, saw him looking, searching, saw him run then toward the river. All other eyes now were on the parley grounds. Quinn made a decision. With a quick glance around him he eased away from the crowds, past the perimeter cordon, then scurried along a shallow wash that came down from the willow groves. Out of sight of the activities then, he set a path that would intercept Darby at the river. Quinn didn't have to test the knife at his belt. It was razor-sharp. He always kept it that way.

VII

Trinidad Salazar was restless. For a time, after the New York City man said something to him and then left the camp, he stayed there mending harness, hauling water and doing other trivial things to occupy himself. Yet, by the time the sun was high and none of the rest had returned, he found himself pacing aimlessly about the hillside, his eyes turning again and again to the town in the distance. He was alone. It bothered him to be so, particularly when there were so many people so nearby.

Trini had known loneliness several times in his young life. He had been lonely when his brothers dispossessed him of the family *hacienda* in Aragon and sent him away. He had been lonely in Madrid when, after a year of devoted attention to the radiant Doña Lucinda Villanova-Madeiro, her father had been transferred to Mexico as a representative of the Portuguese government and she had of course gone with him. He had been lonely in the hold of the old clipper *Cameranth* all the way across the Atlantic ocean—and had nearly starved as well. And he had known loneliness at Montreal and Detroit and St. Louis and a hundred other places where no one spoke his language or cared about his situation.

The ultimate heartbreak—it must have been so—came at Vera Cruz. They told him the beautiful Doña Lucinda had succumbed to the charms of a trader named Miguel Jesus

Montoya and had returned with him to New York City. And yet, he had been lonelier still the day Chance Curtis found him afoot and weary, staggering across high desolate plains while a party of Comanches followed him at a distance, idly curious as to when he might collapse. The old man put him in his wagon, fed him and muttered over him, then he shouted curses at the Comanches until they turned and went away. The Comanches had wanted no part of the crazy old trader who was as a brother to their Kiowa allies and who, it was said, knew the land better even than they did.

Besides, neither the old man nor the peculiar young man he befriended had anything they wanted.

Trini had stayed with the Curtis people, first working for old Chance and now for the son, Darby. He had no clear concept of being a partner in the new enterprise with the Poole man and the New York City man—he understood little of what was said—but he was content to be with good companions. Except that he did not like to be alone. He liked people. The more the better. He was happiest when he was with friends. He was even content when he found himself among enemies, provided there were plenty of them.

But to be Mediterranean and alone was to not exist.

He looked again toward the little settlement by the river. There were hundreds of people there. Even though those on the near side were all—to him—foreigners, and those across the river were the accursed Moros, still they were people.

In his pack he found a bright red shirt and a silver-trimmed short jacket that he treasured. He dusted his wide hat, slicked his boots and put on his best attire. Then he walked to where Hildegarde was grazing. He patted her cheek, rubbed her face and breathed into her nostrils. Then he stamped his foot and pointed at the ground. *"Aqui!"* he told her. That done he crossed himself, grinned and muttered, *"Santa Elena, ven conmigo."* Trini Salazar headed for town.

He was nearing the settlement, making his way through a field full of wagons and buggies, when he saw Edwin Poole coming toward him. He ducked out of sight until the man had passed, then changed his course. He did not want to be discovered just yet and sent back to camp.

Where the *Americanos Ingleses* gathered, there would be Darby Curtis and the others. So Trini eased his path toward the west and circled around the livery barn and the backs of the row of buildings beyond it until he came in sight of the parley grounds beyond the town and his eyes opened wide in admiration. The soldiers were there, crisply ranked in their formations, blue of tunics and gleam of brass brilliant in the high bright sun. And flanking and ranking them were the brilliant-hued societies of the Kiowa, crimsons and yellows, whites of chalk and blacks of fine-drawn soot, plumed raven roaches and bound heavy braids, feathered lances and bright shields, and their horses shared their pigments and were part of them. Trini Salazar's heart rose into his throat at sight of such pageantry. He wished to be part of it, to glory in it, to add his color to the wash of colors before him. And yet, to be found would be to be sent back to the camp. He satisfied himself for a few minutes by strutting back and forth at the corner of the last building, showing off his bright garb and lithe stride for any who happened to glance around. But as far as he could tell, no one did.

So he edged west again, around the parley grounds, toward the river. The people over there, on the other side, were facing this way. They seemed to be only Moros, but they were at least an audience.

He had gone three hundred yards and was nearing the bank of the river, strutting and grinning for the Indian women across the shallow stream, when a bright-painted brave in the near ranks saw him, wheeled his horse and pranced to cut him off. The Indian wore the crimson and plumage of the elite Horse Clan. His chief, Cloud, had shared separately the concerns of the soldier chief Grimes. When the Kiowa with their warriors and the white people with their soldiers met on common ground, the danger was very real. It was well to keep a river between their constituencies.

Trini stopped, looked up at the sombre, painted face above him and backed away. The Indian was alert and looked very strong, and he held his lance as one who has used such instruments many times.

The warrior said something to him and pointed back the way he had come.

Trini glared at him for a moment, then turned and trudged back up the river's cresting bank. His broad hatbrim hid the color in his face, the shifting of his eyes, the tilt of his head as he glanced back. The warrior watched him go, then wheeled his horse and rejoined his rank. He did not look back. If he had, he would not have seen Trini. Before the pigmented horse had stepped into line with its peers, the Spaniard was thirty yards to the west, ducking low and scooting toward the river behind a screen of brush.

It was not that Trinidad Salazar relished the possibility of irritating the big Moro with the sharp lance. Rather, by the time he reached the river again he had forgotten the warrior entirely. In the instant when he had glanced over his shoulder, he had come in line with a break in the screen of willows upstream and his sharp eyes had seen distant movement there . . . movement with a hint of contour and color that sent his blood racing through his veins.

Moving steadily and stealthily, Trini eased through thickets and around stands of scrub and thistle until he found himself on the river's bank, peering through drooping elm fronds. The river's shallow stream bent here, coursing along its gravel bed, forming a pool where the clear water was deep and gentle. It was shaded by a leaning elm which spread long boughs over the stream-bed to catch the summer sun. From just downstream, beyond the bend, he heard women's voices and the rhythmic splashing of water, and an intense excitement grew in him. Away from the encampments, upstream from view of those on either bank, young *Indio* women had come down to the river to bathe.

Trini grinned, strong white teeth flashing. *"Santa Elena,"* he whispered, *"muchisimas gracias."* From where he knelt to the sweeping limb of the elm tree was a few

77

yards at most, and he gathered himself to dash from one cover to the next, then stopped. There was movement to his right and a lean, mustached man in buckskins crept from the shadows of a thicket, pausing at its edge. He was bent low, furtive and tense. He did not look toward the river, but gazed intently to his right, where brush screened a narrow path leading away. It was the same path Trini had come along only minutes before.

As the Spaniard watched the man drew a long, slim knife from his belt and eased back into the shadows of the brush, still watching intently where the path curved away.

Trinidad Salazar knew an ambush when he saw one, but he didn't know what to do about it. The man was tall and strong, and the knife was wicked. And Trini had brought no weapon.

He didn't know who the man was waiting for, but he knew if he tried to interfere the man would turn on him instead. And then, it probably was none of his business anyway.

Movement below the bank caught his eye and he glanced that way, then pursed his lips in a silent whistle. An Indian girl had come into sight, swimming lazily, and as he watched she glided under the drooping elm branch, found her footing in the waist-deep water there and stood up, throwing her long hair back in a sweeping rainbow of spray. She shook her uplifted head, eyes closed as the water flowed from her, and a smile played on a face from the realm of angels. Her trim body was fawn-sleek and tantalizing, a coppery tan lighter by shades than the dusky rose of her face and arms. High-set breasts quivered as she moved, firm but fully round, and the Spaniard's eyes widened in stunned admiration. *"Todos los Santos,"* he whispered. *"Que linda."*

She opened large, dark eyes then and looked around. For a moment she was looking directly at him, and he felt as though he were drowning. But he was hidden in the willows and her gaze moved on. He felt his breath hot and ragged in his throat, and had trouble swallowing. He had never seen a sight so beautiful.

The girl took a step closer to the bank, deeper into the shade of the elm, and the water was around her hips. She spread her arms and stretched luxuriantly. Somewhere in another world someone was calling his name.

He tried to ignore the intrusion, but could not. He glanced toward the path. The man with the knife still crouched there, and there was pantherish intensity about him. Beyond, out of sight but coming closer, he heard a shout. "Trini! Trinidad! Damn your hide, where are you?"

The girl heard the shout too, and she eased down into the water until only her head was visible, her eyes large and frightened. At that moment Trinidad Salazar could have cheerfully strangled Darby Curtis.

He gritted his teeth. The Spanish language was unsuited to the thoughts in his mind then. "Sonomabitch!" he whispered.

The chatter of women beyond the bend had stilled. The girl under the elm bough eased away from the bank, ready to dive or flee. The spell was broken. Trini burst from his cover into the open above the bank, livid with rage, shouting his fury. "Sonomabitch! Sonomabitchsonoma-bitchsonoma . . . !" A violent figure hurtled at him from the thicket three yards away. *Madre de Dios*, he had forgotten the man with the knife. Trini dropped and rolled and the man went over him, skidding to turn at the very edge of the low bank. With the quickness of panic Trini got his feet under him, bent low and charged the man, his head thudding into hard muscle as the knife whispered past his ear. Then Trini was down, half over the bank and scrabbling at brush to keep from falling as a resounding splash sounded and water sheeted over him. He heard pounding footfalls, screams and splashing water, and from a small distance the startled calls of male Kiowa voices, calls which blended into a rush of hooves approaching.

Blindly he pulled himself over the bank, then suddenly he was grasped and lifted, hard hands flinging him up, arms around him, and the sting of parting brush on his flailing hands. He tried to shout and a large, calloused hand clamped over his face, cutting off his breath. An instant later he was thrown to the ground and a heavy body fell across him. Arms pinned his arms, legs held his legs down and a harsh whisper froze him where he was.

"Damn you, Trini, if you move I'll break your head!"

They lay silent then, deep in a thicket and screened from sight, as the sounds from the river a few yards away increased in volume. Running horses on the far bank, then thudding across gravel and into the stream . . . enraged yipping of Kiowa warriors . . . screams and shouts of women . . . a man's pleading voice: "No! Not me!" Then a few syllables of Kiowa cut off abruptly. More splashing, horses and voices going away.

Trini started to move and Darby pressed him down viciously. There were sounds close at hand now, soft, scuffing sounds, voices very low, the movement of brush. The two in the thicket held their breath. Trini's head was turned slightly to one side. The thorny brush concealing them pressed viciously into his chest, his shoulders and his cheek. Blood seeped into his eye and he tried to blink it away. A little tunnel in the brush was before him, a rabbit run, and there was daylight and gray grass at its far end. A beaded moccasin appeared there, stood for a moment and lifted and was gone. Cautiously, above him, he felt the roll of muscles as Darby Curtis turned his head, one way and then the other, slowly so no brush would move as he did. Eternities passed, one by one.

Low voices again, the sibilant discourse of the *Indios*, and then moccasins scuffed the weeded bank and there was the ripple of water, receding.

When Darby Curtis finally crawled out of the thorn thicket and pulled the battered Spaniard out after him, they were alone. The girl was gone, the other bathing women were gone, the warriors were gone and the man with the knife was gone.

They looked around, then they looked at each other and Trini paled before the thunderous anger in Darby's eyes. "*Señor* Darby, *el hombre con cuchillo . . . ,*" he began.

"Trini," Darby gritted through clenched teeth, "Shut

up."

All the way back to the settlement the Spaniard padded along behind Curtis like a scolded puppy, muttering in Spanish and occasionally shaking his head. He was crestfallen and purged of his sins . . . but he was puzzled as to what his sins might have been. He had only gone for a walk.

In the settlement Darby stalked from one place to another, looking and searching, occasionally stopping someone to ask questions. The peace talks by the river had adjourned, and the street was full of excited people. Trini could not make out what all the excitement was about, but he stayed close to Darby, scampering along behind him.

The larger man spoke to someone on the street, then scowled and turned toward a building across the way, his stride lengthening. His big hands were balled into fists. The building he entered had a mast before it, where signal flags flew. Trini had to dodge aside to avoid being hit by the door.

There were people inside, and Darby pushed his way past them to speak to a broad-shouldered, red-haired man at the plank counter. The man said something, shrugged and pointed with his thumb toward a doorway beyond the end of the counter. Darby strode through, Trini right behind him. It was a large, dim-lit store room. The beautiful red-haired young woman he had seen the day before sat demurely on a bale of hay, her eyes wide and starry. The New York City man stood before her, one foot on the same bale, one hand on his hip and the other gesturing eloquently as he spoke to her in tones that were at once persuasive, intimate and boastful.

Trini stared at the woman and swept off his hat. Darby strode to the man, swung a roundhouse punch and knocked him cartwheeling over a stack of kegs to sprawl feet-up among the grain sacks beyond them. Then as Trini and the woman watched wide-eyed he strode around the kegs and stood over the groaning man, lecturing him at length. When he was finished he stooped, hauled the man to his feet, grasped his shirt collar and propelled him out of the storeroom, through the store and out the front door.

Trini blinked at the woman. She blinked at him. He shrugged, swept his hat in a courtly bow and said, *"Buenas dias, Señorita."* With that he hurried to catch up with Darby and the New York City man. One day, he decided, he would take the time to try to understand these *Americanos*. But right now, he had better get back to the mules.

He wondered about the man with the knife. Obviously, the Moros had taken him. He wondered what they had done with him. Then he thought about it further and decided he didn't really want to know. He would think instead of how to repair his beautiful jacket.

Poole and Vince Copple had gathered in the stock and were standing alert guard at the camp, both of them armed. As he hurried a bitter and bleeding Billy Sipe up the hill toward them, Darby counted mules. All thirteen were there, and he noticed Hildegarde had a pair of tin cups hanging from her halter. He counted horses, wagons and equipment. And he counted people. He had Billy in tow, Trini was right behind him and Vince and Mr. Poole were watching them come in. It was time for a meeting.

"It's time we moved out," he told them when he had them all assembled.

"You son of a bitch, I may kill you," Billy Sipe said, nursing an aching jaw.

"Qué dice?" Trinidad Salazar wondered.

Edwin Poole and Vince Copple glanced at each other. "Any special reason?" Poole asked.

Darby made a show of glaring at Billy Sipe, then at Trini, and opened his mouth to speak harsh words. Then he closed it again. The pure, sullen stubbornness on Sipe's bruised face and the bewilderment on Trini's were too much for him. He relaxed and grinned. "Because we aren't making any money being here," he told Poole. "You heard anything about the conference?"

"Not much. Just some talk around the camps. Chrisman offered the Indians a pretty straight bargain. They get their bucks to leave the white people alone—don't take any hair or steal any women or children or burn anybody out—and the Great Father will send in food and clothing enough for everybody in all the tribes."

Darby squatted on his heels and chewed thoughtfully on a blade of grass. "That's a lot of stuff. S'pose we could get the haul on some of that?"

"Be worth a try. Anyway, that's the bargain he offers for a year from this treaty. Meanwhile, he wants the chiefs to go out and talk to the Cheyenne, the Comanche and the Arapahoe and try to get them to come in for a big parley next summer."

"He say anything about the buffalo?"

"He said the soldiers will see to it the white men leave the herds alone."

"Horse feathers."

"Well, that's what he told them, anyway."

"Be nice if it was to work out that way."

"You don't think it will, do you?"

"Be nice if it did. Where they figurin' to make all those deliveries?"

"Someplace west of here. Camp Jacob. They'll put a garrison there and handle the supplies from there. That is, if the chiefs agree. They pulled out to think about it. But if they do, might be good if we was at Westport when the word gets there to start loadin' wagons."

Darby spat out his grass blade and started on a fresh one. "Well, we could pick up a load of cordwood here, I guess. There's Germans at Flat Rock who would pay good money for cordwood. If they had any money. But what they do have is lead . . ."

Trini tapped him cautiously on the shoulder. "*Señor* Darby, *mira* . . .*"

"Hush up, Trini." Darby was deep in thought. The others had gathered around him, all squatting on their heels except Trini, who paced nervously behind him. "They have lead. So maybe we could haul lead down toward the Canadian. I imagine we could trade it along the way for some stuff that needs to go east. Then when we're full we could turn around and . . ."

Trini was tugging at his shoulder. "*Señor* Darby . . ."

"Trini, shut up, damn it! How do you figure we ought to work this, Mr. Poole?"

"Work what?" Vince Copple asked.

"Splits," Darby explained. "You can't have a company without splits."

Poole nodded. He cleared a little patch of sandy soil and prodded his knife at it. "I've been studyin' on that. Way I figure it, we're capitalized at seven thousand dollars."

Copple's eyes grew large. "We are?"

"Good a number as any," Poole said. "Take my wagons. I guess they're worth twenty-five hundred, all told . . ."

"Anybody offered that lately?" Darby asked drily.

Poole ignored him, scratching figures in the sand. "So let's say your thirteen mules are worth about the same . . ."

"They're worth a sight more than that."

"We're not talking a trade," Poole explained. "What I'm talking here is high finance and corporate capitalization. Real money doesn't have anything to do with that. Anyhow, that adds out at five thousand dollars. Then you said Mr. Muldoon will invest two hundred and fifty, and I guess I can sell my bulls for that much, anyway, and if you put up two-fifty of what you got for that wheat meal . . ."

"I'm already in for the mules. Why should I put up any more?"

Poole looked pained. "Because I already figured this out, and if you don't the numbers don't come out even. You don't want to start up a business with odd numbers, do you?"

Darby was outclassed. "No, I guess not. Go on."

Trini Salazar was pacing frantically now, and started to tug at Darby's shoulder again but Darby shook him off.

"So what we have here is beginning capitalization of five thousand, seven hundred and fifty dollars . . ."

"You said seven thousand a minute ago."

"Let me finish. Now comes the splits. There's five of us here to be active partners. Muldoon's a silent partner. I already counted his money. So let's say each of us is worth two hundred and fifty goin' in . . ."

The Spaniard had given up on Darby. Now he was at the black man's shoulder. "*Señor* Vince . . ."

"Wait a bit, Trini," Copple shooed him off. "I'm just startin' to get the hang of this."

"Five of us times two-fifty is a thousand, two hundred and fifty dollars," Poole said, underlining the number with a flourish of his knife. "And all that there tallies out to be seven thousand dollars!"

Darby stared at the scratched equation, puzzled. "What I wondered about was the splits."

"Well, that's easy. We split everything we make twenty-eight ways." Poole nodded happily. "Because if a basic share—which each one of us is—is two hundred and fifty, then two hundred and fifty goes into seven thousand twenty-eight times. See how simple it is?"

Darby's eyes lit. "Sure! So you get twelve shares and I get twelve and these three and Muldoon all get a share each. I like it!"

"Now wait a minute . . ." Billy Sipe erupted.

"It's all right, Billy," Poole assured him. "Darby and me are the one's takin' all the risk. All you got to worry about is to not get snakebit, stomped, drug, drowned, shot, Shanghaied, knotholed, knifed, or scalped. You got it easy. Him and me, we got money ridin' on this."

Trinidad Salazar was frantic now. "*Señores, mira . . .*"

Vincent Copple sat puzzling over the figures on the ground. "Mister Darby . . ."

"Deal?" Poole asked.

"Deal," Darby nodded. They clasped hands and shook on it.

Vince Copple shook his head. "You know you left three-four hundred dollars layin' on the table?" he asked Darby. "I guess you got so interested in the last part of that, that you forgot the first part. Them mules is worth more than them wagons."

"*Señores, por favor!*" Trini shouted, stamping his foot.

"Hope you never try to do business with Mr. Poole and Miss Melissa at the same time," Copple suggested to

Darby.

"Trini," Darby looked up at the Spaniard, "What the hell do you want?" Then he turned to look in the direction Trini was pointing, and his mouth dropped open. He jumped to his feet, followed by the others.

Across the river, on the far hillside, the Indian encampment was dissolving. Everywhere, lodges were coming down, and a cloud of dust clung to the land. Long furrows of dust pointed away, toward the crest of the hill and disappearing over it.

"Mira," Trini explained. *"Los Indios vayan."*

"Well, my Lord, Trini," Vince Copple snapped, "why didn't you say something?"

"What's going on?" Darby asked of no one in particular. "Why are they leaving?"

As he hurried down the hill toward Willow Ford, he saw a puzzled-looking Patrick Muldoon coming toward him. As he approached, Muldoon dug a purse from his shirt and began counting out money. Then he handed the money to Darby.

"Would you mind telling me," he asked, "why I am paying this to you?"

"That's for your share of the High Plains Freight Company. You're a partner. Why are the Kiowa leaving?"

"Oh, they're just pullin' back a few miles, way I heard it. They didn't like being so close to all those soldiers . . . an' then there's a story goin' around that they caught some jasper in the river with a bunch of their squaws. I don't know. They're just pullin' back. The High Plains what?"

"Freight company. You're a partner. They're still talking then?"

"Who? The Indians and the commissioners? Oh, sure. Just from wider back is all. I think Cloud and them will strike a deal, at least for a while. They been closer to white people than some of the other tribes. They don't want war if they can help it. Darby Curtis, have you been flim-flammin' my daughter? Two hundred and fifty dollars . . ."

". . . Would probably buy a man seven real top-grade

harness bulls if he was to dicker just right. I was thinkin' about you and how you need teams now and again to haul cord in. You see that fellow up there? With the beard? That's Mr. Poole and I happen to know he has seven of the stoutest oxen you ever saw in your life . . . and he's hard up for cash money. I bet if you was to offer him thirty-five, thirty-six dollars apiece he'd part with them right this minute."

Muldoon gawked at him. "Oxen? Look here, Darby, I hadn't thought about buyin' any . . ."

"Well, you ought to. Winter's coming on. I'll tell you what. I have two hundred and fifty dollars here . . ."

"Yeah, I know. I just handed it to you."

". . . and I need cordwood. Three high wagonloads. I'll pay you the whole two-fifty . . ."

"What kind of wagons?"

Darby turned, pointed up the hill. "Those three yonder."

Muldoon looked, then snapped, "Hell, those aren't wagons. Those are barns on wheels. You're talkin' about my whole season's cut. Two hundred and fifty . . ."

"But think of the profit, Mr. Muldoon," Darby put on his most persuasive squint. "After all, now that you're a partner, you want to keep purchase costs down just like the rest of us. That way we all make more profit. And you get a full share."

"But . . ."

"And think of the time you'll save. I'll pay you this two hundred and fifty right now—I trust you for the wood and the loading—and you can go straight over there and buy those seven bulls that you need."

With a reassuring pat on the back, Darby handed Muldoon the money. "You tell Mr. Poole that I said he should sell for two-fifty. After all, he's a partner, too."

With that he hurried on down the hill, anxious now to finish up his business at Willow Ford and be on his way. Ever since their arrival, he had sensed trouble here, though he couldn't put a finger on its source. Maybe, he thought, it was just the idea of all those Kiowa and all those soldiers being all in the same place at the same time with nothing between them but a shallow river. Then, there was a lot about that fellow Poling that didn't set right. And the camp of hunters that had been there and then gone. The whole situation was a powderkeg.

Still, it wasn't a sense of immediate danger that bothered him. It was more of a foreboding. It gnawed at him. He felt something had begun here that was beyond stopping, and he didn't like the feel of it.

The town, again, was full of people, but most of them were down on the flats, watching the Kiowa encampment slowly vanish. Between them, along the river, most of Major Grimes's cavalry squadron was deployed.

Despite the high excitement many of those in town had come here to find, there was a vast sense of relief over the settlement. Many of those recently from the east had heard of the savagery of the plains Indians . . . had heard stories that made their hair rise on their necks. And even those who had been here for a time, who knew the Kiowa and had traded with them, were nervous. The long-timers knew the difference between the Kiowa and the fiercer, less predictable Cheyenne and their neighbor tribes. But they knew another thing, too. They knew the Kiowa. And they knew that—if ever aroused—the Kiowa on these plains would be more terrible than the Cheyenne could ever be.

There had been strain on the faces he had seen since coming here. Now there was relief. But the relief had a quality of uncertainty about it that struck a chord in Darby's own brooding anxiety.

"Melly?" he called as he entered Muldoon's store. "Melly Bright-Eyes!"

She came from the back, eyeing him warily, noticing that they were alone in the store, remembering the violence of his assault on Billy Sipe a few hours before. "What do you want, Darby?"

"What do I want?" He scowled. "What kind of question is that? I just came to tell you we'll be movin' out as soon as we're loaded. We're taking your Daddy's cordwood to Flat Rock. What do you mean, what do I want?"

She sidled away from him. "Well, how do you expect me

to feel after seeing you beat that poor man half to death just for talking to me? I mean, after all, Darby . . ." Though she remained distant, the corners of her lips twitched tentatively, as at a sudden, pleasing thought. "I mean, it isn't like you have any claim or . . ."

"I didn't beat him half to death. I only whopped him to get his attention. He was supposed to be lookin' after my mules, not lollygaggin' . . ."

"Your mules!" Melissa's eyes blinked, then fixed on him. "You hit him because of your mules?"

"Sure. Why else?"

"Well, because I thought . . ."

"You see?" he assured her. "You were all upset over nothing." With two long steps he closed the distance between them, took her stunned face between his hands and kissed her. "You behave yourself, now. I'll be back time to time and I don't want you spoonin' anybody while I'm gone."

"D-Darby Curtis . . . !"

"But then, who are you gonna find that's as handsome as me? You thank your Daddy for the money, and tell him we'll do right by him. 'Bye, Melly Bright-Eyes."

He was already out the door when a thrown skillet whistled past his head and clanged off a porch post beyond.

Back at the camp he set Trini and Vince Copple to assembling unfamiliar trace rigging for the mules, as they had seen Poole's oxen yoked but with more freeboard from team to team and with wrapped padding to snug and shape the collars. Then he went to find Poole.

The bearded man was standing beyond his wagons, watching Patrick Muldoon diminish down the hill, toward his woodyard. Poole held currency in his hand.

"Is that the two-fifty you got for the bulls?" Darby asked.

Poole nodded.

Darby held out his hand. "That'll just cover your share of our first payload, Mr. Poole."

Vince Copple walked past, draped in long yards of leather strap. He shook his head and muttered to himself,

"Just like his Daddy. Like peas in a pod, sure 'nough."

Nearly a mile from the town, in a little cove between low hills, two wagons stood and gaunt animals grazed nearby. Frank and Martha tended little Quincy for a time while the woman carried wood so there would be a fire for cooking when the old man and Emmett returned. They had found work over at the town.

Jim had gone off somewhere so Emily took the buckets and went off to the river to fetch water.

It was a fair walk. The road ran along the river here, and the old man had wanted a place not too near the road when they made their camp. There were those in this land who would not welcome them, and he wanted no trouble. Emily strolled, hearing the birds that still welcomed the morning sunrise, seeing the lace canopies of spreading elms pass above her, dappling all below them with green and dancing myriads of shadows.

When she reached the road she looked both ways, and as she hurried across toward the thickets on the river side she thought for a moment she had heard movement not far away. But no one was there.

Humming a tune, she knelt to fill the buckets then passed the hooked ends of the pail-yoke through their bales and lifted it to her shoulders. She turned and there was a man there, blocking her path. He was a man she had seen before. He had come with others to run them off the land they had claimed, and this one had looked at her in a way that frightened her. He had grinned and wet his lips and she had been afraid.

Now he was here and there was no place to go. She stared at him and as before he grinned and wet his lips. "Now, Missy," he said. "Now."

"No," she said, and as he started toward her she whirled, swinging the heavy buckets outward on their yoke. One of them hit him and water flew. He swore and backed away, then he laughed.

He came for her again and she dodged and ran, making

for the path up to the road. For a moment she eluded him, then a heavy hand gripped her shoulder and swung her around, throwing her to the ground. She scuttled backward, trying to get away, but he was above her and when she moved he blocked the way and laughed again.

Then he was on her and his hands tore at the simple dress she wore. She fought him and screamed, and he engulfed her face in one hand, pressing her head to the ground, muffling her screams.

Suddenly there was a heavy thud and the man seemed to sag, his eyes gone glassy. But it only lasted a moment. He straightened then, crouched and stood, shaking his head, and she saw Jim rush at him, saw them go down in a tangle to thrash among the brush. Fist to her mouth, gasping, trying for the breath that had been denied her, she watched in horror. At first Jim seemed to carry the fight, spurred by his anger. But then the man heaved and Jim went over on his back. As he rolled the man came upright, drew the gun at his hip and fired. Jim sagged, rocking on hands and knees, his head down. There was blood on him. Emily screamed then.

From nearby she heard a shout, the sound of her name.

The man had pointed his gun at Jim again, but now he hesitated and turned, confused. The voice had seemed to come from everywhere and nowhere, echoed among the willows by the stream.

She screamed again and the man looked at her, then looked all around again when the voice repeated, closer now, "Emily!"

"Emmett!" she cried. "Be careful!"

The man with the gun ducked into a screen of willow and edged toward the path. He paused when he reached it, turned to look back once, then turned away again and ran . . . right into the heavy shoulder of Emmett, charging down on him, crouched. Emmett lunged and the man doubled across him, flailing. Emmett turned and the man flipped from him to land crashing on the ground, stunned. Emmett glanced at the girl, at her torn dress, and at Jim still on hands and knees, blood dripping from his chest.

Emmett turned then and as the man on the ground tried to raise his gun Emmett kicked it away, then lifted the man full upright with one hand. His fist went back, swept forward and there was the sound of breaking bone as the man's head bobbed crazily on his shoulders. Emmett held him there a moment and then dropped him. The man was no longer breathing.

Emmett helped Emily pull her clothing around her. Then he went to Jim and lifted him across his shoulder. "Bring the buckets," he told Emily. "We'll need water."

Later that day the old man and Emmett went into town, driving their gaunt stock. There was a man in town who had a store. They went to him and told him they were leaving, and needed draft animals in trade.

The man looked at their worn-out stock and shook his head, but his daughter was there and she glared at him and said, "For shame! These animals will heal! Besides, haven't you been wondering what to do with that bunch of oxen you bought? Honestly, Pa!"

The oxen were good stock and would go far. There was traffic on the road when they hitched and moved out, going west, and a pair of gun-belted men glanced at them.

"Ain't that the nester bunch we kicked out back yonder?" one asked.

"They been around town," the other said. "One of them girls of theirs is the one ol' Blue has been sniffin' after."

"One of them's bleedin'," the first one said. "He's bandaged, but he looks like he took a knife or a bullet. You reckon they're tryin' to go back where we ran 'em off, Pasco?"

"We'll be out that way in a few days," the leader said. "If they're there, we'll bury 'em there."

PART II
The Blackleg Men

VIII

Rigged and rolling, the outfit stretched out a hundred yards long from the velvet muzzles of Hildegarde and Madison, the lead mules, to the flag-tail of Trinidad Salazar's mustard pony bringing up the rear. Ahead to the north and away to the east the plains stretched endlessly, bleached grass gold and ghostly-still in the hour of eerie calm that often precedes a storm on the ranging lands above caprock. To the west a pall of angry gray cut off the land and sky as far ahead and behind as the eye could see. All day dark clouds had paraded eastward trailing petticoats of somber velvet. To Darby they looked like thunderous ladies of storm striding across the distances on legs that were glimpses of lightning seen through skirts of rain.

An eddy of breeze came slithering across the miles of prairie, an errant invisible thing marking a path of bowing grass as it rippled toward the jerk-line rig. Darby's nostrils widened as he tasted the air. There was the sweet-clover smell of ozone, and a rich undertint of rain on dusty ground. Beetling thunderheads stood impossibly high to his left—rolling mountains of cloud that towered there leering, full of flash and grumble, moving in to claim the turquoise sky.

Old Chance Curtis had a name for such weather. He called it "batten-down time." To the Kiowa it was "red silence," a time of hush, a time of awe. To Darby it was beautiful. Clouds hid the sun completely, while bright sky bathed the land in hues of color that were vivid beyond belief. The light seemed to come from everywhere and there

95

were no shadows.

Somewhere out ahead Billy Sipe had gone to scout trail, and Darby grinned viciously at thought of the New Yorker's reaction to such grandeur as the weather was showing them today. Sipe would sneer and spit on the ground and say, "Crap, it's going to rain." Darby wondered whether Sipe would ever be comfortable in any space larger than a room. The man seemed lost without walls.

Still, to the surprise of all of them, Sipe had proven to be a competent scout. He might not like what he saw—he rarely did—but he could see. He rode Poole's roan mostly, and rode it surprisingly well. Poole could shed no light on the inconsistencies posed by the sullen easterner. Sipe never chose to talk about his past, and it was not Poole's way to ask. "I usually figure folks will tell you what they want you to know," the gray beard had twitched in a smile as he said it. "Otherwise it probably isn't anybody's business but their own."

On the other hand, the bearded man had no reluctance to talk about himself.

"I was raised up down about the Pontchartrain," he had expounded one evening over campfire coffee. "Did some time at New Orleans over some fool thing or another. That was back about thirty-five. Thirty-six maybe? No, had to be thirty-five because that was when I decided to pull stakes. I wasn't even as old as you fellas are now by a sight, but I taken a notion to go to war."

He puffed his pipe, remembering. "The New Orleans Blues was makin' up to go to Texas, so I made my mark and away I went. The big camp right then was up on the Calcasieu past Alexandria, and they fed us pretty good and lined us up, and some bigwigs made us take an oath then they issued us each a horse, a hundred dollars, two good rifles, a pouch of ball and a keg of powder. Man, you never seen a bunch of poor boys get rich so fast!" He chuckled at it and shook his head.

"Anyhow," he told them, "we was almost to the Sabine before I figured out what a waste it would be if I was to take that horse and those rifles and that money over into Texas and maybe lose 'em all to the Mexican army. The way I saw it right then, that might have done more harm than good, you see."

Darby had shrugged, idly amused, but Billy Sipe stared at Poole aghast. "You mean you deserted?"

"I wouldn't say deserted, exactly. I just left. You might say I took the long way 'round. It wasn't like I never went at all. I just went to Texas by way of Missouri and Ohio and Pennsylvania and Connecticut and some other places that I hadn't seen yet. But I did go to Texas by and by . . . several times.

"Interestin' country," Poole had said of Texas. "People down there ain't like people anywhere else. Then again, they ain't much like one another, either."

In the months since formation of the High Plains Freight Company the partners had worked hard, kept on the move and had made good money, at least on their single-share split. Darby and Poole had found that most of the return on their capital shares went into the maintenance of animals, harness and rolling stock . . . the costs of doing business. Still, as he shifted his callused rump on John Adams's frame saddle in the near-wheel position and looked ahead, admiring the long column of paired mules that were his pride and his responsibility, Darby Curtis was fairly content. He tossed an encouraging flip into the long lead-line gripped in his gloved right hand and watched it ripple from ring to ring, receding. Thirty yards away Hildegarde, in near lead position, stepped out with casual power, leaning into her collar, long strides devouring distance. Darby felt the surge of renewed mule-power as it swept like a wave back along the line and John Adams stepped up his pace accordingly.

Directly behind him tall wheels whispered and tongue-bolts clicked as the wagons responded.

Of all his mules, Darby had developed a special regard for Hildegarde. She was truly a decent mule. She was strong, steady and dependable when she felt like it, not at all like the headstrong Madison with whom she was teamed. They had learned early to harness Madison in off

97

lead position when he was in team. No man could be sure of controlling Madison when he took a notion to go his own way. It took a mule to keep him in line. And in off lead position, the right-hand member of the lead team, he was governed by a jockey-stick set between his halter and Hildegarde's.

Twelve strong mules—six teams of two—drew the three wagons that carried the payloads of the High Plains Freight Company. On this trip the wagons had hauled millwheels from Tascosa to Fort Elliott, then carried a load of mixed supplies up to Shade's Well. Now they were northbound again, the lead and first trail wagon stacked high with block-sawed magnesia rock, the second wagon loaded with cedar posts. There were settlers now at a place called Sly, which was a place by virtue of someone having dug a well and found water. In that treeless prairie native building materials came in one variety. Sod. The curing stone and timbers were in great demand.

Behind the jerk-line rig came Bernice, spelled from harness while Vince Copple treated her for snakebite. The charge of rattlesnake venom that would have killed a man left the big mule with slight swelling and minor discomfort. Still, Darby took no chances with his mules, and the black man regarded them as tenderly as though they were children.

Further back Edwin T. Poole drove the supply cart pulled by a strong horse. Twice the age of the other three partners, Poole had claimed the supply cart as his task and no one saw fit to argue.

The little remuda of saddle and draft horses came next, Vince Copple tending them, and Trini Salazar rode rear guard.

Darby leaned to tug the line. Thirty yards ahead Hildegarde considered the matter, then decided to agree with him. She eased right and the long rig snaked around an old buffalo wallow. Madison blustered and stamped, preferring to go through the depression. But Hildegarde gave him no choice.

Atop John Adams, Darby corrected course again and

glanced once more to the west. The wall of blind rain was only a few miles distant now, and the air was cool and giddy, little breezes tossing in the stillness, ragging the edges of the calm. Darby set his rein, got to his feet atop John Adams's saddle and climbed from there to the lead wagon's high lip to take down his slicker. He rolled it, tucked it under his arm and returned to the back of John Adams.

Dark blots rippling in the distance to the east he made to be small groups of buffalo, drifting as they grazed, and he wondered for a moment as one group, far off, took on visible motion. Something had startled them and they were running.

Miles to the north, disappearing into the shroud of approaching storm, a thread of dark green traced the course of a creek across the pale pastels of prairie. Low hills still further away were a suggestion of blue on blue. "The time of grass greening," the Kiowa called this season . . . a good time to be alive and about and doing things. A hint of dust northeast told of movement there, but too far away to make out its source.

Three more days to Sly, Darby reckoned, then they would begin the circuit back to the south, setting their course according to the cargos to be carried. The outfit had made its first real money carrying government supplies from Westport to little Camp Jacob—a good haul and a profitable one. The supplies were for distribution to the Kiowa in accordance with a truce agreed upon at Willow Ford. Darby remembered vividly the treaty talks—the parade ground atmosphere, the pomp of soldiers and the pageantry of the massed tribes, the presence of danger shrouded by presence of an intent for peace, the discordance of ambitious men gathered around the event, seeking their own ends.

Chrisman had struck his bargain. Cloud and the chiefs had accepted it. They had parted in peace. Yet, when the partners and their load arrived at Camp Jacob they had found the place garrisoned, the same field squadron that had been at Willow Ford.

Darby recalled the sense of danger that had worried him at Willow Ford. He had felt it again at Camp Jacob. Still, months had gone by since then, and while there was talk sometimes of Indian trouble far to the west and the north—and of course, as always, trouble with the Comanche now and then—the plains had remained quiet. Cloud and Kicking Bird and the others had kept their bargain with Chrisman. The Kiowa kept the peace. Of all the chiefs, only Hawk That Hunts Walking had not attended the treaty talks, but there had been no word of the Kana'tenee. The Far Grass People had simply vanished. The outfit had rolled through the winter, trading all the way from Fort Griffin to Black Mesa, and there had been peace.

A mile passed and the creeping storm was nearer still. Again Darby noticed the feather of dust far to the northeast, and now he began paying attention to it. He snugged the jerk-line to the frame of John Adams's saddle and swung down carefully, off the right side, to balance on the long tongue of the lead wagon. The mules paced along undisturbed. One hand each on the rumps of John Adams and Washington, he walked the tongue to the high box of the lead wagon and reached up over its edge to fish out one of his rifles. He unsheathed it. Balancing there he checked the loads, then slipped his slicker over his head and slung the rifle on his shoulder. He sidestepped along the tongue and remounted John Adams. Distances were confusing on these plains, but he thought that dust—which looked so distant—might not be very far away.

If it was near, then it was converging toward their path. Darby wished he had not gotten to thinking about the Kana'tenee. True, he had grown up around the Far Grass People. He spoke their language and knew some of them by sight. None of that would count a lick if they encountered a bunch of Blacklegs out for blood. Given the choice, Darby Curtis would have preferred a run-in with Comanches to a run-in with the eccentric savages who were the Blackleg Society of the Kana'tenee.

Trinidad Salazar rode forward now, to pace beside him. He pointed to the feather of dust. *"Qué es?"*

"Damned if I know," Darby told him. "Might be a good idea if you and Vince was to saddle a couple of horses, just in . . . Trini, why don't you learn English? Saddle!" he tapped his saddle so the Spaniard would understand. *"Dos caballos! Vamos!"*

The Spaniard brightened, nodded and wheeled his pony to trot back down the line. The black man would know what to do.

Meanwhile, Darby found himself suddenly very busy. The mule Madison, thirty yards ahead, had decided to turn right. By the time Darby could snap the jerk-line, reminding Hildegarde of her responsibility, Madison already had the traces angling northeastward with the second team of Hamilton and Jefferson following along and the third team of Fanny May and Monroe beginning to veer.

"Damn you, Madison!" Darby shouted. Then, "Haw, Hildegarde! Haw! Get that knothead back on the track out there!" If he had owned a whip and known how to use it, he would have raised some dust on Madison's rump. As it was, he could only slip the jerk-line free of its half-ring retainers, flip it over the ears of five mules and lean far out to pull on it. Far ahead, Hildegarde considered his suggestion and decided in favor of it. She jerked her head to the right, the heavy jockey-stick rattling Madison's teeth. Then with the patience of a great lady she angled left, dragging the reluctant Madison with her. Hamilton and Jefferson followed, then Fanny May and Monroe, then Lucifer and Longhandle and the rest, and the rig cut a long arc through the grass, back to precisely the direction they had been moving.

Darby swore again, then turned to look back. Past the second trail wagon Bernice ambled along, her head high and curious. Beyond, on the seat of the supply cart, Edwin Poole grinned and shook his head. Trini had gone back to the remuda. Darby could see his hands flying as he tried to explain what Darby wanted to Vince Copple.

Darby flipped the line again, letting it settle into its retainers. Then with another tug to let Hildegarde know she was in charge out there and should pay attention, he snugged the line to John Adams's saddle and swung down from the tall mule. He stood aside, stretching and rubbing his sore back, as the wagons trundled past. Bernice nodded at him and stopped to have her ears rubbed, then returned to her place in line. As the supply cart came abreast Darby turned and trotted alongside. He noticed that Edwin Poole had his shotgun in his lap. He had seen the dust, too.

"You suppose there's any cover up ahead, Mr. Poole?" Poole shook his head. "Not much cover anywhere in this country."

"You think we ought to stop?" Brisk, erratic winds were whipping the grass now, and scattered raindrops sprinkled the cart's sailcloth cover.

"Beats me," Poole said. "You decide."

"I already decided not to, but I thought I'd ask."

Poole put his pipe back in his mouth. Some comments didn't merit response.

Vince Copple rode up leading Trini's pony and looped its reins over the cart's tailgate. "We gonna fight, you think, Darby?"

"Not unless we have to. That could be just most anybody out there."

Out on the plain behind them, some distance now and growing smaller as they moved on, Trini Salazar was tightening cinches on a restive gray horse. He completed his task, swung into the saddle and raced to catch up. As he came abreast he reined in, swung down and handed the reins to Darby. Darby checked the mount's trappings, then mounted as Trini and Vince went back to select another horse.

With a nod to Poole, Darby trotted the gray horse up the line until he reached the lead wagon. With the horse still in motion he jumped off and tied its reins to the left barrel brace. The saddled horses were a routine precaution. If they had to run, there would be no other way but to abandon the rig and run. Privately, Darby had long since made up his mind that he would not do that. Still, there was no sense in being stubborn. He ran to catch up with John Adams. He climbed aboard the high saddle and took up the jerk-line. Out ahead, Hildegarde was still in firm control of the situation.

There were two dust feathers now, the new one smaller and nearer than the first. At its apex rode Billy Sipe, coming at a run, waving his rifle. As he closed Darby called, "Did you see who's making that dust?"

Sipe hauled the roan into a haunches-down, skidding turn. "What dust?" Rain spattered his face as he turned, and he shook his head in distaste. "I don't know about dust, but there's Indians ahead of us. A lot of 'em."

"Where?"

Sipe pointed, ahead and west. "You see that green out there? Hell, you can't see it now for the damned rain, but there's a creek out there a few miles. It runs on up that way then it curves back west again, maybe seven or eight miles. We'll have to cross it."

"Yeah, I saw it earlier." The rain was coming harder, driven before a cold wind. Darby dipped his hatbrim, squinting.

"Well, that's where they are. Just up a ways from there. A whole town. Hell, I couldn't even count the damn teepees."

"Kiowa?"

"How should I know? They're Indians, that's all."

"You better pull a fresh horse . . . ," Darby looked to his right. There was no time. Somehow the distant trace of dust had turned, had grown, was coming directly at them, almost invisible in the rain. There was a rise there in the deceptive prairie and someone was just beyond that rise, coming fast. "Ride the line, Billy! Close 'em up! Close 'em up!"

He hauled the jerk-line. Thirty yards ahead Hildegarde sensed his urgency and stopped in her tracks, forcing the rest of the string to an abrupt halt. Madison began to pitch in his traces and Hildegarde thumped him with the jockey-stick. Darby reached back for the long brake lever, set his brake, then stood on John Adams's back and jumped from there to the high box of the lead wagon. Edwin Poole had pulled the cart close. Bernice was standing over the draft

103

horse, sniffing its ears. Trini Salazar and Vince Copple, dim now in the increasing, driving rain, were hazing remounts toward the cover of the wagons.

Tattered and blackened tumbleweeds scudded across the grasslands and bounded high as fresh, cold winds tossed them. Huge drops of rain splashed and rattled on snapping canvas. A gloom settled on the land as the massed cloud-bank passed above and moved onward, engulfing the sky. Horizons that had been endless dissolved and moved inward, obscured by rain.

Lightnings danced and crashed and their thunder was like cannonfire.

"Jesus," Darby breathed as sheeting rain beat at him. Behind and away he heard Billy Sipe complaining at the top of his lungs. But Darby kept his eyes on the climbing ground ahead and to the east. At first, for a minute or two, he saw nothing. Then there was a hint of motion in the haze and he focused there. He felt his scalp drawing tight below his hatband.

On the rise beyond them lance tips sprouted, then roached headdresses with eagle feathers whipping in the wind. In an instant the prairie was alive with mounted warriors, descending on the stalled outfit at a dead run. Darby clutched his rifle.

"Hot damn!" he yelled. "Blacklegs!"

He dove into the cluttered wagonbox.

IX

Armed with lances and shields, stout bows and fletched arrows, the warriors thundered down on the freight company then hesitated, milled and skidded to a jumbled halt. The leaders were no more than fifty yards away, clearly visible even through the screening rain. They milled in confusion, as though they had not seen the wagon outfit until they were upon it.

Peering over the edge of the wagonbox Darby counted forty or more painted warriors. Their brilliance was subdued by the gloom and the whipping rain which sheeted about them, misted the ground to hide the feet of their animals, and cascaded from shoulder, shield and mount. They were dark forms in the storm, ominous and alert, plumed lances held high. They were dark silhouettes with brilliant, savage highlights in the flashes of lightning that walked across the land.

Then one pushed forward, peering, and Darby saw the hooked lance and black shield of Bird. Glancing around he saw that the mules were standing steady, resigned to the storm but intensely curious about the Indians. He heard horses prancing and neighing on the upwind side of the wagons and wondered where the others were.

Dimly in the rain he heard Bird's voice, commanding. Then the massed warriors divided, half racing toward the head of the line, the rest galloping away to veer around the tailgate of Poole's cart. In a moment they regrouped on the other side of the trading rig and Darby nearly gutted himself on a hay rake trying to swap ends in the crammed wagonbox without exposing himself to arrow or lance.

Strangely, the Kiowa seemed not greatly interested in the long trading rig. Their attentions seemed focused past it, back the way they had come. There was a thump, a rattle of tools and Vince Copple tumbled into the wagonbox with Darby. The black man's eyes were round in his dark face. Darby had no idea where Poole, Billy Sipe and the Spaniard had gotten to. They were not in sight.

As Darby raised himself again to peer between the top of the wagonbox and the brim of his hat, Bird was directly before him, just a few yards away. The rest of the warriors had gathered around him. Bird raised himself tall in his saddle, looking up and down the length of the outfit, then he spoke and gestured with his hooked lance. Most of the warriors slid from their mounts, handing reins to a few remaining who took the horses and backed away into the screening downpour. Bird dismounted and a young brave came forward to take his horse. The crook-bearer surveyed the length of the rig again, then stabbed his lance into the wet ground. Its shepherd's-crook end stood tall, eagle feathers and beaver-hide festoons whipping like pennants in the wind. He shouted—quick, melodic phrases that Darby couldn't catch—and the warriors afoot spread out, moving close to the line of animals and rolling stock.

"What in God's name . . ." Darby muttered.

Copple glanced at him. "What did he say?"

"I don't know. Something about a good place to fight."

"I don't suppose he'd be willin' to talk?"

A mounting clamor filled the air, clanks and rattles and the drumming of hooves on wet ground. Vince Copple raised himself to turn and look east. "Geez Gawd," he yelped. "It's the cavalry!"

Down the rise, glistening in the rain, came soldiers spread in forager line and approaching at a canter. They outnumbered the Kiowa at least two to one, a full troop at field strength. Darby found himself in a frenzy of motion, trying to turn in the confines of the wagonbox, trying to stay down, trying to see both ways at once. The soldiers were straining, peering, trying to make out the silhouettes

ahead, trying to see the long line of standing rigs and trying
to see through them. They were at a disadvantage. The rain
was in their faces, whipping on storm-front winds. An
officer—a captain—at the center of the forward line raised
his saber and shouted. The lines moved then, at a trot,
gaining speed.

For a moment Darby lost sight of the field. Vince Copple
had become entwined with the clattering hay rake and had
rolled over onto him. They struggled in the bottom of the
wagonbox.

A feathered warrior vaulted to the back of John Adams,
stood there for a moment, then drew and released an arrow
into the approaching line of soldiers.

"Here!" Darby erupted from beneath Copple, raising
his rifle. "Get off my mule!" Before he could fire there
were shots from the closing soldiers and the Indian pitched
backward to fall in a heap in the tall grass.

The Blacklegs were spread all up and down the line,
running and crouching to release arrows between the legs of
the startled mules, through the spokes of high wheels. A
few of them had guns. Most had bows, and a volley of
shafts plowed into the charging line. Soldiers fell, holes
opened and the charge collapsed.

An Indian crouched on the wagon tongue directly below
the box and aimed over the back of Washington to take a
soldier out of his saddle twenty-five yards away. Darby
leaned out above him, swinging his rifle, but the warrior
had dropped from the tongue and was out of reach. Bullets
from the milling soldiers screamed past and Darby ducked.

"As skirmishers!" the officer shouted. "Dismount!"
Bullets thudded into the wagons, whined off their loads of
stone. In the traces, the mules pawed and danced. Darby
tried to reach the brake lever but was driven back as a pair
of arrows burried their heads in the planking inches from
his arm. He dodged, started to drop again into the shelter
of the box, then went white as big Jefferson, far ahead in
the second team, reared, brayed and collapsed. A soldier's
bullet had taken him dead center. Wild anger roared up
from Darby's gut and he raised and fired, directly into the

line of dismounting soldiers, dim in the sheeting rain. A cavalry mount reared, wheeled and raced away, dragging its rider.

Then the waves of battle burst onto the rig. Indians swarmed over the wagons and teams. Soldiers darted and pushed through the openings. Darby fired and a Blackleg sank beside the prancing Fanny May. Something tore into the brim of his hat, skewing it half around on his head, and Vince Copple yelled. Darby turned to find himself face to face with a Blackleg warrior coming over the side of the wagonbox. The painted face met Vince Copple's boot and was gone.

Darby raised his rifle again and a lance tip sent it spinning from his hands. He sprang upright to grab the leg of a warrior standing atop the lead wagon's load. Twisting and pivoting, he threw the Indian outward in a somersault, bowling over three running troopers.

"The stock!" he yelled. "Protect the stock!"

He heard the roar of Edwin Poole's shotgun. A running horse—one of their remuda—swept past the wagons, an Indian pitching from its back. The panicked horse bowled into a soldier climbing through tangled traces, throwing him into the hindquarters of Lucifer. Lucifer went wild. A lashing kick sent the trooper sprawling between two Blacklegs. All three went down.

From the north a thunder grew, its source lost in the veil of pouring rain. Darby glanced that way. Rain pelted and steamed. He could barely see his lead team. Beyond was blindness. From somewhere behind he heard the bark of Billy Sipe's carbine. Vince Copple had climbed to the top of the stone load and was firing from there, methodically, in both directions.

A rattle of fire and a high-pitched, ringing voice brought Darby's head around. Rain pelted in his face, into his eyes, and through it he saw the wild, raving figure of Trinidad Salazar in full charge, revolver blazing, mustard pony as wild as its rider as they swept into a knot of Blacklegs and scattered surprised Indians in all directions. No Indians fell, but before they could react the Spaniard was gone into the curtaining rain.

Again, between clamors of battle all around him, Darby heard that growing thunder from the north. Now there were shouts.

Soldiers in force had filtered through the line of wagons, but now at commands from the east side they began to retreat, firing and falling back. The thunder was louder, nearer. Darby looked around, trying to spot his rifle in the grass below. Almost under the high wagonbox a Blackleg was on hands and knees, blood dripping from his head. A soldier scurried past the wheel and raised his carbine like a club. Darby reached down, caught it and took it away from him, then turned to fire at an Indian heading for Beelzebub. The gun was empty. He swung it, threw it a running Blackleg and picked up the hay rake. He realized he was shouting, raving, a mixture of babble and war-cry.

Away to his right the officer with the saber was circling his mount and shouting. Other voices echoed his. Darby made out only one voice, shouting "Horse handlers . . ." The rest was lost in the seeth and hammer of rain, the mounting thunder and the yells and yips of fighting Kiowa.

Ninety feet away, veiled and dim, an Indian was clambering onto the steady back of Hildegarde. Darby howled and jumped from the box, waving the heavy hay rake. "I said stay off of those mules!" As he vaulted from John Adams's back to Beelzebub's and from there to Longhandle's, avoiding the wicked Lucifer, he shouted it again, this time in Kiowa. Several painted faces turned toward him in surprise as he jumped again, across to the back of Fanny May, then to Hamilton in a long vault that took him over the ears of the startled animal to land on its rump. Jefferson's fall had broken his collar loose and Hamilton somehow had turned completely around in his traces.

As the Indian on Hildegarde saw him and raised a lance Darby brought the hay rake around in a sweeping blow to the warrior's belly. The Blackleg doubled over and fell backward off the mule.

"And stay off!" Darby yelled. He stepped to the back of Hildegarde and dropped astraddle to pat her on the neck.

"Steady, steady now. Good girl." A barbed arrow stood in the tough leather of her collar. He yanked it loose, broke it in half and flung it into the face of a Blackleg coming at him with a war club. "At-ska-ho'idi!" he shouted, at the same time seeing a face he had seen before, seeing the big bell that clanked in the center of the brave's shield as ornament and medicine. "Stalking Horse! Stay away from my mules!" The Indian paused in mid-stride, puzzled, then spotted a retreating bluecoat and raced after him, yipping.

Hildegarde skittered beneath him, shaking her head to control Madison alongside and Darby noticed that of all the mules except Hildegarde, only Madison had not moved during the battle. The off lead animal stood rock steady, head up, hampered by the jockey-stick but firm and sure. His lip was curled in something like innocent glee. Someone was screaming. Darby looked down.

A soldier lay flat on his belly, squirming and hollering, pinned to the ground by Madison's right forehoof. The mule seemed to be massaging the man's spine. From a distance a soldier fired and something hit Darby in the shoulder, knocking him off the mule. He hit the ground rolling and came up directly in front of a yipping, running Blackleg. He crouched, raised and flipped the Indian over his back, then took his lance away from him and broke it, raging at him in a mixture of English and Kiowa with bits of Spanish thrown in.

Darby Curtis had never been known for his patience. The startled, tumbled warrior looked up at a furious unarmed white man scolding him roundly and shaking the pieces of his shattered lance. Wide-eyed, the warrior drew back, got to his feet and ran. A sheet of pounding rain hid him after a few feet.

Darby was dizzy. His vision seemed blurred more than by the rain. He was aware of blood dripping from his fingers, staining the flowing water at his feet. He looked at his tangled, pitching team. He looked at Hildegarde, gazing down at him affectionately. He looked at the fallen Jefferson lying dead in his traces. Waving the lance-ends with their bright festoons he stumbled and stalked along the line of wagons, shouting at the Indians who drew back from him hesitantly, cursing them in their own language, turning then to curse the soldiers fleeing between the wagons and teams. One of them turned to look and stumbled too close to Lucifer. He somersaulted backward, propelled by lashing hooves.

Then, momentarily, there was an odd silence within the pummel and hiss of the pelting rain. Darby stood swaying, seeing all that was near him with bright and unreal clarity.

Beyond the wagons dim soldier-shapes were regrouped, mounted and in full retreat, thundering away toward the south. From the north came Indians. Hundreds of them, pouring out of the curtaining rain, bright colors vivid in the pall, rain streaming from glistening bodies, racing hooves sheeting water from the flood prairie.

"Well, hell!" Darby breathed. He dropped the lance pieces, started to move toward the wagons and dropped to his knees. A bell was clanking somewhere. He looked around for its source.

The Indians streaming down and around the train now were not Blacklegs, but they were Kiowa, and Darby saw with a start the colors of the Real Dog Men, the senior warriors of the Kana'tenee, the most feared horsemen on the high plains. They thundered down on him and he could not move.

But someone was there. Lightning flashed, starkly outlining the shape of a tall, feathered warrior standing with his back to Darby, feet spread and arms raised high, a round black shield on one, the other hand holding a sheperd's-crook lance. The charging warriors broke and flowed around him. Sheeting water from the hoves of painted mounts cascaded outward, thin dark mud drenching Darby from both sides. He barely noticed that there was another Indian standing directly above him, also holding his arms high, shielding him. And the shield of this one was decorated with a bell.

They swept past and past, endlessly. Then they were gone and Darby Curtis crawled across the muddy, bloody

111

field until strong hands found him and lifted him into the shelter of a wagon. He lay there huddled, with Vince Copple and Edwin Poole, among stacked cedar posts, waiting for the weakness to pass and his vision to clear.

Mostly he noticed the quiet. The squalls had moved on and now the rain fell soft and steady. No clamor of battle remained, no shouts and screams and thunders. There was only the rain and the sounds of people working, trying to sort out teams, make repairs, reassemble. Vince Copple muttered as he worked on Darby's shoulder, salving and bandaging. Edwin Poole wandered past, taking inventory in the rain, and somewhere Trini Salazar swore in Spanish as he labored to reset a headstall on the stubborn Madison.

The only discord was the high, shrill ranting of Billy Sipe. "Dead soldiers! Look at this! Dead Indians and dead soldiers! Cheez! Crazy! You're all crazy! My God!"

"I guess we killed some Indians," Darby said, his shock beginning to wear away.

"I guess we did a little more than that," Vince nodded. "I guess we might have got a couple of soldiers, too."

"I guess we're in big trouble," Darby breathed.

X

The Board of Directors of the High Plains Freight Company assembled that evening at a buffalo wallow three miles east of a little creek where they had watered the remaining stock before moving on, gaining as much distance as possible from the site of that day's battle.

The outfit was reduced and hurt. Darby's shoulder around the bullet crease was bruised and painful, and he was still a little giddy from loss of blood. Trini Salazar limped on a leg bruised by a war club's glancing blow. Vince Copple had several small cuts and a stab wound in one thigh from a lance thrust. Only Poole and Billy Sipe had not suffered injury. Twelve mules remained, and four horses. The roan had been nicked by an arrow, and Trini's mustard pony had a long bullet burn across its rump. Bernice now hauled at offside second team behind Madison, who sported a notch in one ear. Both Sam and Longhandle had arrow cuts, and they had dug a flint point out of Fanny May's haunch and filled the puncture with Vince's salve.

It was a miracle, they felt, that the mules had stayed in trace. But Darby was concerned. Through the day, the big animals had remained nervous and skittish. He wished now that they had replaced Hildegarde's bell. It might have soothed them. It was his idea to put hobbles on them now when they made camp, and the mules made it plain they did not approve. Hildegarde gazed at him in sorrow when he placed the restraints on her feet. He felt he had betrayed a friendship. Lucifer tried to kick, stumbled and almost fell, then went off to pout. Madison stood still, staring at the strap on his ankle, and was still standing there when the men turned away and made their camp.

"As I see it," Edwin Poole said after their tiny fire had produced coffee and a tasteless meal, "we've taken ourselves a hand in somebody else's fight—not that we had the choice, mind you—but it looks to me like we've come out squarely crossways of both sides. Whether we end up gutted an' scalped or stood in front of a firin' squad just kind of depends on who finds us first."

"We got to make a run for it," Vince Copple allowed.

"Yeah, except a jerk-line outfit loaded up with magnesia rock and posts ain't exactly hard to catch. And there sure ain't anyplace to hole up."

"We got horses and those damn mules," Billy Sipe pointed out. "And saddles."

Darby glanced at him. "We aren't going to abandon the wagons. Those are half of our investment."

"Yours and Mr. Poole's," Sipe sneered. "Me, I got one share and I'm it. All this stuff about a company, that's fine and good as long as we're makin' some money. But I got nothin' tied up here. You do what you want."

Vince Copple sat brooding, staring at the tiny fire. "What you suppose they do to folks that shoot at soldiers?"

"I don't know," Poole said. "I never heard of anybody doin' that before. 'Cept other soldiers . . . or Indians."

"And how come those Indians didn't finish us off? We were shootin' at them, too."

"I told you about the Blacklegs," Darby shook his head. "That wasn't what they were out there for today. That doesn't mean they won't be after us tomorrow, though. And now if the Real Dogs are involved, that means we have a whole tribe out for our blood. Those Blacklegs, they're sort of a guerrilla bunch. And they're weird, the way they think. Real strange sort of codes, but they stick to them. But the Real Dogs, that's like their regular army. God Almighty . . ." he started to say more, then decided not to. He felt sick.

Trini Salazar looked from one to another of them,

concerned and confused. He understood almost none of what was being said. "*Señor* Darby, *qué pasa? Los solda-dos . . . los Indios . . . a donde van?*"

"I don't think we had better go to Sly," Copple said.

"I don't know where we can go." Poole scratched his bearded chin. "Anyplace we head for with this load, they're gonna catch us. An' there isn't anyplace we can go, anyways."

"How about right here?" Copple wondered. "With the stuff we got, we could build our own fort right around this old wallow. We could stand off some Indians if we had to, with a fort."

"And cavalry?" Poole asked mildly. "You think we might stand off the U.S. Army?"

"I don't want to fight the army," Darby said. "Hell, I don't want to fight anybody. The thing is, if we can't go to Sly, then there isn't any reason we should carry this load around. I say we leave it here. Maybe if things change, we could come back for it."

Poole glanced at him. "Wonder how fast we could move with empty wagons."

"That's up to the mules. We have twelve left. I'd like to kill the son of a bitch that shot Jefferson."

"We may already have," Poole reminded him. "That's the problem."

"Leave the load," Copple muttered.

"I agree," Poole said. "Leave the load."

As a quarter moon climbed in a sky now spangled with stars the partners labored, emptying the big lead wagon and the first trail wagon of their loads of building stone, emptying the second trail of its cedar posts. The combined loads filled the buffalo wallow almost to its brim. Then they worked for another hour with spades and rakes, throwing a thin cover of dirt and sod over the entire treasure.

"You know this isn't going to fool any Indian for a minute," Copple pointed out.

"It ain't Indians we're worried about here." Darby mopped his brow. "What's an Indian goin' to do with magnesia rock? Build a stone teepee? This is to keep it from curing out. Settlers won't pay much for it if they can't cut it. Besides, maybe the soldiers might not notice it. They'd steal this stuff quicker'n you can spit."

"Liable to be some surprised buffalo," Copple noted, gazing across the wallow that was no longer there.

"Be morning soon," Poole said. "We better move out. Where's Billy?"

Sipe was gone. So was the roan horse, a saddle and a good load of supplies. Sometime while they worked, the easterner had simply packed what he wanted and left. Poole stamped around, swearing, but there was nothing to be done about it now.

"We'll head southeast," Darby decided when they were rigged. "That's the only direction I can think of that there might not be anybody waiting for us." Besides, he thought, if they got out of this mess the Cherokee Strip was somewhere southeast, and beyond that Texas. Maybe they could go there. And if they did, maybe they could start over. He thought abruptly of Melissa Muldoon, and it dawned on him wrenchingly that he would miss her. Not that he thought much about her for months on end, but if he were to know he would never see her again . . . he would miss her.

The mules were subdued and thoughtful. It was the first time they had ever worn hobbles for a night, and Darby had a vague impression they were still thinking about that . . . and that the vote was not yet in.

Copple tended their cuts and bruises again, then they got them hitched up. Bernice again had second off lead.

Relieved of their burden the three tall wagons sailed easily across the dark prairie, the twelve surprised mules moving out at something like a canter. It was in Darby's mind to make some miles before morning.

Behind them in the moonlight a lone rider approached from the west, skirted partway around the filled wallow and reined in, sharp eyes gazing at the place with something like amusement. He turned then, head high, eyes seeking out the speck of movement where the running jerk-line team grew distant on the moonlit prairie.

116

He dismounted. Walking, leading his horse, he paced out the ground where they had stopped. He saw where the stock had grazed, saw the imprints in still-damp grass that told of hobbles, saw where one man had saddled a horse, distantly from the rest and slowly—surreptitiously?—then had ridden north, away from the wagon outfit. He read the tracks of the big wagons and knew they could now run. He squatted on his heels in thought, adding what he found here to what he had found earlier.

Cold gray eyes caught the lingering moonglow as he removed his hat to wipe its band, eyes that missed nothing and told nothing—eyes that could be at once serene and lethal.

Only a few days before Ernest Kichener had found what he had been looking for off and on for months. It had taken that long to find it because the country was vast, and because it was only one of several quests he had begun.

South of this place two days' hard ride he had followed an old buffalo trail, unused since the fall. It had been a small herd, maybe no more than a thousand head, months ago, in late winter, at the latest, and they had grazed southward. He made out the old path and followed it, and he found them: hundreds upon hundreds of rotting carcasses hidden by winter then exposed by the melting snow. Hide hunters had been at them, had nearly wiped out the herd. Shooting ground after shooting ground they had pursued, relentlessly, until the herd was gone.

More than that he found by the sign. Indians had been there not long before him and what he had seen they had seen too. Pony tracks only days old overlaid the faded faint ruts of many hide wagons heading northeast.

He had gone north from there, scouting out the country. He had intercepted fresh tracks of heavy wagons and had followed. Waiting out a storm, tarp-sheltered in a high cove, he had mapped the things he had found. These wagons were not hide wagons. They had come north, but had missed by miles the evidence of slaughter he had found. Still, when the rain was past he moved on. It was almost dark when he came upon a battlefield, its dead still fresh where they fell. He had stayed only minutes, but long enough to read the story, then had followed the wagons east.

Now he reviewed again the things he had seen, fitting them into sequence, relating them to other things he knew.

Finally he swung into his saddle, took one last look in the direction the empty wagons had gone, then eased his reins and set heels to his mount. He headed north, silent and alone across moonbathed prairie still hours from its new sunrise.

It was with a heavy heart that Twenty Buffalo led the warriors of the Far Grass People northward across the sunset plains to the village by the stream. More than two hundred strong they rode, warclubs slung from waist straps now, bows sheathed and lances carried low in the home-coming fashion.

Theirs had been honor in the field this day. The blue soldiers had fled before them like smoke before a wind. Many of the warriors had tied white feathers to their lances and shields. These had touched the enemy and lived to touch again. On this day many a brave had won honor.

Yet Twenty Buffalo was worried. He knew the white men. At an age when most warriors turned over the lance to younger men and joined the wise ones at the council fires, Twenty Buffalo remained a strong hunter, a robust fighter and a stern leader. But his age gave him memories and the memories were knowledge. He had known white men better and longer than most, from a time when they were few on the plains and encounters were rare except to trade . . . or to fight over horses. He spoke bits of their language. And he dreaded them.

They would be enemies now, but the white men would not be good enemies to have. The white men and their blue soldiers lacked the etiquette of honor. They were like the Apache of the desert—fierce, formidable and bound by no codes that Twenty Buffalo could understand.

He took little comfort in the words of Bird and the sharp-eyed Stalking Horse. The Blackleg men were respected warriors, and their society was held in high regard. Yet theirs was not the duty of guarding the People and their welfare. The Blackleg men were mystics. They hid their rituals always from the eyes of others and kept their own counsel and often spoke in riddles. Therefore when Bird said the Blackleg men had shared a vision of what the Kana'tenee must do, and when Stalking Horse said the Blackleg men would bring new medicine, Twenty Buffalo had only nodded and brooded and watched them ride away. They had not told him where they were going, or why.

He knew only that the Blackleg men had found a great killing ground of buffalo, and had gone to revenge themselves upon those who wasted the earth, and had been chased and attacked by blue soldiers. Now he must counsel with the wise ones.

By virtue of their eminence in the tribe the society of Real Dog men rode at the head of all the warriors of the Kana'tenee. And as leader of the Real Dogs, Twenty Buffalo rode first. Racing out from their village, alerted by scouts to a fight taking place, he and the others had painted themselves as they rode—red on their faces, red on their arms, red on their leggings and red on the necks of their galloping horses. It was the custom of the Real Dogs. It was their oath. No enemy should fail to see the leading warriors of the Kana'tenee.

But now, returning, they had removed most of their paint and splashed themselves with mud to dim the rest. Twenty Buffalo believed, and the others of the Real Dog men agreed, that today's adventure would bring evil before it was done. He heard the keening voice of old Keeps His Horses singing of bad times to come, and he remembered the implacable pale men he had known in earlier times . . . men who could live without honor as he knew it. Men who nonetheless knew well the ways to kill.

Crossing the creek the Real Dogs dismounted to wash away the remnants of their paint while other, lesser warriors and braves filtered into the village, each toward his lodge or his tipi.

"Hawk That Hunts Walking will be waiting for news," Turns The Wind said. "The people will wonder why the Real Dogs do not raise their lances, why we do not dance."

"I will talk with Hawk That Hunts Walking," Twenty Buffalo told him. "You and Little Wolf may speak, as well. Let Broken Bow and Dog That Runs With Horses stand at the entrance to keep people away until we finish."

As he remounted and turned his horse's head toward the center of the village, Twenty Buffalo was thinking hard. He must explain to the old chief that their rescue of the Blackleg men might sing in the thunders for many moons to come, and that their enemies would not be good enemies. They would be the blue soldiers.

Although the prairie air was cool, it was hot in the tipi of Hawk That Hunts Walking. The vents had been closed to only a tiny slit of evening sky, and the flap was secured until Twenty Buffalo and the others entered and closed it behind them.

It was hot, yet Hawk That Hunts Walking sat wrapped in heavy robes and kept a bright fire burning as though the winter past had not yet left him. His hair unbound was silver with only small streaks of dark remaining. His face was a rich weaving of the tracks of years and wisdoms. Yet there was a firm jaw there, and his wide mouth with its age-creased lips was strong. Eyes that had lost some of their sight to the long years remained no less bright and thoughtful.

"Many braves display bright feathers now who did not this morning," he said when the ritual cup and pipe had gone around. "Yet the Real Dog men have removed their paint and lowered their lances."

Twenty Buffalo bowed his head. "Many young men have touched the enemy and gained honor today. Some can now be warriors. The sun shines upon them."

"Honor comes to the Kana'tenee this day." The old man nodded. "Then why do the Real Dog men not dance?"

"Keeps His Horses sings of bad times," Twenty Buffalo said softly. "And the Real Dog men have seen the enemy our young men chased." He glanced at the old chief's trophied shield beside the flap, with its bright paint and festoons of trophies from many battles. "The Kana'tenee have been fortunate in the time men can remember, wise one. Our enemies have been good enemies. But now comes one that is not good."

"You have touched the blue soldiers."

"It is as you said, in the last season of grass greening when word came for council with the chiefs of the Great Father. The blue soldiers have come. The Blackleg men have gone to find new medicine, but the Real Dog men hear the song of Keeps His Horses and find it hard to see the sun."

Hawk That Hunts Walking pulled his robes more tightly around him. His dark eyes seemed to see beyond the smoky lodge, beyond the village, beyond the waning day. For a long time no one spoke. Then the old chief seemed to return to them, and he put his robes aside and arose. "Come out," he said. He went to the flap and it was pulled open by those waiting outside. As he followed, Twenty Buffalo noticed how frail the old man had become.

In the waning light of dusk fires danced bright before a hundred lodges. The day's rain had bathed the plains and scrubbed the air clean, and people were about. Women cooked and carried water, men tended their horses and tended their weapons. Children darted here and there, playing, scuffling, taunting one another.

"Those who were old when I was young," Hawk That Hunts Walking said, "saw what I see now—the people of Kana'tenee and the land and the sky. And there was no end of anything. Yet of all I see now, only the sky has no end.

"Long ago our people hunted with the Cut-finger people on common ground. Sometimes we were at war with them. Sometimes we fought too with the Lakota, but sometimes we hunted together. Then the white men came and drove the Lakota back, and the Lakota made a pact with the Cut-finger people and drove our people back. I was a young warrior when our people made a pact with the Comanche," he made the sign of the snake, "and we took back the hunting grounds taken by the Lakota and the Cut-fingers.

121

Now we do not hunt with them, and we war whenever we meet. And now Cloud and the other chiefs have made pact with the white people. They do not want war with the white men." He shook his head and looked about him, dark eyes large and bright in the light of the fires.

"The Lakota did not want war with the white men," he continued. "They moved back. But now they have war anyway. The Cut-fingers did not want war. They went to the white man's grounds in peace. Now many of the Cut-fingers are dead and the rest are at war. All around the Kiowa are people who wanted peace with the white man and now have war. Only the people of the snake, the Comanche whom we name 'enemy' and treat as friend, did not go to the white man seeking peace. And now only the Comanche are secure on their lands. What does all this mean?"

Twenty Buffalo and the others stood around him and had no answer.

"The chiefs of five tribes have made a pact with the white people," Hawk That Hunts Walking said. "Of all the Kiowa only the Kana'tenee have made no treaty. Still, who knows what is in the mind of the white-eyes? I see the sky and it has no end. But I cannot look at the sky." He lowered his head and swept an arm, pausing to point toward an open space where youngsters were playing. "I must look at the children."

XI

Captain of Cavalry Jack Sinclair came awake, groaned and rolled stiffly out of his blankets. The quarter moon was well down in a sky brilliant with stars, which meant that he had slept several hours. Yet it had been an interrupted sleep and he felt more stiff and sore than rested.

The old nightmares bothered him often, the grim montages of fallen men, of blood on trampled ground, of charging gray lines blossoming with musket fire . . . of cannonfire walking across a hillside, each stride a tower of shellburst and acrid smoke. They tormented him, those dreams. And now they had new faces—wild, painted faces with glinting black eyes—faces that yipped and howled and darted from cover to cover.

It had been a restless sleep, twice interrupted by alerts. First there had been Private Mulcahey with that idiotic story of seeing ships sailing on the horizon. A big ship and a small one, he had said. Sailing eastward. The first had three short sails, the second only one. The camp had come awake, sentries doubled and the best eyes among them trained northward. He was so certain he had seen something out there. But there was nothing to see.

Then—it had seemed only moments of sleep later but had been an hour or two—it was Mulcahey again. This time he reported seeing a band of Indians riding by moonlight, far to the north and also going east. Again, the camp had come to full alert. Again, there had been nothing.

Sinclair sat up, rubbed his eyes and put on his hat. Then he found his boots, thumped their heels on the ground and tipped them to evict anything that might have taken up residence, and pulled them on. Wadding his blankets over one arm he stood, breathing the cool night air which still carried the spice scent of yesterday's thunderstorm on the plains. A few yards away there were men at a small fire, and he walked toward them.

Master Sergeant Boyd Hanlon glanced up as he approached, then scuttled aside to make room. "Mornin', Captain. Can I pour you some coffee?"

Sinclair dumped his bedroll with others on a spread groundsheet and squatted by the fire. Hanlon handed him a scalding cup and he sipped at it, still rubbing sleep from his eyes. "Morning, Sergeant. Men." He nodded at the platoon sergeant and the pair of corporals sharing the fire. "What time do you make it?"

"It's well past four, sir. Corporal Riley's just about to start kickin' em awake. The lieutenant said you'd be wantin' to move out early. He's already gone out to tell off the sentries an' get the mounts brought in. Sleep all right, did you, sir?"

"Not worth a damn, thank you." He sipped again at the strong coffee, drawing its steam into his nostrils. It made him cough. "No more sightings, I take it? No more Indians . . . or sailing vessels?"

"Nothing, sir." Hanlon kept his gaze on the fire. The others looked away. "But sir, if you please, Private Mulcahey was real sure he saw somethin' out there. Whatever it was. Moonlight can do funny things, sir, but I'd say he did see somethin'."

Sinclair coughed again and sighed. "I don't doubt that, Sergeant. I am sure something moved out there. I just wish I knew what it was."

"An' the other alert, sir. The lad couldn't be sure it was Indians. They were a long ways off. But they might have been."

"He did the proper thing, Sergeant. I'm not complaining. It might have been elk. Or buffalo, or wolves. But he saw something, and he reported it."

"Yes, sir." The master sergeant was satisfied. His trooper was vindicated. "Will the captain be wantin' a burial detail today, to go back there?"

Sinclair brooded, gazing into the fire. Five men missing. Three of them known dead, maybe all five. He tried to feel at least a little remorse, and found he couldn't. The war had taken that from him. He couldn't take the whole troop back there. It would cost a day or more, and his command was a wreck. Three-fourths had wounds of some sort. And his report was needed at Camp Jacob. Nor did he want to split his forces. Yesterday's battle had been a rout. Instead of thirty or forty savages, they had found themselves pursued by hundreds, coming out of nowhere. Sinclair was new to the plains, but he was beginning to learn their secrets.

Still, those fallen men . . . they deserved a decent burial.

". . . Because if you do," Hanlon continued, "I'd take it as an honor to take th' detail. An' there's volunteers already come forward, sir."

"We shall continue north until sunrise, Sergeant. When I can see what's around me, I'll decide."

Gazing into the fire, he began again to formulate the report he would make at Camp Jacob. A Troop had surprised a band of Indians preparing to attack an encampment of white men at a place where a small creek flowed through a canyon and was joined by a wide, dry creek bed, about midway in the sector called C-9 on company maps. The Indians had been painted. Faced with cavalry, they had turned and run, south of west. A Troop had given chase, had tracked and chased the primitives repeatedly over a distance of approximately twenty miles.

The Indians had headed directly into a building storm. He had expected to lose them then, had been resigned to turning back. But the Indians had stopped. They had encountered a wagon outfit, apparently northbound, and

125

had grouped behind the wagons. Then when A Troop approached, the Indians attacked. With the wind and rain at their backs, they had opened fire on A Troop.

He tried to sort out the rest. It had been so hard to see. A Troop had sustained casualties. He knew the Indians had, too.

There were people with those wagons. What had become of them? He had glimpsed them, at least one of them, in the midst of the fighting—a man standing on the back of a mule, doing something . . . what? Using a weapon of some sort?

Then more Indians had come. Hundreds of them. He had withdrawn A Troop. Withdrawn? Hell, they had run for their lives.

They would want identification of the Indians. Kiowa? Cheyenne? Comanche? Sector C-9 was a long way west and south of Camp Jacob. They could have been anyone. War paint, bright colors, warriors' hair standing in tall crests with feathers waving there . . . maybe someone at Camp Jacob would know. Lances and shields. Mostly bows and arrows but maybe some had guns. He had seen muzzle blasts.

Strange, that the field order which sent A Troop to Sector C-9 had been carried by a civilian. He had wondered about that at the time. But this was new country, long on miles and short on people. And it was a damn good thing the order had come. That encounter at the dry creek bed had the elements of a full-fledged battle between Indians and white civilians. An all-out war could have started right there. Somebody had acted on knowledge received, and A Troop had been just in time.

Captain Jack Sinclair finished his coffee and got to his feet. The dark of morning lay vast across a prairie endless under a waning quarter moon. Somewhere coyotes chorused. Were they really coyotes? They sang and yipped and they sounded like Indians.

No reveille this morning. No "Boots and Saddles." Jack Sinclair, new to the high plains, looked out on the dark prairie and decided he was not ready to issue any chal-

126

lenges. "Get them up and moving, Sergeant. Quietly if you can. We're moving out."

At his sutler's cabin beyond the perimeter at Camp Jacob Cain DeWitt cursed and muttered as he pulled a robe around him and lit the wick of an oil lamp. His hair was matted, his eyes gritty with interrupted sleep. Again he heard the light, persistent knock at the door.

Carrying his lamp he opened the door, then stepped back in disgust as night air washed a high stench into the room. The man who hurried in, closing the door behind him, was a bearded, unkempt creature wrapped in layers of foul clothing and sewn hides. He stank of filth and old death.

"What are you doing here?" DeWitt snapped. "You know you aren't supposed to come here."

"I ain't moved 'cept in the dark," the man drawled. He kicked a chair around and sank into it, sighing. "Nobody seen me come. But I figured you'd want to know we finally drawed us redskins. Shit, we had to wait long enough, but they finally come."

DeWitt's eyes brightened. "Kiowa?"

The man nodded. "Kiowa, I think. Some kind. I don't know which kind. But Kiowa. Trouble is, we kind of got interrupted. We was layin' for 'em, like you said. We was forted up good an' we was ready. Shit, we coulda' covered a quarter-section with dead Indians for your soldier-boys to see. But it didn't happen just that way."

DeWitt frowned. "Something went wrong? What?"

"Your friggin' soldier-boys, that's what. Them redskins was just ready to come down on us an' meet their maker, an' we was pickin' our shots, when a bunch of soldiers showed up an' chased 'em away. Shit, we didn't even get off a shot. I thought you said the Army wasn't gonna come near them canyons."

DeWitt sat down hard on the edge of his tumbled bunk. He was still holding the lamp and its glow danced weird shadows on the cabin walls. "Cully, you told me this would go off without a hitch."

Hard eyes fixed him, eyes gone from tired to cold. "If you're thinkin' of puttin' the blame on me an' the boys, DeWitt, you better think again. Hadn't been for them soldiers we'd of sowed your field with dead Indians for you, just like we said. Shit, ain't we been squattin' out there for months now, just waitin' for 'em to come? It ain't like we made nothin' off them buff hides. Shit, that far out it weren't even worth the haul. But we done like you said. We left a killin' ground down there, and sure enough they found it an' they come. Blame the soldiers, DeWitt. Not us."

"My friends won't like this, Cully."

"That's your worry. We need a stake now. I don't aim to be waitin' out there when them soldiers gets around to wonderin' why we was there and comes back askin' questions. There's plenty hides to be had on west. We're packin' it in. That's why I'm here. We done our part. Now I want my money."

"We don't pay for misses, Cully. Only for dead Indians."

The stinking man seemed hardly to move—only shifted slightly in the chair where he sprawled—but now there was a pistol in his hand. "I'm too tired to argue, DeWitt. Just give me my money."

With moonset the mules had decided to stop. It was too dark for them to see their footing, and no amount of coaxing would persuade them to continue. It was the first time Darby had known Hildegarde to balk. But then it was the first time he had ever asked her to travel at night. Still, they had covered a lot of ground by then and the horses were near to exhaustion.

For the second time they placed hobbles on the animals, and Darby was too near exhaustion himself to even wonder about the mules' reaction this time.

They built a tiny fire under a claybank with deadfall from scrub cottonwoods that stood beside a seep. They lay sprawled and aching, waiting for the coffee to boil, and they talked just to keep themselves awake. Sleep now was a luxury they wanted to avoid at least until they were moving again. The more they considered their situation, the more imperative it became that they put this country behind them. Their eyes were those of hunted men, turning often to their backtrail.

"Seems to me like I've spent most of my life wonderin' just why I'm wherever I am an' how I got into a mess like this," Edwin Poole allowed. "Right now I'm wonderin' how come I ever come to the territories."

"I don't have that problem, mostly," Vince Copple told them. "Anyplace I am is better than were I was. 'Course, right now I can think of better places to be than right here."

"I guess a man doesn't wonder why he's someplace if that's where he was born," Darby said. "He can just blame the whole mess on his daddy. Mine decided he wanted to be a buster."

He broke a dry stick and worked the halves of it into the little fire below the blackened pot. "Maybe thirty years ago Daddy took a notion he could do better out on the Missouri Plains—back then that's what they called all this—than he could tending store back east. So he made a run across the 'permanent frontier'—they still called it that, then. Before they started movin' it every year or two. He got past the border forts and the picket zones and the tame tribes, and picked himself a place up on the Smoky Hill and settled in. That was all Kiowa country then. He traded with them."

Poole removed the rank pipe from his face and knocked out the dottle on his hand. "Run whiskey to 'em, did he?"

"That's what he started out to do. Best profit for the least payload. But the first wagon he brought in, a bunch of bucks got likkered up and butchered his milk cow and tore down his shed for firewood. So he got out of that business. But he did all right free tradin'. Always got along with the tribes, and they liked havin' him around. He used to say the Kiowas would send out raiding parties whenever the soldiers patrolled near the Smoky Hill, just to pull them off some other direction."

"You really was raised up with Kiowas, then." Poole's brows lifted. He had never been sure what to make of all that. "You really *are* a native."

Darby yawned, nursing the aches that tormented him, striving to stay awake. "Sure. I was born right there on the Smoky Hill. My ma was a schoolteacher. Daddy traded a Pawnee chief four good horses and ten blankets for her."

Poole glanced around, intrigued. "He traded? For a schoolteacher?"

"She was from Iowa. Used to teach at a mission school, but a bunch of Brules picked her up on a raid. They swapped her to a Pawnee and my daddy got her from him."

"I never heard the like."

"Oh, Indians don't think anything of tradin' people around like they was merchandise."

Across the fire Vince Copple grinned. "Do tell," he muttered.

"Damn wonder you wasn't born a halfbreed," Poole said.

"Not likely. Strong-willed woman, my mother."

Poole lifted the lid on the pot, letting a banner of steam rise. He peered inside. "Won't be long," he yawned. Darby yawned too. He couldn't help it. Light snores from the right told him Trini Salazar was sound asleep, and he could see Vince Copple's eyelids drooping.

"Somebody better stay awake, here," he told Poole. "Soon as there's light, we have to move."

"Yeah. Little coffee would help. Come on, damn it," he told the pot. "Boil!" He lay back against the claybank. "Damn, I hurt all over."

Shortly after that Darby became aware of the coffee pot rumbling rhythmically. There was a scent of coffee, and he wondered vaguely why Poole didn't do something about it. The sound was soothing, though, and he didn't care very much.

He awoke with a start. There was light, and there was birdsong. The fire was out. Around him Poole, Copple and the Spaniard sprawled like dead men, snoring in harmony.

He moved, and everything he owned hurt. He swore softly, got to his feet and stepped up on the claybank. Rose light played on high ground in the distance, creeping toward the low meadow where they had stopped, driving purple shadows inward to the crush of morning. First dawn touched the top of the lead wagon's beacon pole and started moving down it.

He had slept for two hours—maybe three—and the need for flight came back to him strongly. They were still a long way from being out of reach of the Kiowa—and a far longer way from being beyond the reach of the army. Limping at first, then walking more strongly, he strolled out into the high grass. The horses were close in, starting to graze. They had been too exhausted to stray. Of the four, only Trini's mustard pony was at any distance. It looked at him from a rise a few hundred yards off, then dropped its head to graze again.

Yawning and stretching, Darby looked around, counting the mules, then stopped almost before he had started. A discarded hobble lay in the grass at his feet. Its ends had been untied and showed the marks of large teeth.

Madison was gone. Wide awake now, Darby surveyed the tall mules scattered across the near meadow. Only ten remained, and he discovered with a shock that Hildegarde also was missing. He started to climb the wagon, to see further, then stopped. They wouldn't have gone far. He would send Vince and Trini to find them.

He shrugged. He knew his animals. The hobbles had been a mistake. Hildegarde was showing her displeasure by wandering away. Madison . . . well, Madison was just being Madison.

Sunlight crept down the beacon pole on the lead wagon. He decided he could give the animals a few more minutes to graze, and give the other men a few more minutes of sleep. When the sunlight reached the wagon hubs, he decided— then they would hitch up and move on. Two more days of good speed should give them some breathing room. The prairie was huge. Two more days and they would be pretty hard to find.

He had only a vague idea of where they were going— southeast across a couple of rivers, then maybe due south as long as their supplies held out. Though he had never traveled past the post oak country south of the Red River, he knew there were other lands down there—piney woods where a lot of folks didn't hold with the U.S. Army and where the Kana'tenee and the rest of the Kiowa were a long way off.

He had given up any thought of ever reclaiming the load of magnesia rock and cedar posts. He recalled vividly the painted face and agate eyes of Bird, and knew the load wan't worth it. And even if Bird should forget, the army never would.

Again there was the bittersweet memory of Melissa Muldoon. Melly Bright-Eyes. Where he was going, it might be a long time before he would return. He could get word to his family when he was safe . . . and to Melly. But he might never see her again. His regret was partly guilt for not having thought of her more, partly stark awareness that the awkward girl-child he had known and taken for granted was something quite different now from what she had been back then. And it was partly something else . . . something he had felt before but had not taken the time to explore. He felt for her . . . the thought betrayed him. He felt for her.

Deeply, as he watched the sunlight creep down the wagons' canvas tops, he said his goodbyes to these high plains. He might never come back. He looked around and saw vastness . . . a great open that was comfortable to him.

It was home. It was time to start again, in a new place.

He took another long look around at the empty grasslands. There was no sign of pursuit. But then there wouldn't be, necessarily. The land only seemed flat. He knew its deceptions. It rolled and rippled in the distance to the west, and those ripples could hide most of what might be there to see. One who has lived his life on such plains knows what they can hide.

Climbing onto the nearside hub of the lead wagon he placed his rifle in the box and tossed his coat in after it. The morning air was cool, but it would warm soon.

Six hours at a stretch, he figured. Six hours on the move, an hour or two of rest, then six hours again. He wouldn't run the mules gaunt, even if they would let him. Six hours in trace would be a fair limit, at the pace they needed to maintain.

Sunlight found the slab side of the lead wagon. A few more minutes. Darby yawned. There was a long, long way to go.

He still had seen no sign of Hildegarde or Madison. Probably they had wandered over a rise. By now, though, they should be returning.

Something seemed wrong. He glanced around. The wagons stood as they should, harness spread for rigging, most of the stock nearby, shadows still on the wash where the rest lay sleeping, a hundred yards away. Morning on the prairie, sunlight seeking the pale grass that seemed the entire world . . . he caught his breath. Hackles rose on his neck.

There had been birdsong. Now there was none. The meadowlarks were hushed.

He tensed. He turned slowly, looking out into the grass—not across it this time, but into it, close at hand. There was movement.

He turned to go after his rifle, then froze. Five yards away a painted warrior crouched in tall grass, bow bent full, arrow aimed at Darby Curtis. Beyond him another appeared, then several more. To left and right, everywhere, the prairie sprouted Kiowas.

He should have been watching the mules. They would have told him. But he had been daydreaming. He saw now what he had not seen before, had not noticed when they arrived in darkness. To his left, not fifty yards away, feathered crests appeared above an invisible rise and lance tips rose above them. Ghostly they grew, a rank of silent, mounted fighting men bright with paint and feathers. The first one bore the crooked lance.

Suddenly they were on him, bearing him down, pulling him to his knees. Strong hands imprisoned his arms. Strong scent of smoke and rawhide and tallow was in his nostrils. Indian smell. In the distance behind him there were shouts, a single gunshot and the fierce yipping of Kiowa Blacklegs on their prey.

A hand gripped Darby's hair and drew his head back.

Above him, bright in the morning sun, stood Bird. Round black shield slung behind his left shoulder, he held the shepherd's-crook lance in one hand, a war club in the other. Just beyond stood Stalking Horse, compact and tough, dark eyes deadly in his painted face. He had removed the brass bell from his shield and was tying it to a piece of rope.

Yet it was Bird who held the captive's eye. The Blackleg leader was, he noticed dully, a magnificent savage, tall even among the Kiowa, muscles rippling beneath skin the color of dark apples flushed with sunlight, raven hair pulled upward, eagle feathers fluttering in the breeze.

For a moment, Bird stared solemnly down at Darby. Then without a word he raised his club and brought it down on the captive's head.

XII

Three mules and a mustard pony ambled westward across endless prairie, stopping sometimes to graze for a while where the tall grass was lush but moving on each time, always westward. Hildegarde, the natural leader, set the direction and the pace.

Strong teeth and quick intelligence had enabled her to free herself of her hobble in moments, after watching Madison struggle for a longer time with his. Once freed, she had wandered some distance in her annoyance, putting a rise between herself and the camp, Madison following along. She didn't like hobbles, and was demonstrating that. Once having made her point, though, she was on her way back when strange noises in the distance stopped her, and then she caught the strange scent of painted men and painted horses, scents that reminded her of unpleasantness. So she had crept up a rise, just far enough to see the camp below, and had stopped there to watch, snorting to keep Madison back from the crest. Most of what she saw was beyond understanding. The wagons were there, and the other mules, but everywhere were strange animals and bright-colored men.

She had seen Lucifer get free. The dark mule had stood placidly while one of the Indians removed his hobbles. Then he had switched ends abruptly, lashed out with his hind legs and sent the Indian looping and howling through the air. Then he had run. She had not seen where. But when she returned to the standing wagons later he was there. The rest were gone.

Vaguely, after a time, Hildegarde had felt the need to travel. So she followed the broad trail of men and horses, pausing now and then to sniff the ground like a dog. There were familiar scents among the strange ones—mules and horses that she knew.

Somewhere along the way the mustard pony had appeared and decided to follow along. It kept its distance, realizing after one approach that Lucifer did not consider it welcome. Yet it followed.

At a shallow creek they paused to drink, then to browse for a while on succulent brush. The sun was high and warm. Madison found a place he liked and rolled in the grass, raising clouds of whitish dust. Then, satisfied, he shook himself and turned north, trotting along the creekbank. Hildegarde watched him go, then went back to browsing. Some distance away Madison stopped, turned, saw that he was alone and pawed the ground in irritation. When that produced no result he grazed for a few minutes and then returned to the others, ears high and eyes bland as though he had never had any other intention. The mustard pony had moved too close and Lucifer rushed it, trying to get into position to kick. But it retreated nimbly and he decided to ignore it again.

After a while Hildegarde crossed the creek, found the trail and continued westward. Madison, Lucifer and the pony ambled along behind her.

Corporal James Finnegan mopped sweat from his brow, replaced his hat and climbed out of the five-foot-deep hole he and Private Mulcahey had made by lifting building stones out of the old buffalo wallow. He shook his head and shrugged at Sergeant Hanlon. "Nothin' down there but some logs, Sarge. Under that is just dirt. Bottom dirt. You want us to try someplace else?"

Hanlon tipped up his hat to scratch his head, staring around him at the circular patch of replaced sod. It would take hours to uncover it all, and he really didn't know what they were looking for . . . if anything. "Jamie, can you think of any reason people would bury a bunch of rocks an' sticks? Unless there was somethin' valuable under 'em?"

There was no answer to that. He sighed, gazed out across the empty flatness of the prairie, miles of grass vanishing in every direction. Empty. Vast and empty. Yet Hanlon knew it was not empty. Out there somewhere were hostiles. They could be anywhere. And the main body of A Troop was miles away by now, bound for Camp Jacob.

He was anxious to be on his way. He had volunteered to head the burial detail, to find and bury those men who had died in the skirmish with savages, and the six with him also had volunteered. But that didn't make this wide country any more comfortable to him, or make the seven of them seem any less alone. It was as though, in all the world, only the seven of them remained.

They had come across this mystery, and had stopped to investigate. But now it remained more of a mystery than ever, and Sergeant Hanlon was acutely aware that time was passing and they still had a long way to go.

"Put the rocks back and cover 'em over like they were," he told Finnegan. "Then let's get out of here. There's men out there to be buried."

"I hope we get to 'em before the wolves does," Private Jake Bloom said earnestly. "Lord, I hate a mess like that."

"They swell up an' go to stinkin' the buzzards 'll be on 'em, Jakey," Private Tom Pedigo pointed out. "Me, I'd rather handle wolf-leavin's. You ever been right up close to a ripe . . ."

"Pedigo, shut up!" Finnegan swore. "You got so much time on your hands you get down in this hole an' set rocks. Bloom can hand 'em down to you. Mulcahey, come out of there."

"I'll bet I know what all this stuff is," Pedigo muttered as he traded places with Mulcahey. "It's a shipwreck. I bet there was this ship out sailin' around on the prairies last night an' it fell in a hole an' sank, an' this stuff is its remains."

Mulcahey flushed. "Damn it, I know what I saw!"

"Easy, Irish," Pedigo said, looking up innocently from

the hole as Bloom wrestled a stone block to its edge. "I believe you. Man, didn't I help dig a canal one time? I know about stone boats."

Hanlon frowned. "Shut up and get this stuff put back. We ain't got all day."

Mulcahey mopped his brow with his sleeve, wiped out his cap and settled it on his head, gazing out across the undulating expanse of prairie. Suddenly he squinted, then wiped his eyes and stared eastward. His mouth dropped open and he blinked and wiped his eyes again. Then he shrugged resignedly. "Sergeant, I got to tell you somethin'."

"What is it, Mulcahey?"

"Well, it's . . . Sergeant," he pointed, "I seen somethin' out there, just now. I don't see it now, but I seen it just a second ago."

Hanlon shaded his eyes, squinting across sun-baked plains. "What was it?"

"Well," Mulcahey gulped. "Well, it was like . . . what it was . . . uh . . . well, maybe it was some camels, Sergeant. Three of 'em. And a dog."

Private Bloom let out a whoop and lost his grip on a stone. In the hole, Pedigo howled. Sergeant Hanlon gaped at Mulcahey. Slowly, sadly he shook his head and turned away.

Through the long day Billy Sipe had pushed the roan, pushed it just short of its limits, pausing only now and then to let it rest and graze, once at a little creek with an inch of water lazy along its sand bottom, twice on the open prairie where no landmarks could be seen and where every direction looked like all the others. He needed the horse, needed it desperately. Each time he rested he inspected its worn shoes, its trim pasterns, its fetlocks, cannons, knees and hocks. Then he gave it a hatful of water and a hatful of grain, while rubbing it down with sacking.

He was grateful now for the time he had spent as stable boy for a hack company, and later as liverer for a field regiment. He had no love for the vast, depressing openness of these plains, the huge distances, the nothingness around him. There was no comfort here, and his ticket out was the roan horse. Many things Billy Sipe had never found the opportunity to learn, but he did know about horses. His street-urchin education had taught him to fight and to run, to hide and to steal. But nothing had ever prepared him for the immense loneliness of the prairie. Here there was no one to fight and no place to hide, and nothing to steal beyond what he had already stolen. Nothing remained but to run, and the sheer distances daunted him. The horse was his only means to escape.

Escape where? He had no idea, but he had chosen a direction and he kept on. Somewhere there must be a town, he thought. A place with buildings and people, with streets and walls and roofs. A place where he could function. For a time after the elation of his escape from the trap of the wagon outfit had worn off, he had felt very small. And yet, there had been no choice that he could see. Those people were doomed. The Indians would get them, or the soldiers would. It didn't matter. They were dead men, and it was their worry, not his. He had survived alone before. He could do it again.

Yet the distances pressed down on him. Mile after mile he had no sense of having progressed. It all looked the same.

He wished he had been able to find Poole's money. He suspected it was in the wagons somewhere, but had never known where. He would need money when he arrived at a town. But, he did have his own, and it was enough. The horse he had taken he felt was his due, along with the sack of grain, the three big canteens, the carbine and the supplies. They had made him a partner, they said. Therefore, he had taken his share.

He felt small. He didn't like feeling small. It was this emptiness getting to him. He tried whistling as he rode, then stopped. It made him feel small. Out here there were no echoes. He missed walls.

Before wandering into the western plains—a journey he

tried hard to forget, full of fear and hunger and looking always over his shoulder—the worst place Billy Sipe had ever been was the Santee swamps. Men had died there, and they had died wet and cold, and he had not been ready to die. But even there, even in that hell, there had been echoes. The dismal forests had at least obscured distances and bounced back mournful sounds. Out here . . . there was nothing. Nothing.

The plains receded in all directions, distances beyond reckoning, and there was only land and sky. He rode on, more slowly now, keeping his eyes on the ground, trying not to look at the distances. He felt very small.

The land rose steadily ahead, the horizon receding hour by hour. Then abruptly he saw that he was approaching the crest of one of those elusive swells, long rises that were invisible in the distance yet could hide all sorts of things—settlements, buffalo herds, Indians. In his months of travel in these lands, first with Poole and then with the "company," he had noticed this phenomenon and been awed by it. Whole armies, he knew, could be swallowed up on these "flat" prairies and not be seen at all.

Cautiously he walked the roan toward the final crest—it was deceptively far—then dismounted and eased forward until he had a view of the lands beyond. He raised, looked, then stepped back as though he had been hit. Beyond were more plains, endless and fading into blue distance that lost itself in sky. The nothingness he had covered was nothing. The nothingness ahead was crushing.

Still, it was a direction.

After a long time he mounted the roan again and tapped its sides with his heels. The sun that had been high now lay low on the horizon to his left, and the world out there was afire with its glare. He went on.

The damned fools . . . they could have come with him. They could have run away. The wagons were nothing. They could get more wagons. Let the stinking Indians have the wagons. Let the soldiers have them. That old man . . . he was a fool. He had found Billy Sipe down-at-heels and hungry in a squalid little hill town and had fed him, then taken him on as driver. He had never even asked him any questions about who he was, where he came from, or why. A dozen times, if he had felt like it—a hundred times maybe—Billy might have brained the old fool in his sleep and taken what he had. He just hadn't ever felt like it, he told himself. Stupid old man. He wouldn't have lasted a week where Billy grew up. Yet the contempt that should have come never quite did.

Billy shook his head, exasperated with himself.

Then Poole had tied them up with those others. That crazy Spaniard—Sipe still couldn't believe some of the things he had seen him do, like single-handedly charging a bunch of armed warriors, yelling like a madman. He was plain crazy. And the negro, Copple—a damned black cow, Billy thought. Placid, good-natured, never rankled . . . a cow. Yet, there was something about him. Billy had never quite been tempted to push him. He had thought about it, just for the hell of it. Goad him and see if he gives . . . but something had cautioned him and he had never done it.

He scowled when he thought of Darby Curtis. A bully, he thought. A strutting, arrogant bully, big and strong and always pretending to be somebody else, always seeming to hide the cruel callousness that men of that size always had. Not until the bastard had walked into that storeroom and slugged him had Billy's suspicions been confirmed. Picking on the little guy . . . that was how they were. All of them. Curtis just hadn't shown it until then. The fact that Sipe was almost as big as Curtis didn't enter into his thinking on the matter. He had always been an underdog. He would always be an underdog. The streets had taught him that. Curtis and his damned mules reinforced it.

He glanced at the inconceivable distances around him and he felt small.

The roan's ears came up and Billy caught his breath, grasping the carbine as something moved suddenly, far ahead in the evening light. Then he shrugged. Antelope. A small herd of them. They had appeared suddenly from some invisible ripple in the prairie. He watched them go, sleek and distant and incredibly graceful. They belonged

141

out here. The distances were home to them. Not to him.

Had the Indians come on them by now? He wondered. Were they lying on the prairie back there somewhere, dead and maybe scalped, with turkey buzzards circling over them? Or had the soldiers found them? Were they on their way to a firing squad . . . or already summarily executed? Maybe they were still running, or holed up somewhere under fire, needing another gun.

The thought tormented him and he tried to shake it away. That kind of thinking was no good. That kind of thinking, back there in the Santee swamps, would have got him killed. He wasn't ready to die.

It had been easy back there on the Santee. Nothing there had taunted him, haunted him, goaded him to stay. He had run.

Somehow, though, out here there were spirits. With evening a breeze drifted across the grass and whispered to him. Shame, it said. Shame. Ssss-sshame. Poole, it said. Damned old fool Poole. Yet Poole had run one time, so he said. From Texas. Did he run, though, or just go?

"What the hell difference does it make?" Billy Sipe shouted, and the sound of his voice was lost in distance. There were no echoes. He felt small.

Day had faded to long evening. Blues and purples underneath magenta fleece in a sky impossibly deep.

It took him a while to realize he was not moving. He had reined in, somehow, and sat now looking back the way he had come. The roan turned its head to look back at him, curiously.

"What the hell difference does it make?" he whispered. Then, "That damned old fool. All of 'em. They're damn fools."

Maybe it was a land of fools. What does a man do when the land is too big for him? Unforgiving land that would not shrink, would never accommodate?

Nobody but a damn fool would try to overcome this land, try to be bigger than he was. Only a fool . . .

"You haven't got a brain in your damn head!" Billy Sipe told himself as he turned the roan and headed south at a mile-eating lope. Still, the land in this direction swept toward horizons not quite so distant and he didn't feel quite so small.

It was nearly dark when he stopped. He checked the roan's shoes and its legs, rubbed it down briskly, gave it a hatful of water and a hatful of grain, hobbled it and then found a low spot to make a tiny fire of sun-dry buffalo chips. The fire was low and blue and gave almost no light. Billy cradled his carbine in his arms and lay back against his saddle, listening to the coyotes chorusing somewhere far off.

He might have gone to sleep. He had heard no sound. Yet suddenly there was someone beside him, crouching there, and a low calm voice said, "No, you won't need that," as he started to raise his gun.

The man was only a silhouette against starlight. "I have a little coffee," he said. "We'll use your pot. You came a long way, William Sipe."

The name froze him. No one had called him that, not since . . ."Who are you?"

The man's voice was gentle, somehow approving. "My name is Kichener. I have been following you. I wouldn't have followed much further, though. If you hadn't turned around I wouldn't have needed you."

As the man turned away to tend the little fire, Billy sat up. He still held his carbine and now the stranger's back was to him. He hesitated, and the stranger chuckled.

"That answers my other question," the quiet voice said.

"What do you want with me?" Billy lowered the gun. He knew he wouldn't use it now.

"I need your help, William. In return, I offer you a chance to clear your record."

"Of what?"

Suggestion of movement as the man turned. "You know what, William. Desertion in the face of the enemy. Yes, they knew you ran. Three of your patrol made it through the swamps. The report is on record."

"What are you . . . Army or what?"

"No, not Army. I'm on business of my own. But I can

arrange some things for you . . . if you're worth it."

"What do you mean, 'worth it'?"

"We'll see. You took a big step when you turned back."

"Stupid. That's what I am. That old man, Poole, him an' the rest, they're probably dead by now. Indians an' the army both after 'em. They haven't got a chance."

"Maybe." A quarter moon was rising now in the eastern sky. As the man turned he raised his face and Billy saw his eyes below the shadowing brim of his flat-crowned hat. They were startling eyes, pale and cold yet burning with hidden fires. "Still, I think not. Have you noticed, Billy, that the people out here—those who belong here, who survive here—are . . . shall we say . . . unusual?"

"I've noticed they're crazy. They're all crazy. That's all. What are you drivin' at?"

"Darby Curtis is a native of these plains. This is his home. And in a way, Edwin Poole has found a home here, too. They won't die easily."

"Those Indians belong here, too. Hell, they're even crazier than Curtis."

"Yes." The man turned again and Billy noticed he was smiling—a cold, serene smile. "Yes, I am counting on that. Come with me, Billy. I want to show you something."

Billy trailed after him, baffled. From the top of a rise they looked out across a moon-silvered world that stretched away into infinite darkness. Kichener stood lithe and gray in the moonlight. "Tell me what you see, Billy."

Billy looked, then shook his head. "Nothing. Just a thousand miles of nothing."

"They're not so different from you, these western people. They just have other skills. But you have good eyes, Billy, if you know what to look for. Now look here." He pointed. "Just off there. Not so many miles. Do you see a glow?"

"Well, yeah. Something, I guess. What is it?"

"Buffalo hunters. A camp of them. The Indians you fought weren't after you. They were lured to fight. Someone wanted an incident, and the Indians were supposed to have attacked those men out there. As it happened, the cavalry intervened."

"And chased 'em right down on us. I know."

"An odd coincidence. Singular. And interesting. Now look beyond, Billy. Far beyond. What do you see?"

Billy stared across the prairie until his eyes watered. Then it seemed he saw something. "Well, maybe there's some lights. Kind of like they're moving a little. But my God, that's a hundred miles away!"

"Only about twenty. Take note of the direction. It's important. This time tomorrow, that is where you will be. There or somewhere beyond. Those are the Kana'tenee. They are Kiowa, and it's their warriors you fought."

"And you want me to go there?" Billy gawked at him. "You're crazy! No way in hell am I goin' to . . ."

"You turned around. You changed your mind and started back, to help your friends. I don't think you will turn away again."

"I ain't ready to die!"

The gray man looked at him in the moonlight and again Billy glimpsed those strange, cold eyes. Eyes of a cat, he thought. Yet not a cat. A hawk. A hunting hawk. He shivered. He wanted to be away from this man, away from whatever he was. Yet the eyes held him, and there was something there that was like approval. The man nodded.

"You aren't ready to die, but I think you are finally ready to live. These lands can get in a man's blood, Billy. They breed men to match them. An odd breed, possibly a sundown breed, but remarkable in many ways. In these lands a man can either shrivel away or grow to match them. When you turned around, you began to grow. How does it feel?"

"I don't know what you're talking about. What is this all about, anyway? What do you want from me?"

"I want you to do what you set out to do. I will show you how."

"What is this 'business' of your own, Kichener?"

"It's very simple. There are people who want an Indian war. One of them is a man named Mercer Poling. No, you don't know him. It doesn't matter. Poling isn't for you. He's for me. That's my 'business' out here. War with the

145

Indians may come . . . in a year, or two, or three. But not the war that Poling wants, and not now. You want to help your friends. You can do me a favor on the way. In return, I'll do one for you. Your horse is fresh, Billy, and you have rested. Let's get you ready to travel, and I'll tell you what you must do."

The sun was still above the horizon when Lieutenant Thomas Spradley, riding ahead of the main column with a scouting detail, reined in and squinted across prairie that had been empty . . . and suddenly was not. Three tall mules and a small horse ambled toward them, not a hundred yards away. They had appeared as if by magic, cresting a shallow swale hidden by the gently waving grass.

Flanking the lieutenant, Private Rusty Anderson rasped, "Well, I'll be . . . where did those come from?"

Raising a hand, Spradley halted the little column. The four unfettered animals came on at a casual pace. The mules raised their heads and turned their ears at sight of the soldiers, but didn't pause. Ten yards away the leading mule, a big mare with dark bristling mane, snorted and turned aside to veer around the intruders in her path. The others followed. Some distance back the yellow-gray pony paused, stared at them, then turned to begin a wide circle around.

Spradley looked back. "Some of you men, catch up those animals, will you?"

"Yes, sir," Anderson said. He and some others dismounted, uncoiling hackamore ropes from their saddle gear. The mules stopped, gazing at them curiously. Anderson walked to the tall mare. "Nice lady," he said softly. "Just stand still, lady. Let's have a look at you. Lordy, but you're a big one, ain't you? Nice lady." The mule gazed at him thoughtfully. He approached, let her sniff at his outstretched hand, then ran gentle fingers up her muzzle, toward her ears, his other hand readying the rope. He was standing on tiptoes. "That's a gentle lady," he said, pleased.

146

At that moment someone shouted, "Look out, Louie! Watch it! Oh, Christ!"

Anderson spun around in time to see Louie Gifford hit the ground rolling. Behind him one of the mules, the big dark one, was doing a spiral handstand, lashing out with powerful hind feet as it turned. Beyond it the other mule reared, pawed the air and brayed in ear-splitting challenge.

"You men!" the lieutenant shouted. "Control those animals!"

"Yes, sir," Anderson muttered. He turned again to the female, but she was no longer there. She had backed away from him, and now she responded to the snorts and brays of the others. She crouched, spun away and headed west, turf flying from her thudding heels. As if on signal, the others followed, scattering soldiers as they went. In an instant they were past and beyond the patrol, the mustard pony running belly-down in their wake.

Anderson bent to help Louie Gifford to his feet. The soldier was pale and gagging, the wind knocked out of him. But nothing seemed to be broken. Spradley had turned his mount as though to give chase, then changed his mind. He glared around him. "What kind of cavalry can't get a rope on a mule? Damn! You men are in the army! Haven't you ever handled mules?"

Anderson shook his head. "Yes, sir, all of us have. But those wasn't army mules, Lieutenant. Not by a long shot. I never seen mules that big . . . except with them wagons."

Anderson was helping Gifford back into his saddle when the rest of the troop arrived at a gallop. While Spradley reported to Sinclair, First Sergeant Ben Foley and the Tennessean, Andy Pell, scouted tracks.

"These was like those with the wagons," Anderson told Foley. "Big. Biggest mules I ever saw. And not wild, exactly, they just didn't want to be caught."

"Awful lot of sign out there," Pell pointed westward. "More mule tracks, and horses. A lot of 'em Indian ponies. No shoes, an' no grain in th' droppin's except what would be wild here. They come up from southeast, sometime after daybreak."

Sinclair rubbed his tired eyes and squinted into the glare of the setting sun. Out there was where they had fought Indians. And out there, somewhere, were Sergeant Hanlon and his burial detail.

Spradley sat his mount, facing him. His lean face was drawn in harsh planes. "If those were the same mules, then those Indians are the same Indians, Captain."

"Yes. Pell, can you tell how many?"

"Not really, Cap'n. Maybe forty-fifty animals altogether. Too many to sort out."

Spradley pushed back his hat. "Orders, Captain?"

"Very well, Lieutenant. First Platoon, full field gear, pull the supplies and equipment you need from the rest of the troop. Take the remounts, they're fresh. Pell can scout for you. Follow this trail as long as it holds westward. If you sight hostiles do not engage them. I want you to find Sergeant Hanlon and his detail and bring them back. If you can get me a report on the hostiles, do so. Otherwise just find that detail. You understand."

"Yes, sir." Spradley turned to Foley. "Sergeant, you heard the captain. Get the platoon's gear on those remounts, and see to supplies. On the double."

By evening light eighteen men headed westward across the plains. Sinclair watched them go, then turned northeast toward Camp Jacob. He knew what would happen next. Major Alfred Grimes was anxious to test his full squadron in the field.

XIII

Without their paint, and with their gawdy finery packed away for another day, the Blacklegs looked like any other Indians—firelight soft on dark features that ranged from severe to sullen to faintly humorous, jet eyes hard and quick, strong teeth white as they talked among themselves and kept a watch on their prisoners. Bird, Stalking Horse and a few others sat at a small fire at the east point of the wide, hidden shelf where they had camped. Other braves came and went around a separate fire to the west. A haze of faint smoke and a smell of cooking meat hung in the fragile stillness of the little valley, taken often by erratic winds and coming again when the silences returned.

Between the fires Edwin Poole and Vince Copple sat on stony ground, dividing their attentions between the padding braves who were always near, always watching, and the blanket-wrapped form of Darby Curtis asleep between them. Sometimes he would stir, sometimes snore, and they would turn to him to listen to his breathing.

A short distance away Trinidad Salazar squatted alone, unbound except for an eight-foot cord tied loosely around his neck, its other end fastened to a stake driven into the ground. The little Spaniard was a thing of wonder to the Kiowa. Twice during the day he had attacked them. All of them.

Out on the flat, just visible by starlight, horses grazed and nine tall mules clustered apart and aloof, staying close to Bernice and the comforting bell she wore. Only Bernice was hobbled. Stalking Horse had studied well the magic of

149

the mules.

Edwin Poole rubbed wrists chafed by the bindings they had worn through a day of fast travel, and grumbled. The black man kept his silence. He knew far more of bondage then did the others.

"Wonder what would happen if we was to try to light ourselves a fire," Poole muttered. "I'd feel better if we had a fire. I see some firewood yonder. Where you suppose they got it?"

"Down in the bottoms there," Copple tipped his head, though there wasn't enough light for Poole to see the motion. "Plenty of deadfall down there. But I wouldn't try to go down there to get some. Prob'ly wind up clouted like him."

"Stupid Indians," Poole spat. "Damn wonder he ain't dead after that rap. I thought he was dead for a while. For that matter, I haven't figured out yet why any of us are still alive. Where you suppose they're takin' us, Vince?"

Copple pondered on it for a time, then shook his head. "I don't know. All day long, I thought they was goin' home. We been movin' straight west all day. You recollect when we was fightin' Indians and cavalry, when it rained . . . all those Indians that showed up comin' from the north? Those was fresh horses they had, so they hadn't come far. I was thinkin' it was that big village Billy Sipe saw, and that we been headin' toward that. But then when we turned south 'bout sundown . . . well, I don't have any idea now."

"I saw some of 'em take fresh mounts and go on ahead," Poole said. "That was earlier. Then they came back, and that was when we turned. I didn't see much else. It was right about then that your Spaniard let out that whoop an' charged into a bunch of 'em that had their backs turned. Hoo! That's the craziest yahoo I ever seen. Hadn't been his hands was tied, he might have got hisself a few. An' up on one of their own horses, too." He shook his head.

"He gets like that sometimes," Copple allowed, mildly. Between them Darby Curtis snorted and turned over, drawing the blanket around him. Copple adjusted it, making sure he was covered. He listened to his breathing. "Sounds like he's just sleepin'," he said. "Earlier on, when they stopped in that draw an' he woke up an' had to pee, I thought they'd scrambled his brains. He thought he was at Antietam. Said if Captain Somebody-or-other didn't pull back he was goin' to shoot the son of a bitch."

Poole looked up. "I never heard him talk about the war."

"He don't talk about it. He just went off to it, an' was gone for a time, then he came home and took up where he'd left off . . . that was last year. Never hardly said a thing to anybody 'bout where he'd been. Only thing he ever said to me was that was the last time he was goin' east. He said those folks back there was a bunch of lunatics."

Poole nodded, his whiskers a blur in starlight. "Amen," he muttered. "I wish we had a fire."

Copple gazed at him, a shadow in the night. "You hurtin' too, Mr. Poole?"

"Just aches. Get 'em now and again. Especially when I'm waitin' to be gutted and scalped. Aches comes with the dismals, mostly."

"If they're fixin' to kill us, why didn't they already get it done?"

"I don't know. Maybe takin' us home so the squaws can have some of the fun. Man, haven't I heard some tales . . ."

"I'd just as leave not talk about things like that, Mr. Poole." Copple shivered. Then with another glance at Darby, he got to his feet, groaning. Bruises taken in their capture and ignored all day had begun to throb and stiffen. He stretched, gazing around, and several Blacklegs appeared in the darkness, watching him. "Gotta see about somethin'," he said, and walked away.

Before he had gone twenty feet there were warriors in his path, chattering at him, gesturing with their lances. He stopped, spread his hands wide, palms up, then pointed toward the nearest fire. When the Indians hesitated, he continued walking. The two with lances eased back, letting him pass between them, then fell in behind. Copple noticed that he was sweating, despite the cool of night. Keeping his hands outspread, he approached the cluster of Indians at the fire. Several of them stood as he neared, weapons in their hands. He stopped just short of them, where dry wood was piled, and bent to pick up a good armload of the fuel. Then with his heart pounding and pulse racing, he strode through them and past them to kneel by their fire. All around him weapons glistened and dark eyes glinted.

He selected a stick with good coals most of its length and pulled it from the fire. As he held it aloft a breeze caught it and fanned a flame. The Indians had gone silent, and he felt he should say something. "Need to borry a light," he said, feeling very foolish as he said it.

As he turned a husky warrior with a warclub barred his way.

"A'as steche'an akada," the Indian demanded.

Holding his faggot, Copple gestured toward the firewood in his arm, then pointed toward the darkness where the scrub forested bottoms lay. "You want me to go get my own?"

The Kiowa scowled at him, then said something harsh and stepped aside. Copple drew a deep breath and expelled it. He started forward, then turned back, pointing with his smoking coals. "We could use some of that meat, too." When there was no response he returned to the fire. With the cold end of the firestick in his teeth, keeping his head turned to that its smoke would not blind him, he extracted a large chunk of sun-cured buffalo meat from a noisome hide pouch, then shouldered through a growing cluster of curious hostiles and returned to where Edwin Poole sat beside Darby Curtis. Several Indians followed and flanked him, but when he dumped his firewood and squatted to make a fire they faded back, apparently unconcerned.

"That took some nerve," Poole said. "Wonder they didn't kill you."

"Been better than what you was startin' to talk about," the black man assured him. When he had a fire going he spitted the chunk of meat on a stick and rested it over the blaze. "This don't smell very good, but they eat it and it don't seem to hurt them any. Maybe I can cook th' high out of it."

They had finished half the meat when Darby Curtis rolled over, flung his blanket aside and groaned, "Melly. Melly Bright-eyes . . . ohhh!" With a shudder he rolled again, came to his hands and knees and stopped there, breathing hard. "Oh, God. My head."

"Prob'ly needs to pee again," Copple said. "You awake, Mr. Darby? Where you think you are this time?"

Curtis eased into a sitting position, his long legs spread, face in his hands, cradling his aching head. "Right here, I guess," he murmured. "Oh, Lordy, Lordy. Never again, Vince. That musta' been some party. Ow!" He had discovered the lump on his head. He lifted his face, glanced at the fire, then at each of the men sitting with him. "I guess I missed something. Where are . . ." his eyes lifted then, caught the motion of figures in the background. "Holy . . . Vince! Blacklegs!"

The black man's strong hand on his shoulder restrained him. "Easy, Mr. Darby. You been out a while. Look like your eyes is focusin' now, though. You want some water? Maybe some high meat?"

He stared around in the fire-touched darkness. He tried to remember, then did. "Vince . . . the mules? Where are the mules?"

"They got most of 'em, Mr. Darby. They got nine an' most of our horses. An' all of us."

"Trini? Where's Trini?"

"Right yonder. They put a string on him. But we fed an' watered him. He's doin' all right. Here, you better least-ways drink some water."

Darby staggered to his feet. "In a minute. First I got to pee." He walked a few steps away in the darkness, glaring at the dim forms of Kiowa braves just beyond the light. When he returned to the fire he sagged onto the blanket. He drank water, ate a few bites of meat and lay down again. Within minutes he was snoring.

"I guess he'll be all right," Poole said. "For whatever that's worth." He stared morosely at the east fire, distant from where they sat. Vaguely, he could make out the silhouettes of packs strung to thrown travois. The Indians had gone through the wagons, taken what they wanted. "Wish I had my pipe right now," he grumbled. "And some of that good tobacco."

Vince Copple shook his head, gazing at the old man across the dying fire. "I done used up all the nerve I had, Mr. Poole." He lay down then, to see if he could get some sleep.

When Darby Curtis opened his eyes again, the pain in his head had receded to a constant but distant throb. His mouth was dry, his throat parched and his belly felt as though his gullet had forgotten the way. He closed his eyes, groaned dismally, then opened them again. First dawn was in the sky, and smoke wafted on the morning breeze carrying the scent of slightly-tainted meat roasting. The bulk nearby he made out to be Vince Copple, asleep with a glisten of dew on his dark-wool hair.

Darby groaned again, then raised himself to one elbow to look around. A few feet away white ashes marked the remains of a small fire. Beside it Edwin Poole lay curled like a child, snoring faintly. Beyond, a little distance, Indian braves moved around a cooking fire. Beyond them, a hundred yards away or more, stock grazed on a meadow and he saw the tall, dark shapes of some of his mules. Near his feet was a hide water-pouch, and he dragged it to him, hoisted it and drank. The water was no worse than water he had drunk before. It refreshed him. It also made his stomach clamor. He was ravenous. A spit that had been rigged beside the fire had long since collapsed, whatever scraps it had held destroyed in the coals. There was nothing else to eat. He got to his knees and hunkered there, reaching for his knife and realizing it was gone. For a moment he fought dizziness, then his vision cleared and he was fully awake. He rubbed rough hands through the stubble on his cheeks, wiped his crusted eyes with a dirty sleeve and explored the knot on his head. It was sore, but subsiding and the skull beneath it seemed firm.

Bird, he thought. That bastard, Bird.

He drank again, then turned slowly, trying to see details in the dim light of pre-dawn. There seemed to be no

Indians nearby. The closest were at the first fire he had seen, thirty or forty yards away. Looking east he saw another fire, more Indian shapes and something lying on the ground nearby. Cautiously he crawled toward it. It was Trinidad Salazar, asleep. Darby crouched near him, puzzled, then he saw the thong tied to his neck, its other end fastened to a stake.

"Hell, Trini," he breathed. "You poor little bastard, what have they done to you?" He moved close, reached to remove the loop from the Spaniard's neck, and suddenly was caught by a hard grip on his wrist. A flurry of silent motion and he was rolled onto his back, a whipcord body pressed him down and the Spaniard's arm hovered above his head. He had a rock in his hand. Darby caught the arm and held it, gasping. "Trini, damn it," he whispered. "Let go. It's me."

Instantly the Spaniard subsided and edged away. Darby glanced around. No one had heard the struggle. He took the rock from Trini and gazed sadly at the Spaniard's happy grin. "My God," he whispered. "Don't you ever quit? Christ!"

Carefully, staying low, he deciphered the knot in Trini's constraint and untied it. Then he worked the heavy stake out of the ground and coiled the eight-foot thong. He didn't know what to do with the things, but at least he had something now. He looked to the west, beyond the nearer fire. Again he could make out the shapes of animals grazing. He also thought he could see men out there. He nodded. The Kiowa would have guards with the animals.

Some distance away to the south the shadows revealed a bottom where brush and a few trees grew. With Trini following, he crawled back to where he had started and laid a hand on Vince Copple's thick shoulder. The black man awoke with a start, but Darby hushed him. Hands close to his face in the vague light, he signed for him to follow. Then he crawled to Edwin Poole, awakened him and held a hand over his mouth to stifle his groans. When he was fully awake they gathered around Darby and he pointed toward the still-dark bottoms. Vince picked up the water pouch,

Poole found a sturdy stick beside the dead fire and Trini recovered his rock. Then as one, Darby in the lead, they snaked into the tall grass and began crawling. Darby kept Trini near him so he could swat him down in case he decided to raise his head for a look around.

Minutes that seemed like hours passed, and a sweat broke out on Darby's face. They had heard no sound from the Indians' fires, no evidence of alarm. It occurred to him that this was easier than it should be. He knew the Blacklegs and he knew their methods. Still, this was the only plan he could come up with. He had no hope of making it to the animals . . . of getting horses or even of recovering his mules. He didn't even know why he was still alive, he or the others. But the shadowed bottoms were the only way out if there was a way at all. Silently, steadily he snaked through the grass, feeling the slight downslope of the ground, knowing when it became more pronounced, visualizing where they were by the sign.

He sensed slight motion ahead and froze, willing the others to make no move or sound. An inch at a time he crept forward, then stopped when he saw motion. A dimness moved, stopped and moved again, a low roundness barely stirring the grass, coming toward him, hardly an arm's length away. Grass-tops rippled above him in a steady breeze from the southwest, blowing his scent away. He squinted. The thing moved again and he saw a wide, flat head with light stripes on dark side-fur. Small, bright eyes glinted and a quivering nose above visible sharp teeth tested the air.

At first glance he had thought rabbit. He had been afraid it was a jackrabbit, that would discover them and go bounding away, alerting every Indian for a half-mile around. Now he gritted his teeth, wishing it had been only a rabbit.

The last thing on earth he needed right now was a run-in with a badger. He had no idea what a full-grown badger could do to a man on the ground, but he had seen what one could do to a pack of dogs and he wanted no part o fit.

Still, the badger edged forward again and he braced

156

himself. Then there was quick motion beside him and a rock thudded into the ground directly in front of the animal's nose, skidding into it. The badger seemed to turn inside its skin, rolling, doubling back. It disappeared, and he heard the receding hiss of its passage through the grass as it hurried away.

"*El diablito parten*," Trini breathed beside him.

Christ! Darby thought, sighing. What would the idiot have done if it hadn't run away? Tackled it with his bare hands? He had wondered before how the Spanish had managed to conquer whole continents. But, as now, every time he started thinking about it he decided he didn't want to think about it any more. He kept imagining armies of Trinis. The very thought was awesome. No race or culture would ever be prepared for a phenomenon like that.

He lay still, getting his nerves back in order, then started crawling again and stopped. Some distance away there was a startled cry and the sound of something—someone—plunging through brush. He knew then. They had been waiting for him. The badger had found them instead. He edged away from the direction of the sound. The light was growing minute by minute, dawn coming on. Hurrying now, but still staying within the grass, he crawled on, angling away from the sounds he had heard. There was still a chance.

Ten yards became twenty, and twenty became fifty. The ground's slope now was pronounced, and they moved faster. If they could reach the shelter of the brush, he thought, there might just be a chance. At least they could run then . . . or maybe they could hide. He knew it was impossible. Those were Blacklegs back there. Skilled horsemen, fine trackers, formidable hunters and fighters. Still, there was no other chance.

He knew the brush was close. It had to be close. Then the hair rose on the back of his neck. Behind him he heard Vince Copple's voice. Just a grunt, but he knew what it meant. He raised his head slightly. A line of warriors stood ten feet away, watching him solemnly. He turned. There were others behind.

Defeated, he got to his feet. The Blacklegs made no move, except that a few grinned wickedly at him. When the fugitives were standing, the line parted and Bird stepped forward, bearing his hooked lance.

"Good," he told Darby in the Kiowa speech. "You do well, wild one. Some of the young braves might learn from such as you. Come back to the fires now. A new day is here and we have far to go."

Darby struggled for words. He was far too angry at the Blackleg leader to address him using the forms of respect, but he was in no position at the moment to insult him. He resolved his dilemma by turning from Bird to another warrior nearby. "Where are the Blackleg men taking us?"

The warrior grinned at him and said nothing. Bird looked at him thoughtfully, then nodded. "You are like your father, O'gatedota. But the time of our fathers is past. Hawk That Hunts Walking has moved his people to the south. We will take you to Hawk That Hunts Walking. We have promised him medicine."

Darby swung back to him in disgust. "We have no medicine!"

"Stalking Horse has had a vision," Bird said. "We must take you to Hawk That Hunts Walking."

XIV

Billy Sipe found the hide-hunters' camp before morning touched the sky. A west wind brought the smell of it to him and he almost changed his mind about this thing the pale-eyed man had set him to do.

The smell on the wind was the stink of death.

For the hundredth time since nightfall he wondered what in God's name he was doing, taking a hand in things that were no concern of his. If there had ever been a guiding principle in his life, it was that other people's worries were no skin off his nose. Yet, somehow out here where a man could see no confines—where the world just went on forever—that principle was lacking in comfort. Here, in these foreboding distances, there was no place to hide from himself.

"I'm about to get myself killed," he muttered as he walked the roan westward in the pale of morning. "I'm just plain headin' for the place I'll meet my maker and I've had all night to turn around and here I am still goin'. I'll ride in there and those men will shoot me down and that's the last the world will see of Billy Sipe. And who cares, anyway? It won't matter to anybody if Billy Sipe is dead. Never has mattered to anybody . . . except me. So why am I doin' this? That Kichener, he's as crazy as the rest of 'em. And spooky. All he wants me to do is ride in on a bunch of wild buffalo hunters out here where there ain't a witness in a thousand miles . . . then if I live through that—and no way in hell am I goin' to live through that—then I'm supposed to go find a bunch of hostile Indians. I don't know what

I'm doin' here at all."

Still, the roan walked westward unimpeded and Billy Sipe sagged in its saddle with the first peach hint of dawn at his back and the stink of death before him, carried on the wind.

When the camp was in sight—a sprawl of untidiness centered by a ring of sideboard wagons and a drifting plume of smoke—he stood in his stirrups to shout, "Halloo, the camp! Halloo!" He saw no evidence of response, then realized with a tinge of embarrassment that he was still nearly a mile away. "I hate this country," he swore. "I don't see how anybody can stand this." He tapped the roan with booted heels and rode on.

A half-mile further and he saw motion. Men appeared between wagons, looking his way. They all held rifles. He reined in again and stood in his stirrups, waving his hat.

"Halloo the camp!" he shouted. "Can I come in?"

No sounds carried to him at this distance, and he knew they had not heard him. But they saw him, and after a time one of them stepped out in plain sight, waving a hat. No sense thinking about turning back any more, he told himself. It's too late now. The stink on the wind was a living thing. Those men killed for a living, and the mark of it rode with them.

Straightening with an effort, his face a mask of innocent purpose, he rode into the hunters' camp.

In silence they gathered around him, rough men with dirty beards, smoke and grime heavy on the soiled garments and foul hides they wore, brutish men who carried large rifles of a dozen varieties and handled them with the ease of long acquaintance.

Billy looked around at them, wet his dry lips and pulled off his hat. "Which one of you gents is named Cully?"

The one who spoke was behind him, and Billy turned in his saddle. The man was big and gaunt-seeming, hard eyes in a face like leather above a heavy beard.

"Who wants to know?" he asked.

Billy wet his lips again. "I come from Cain DeWitt," he said. "He's got one more job he wants done. I'm supposed to make you an offer. Ah, can I get down?"

"No reason to," the man rasped. "You can just stay up there an' speak your piece. Then I'll decide what to do with you. Where have I seen you before?"

"I don't know. I used to drive for a tradin' rig, but DeWitt pays better money."

"Only when he has to," Cully spat. Some of the others chuckled at this. "So what does he want done now? He want us to bait some redskins again?"

"No. This is a lot simpler. He wants you to *be* some redskins. He'll pay. He'll pay good."

"What do you mean, *be* redskins? How we gonna do that? Keep talkin'."

"West of here and a little south, there's a place that a bunch of Kiowa have had a village. It's on a creek, just up from where there's a wide bend . . ."

"We know the place. Fisher an' Silk seen it. Big bunch of 'em. Lot of lodges. What about it?"

"Well, DeWitt says those Indians will be movin' out. Maybe they already have. But a few days from now, week or so maybe, there's going to be a cavalry patrol checkin' the place out. DeWitt says it's worth plenty if that patrol doesn't come back. If the Indians get 'em instead."

"You said the redskins was leavin'."

"That's right. And if you fellows were there when the patrol comes, you could make it look like anything you wanted to, couldn't you? Poke an arrow in a bullet hole and who knows the difference? Take a scalp and who knows who took it? That's what DeWitt says."

The man squinted up at him. "That sounds like a crazy notion to me. How's he know we can jump th' army an' get away with it? Shit, it ain't like Indians. You're talkin' about soldiers now."

"With them," Billy pointed at the heavy rifles several of them carried, "what's the difference? Cavalry ain't got anything can shoot like those."

"What does he mean by patrol?"

"Nine, ten men at the most. Just a circuit detail. That's all bein' fixed. DeWitt says you fellows go to that abandoned village an' set up like it was Indians there, and wait. When they come, you know what to do. Just so it looks like redskins did it."

"Then when it's done," Cully sneered, "how do we know DeWitt will pay? We already know about him. Shit, the bastard's only honest when he's lookin' at a smoke hole. I don't think . . ."

"I brought money with me." Billy reached carefully into his coat, aware of quick shifting of rifles all around him. "DeWitt said you'd have to see the money. I got $500 here for you." He held it up so they could see.

Cully blinked at the money. His tongue darted from his whiskers, licking his lips. Then he grinned evilly at Billy. "Why, that's decent of you, pilgrim, just bringin' all that money out here like that. Lot easier just to take it off of you than to fuss around with a bunch of cavalry for it, ain' it?"

"Yeah," Billy nodded. "I guess so. But then you wouldn't get the other half. All I brought was half of what he's payin' for this job. DeWitt said it wouldn't be real smart for me to bring all of it."

"A thousand dollars?" Cully's eyes widened. "He's payin' a thousand dollars for this job?"

"It's worth it, he said. But only if it's done right. He'll have the rest of it for you when you're done. But he wants to see scalps an' sidearms. And badges and stripes. You take what Indians would take, and leave sign like Indians would leave, and you show him things he can count so he'll know the job is done. Then there's another $500, just like this." Leaning down from the roan, he handed the money to Cully. "Well, does he have a deal? He's waitin' for me to say."

Cully looked at the money in his hand, then exchanged glances with some of the other hunters. Several of them nodded. He looked up again at Billy, scowling. "I ain't real sure I like everythin' you said about this. You keep sayin' DeWitt this an' DeWitt that. Ain't somebody else in this? What does he say?"

Billy suppressed a shudder. What if the man questioned him further? All he knew was what Kichener had told him

162

to say. "I don't know anything about that. All I know is DeWitt said I was to come and find you and tell you what I said. Is it a deal or not?"

"It's a deal," the man said. "You just tell DeWitt the next time I have to show a gun to get my money, I'll use it."

When Billy rode slowly out of the hunters' camp, going east, he was wringing wet under his coat. He kept the roan to a steady lope and didn't look back. The smell of death clung in his nostrils, and his stomach was knotted into an iron ball. It was nearly a mile before he noticed the hard tension in his shoulders and back, and stretched himself to relieve it. Even that far away, his backbone had been expecting the impact of a slug from a buffalo gun.

When he was well beyond sight, over a broad swell in the prairie, he turned right and headed south. In his mind was the terrain of the land as Kichener had showed it to him by the light of the quarter moon. Beyond and away from the hunters' camp, many miles beyond, had been an impression of lights moving. Indians, Kichener had said. The Kana'tenee. People of the far grass.

"I can't believe I'm doin' this," Billy Sipe muttered to himself. "Here I am, headin' out to get myself killed, and for what? This isn't my business. None of it's my business. Why should I care? Does anybody care what happens to Billy Sipe? Hell, no. So what am I doin'? I'm on my way to get myself killed, is what I'm doin'. 'Go ahead an' get yourself killed, Billy,' says I. 'It'll make you feel better.' That old fool Poole. An' that struttin' cockajay Darby Curtis . . . if he's still alive an' they don't kill me right off I might just kill him. Leastways beat hell out of him. Serve him right . . ."

Three fresh mounds stood bleak and lonely on the prairie, little mounds of gray-brown sandy soil topped by slabs of sod cut away for the digging then replaced to keep animals from digging them up again. The mounds were neatly ranked, side by side, each with a small wooden stake to serve as a headstone.

163

Some distance away, downwind, a broken lance and the ripening carcass of a large mule were all that remained now of the first encounter between Kana'tenee Blacklegs and A Troop. The people of Hawk That Hunts Walking had returned long since to clear the field of their dead and wounded—and of anything useful.

By high morning sun five men in travel-stained uniforms stood gazing down at the three little mounds.

"Smith, T.," Master Sergeant Boyd Hanlon extolled, standing at rough attention, hat in hand. "Smith, J., Dorchester, H. . . . privates, First Squadron, detached, Fifth Regiment of the Ninth Division, United States Cavalry." He paused, glanced around at the four young troopers standing bareheaded behind him. Then he faced the graves again.

"A known thief,' he continued in a softer voice, "a fornicator and a released arsonist . . . may God forgive them. They were good soldiers all."

"I'm glad the wolves didn't get to them," Jakey Bloom whispered to Tom Pedigo. "I hate a mess like that."

"What I'm glad of is the Injuns didn't lift their scalps," Pedigo nodded. "You ever see a man that was scalped? Way I hear it their faces sort of fall down an' they look like dead Chinamen."

"Scalps ain't all Injuns take," Barney Studely whispered. "There used to be a old Injun up in Illinois that had a tobacco pouch made out of a man's . . ."

"Studely!" Sergeant Hanlon snapped. "Shut up! Let's have a little respect here." He turned back to the fresh graves.

"A man's what?" Bloom whispered.

"Well, you know, his . . ."

Private Mulcahey had turned away, shielding his eyes. "Somebody comin', Sergeant," he said.

"Which is it this time," Bloom snickered. "Ships or camels?"

"Two riders," Mulcahey snapped, then turned to Hanlon. "Could be Corporal Finnegan and Private Crump. Matter of fact," he grinned, "I guess that's who it must be since they're all that's out."

"Irish logic," Bloom breathed. "One of the marvels of the world."

The sergeant glared at them. "Bloom and Studely, bring in our mounts. And you two, get this equipment tied. Move it! We haven't got all day."

The mounts were retrieved and saddled, spades and picks stowed aboard them when Corporal Jamie Finnegan and Private P. T. Crump rode in at a trot. "We circled out two-three miles, Sergeant," Finnegan reported. "Not a sign of anybody. Maybe them two got away, do you suppose?"

"Maybe," Hanlon shook his head. "But not likely. And if they did, God help 'em because they didn't have a brain between them, rest their souls. No, Phillips said he thought he saw Jones fall when those Indians were chasin' us. And that's what probably happened to both of 'em. We'll just have to follow out that way and find 'em and plant 'em. You men, mount up."

They mounted and fell in behind him as he headed his mount south, following the barely-visible trace of the retreat in the rain. Two more graves, then they could turn east again and head for Camp Jacob. Hanlon thought of a basin of hot water, a razor and soap, and a soft bunk. He was ready to put in some bivouac time.

Behind him Private Jakey Bloom loped his mount forward to pull alongside Tom Pedigo. "I hope the wolves haven't got to'em before we get there," he said.

They had gone eight miles, without trace of the two missing men, when Private Mulcahey at right flank reined in his horse and stood in his stirrups open-mouthed, gawking at the distances to the west. He blinked, squinted and stared again. The sun was high and the grass ran away for miles to dissolve finally in a seeming ocean of rippling blue water, infinitely far yet invitingly close, elusive as only a high plains mirage can be. Mulcahey had seen mirages before, and though they puzzled him he had learned to ignore them. Yet this one was different. Out of its mist and across its blue surface rode a long file of Indians, haze-distorted and shimmering, their silhouettes immensely tall and close together, hundreds of them it seemed, a line that continued from mist to mist in the mistless distance. Among and behind them walked others, squaws and children, tall shapes of tiny people captured by the convex air and displayed for his amazement.

"Sergeant," he whispered, then gulped and tried again. "Sergeant, look. There's . . ." The silence mocked him and he turned. The others were a hundred yards away and going, unaware that he had stopped. Again he looked into the west and still the file continued—tall thin people and tall thin animals moving between earth and sky, part of both and part of neither, so near he could see features here and there and yet so far away that he knew a day's hard riding might not take him where they were.

Somewhere out there a cloud scudded shadow across the land. The imaging air shifted and the visions swayed, blurred and were gone. He stared across endless prairie, straining his eyes for some glimpse of the reality of what he had seen, but there was nothing.

With a shrug of resignation he turned away and tapped heels to his horse. He let the animal take its time, closing slowly on the rest of the burial detail while he tried to work out in his mind how he might tell Sergeant Hanlon what he had seen.

He wondered if he should even try.

Through the day the First Platoon followed the trail left by the band of Indians and their stolen animals. The trail was faint, but discernible to Private Andy Pell. Though he was an easterner, Pell was not a product of the cities. Most of his young life had been spent in those wild, weather-haunted lands beyond the sound. He had trailed with Pequots and learned their ways, and he knew where a man or beast had gone by the traces of its passage. At places through the day he even saw prints, among them shod tracks he would have taken for mule prints had they been smaller. Then he remembered the huge mules they had seen. These then were mules as well.

With evening they camped on a high place and when it was dark they caught the tiny glow of firelights far away. Those ahead of them they knew were the party they had trailed. But there was one little glow apart by miles, southwest of their position.

"Sergeant Hanlon's detail," Lieutenant Spradley decided. "And so we have followed those savages far enough. With dawn we go southwest to pick up those men."

Shortly after noon they found the three fresh graves and clustered around them, removing their campaign hats and glancing about in silence while Private Rusty Anderson read the markers. "Both of the Smiths," he told the lieutenant, "and Dorchester. They must not have found Jones and Heath."

From a distance away Private Pell waved his arm and shouted, "Lieutenant!" When Spradley reached him he pointed at the ground. "They went this way, sir. Just about due south, it looks like. Not far ahead of us, either. That dung there is still wet."

Several miles to the northwest three mules and a mustard pony cropped at tall grass in a place where many men and horses had camped very recently. After a time Hildegarde started west again, then stopped, puzzled. The trail had disappeared. As she stood, head high and ears up, bright eyes studying the land, Madison trotted past her, heading west. Some distance behind her the mustard pony sidled close to Lucifer, then dodged nimbly as he whirled and kicked.

Minutes passed, then Hildegarde ambled southward, snuffing now and then at the tall grass. Approaching a brushy bottom she found scent and followed it. After a few hundred yards she had the trail of passage again, and set out upon it in a long, easy lope. Lucifer left off chasing the mustard pony to look after her and then follow. The pony in turn followed Lucifer. Some distance to the west Madison looked back, snorted and tossed his head. Then when that accomplished nothing he set himself a course that would intercept them eventually.

He had gone a half mile when he noticed he was being followed. A pair of curious prairie wolves, male and female, were trotting along behind him, zigzagging across his path, moving up to flank him on both sides. He extended to a long trot, and the pair stayed with him, seeming to enjoy the run. But then the male dashed in and made a try for his rear tendons. He lashed at it, missed and began to run. The female was beside him, coursing him for a moment, then he gained distance. He topped a low rise and the others were there. At sight of the wolves Lucifer brayed, lay back his ears and charged. The female swerved aside and he stomped and danced, trying to catch the male. In a moment the wolves changed their minds and hurriedly left the scene.

Hildegarde glanced curiously at Madison but did not break her stride. She had places to go. Grouped again, the three mules trotted southward, the pony tagging behind them.

XV

With their prisoners mounted now, unbound but closely watched, and plenty of animals to carry the things taken from the wagons, the Blackleg men moved with a speed that left Edwin Poole profoundly impressed.

Reining his loping mount close beside that of Darby Curtis, he waved a hand. "I don't see how they do it, Darby. If soldiers was to try to cover this much ground, they'd kill their horses."

"That's because soldiers don't know how," Darby said. "The army goes by the book. The book says you run and stop, then run and stop. If you notice, these people hardly ever do either one. The army uses horses by the book. The Kiowa use 'em the way God made 'em." He glanced back, fretting. Some distance behind, two warriors held thongs attached to Bernice's belled bridle, pulling and guiding her. The other mules trotted serenely behind her, content to follow the bell mare even if she was only Bernice and not Hildegarde. Of all the animals, only the mules showed no signs of wear. A prolonged pace that strained horses to their limits—limits known intimately by the Kiowa—was for them nothing worse than boring.

Through the morning, Darby had tried to persuade first Stalking Horse and then Bird that they should allow the prisoners to ride the mules. He had used his best logic. If he and his friends rode the mules, there would be that many more fresh horses for the men of the Blackleg Society.

Stalking Horse had ignored him. Bird had laughed. Neither of them was quite sure what the ugly horses could do, but they had noticed that a loping pace for their mounts was only a trot for the big animals. "You will ride ordinary horses, O'gatedota," Bird said. "The path is long, and we do not have time to waste chasing you."

Among the pack stock were their horses and his remaining nine mules. He assumed the others were dead. He thought of Hildegarde lying lanced on the prairie, and a tightness came into his throat. He had become fond of the big lady.

"I guess there isn't anybody gets along better on these plains than the Kiowa," he told Poole. "Somewhere along the way they've learned everything there is to know about everything it takes to live here."

"They ride like Comanches," Poole noted. "It's like they're part of their horse. Or it's part of them."

"Probably learned it from the Comanche. Or the Sioux, or maybe the Cheyenne. But they're better than any of them at coverin' distance. I guess they have to be. That's what their land has the most of, is distance."

Just behind them Vince Copple rode bleakly between curious Blackleg braves who now and then edged close to study his skin, wondering what made it black. And close behind Copple, Trini Salazar sat stiffly aboard a half-tame steeldust, minding his manners very carefully. He was still pouting from the tongue-lashing Darby Curtis had given him about attacking their captors. He had understood little of it, but had got the message. He was to behave himself. Still it chafed him.

The incident had been early in the morning. Trini had let himself lag slightly behind the other captives in their circle of swift-riding guards. Then he had heeled his mount suddenly, veered alongside a warrior and wrested his war-club from the thong that held it, and turned swiftly, swinging the weapon, intending to charge gloriously among the accursed Moros and lay them to waste. Unfortunately, the horse he was on had no spirit. Instead of charging it had wheeled and pitched him off.

At first they had tied him across a saddle, then Darby Curtis had chattered at them and one of them chattered back, and they reluctantly untied him and Darby Curtis had scolded him while the *Indios* sat in a circle about them and watched.

They had let him ride again, then, but he was not to fight them. He understood. Therefore, he held himself in check and passed the time by frowning and pouting. It was not his way to go placidly among the enemy and allow them to live. It was not Spanish.

The path of the Blacklegs now paralleled a small stream whose course at first was a gentle valley a half mile wide. But as they pushed southward the land around the stream became rougher and more broken, the valley deeper. Side canyons grew from it, and the formation widened to more than a mile. When the sun was high the braves riding point turned right, into one of these canyons, and the party angled downward, deeper and deeper into what had now become a terrain of broken land. Stubby towers of mesa stood among scoured, wild walls of red, yellow and chalky stone. Scrub cedar grew above the bottoms, and stands of brittle-looking juniper vied with clumps of stunted oak for space to sink roots among the tumbled stone.

The wind in the canyons was erratic, shifting and darting through vast mazes of wasteland. As they neared the stream-bed, winding through snakelike corridors flanked here and there with willow and cottonwood, Darby had a momentary impression that the Indians might be lost. For long minutes they would ride down one sheered canyon, then double back up another to follow pale trails across ridges and turn downward again. The high sun was confusing, the shadows directionless, and they seemed to be going in circles. Then he glimpsed greenery below again, and realized they knew exactly where they were going.

Through the morning, riding across high rolling prairies, the Kiowa had seemed to make no effort to obscure their trail. Not that there was likely anyone within a hundred miles to obscure it from, but it had puzzled him that they should be so careless, these wild red men who lived by wit and by their wisdom of the ways of the high plains. But now he understood. Even if anyone should find and follow their trail into these breaks, he would follow it no further. It would take extraordinary luck to even find, much less follow, a trail in these lost mazes.

He recalled then something about the Kana'tenee, the people of the far grass, that he had forgotten. Even among the Kiowa, the people of Hawk That Hunts Walking were considered strange and elusive. Sometimes everyone knew where they were, from the Evening Wind people to the Fire Dancers, from the people of Spotted Horse to the powerful tribe of Cloud and White Bear. For seasons at a time the village of the Kana'tenee would be as other villages, on a stream somewhere, or between two hills, and the people of the other villages would know its presence. Then, abruptly, the Kana'tenee would be gone and even messengers provided by the crafty Fire Dance People could not find them. Of all the Kiowa people the Kana'tenee ranged the farthest, and were the least known. Sometimes it was as though they had fallen off the edge of the world.

He had known the Kana'tenee when he was a boy. For a year or two they had been the principal Indians around the Smoky Hill River lands where Chance Curtis settled. Then they had gone, returned and gone again. He had listened to men of other villages speaking of them, wondering where they went when they were gone.

Now he looked at the pattern of canyon walls around him and began to understand. If the Kana'tenee were not like other Kiowa it was because they did not choose to be. Certainly no other band had produced clans any more colorful and respected than the Real Dog men, or the unpredictable Blackleg men. Even such great warrior chiefs as Cloud and White Bear held them in high esteem, and it was partly because of them that Hawk That Hunts Walking was a respected name in all villages—even in those times when no one knew where he was.

In the vastness of the caprock plains, in their generations of far-ranging nomadic travel, the Kana'tenee had found hidey-holes that were theirs alone.

Even the fierce Comanche who could ravage the lands for hundreds of miles in a sweep then disappear like smoke before their pursuers . . . even the stealthy Pawnee who came and went like shadows by day and like ghosts by night . . . were no better at going to ground than were the Far Grass People of the Kiowa.

"I never knew there was breaks like this out here," Poole said, gaping. "I don't even know where we are."

"I've heard of the badlands of the Purgatoire," Darby nodded, "but I think those are 'way west of here. I don't know what this is. But you notice, the farther we go the deeper we get? Must have been a hell of a river here one time. But the only water I can see is that creek down there and I'd swear it's the same one we saw back there before the Blacklegs and the cavalry jumped us, where Billy said that village was. And speakin' of Billy, I wonder what's become of the son of a bitch. Not that I care. Good riddance, far as I'm concerned . . . no offense meant, Mr. Poole, if he was your friend."

"None taken," Poole shrugged. "I guess I didn't think he'd pull stakes like he did, either. But then, I never knew all that much about him, when I stop and think on it. I needed a driver, and he come along. That's all. Never talked about himself, an' of course I never asked. He's from New York City, originally, an' wound up out here for some reason and never liked it much. I guess I was sort of disappointed, though. It didn't ever occur to me he'd leave."

"Well, he did. Maybe he was smarter than the rest of us. It's us the Blacklegs are takin' who knows where to do who knows what to, not him."

"Sonamabitch!" a voice said behind him and Darby turned, startled. Trini Salazar rode there, beside Vince Copple, and the Spaniard looked as bleak as Darby felt.

"Sonamabitch!" Trini said again, and they all stared at him.

"Is he talkin' about Mr. Sipe?" Vince Copple wondered.

"Miguel Jesus Montoya sonamabitch," Trini explained. "New York Ceety. Trinidad Salazar go New York Ceety keel Miguel Jesus Montoya. Sonamabitch!" With that he subsided into a bleak soliloquy in soft, fast Spanish and the others looked at one another.

Around and behind them glowering Kiowa warriors barked sharp commands.

"They say to stop talkin' and go faster," Darby told them. He stepped up his pace, heels drumming the tired horse he rode. The others pushed ahead, down a winding, rocky trail between beetling canyon walls.

Vince Copple stared at Trinidad Salazar. "We all on our way to get out scalps lifted at the pleasure of these red heathen and there he is plannin' a trip to New York City," he muttered. "Swear to God I ain't never seen anybody act like he does."

Miles of twisted, serrated canyon unraveled behind them, a world of standing towers and hidden recesses, of false trails and puzzling twists, and still they rode, keeping a pace that never quite exhausted their horses. Only when the sun quartered into the west did Darby regain his sense of direction. They were still pressing southward.

The depths were in shadows when Bird, now at the head of the file, called a halt and they dismounted, slumping to the ground to rest while they could. Indians led the prisoners' horses away with the others, toward a secretive bend where water flowed in a rocky cut.

Darby paced the confined space their guards allowed them and studied the canyon walls, the vague trail back the way they had come, the endless mazes ahead. He wanted to get them out, to escape, but he could find no slightest possibility. Nearly forty warriors made up the Blackleg band, and there were always a dozen on guard, watching them closely. A few carried guns, but Darby knew the guns were not the real threat. Should they make a break, they might—one or two of them—elude gunshots. But the ready lances would not miss, nor would the arrows that could fly like a cloud of death to pincushion them before they had gone ten yards. These were the Blackleg men of the Kana'tenee. No prisoners would escape them and live.

Ahead, several braves were clearing brush, rolling back stones alongside the canyon trail at a place where the little stream seemed to disappear into a hillside. The prisoners settled themselves on sandy ground beside a stone ledge, waiting for what might come next. Darby squatted on his heels, still studying the canyon and its towering walls. Poole sat crosslegged, tired and gray-hued with worry. Vince Copple rested his head on his arms and thought his own thoughts. Trini Salazar glared at *Moros*.

The braves had finished whatever they were doing ahead, and now Darby saw several Kiowa opening little pouches, getting out paint pots and pieces of ornamentation. They began painting themselves in ceremonial grandeur, pulling their hair into tall roaches tied with strips of hide or beaded thongs, putting on their bright quilled warshirts and many-colored adornments of shell and plume.

When Bird padded back to where they sat, the Blackleg chief was as Darby had seen him once before—a vivid, splendid savage in full regalia, inscrutable and fearsome. He carried his black shield and his hooked lance, its plumes dusted and brilliant in the shadows of the canyon.

Bird stood over Darby, looking at him across the top of his shield. "You tell them now there will be no more escaping, no more trouble. Soon we bring you to Hawk That Hunts Walking. If you cause no trouble we bring you alive. If you make trouble we bring you dead. You tell them."

Darby got to his feet. "What does Bird want with his white brothers? It would be the best thing if you let us go. Give us our horses and let us go. We will find our own way back. We are no use to Bird and the Blackleg men."

"Stalking Horse has had a vision," Bird said. "You will make medicine for Hawk That Hunts Walking. You are our gift to the Kana'tenee. Over there," the Kiowa pointed with his lance, "is the trail no one knows. On that trail we will find the people. Then you will make medicine."

"Bird, I have no medicine for your people. You know me, as your father knew my father. I know nothing of medicine for the Kana'tenee. I have nothing for you."

But the tall warrior had turned away, not interested in argument. He knew what he was doing. Darby wished desperately that he had some inkling of it, himself.

Where the braves had cleared trail there was now an opening in what had seemed only a brushy draw, and beyond that opening the canyons opened out, widened into a bizarre world of standing fortress stone and sweet-meadow bottoms.

Indians brought their horses again and they mounted, tightly cloistered now by painted warriors in full finery. There was no talk now among the Kiowa, no banter as he had heard before. They rode painted and grim, and the needle tips of their lances were always toward the prisoners.

Two abreast, they passed through the hidden cut and into the secret place of the Kana'tenee. Far ahead, miles still, deep in the heart of these vast canyons, Darby sensed movement and glimpsed a bit of smoke.

Warriors on foot stood aside as they passed. Looking back Darby saw them beginning to close the brushed passage, working with sticks and sage brooms to wipe out every trace that someone had gone this way. A dismal dread settled over him. Deep down, he had considered the remote possibility that someone—someone with guns and a striking force—might just have found their trail, might somehow have followed. But no one would follow here. They were alone now with the Kana'tenee, and no one ever would come to find them.

The vanished stream had reappeared, coursing from beneath a limestone ledge, and now it widened into a rippling expanse flowing over a broad gravel bottom. The water was clear and fresh, a swath of bright ribbon bordered by tumbled stone and stands of gnarled cedar. Tall trees grew here and there, their roots in crumbling rock and fans of topsoil fed by the stream. The sky was wide here, but far away and bounded by receding cliffs of lined stone. Up there somewhere was the endless caprock prairie, the land Darby had known since birth. Yet here, far below in these vast breaks, was another world, impenetrable.

He saw his mules led forward to the point of the march, saw bright warriors flanking them as they approached the sheltered meadow where he now knew rested the village of Hawk That Hunts Walking. More Indians were riding out now, flanking them, escorting them in, and still others stepped from shelter at vantage points along the near canyon wall to watch them pass. There were hundreds of them. Darby felt his hopes receding beyond recovery.

"What is this place?" Edwin Poole gawked around him, astonished at the magnitude of the canyon complex. "Where are we?"

In the distance, where Darby had seen smoke, a village was going up. Many lodges already were standing. As he watched others arose. Children drove horses into fresh pastures. Women tended cooking fires that had no base of ash.

"They just got here," Darby said softly. "We must have been right behind them."

At the edge of the new village a long line of horsemen appeared, sitting silent and alert, waiting for them. They wore paint, mostly red with traces and slashes of white and yellow, and the necks and rumps of their horses were painted. Darby's hackles rose. "The Real Dog men," he told Poole.

The Blacklegs rode in a tight diamond formation as they waded their mounts across the creek—Bird at point, followed by Stalking Horse and another senior warrior, then the main body with flanking riders and younger braves bringing up the rear. Bird raised his lance and the line of Real Dog men parted, then wheeled two by two to flank the Blacklegs and their prisoners. Off to one side Darby saw a lot of curious Indians gathered around his mules.

The village was large, at least two hundred lodges, and bustled with activity. They rode to the center of it, where a tall lodge stood, ranged by others. A group of old men in elaborate finery stood there, waiting for them. One of them was truly ancient, a white-haired elder with a face of deep bronze wrinkles. He held a blanket wrapped tightly about him. The two on each side of him stepped forward and held up their hands. Bird responded and the column came to a halt. Bird and the two with him raised their lances, point down, then thrust them into the ground. Dismounting, they approached the standing chiefs and talked for a time.

177

Then Bird turned and made a signal.

Hard hands grabbed Darby and hauled him down from his horse. He struggled, but was held secure. Around him the other three also were stood down. Then they were released and prodded forward. When they were ten yards from the old chief Bird signaled them to halt.

Darby heard the clanking of a bell. He turned. The young leader, Stalking Horse, was coming in leading Bernice. The mules had all been stripped of packs, and the rest of them followed placidly behind the bell mare. Stalking Horse led Bernice forward until he stood beside Darby. Then he handed the lead rope to the white man and walked away.

Bird held up a hand. "Hawk That Hunts Walking is troubled. Many things are happening in the lands of the Kiowa people that are not very good. Hawk That Hunts Walking awaits a sign. The Blackleg men have brought him a sign. This is our gift to Hawk That Hunts Walking and the People of Good Grass Far Away. This is our medicine," he pointed at the prisoners and the mules.

Throughout the village there was silence. Hundreds of Indians encircled them, watching, waiting. The prisoners scuffed their feet and looked around. "What did he say?" Copple muttled.

"Something about us being medicine."

The silence grew. They were waiting for something, expecting something. Darby stared at the Indians and they stared back. He looked at the unreadable face of Hawk That Hunts Walking, then at Bird. Bird gazed at him serenely . . . smugly, Darby thought.

"What's s'posed to happen now?" Poole asked.

Darby shook his head. "I'm damned if I know."

The silence went on and on. Long minutes passed. One of the chiefs next to the old chief said something to another and shrugged. The other shook his head. Hawk That Hunts Walking stood like one carved out of stone, waiting.

Off to one side, Stalking Horse scowled and scuffed his feet. Bird glanced at him, then strode to the prisoners. Shield resting at his shoulder, he unfastened his warclub and glared at Darby. "Do not keep Hawk That Hunts Walking waiting," he said. "Make medicine."

Darby shook his head. In his best, most courteous Kiowa he said, "Honored one, it saddens me to say such truth, but you are as crazy as a buffalo cow in a mud bog."

Bird's mouth dropped open. His breath hissed and he raised the warclub.

"And if you try to hit me with that thing again," Darby continued quietly, "I'll break your arm. Now it would be a good thing if Bird would tell me just what the . . ." finding no suitable epithets in Kiowa he threw in a few colorful examples of the English language then continued ". . . you expect us to do."

Bird's face darkened beneath its elaborate paint, but he hesitated. "Stalking Horse had a vision. In his vision the Blackleg men have brought you and your ugly horses to the place of the Kana'tenee. Then a medicine comes and tells Hawk That Hunts Walking what he must do to protect the people from white men's war. You must make a medicine so he will know."

"We don't know anything about a medicine," Darby spat.

"Then I must kill you," Bird said flatly.

Pivoting he arced the heavy warclub in a whistling swing at Darby's head. Darby dropped to one knee. The heavy club passed over him and he surged upward to grip the Indian's wrist with his right hand, his shoulder with his left. Following the club's momentum he diverted the swing down and back, full circle. As Bird straightened, reacting, Darby pivoted and kicked his legs out from under him. The warrior crashed to the ground and Darby was on him, wresting the warclub away. It had all happened in an instant. Darby came to his feet. With a stride and a leap he swung himself to Bernice's back and shouted, "The mules! Run for it!"

Waving the club he hauled Bernice's head left and the tall mule turned, haunches-down, those behind her following suit. Vince Copple bounded aboard Monroe, and Darby saw Edwin Poole struggling to climb onto Sam.

Trini somehow had disappeared. But then a knot of Kiowa braves behind them burst apart, some falling, rolling, some caroming to each side. As Indians scattered the Spaniard raced through brandishing a feathered lance, shouting, *"Viva Aragon!"*

As one startled warrior danced to avoid the lance, Trini upended another with the haft of it, then ran and vaulted to the back of Longhandle, drumming the surprised animal with his heels. *"Adelante! Vaya!"*

As a pack the mules charged and startled Indians scattered before them. Darby saw lances raised and he ducked low on Bernice. They plunged through a scattering line of braves, then into the ranks of women and children. Darby set his knees, raised a hand to swat his mount . . . then hauled up short, stopping Bernice in her tracks. Another mule plowed into her from behind and she danced and braced, almost falling. In the skidding, halting herd a mule went to its knees and then surged upright under another, upsetting it. From the corner of his eye Darby saw Monroe upright, pawing the air, Vince Copple tumbling from his back.

Darby gritted his teeth and drew a deep breath. Just in front of Bernice, almost under her, two tiny Indian children stood shocked, staring up at him with huge eyes. If he had not stopped her, Bernice would have trampled them . . . would not even have seen them. Even while the mules were colliding, were still impacting, a young Indian woman screamed and ran to scoop up the children, dashing away with them in her arms.

And it was too late to try again. In that moment, the warriors had reacted. Ahead of him now, barely fifteen yards away, Real Dog men in ceremonial paint plugged the gap—an unbroken rank of seasoned fighting men with arrows in their bows, the shafts homed squarely on the fugitives.

"Aw, hell," Darby muttered. He let the warclub drop to the ground. Then at a rush of hooves he whirled, just in time to shout at the Spaniard, "Trini! No! Drop it!"

With an accusing glare Trini lowered the lance he had

been ready to throw.

Blackleg men were among them then, leading them back to where they had started, pulling them roughly from the mules to dump them bruisingly on the ground.

Darby got to his knees. The chiefs had not moved, nor had most of the Indians. Only in the east ranks where they had made their charge was there any disruption of the waiting silence of the village, and now that died and again the valley was still.

Darby clambered to this feet, shaken and angry. He stalked forward to where Bird now stood talking quietly to Hawk That Hunts Walking. The Blackleg leader turned to stop him but Darby pushed him away and bent to stare straight into the ancient eyes of Hawk That Hunts Walking. "Damn your red hide, let us alone," he demanded. Pointing with a stiff left arm he shouted, "Tell those people to stand aside and let us go! You can tend to your own damn medicine!"

Fuming, he realized he had been shouting in English, and he shook his head and started over but Bird stepped between them, shoving him backward. The Blackleg leader's face was a murderous mask of paint and hard features, but his voice was quiet and calm. "We have seen," he said. "Hawk That Hunts Walking is satisfied. The medicine has begun. Now he will think about what it means."

PART III
Hawk That Hunts Walking

XVI

There was no sign of either Jones or Heath. Alive or dead, the great plains had simply swallowed up the two troopers. The platoon had searched a full day, scouring miles in teams of three, and Sergeant Hanlon was forced to agree with Lieutenant Spradley that there was no more to be done. They had come a long way south, further than A Troop had retreated by miles, yet the vast prairie remained always the same, unbroken horizons of windblown grass featureless except for the shadows of clouds drifting overhead.

"We'll camp here," the lieutenant said as evening light began to fade. "At dawn we head northeast. I'd guess three days' ride will put us in sight of Camp Jacob. Keep the men close for the night, and a tight guard on the stock. I don't want anybody else disappearing in this wilderness."

The burial detail had melded with the platoon, become a single unit as automatically as the book of army drill required. As master sergeant, Hanlon became chief noncom and Sergeant Ben Foley took charge of the assignment of men and provisions. They were twenty-five in all now, counting the lieutenant, but they would function as a single platoon until they could rejoin A Troop and the rest of the squadron.

Still, it was not Foley that Private Mulcahey came to when they had been fed their rations of salt meat and hardtack and the coffee pots were bubbling over low fires of dried prairie coal. Mulcahey came to Hanlon and stood before him ashamed and confused.

185

"I should have told you earlier, Sergeant," he said. "But it seems like every time I see somethin' I get shellacked over it . . ."

Hanlon cocked his head to look up at the private. "You saw something, Mulcahey?"

"I did, Sergeant. But it wasn't hardly anything I knew how to tell you about. It was . . . well, you know how sometimes you can see lakes an' things out here, where there aren't any such things? An' sometimes there's things out in the lake that you know can't be there but at the same time if they wasn't somewhere you couldn't be seein' 'em?"

"Mirages." Hanlon nodded. "What was it you saw, Mulcahey?"

The private squatted on his heels, speaking softly. "Indians, Sergeant. A great long line of 'em out on one of those lakes. An' I know they had to be a long ways away, but they was *tall*. An' sometimes I could see 'em close-like, except I know they was a long ways off, prob'ly too far away to see at all . . . Sergeant, I should have said right off, but I been thinkin' all day about how to tell you without it soundin' . . . well, you know . . ."

"Like ships and camels."

"Yeah. Like them."

"When did you see this, Mulcahey?"

"It was earlier, right before th' lieutenant an' his platoon come up to us. I was lookin' west an' I saw them. Then a cloud went by an' there wasn't anything out there but grass."

Hanlon sipped at his coffee. "Well, I'm glad you told me, Mulcahey, though I don't know what difference it'll make. It isn't Indians we're looking for, and it's my guess Jones and Heath are both dead. There's just too much prairie out here to find 'em on it."

"But Sergeant, that's why I thought I better tell you. I thought about it for a long time, goin' over what I saw. I guess there might have been a white man with them Indians. Maybe more then one. I can't be sure, but maybe there was."

"You think they had . . ."

"I don't know, Sergeant. But I guess they might. Maybe it would be best if we was to just . . . ah . . . kind of look before we go back." The private, Hanlon noticed, looked immensely relieved. Now the burden was someone else's, not his.

"You don't have any idea how far they were, then?"

"I been studyin' on that, Sergeant. My granddad was a sailor, name of Charley Duncan. It was him that sailed with Dalton on the *Faith*. Anyhow, he'd learned his navigation an' gunnery an' could cypher in trigonometry an' the like, an' he used to say a man on top lookout of a frigate could see the top royals of another frigate 22 miles away in fair weather, give the curvin' of the world an' all. So I took to thinkin' about that, an' supposin' top lookout was a hundred an' twenty feet high an' the top royals was a hundred an' eighty, an' supposin' I was ten feet off the ground standin' in my stirrups an' I wasn't seein' just those Indians' top royals but the whole Indian so to speak . . . well, ten from a hundred an' twenty leaves a hundred an' ten, plus a hundred an' eighty makes two hundred an' ninety, an' ten is one twenty-ninth part of that . . . well, it's like twenty-two miles less twenty-eight twenty-ninths part of what you'd have if you could sort of fold twenty-two miles into thirds . . . uh . . ." a sweat was forming on the private's brow. He was using up his fingers. "Uh, I sort of forget how I calculated it, Sergeant. I worked at it all afternoon. But anyhow, I don't see how they could have been more than twelve-fifteen miles from us at the time . . . do you?"

Hanlon had forgotten his coffee. He stared at the young trooper in awe. In all his years with the cavalry, he had never heard anything quite like that. After a time he got to his feet and went to talk to the lieutenant.

Faint dawn had touched the sky when the puzzled troopers of the First Platoon mounted up and angled north of west, riding into a new day that would begin behind them.

Private Jakey Bloom edged his mount close to Tom Pedigo's. "Our remarkable Irisher has done it again," he

187

whispered.

"Done what? Another sighting? What is it this time?"

"I don't exactly know. I didn't hear much of it. But whatever it is it's twenty-two miles long and a hundred and eighty feet high and it's got Jones and Heath."

Pedigo's jaw dropped, his eyes searching Bloom's for hint of a joke, finding none. "I don't believe it," he said finally.

"I don't either, but he said he went ten feet off the ground when he saw it. Fact. He said that."

Near noon, as best Mulcahey could estimate by dead reckoning, they were in the vicinity of the place from which he had seen the mirage. But there were no mirages now. The sky was faintly overcast, the wind had gentled and the prairies rested luxuriant and vast beneath a sun-touched haze.

"I hope you realize how far I'm stretching the captain's orders," Spradley said, squinting at the master sergeant from beneath his campaign hat. "It's only because he said to find your detail and escort you back *when you finished.* At least, it does seem like he said that."

"Yes, sir," Hanlon assured him. "I realize, Lieutenant. And the minute we finish buryin' Jones and Heath we'll head right back to Camp Jacob. Of course, we have to find them first, like I pointed out."

"Exactly," the lieutenant nodded. "And in the meantime, it might be a very good idea if we could get a glimpse of those Indians and some idea where they were going. Mulcahey said there were a lot of them. It might have been a whole tribe. And if so . . ."

"If so, and if they're Kiowa, then maybe we have found Hawk That Hunts Walking. We know where all the other bands are."

"It could be their warriors as chased us the day it rained, too."

Spradley nodded. "I don't see how it could be any others."

They pushed west.

"You know when this all started, Sergeant?" Spradley paced through knee-high grass, stepping wide around a

188

clump of thistle. The sun quartered ahead of them now, and nearly ten miles lay behind, beyond the place of the mirage. The grass here was sparser, more studded with yucca and sage, here and there low gray islands of mesquite and spreading growths of prickly pear.

"It was that civilian that intercepted us out of Camp Jacob and alerted Captain Sinclair to an Indian attack in Sector C-9. That was strange, wasn't it? The man just appearing like that, I mean. Sort of out of nowhere . . ."

"But he was right," Hanlon nodded, turning to look back at the patrol. The men were dismounted, leading their horses, giving them rest. "Those Indians was almost on top of that canyon and those white men when we got there."

"Yes, he was right. But who was he? Captain Sinclair said he recalled seeing him, maybe back at Willow Ford when they had the treaty talks. But who was he and how did he know there were Indians after those hunters? I don't think the whole thing makes sense."

"I don't know, Lieutenant." Hanlon paused a moment to remove a devil's claw lodged on his boot, then strode on. "But he was right. Right as rain."

"There isn't anything out there," Spradley waved toward the sun-fired prairies ahead. "Nothing. Just more of this. God, it's like it goes on forever. Just flatness . . . grass and nettles and more grass, clear to the end of the world. How can people survive in country like this, Sergeant? Why would anybody even want to?"

"It's big, sure enough." Hanlon was noncommittal. Place like this could get to a man, he thought. The distances had a magic to them that affected people. And yet, it wasn't the distances that did it. It was the people themselves. The prairies were so vast that they dwarfed a man, made him take a hard look at himself. And maybe it was what he found there that was hard to deal with. Without walls, even the walls of visible terrain, without limits or landscapes, a man had nothing to compare himself to except himself.

They walked, and the sun quartered a gold-hazed sky ahead. It was hard to see ahead, and hard to look at the distances.

Suddenly, far out, there was movement, and he squinted trying to make it out. He held up his hand and the column halted. In the distance, hazed and indistinct, were animals. Private Mulcahey hurried forward, excited. "It's them, Sergeant! I told you I saw camels! That's them!"

Hanlon and the lieutenant squinted, their eyes watering. Private Pell had joined them, and he peered ahead, shading his eyes, then nodded. "It's those mules we saw, Lieutenant. The ones that got away from us. See, the little horse is still with them. They're moving south, best I can tell."

The hazed sunlight dazzled their eyes. The distant specks wavered, then became clear. Then, as they watched, they disappeared one by one. It was as though they had fallen into the earth.

"Mount the men, Sergeant," Spradley said. "Let's take a look."

With a goal now sighted, at least for a moment, the patrol made good time for a mile, and then part of another, then Lieutenant Spradley raised a hand and looked around him, confused. Surely, he felt, they had come to where the mules had been. Yet ahead was only emptiness and distance—the same distances they had seen since leaving Camp Jacob, distances that swallowed everything and told nothing.

"They can't just disappear," he said. Then he turned. "Pell! Forward, please!"

The scout reined in beside him.

"Ride ahead and look," Spradley said. "They have to be out here somewhere. They didn't just fall in a hole."

With a quick salute Pell spurred his mount and headed out at a canter. They watched him receding, growing smaller with the distance, and Spradley removed his hat to wipe its band. The day was calm, the calmest he had seen on these plains, and the silence of it was spooky. Beside him, Hanlon sat his horse, squinting against the lowering sun. "There's nothin' out there," he muttered. "Just nothin'."

He looked away for a moment, then looked again and his

mouth dropped open. Beside him the lieutenant drew a sharp breath, and behind him there was exclamations in the ranks.

Private Pell had disappeared. As a man, the patrol touched spurs, drew sidearms and thundered westward at a gallop.

The canyon when they reached it was narrow, its cut hidden in the sameness of the prairie until they were at its lip. Yet it seemed to widen toward the south, and distantly, on its floor, they saw three mules and a pony, trudging southward.

Pell was waiting for them on a ledge below the rim, watching the animals below. When they descended to him he pointed at markings on the ledge. "Indians been by here, Lieutenant. Not very long ago. Some horses shod, some not, but I'll bet it was Indians. I ain't sure, but I think it's the same bunch we followed trail on before we cut off to pick up Sergeant Hanlon's detail. Maybe those animals down there have been followin' 'em too."

The faint trail from the lip to the canyon's floor was tortuous, and the stray stock was out of sight by the time the soldiers reached there. But they knew which way they had gone—down-canyon, into what seemed as they rode to become a larger and larger world of standing ridges, maze-like scours and box side-canyons. They rode for nearly an hour in deepening shadows through a widening world completely unlike the endless plains that hid it. They followed the meanders of a pretty stream and sometimes Pell found tracks or droppings that said they were on course.

"Hard to believe there's a place like this out here," Spradley said. "And you can't even see it until you're in it."

"I never saw the like of this country," Hanlon agreed. "Up east, the Irish folk would say it's fey. It can look like one thing and be another and you can't tell which is which."

Complex canyon walls caught their voices and echoed them back, eerily. In the column Private Mulcahey heard the comment and shivered, gazing around at the clustered spires and mazes of tall buttes that stood above the canyon floor—striated layers of dull red and vague yellow stone scoured by ancient floods, carved by winter winds. Tumbles of boulders skirted their bases, pedestals of rubble from which rose monoliths. White sandstone protruded from the lower shelves, and flood-rounded pieces of it reminded him of discarded skulls in the shadows.

The sky was a golden dome standing atop the pillars of canyon stone.

Pell came back from scouting ahead. "There's a box in front of us, sir. Little ways on. The creek disappears and there's a dozen canyons openin' all different ways. I found a few tracks, but it's only those stray mules and the horse. The Indian tracks just go out into the middle of it and quit."

"They might have swept their trail then," Hanlon said.

"Can you see where those animals went, Private?"

"Yes, sir, but that's all. There's a little brushed-over draw kind of at one side, and they went in there but it doesn't look like there's any way to get through."

A few minutes later they were at the place. Pell had described it well. Here the main canyon was a walled amphitheater, with exits in all directions but none appearing usable or used. Hanlon followed Pell to the nondescript little draw where the mule tracks led. It looked like a dead end, yet the tracks went into it and did not come out.

The sergeant stepped his mount forward, slowly. Rocks and brush obscured the ground, but then he saw a broken twig dangling from a clump of dwarf cedar and pointed it out to Pell.

"It's fresh," the private said. "The pitch hasn't crusted."

They moved on, guiding their mounts around and over strewn rubble, pushing through screens of twist cedar and dry willow. The rest followed.

Sheer walls pressed close on either hand. The draw closed on them until there was room only for single-file travel. Again, Pell found the track of a shod mule. Wherever the strays were going, they had come this way. Hanlon looked up. Above and ahead, the beetling tops of the canyon walls seemed to spread apart. Acting on instinct, the sergeant drew his carbine. Behind him he heard whispers of other guns clearing leather.

The draw they had entered was not a draw. It was a cut. Somewhere beyond it were Indians, and maybe those Indians had two of his men. He turned, looked back at the lieutenant, saw his nod. Whatever was ahead, they would have a look.

A hundred yards beyond, the cut ended abruptly and they rode out into wide, wild canyon country far larger than what they had seen before. And now, again, there were tracks of many horses, far more than there had been. Pell puzzled over the droppings he found. Some were two or three days old, some just a day. And one, he guessed it to be one of the strays', had been dropped within the hour.

Spradley moved up and halted them. "I don't like this, Sergeant. Not one bit. We could be walking right into a trap."

"If you like, sir, I'd take a man or two and go forward, just to have a look."

"No." Spradley studied the vast, spreading canyon land ahead. "No, we'll stay together. I want every man's eyes open. No surprises."

"The creek's back," Jakey Bloom noted after a time.

The traveled trail led out across wide meadowed flats toward shadowed distances to the south. But now, rather than follow the trail, the patrol stayed to the ridge-line, keeping good cover at hand as they moved.

"I see horses or somethin'," Mulcahey pointed. "A lot of 'em."

The erratic wash through which they rode played out ahead of them, and would leave them open and exposed. But not far to their right the creek dipped lower between widening banks and offered cover. Gnarled cedars and taller trees dotted its course at intervals. Spradley led them at a trot across the open ground and into the streambed. The creek here was wide and shallow, rippling over its gravel bed as it wandered between rock-strewn banks.

At a bend Spradley sent Pell forward. The scout was

back in a few minutes. He had seen nothing out of order. The troopers rounded the bend.

A sharp plume of spray erupted from the creek's surface and a gunshot echoed back and forth across the valley. Another shot exploded bark and splinters from a twisted cedar on the right bank, and a third ricocheted from pink stone almost under the nose of Sergeant Hanlon's mount. Weapons drawn, the patrol milled in the stream, looking everywhere at once, trying to find sources.

Again there was gunfire, and now there were Indians on the bluffs above them. Jakey Bloom's horse reared, pivoted and went down, throwing the private sprawling in the stream. He struggled to his feet, wild-eyed, and Mulcahey brought his mount around in a hard turn to shield him. "Get up behind me," he shouted, extending a hand.

"Fall back!" Spradley ordered. "Fall back and regroup! Form a cordon!"

"That cut, sir!" Hanlon pointed. "There's high banks!"

The patrol wheeled, driving for shelter. Spradley spurred to the lead, then hauled on his reins. The cut was two hundred yards away. But it was no longer empty. Painted warriors, mounted and armed, filed from it, spreading to form a long line, blocking the only exit upstream. Spradley swore. There were a hundred of them or more. And as he looked more and more appeared on the bluffs, above, ahead and behind. He wheeled his mount. From downstream came a band of brilliantly-garbed warriors, driving toward them, a wedge of painted savages led by a warrior who carried a round black shield and a hooked, feathered lance.

XVII

The old man was not old. He was barely middle-aged, but a lifetime of hard work and scant return had left the marks of time etched deep upon him.

The journey had been a difficult one, for all of them. One disappointment had led to another, until he wondered if he could handle any more. He trudged beside the rickety lead wagon, leaning sometimes on its cask frames to take the ache from his shoulders, and the old rifle he carried was heavy in his hand.

Still, there was a hope within him that refused to die. He was used to hard times and hard knocks. He had never known anything else. Gazing about now at the endless sameness of the prairie where cured grass nodded in the wind, he thought about the land from which he had come . . . high-up hills dressed in shades of green and blue, rock crags that thrust above the narrow valleys, encroaching upon the tillable spaces until those that remained were precious and heavily worked.

Those bottoms had been good land, land that a man could appreciate as he worked it even though it belonged to someone else and could never belong to him. Land that always promised more than it gave, but still the promise was worth the having. All his years he had worked such lands, worked them good years and bad, made some good crops from time to time, and worked harder after poor ones. His fare had been the tenant's share, and it always came to not quite enough. Still, with grown sons to put meat on the table now and then, and growing daughters who could catch the eye of good men and maybe one day go with them to better places, the family had survived.

Mighty pretty country, he had always thought, even in those times when the country and its people had been cruel. But finally the time had come to move on, and he and the woman had gone in the night to retrieve their poke from its post hole. They had counted the money, the savings of their lives of hard work, and had sat for a time by candlelight, across a plank table with the little bit of money between them, and wondered where such a small fortune might take them. Then with her wisdom of his concerns she had gone and got out the Bible, and placed it there beside the money. "We can go as far as we have to," she had said.

The family was smaller now. Of the nine living children, three had remained behind. Sally June had a beau at Crockett's Fork, and she stayed on to get married. Billy Joe, the forth in line but man-grown at sixteen, had strapped on his gun and kissed his mother. "There's places on the river where a man can make do," he had said. With Bubba it was different. He helped them load the wagons and harness the teams, then he looked at his brothers and hugged his sisters and took down his banjo and went to sit on the porch. He said not a word, but when they looked back from the road he waved at them.

They had come a long, long way. The old man and Emmett found work at a place called Cairo that kept them for a season and gave them the means to go on. They had worked again in Missouri, but the war had come there and they had moved on again, staying to the back trails and the secret places. They had moved and they had survived, yet nowhere was there land to be had for such as they, and this was the old man's dream.

"A man needs land," he told the woman, and he said it many times. "A man without land has nothin' to give his children that will let them be better than him."

"There's land somewhere," she told him each time. "We keep lookin' we'll find a piece to claim."

The hope had been strong in Kansas. There was land to the west where folks could settle. The war was over and they'd made a treaty with the Indians and there was land. The old man and Emmett had worked at a place called Willow Ford, for a storekeeper, and had heard talk of land. But when they packed and moved and tried to claim some, men had come and driven them away.

"All this is consigned," they said. "No squatters here. You want land you pay Mr. Poling's fee. He's the land agent. You pay the fee or move on."

From the storekeeper at Willow Ford the old man bought a team of oxen for each wagon, and paid the price of them from their work. That was because one of the land agent's men had set his eyes on little Emily who was coming of age, and thought he'd have her, and Emmett had killed the man in a fight. They needed animals to move on.

The storekeeper had a red-haired daughter, and she had been kind to them while they were there. "The last outpost is Camp Jacob," she said. "Past there, that Poling and his men don't have the law. I don't know what's out there, but I hear there are settlements. And the land is open, and there are traders who can help you with supplies. You keep a lookout for some big wagons and some big mules, and if you see them you tell Darby Curtis to light down and give you a hand. You tell him Melissa Muldoon said that."

So they were still moving, and the old man kept a good watch as they went, and each day Emmett and Jim rode out afield to see what they could see. Sometimes there were buffalo, and deer and antelope in plenty, and they kept themselves fed, but for a long time now they had seen no people. Jim's wound had healed clean from the woman's tending.

"We've missed Camp Jacob," the old man said. "I guess

we've come too far south, and passed it by."

He looked at the endless land and wondered at how different it was from what he had known all his life. Mile after mile, day after day, it was changeless and when the noon sun was upon it it had no color and seemed barren and bleak. Yet sometimes when they stopped he put a spade in the sod and squatted to get a handful of the soil that was beneath. He rubbed it in his hands and watched it fall in the wind. He spat on it to see its color and he tasted it to know its worth. It was good soil, rich and fertile, and when rain fell on it there was the scent of heavy loam.

"Bottom lands," he told the woman. "A whole world of bottom lands and all it needs is water."

"Is this our place, then, Joshua?" she asked each time. And each time he would think on it and then shake his head.

"There'll be a sign," he told her. "We'll know when there's a sign."

It was Jim who found the buffalo, just a little herd of them, no more than a dozen, and he came for the old man and they went out to shoot meat. They rode a mile, then picketed their horses and crawled through the grass until the old rifle had its range. He picked a young cow and put her down, then reloaded for another try. But then he stood, letting the rifle droop. In the distance the animals saw them and turned to drift away.

"That cow will do us," he told Jim. "There's no sense to wasting good meat."

They got their horses then and led them to where the cow had fallen. But when they were there they stared in wonder. The buffalo lay in a circle of patchwork sod that had been cut and then relaid, and in one place was a hole where they saw blocks of stone and posts of cedar wood, all buried below the surface of the ground.

While Jim went to work with his knife the old man dug around beneath loose sod and a hope grew within him. He stood then, turning slowly, and his eyes found a strip of green to the west. There would be water there. He mounted his horse.

By the time Jim had finished skinning out the cow and was cutting meat in strips, the old man was back and he carried a fork of fresh willow, cut at the buds. Holding the fork-ends in his hands he began to pace, back and forth across the sodded circle, then in rings around it. Fifty paces from the circle, the willow wand dipped and danced, and he straightened his shoulders and took a deep breath.

"I'll finish cutting, Boy," he told Jim. "You go yonder and tell your mother to bring the wagons here. And you tell her when she makes her fire this evening, where that fire is we'll build our hearth."

Emmett came later, when the sun was almost down, following the fresh tracks of the wagons. He saw fresh meat hanging on cut cedar poles. He saw his brothers building a lean-to and his sisters cutting hay. He saw his mother cooking over an open fire, and her hair was done up and there was a radiance on her face that he had not seen for a long time. He saw his father setting a spade, beginning to dig a well.

He went to the old man. "Yonder a ways I seen wagons, three high-sides and a cart. They've been left out there."

"We'll take the bulls tomorrow and bring them here," the old man said. "Whoever left them may be wanting them back."

When it was too dark to work they gathered at the fire for their supper. Joshua read from the book, not seeing the words by firelight but knowing what they said. Then they passed around the food and each took a share. They had almost finished when Emmett's hound dog bristled and stared into the darkness. Joshua took up his rifle.

"We saw your fire," a voice called from the night. "Can we come in? We're awful hungry."

They were soldiers. One limped on an injured leg and the other had an arm in a sling. Their uniforms were stained with old dried blood, and their faces were gaunt and frightened.

There had been a fight with Indians. They had been hurt, but had escaped. They were afoot and they were lost. The only food they'd had in days was a rabbit the limping one shot with his carbine.

Mary Todd and her daughters fed them and tended their wounds. They talked for a time, then their eyelids drooped and soon they were asleep by the fire. Emily and Martha brought blankets to cover them, and the old man lit his pipe.

"Tomorrow we will begin to build," he told his sons. "The good Lord led us to this place, and there's stone and timbers here to fetch up a good, strong house. If there's Indians about, we'll want that. We'll not harm the heathen, but it's ours to do to see they don't harm us."

Far into the night Emily and Martha tended the fire and seldom did their eyes leave the sleeping forms of the two lost soldiers.

Not since the march to Camp Jacob had the First Squadron taken the field in force. Though it had chafed him, Major Alfred Grimes had spent most of his time for almost a year deluged with trivia. Papers and reports, squadron ritual and parade-ground pomp, the sending out of patrols that brought back reports of nothing, the murmurs of Indian uprising that persisted yet never materialized, all these things had added to the mounting impatience of Major Grimes.

A lot of strings had been pulled to put a crack squadron of cavalry in the field with him at its head, strings he knew were attached to favors owed, and this bothered him very little. It was the way of the world. And the favors had been small, had been no trouble to grant. Placing Cain DeWitt as sutler at Camp Jacob was simple. It was Grimes' prerogative as commanding officer to place as sutler anyone he chose. The man had done an adequate job and had abided by the rules of the camp, and Grimes was satisfied.

Some of the things—turning his back on abuses of authority by some of Poling's men, for example, had been a bit harder to swallow, but Grimes himself had heard few complaints. Those who might have complained generally were not available to do so. The land agent was, he realized, operating somewhat beyond his precise authority in demanding settlement fees and administrative fees far beyond those prescribed by territorial mandate . . . but that was civilian politics, not military concern. And Poling had kept his operations quiet enough that the army had never been forced to intercede. Grimes was quite aware that the man and his associates were making great amounts of money and exercising vast amounts of power. But again, that was not the army's concern.

He had almost balked several times at issuing orders to keep his patrols out of certain sectors at certain times. Such demands went against the grain, and he assumed he was abetting Poling and his men in some nefarious night-riding activity against squatters when he did so. But again, no formal complaints had surfaced.

The policing of a frontier against possible swindles and the natural course of settlement friction was not what interested the major.

What did interest him was to recover permanently the rank he had held temporarily during the last year of the war. It pleased him to be called "Colonel," and he could foresee situations that might gain him that rank again, and maybe ranks above it if the cards fell right.

Still a year had passed and there had been no occasion to exercise his command in the field against an enemy. The Kiowa—or five tribes of them, at least—had agreed to a treaty and they had maintained their agreement. The biggest tribe, led by Cloud, White Bear and Kicking Bird, remained south of the Smoky Hill River and away from trade routes and settlements. The other four smaller bands had evaporated into their own distant terrains with assurances to the commissioner, James Chrisman, that he would have no trouble with their people.

Only one tribe, that of Hawk That Hunts Walking, had not agreed to the treaty, and Grimes held his squadron alert for trouble from that quarter. But it had not come—until now. For a year, no one had even known where the Kana'tenee were, much less had any hostile encounters with them.

201

But now Captain Sinclair's report had galvanized the force at Camp Jacob. There had been an attempted Indian raid in Sector C-9, avoided only by the intervention there of A Troop. Grimes was aware that A Troop had been ordered to stay away from C-9, but he avoided asking why they had gone there beyond Sinclair's comment about an alert from a civilian. It might have been difficult to explain, in the face of the report, why he had told them not to go there.

Had the attack on innocent hunters taken place, they would now be in a state of war. A Troop had averted the attack. But then, pursuing the hostiles, A Troop itself had come under attack and had suffered casualties. It was enough.

Grimes had intelligence—by the vague grapevine that seemed to operate in this country—of the location of a large encampment of Indians. That location coincided with the location of the attack on A Troop. Therefore that encampment was hostile and could be dealt with in a military manner.

While the men of A Troop got a few hours' needed rest, the squadron had been in feverish preparation and now, with first light of dawn, they were on the move. There was a crisp freshness in the air, and a crisp precision in the sounds of many horses at field march.

Grimes looked around him. To his right rode A Troop, Captain Sinclair in the lead, a full troop short twenty-five men not yet back from patrol. To his left rode C Troop led by First Lieutenant George Christy, a first-rate young officer and a handsome figure on the parade ground.

Behind the major came B Troop, First Lieutenant Gregory Pine leading, and in the van came his mountain howitzer unit.

Finally, after almost a year of debilitating peace, the First Squadron would have its day. Grimes smiled to himself. They would make short work of a band of nomads. Short work indeed, and the reports to regiment—and direct to division headquarters—should put the major well on his way toward his colonelcy.

Only a garrison guard remained at little Camp Jacob, a

handful of soldiers and the civilian contingent of the place.

Cain DeWitt strolled across the compound to watch the squadron move out, and he stood for a time in the open gateway, watching the unit dwindle into the distance of the morning plains. Finally he turned and walked back to his cabin, thinking of breakfast. He felt very pleased. Somehow the scheme that had seemed to fail had ultimately worked. Although the hunters had failed, there had been a clash with the Kiowa, and now the calvary was on its way to complete its task.

He turned and looked westward again for a moment. The lands out there were endless. Only the sham of a treaty barred Poling and his group from setting up as territorial land commissioners over an area the size of some New England states . . . and eventually, with Poling's connections, governing a new territory settled by people beholden to him.

The First Squadron would punish Indians. They would do so very thoroughly. DeWitt felt it would be only a matter of time between the disciplining of the Kana'tenee—or whoever was out there—and violations of the treaty by the other tribes of Kiowa. Of all the plains tribes now, only the Kiowa had kept the peace. But the fact they had was the obstacle in Poling's way. It was the foundation upon which idiots like Chrisman built their structures.

DeWitt continued toward the sutlery and his cabin. He noticed as he approached that two saddled horses were reintied before the sutlery. They hadn't been there when he left. Behind their saddles, both carried bedrolls and packs, and canteens were suspended from both horns. One of the rigs also included a rifle in a boot.

With a shrug he pulled the latch-string and let himself into his cabin, closing the door behind him. He crossed to the shutters in the gloom and opened them wide to let in the sun . . . then spun around when a boot scuffed on the floor behind him.

"Good morning, Mr. DeWitt," Ernest Kichener said. "It is a beautiful day for a ride. If we leave now, we should be in time to see all the fun."

DeWitt's mouth dropped open, speechless. He recognized the man, had first seen him a year ago at Willow Ford and had seen him once or twice around Camp Jacob. Further, he knew his name because Poling had inquired about him after the interpreter incident at Willow Ford. Unfortunately, beyond a name and the fact that he carried credentials from the Department of Interior, they had learned nothing more.

"What are you doing in my cabin?" DeWitt managed.

"Waiting for you." The man's voice was soft, his words cordial, but there was something about his eyes . . . DeWitt shivered. "We have a long way to go, Mr. DeWitt. You'll want that coat there on the peg, and I suggest you remove your shoes and put on those boots. I have arranged everything else that you'll need."

"I'm not going anywhere!" DeWitt erupted. He started past the man, his hand reaching toward the door latch. The hand that stopped him was like an iron clamp on his shoulder, bearing him back, thrusting him casually as though he weighed nothing, forcing him down until he sat with a plop on the edge of his bunk.

"I suggest you put on your boots now," Kichener said. "You see, we are going to war."

Two horsemen rode silently past the guards at the open gate of Camp Jacob. The tall, slender one touched his hat in casual salute as they passed. The other was the camp sutler, Cain DeWitt, who sat stiffly in his saddle, his face very pale.

It was nearly a half hour since the departure of the squadron, but they were still clearly visible, far away and tiny, westbound across an endless grass sea. The pair of civilians took the same direction when they left the gate.

XVIII

"I can't believe I'm doin' this," Billy Sipe proclaimed to the errant winds. "Me, Billy Sipe. Why me? Hell, I ought to be goin' the other way just as fast as possible . . . if I knew just exactly where the other way was."

Climbing aboard the roan he stood tall in his stirrups, looking all around, shading his eyes. Everywhere was prairie. He dismounted again and resumed his walking, leading the roan, preserving it. Never in his life had he felt so alone. Hours before, he had lost the trail of the Indians. Now he was lost, and the prairies mocked him. Still, he believed he was going the right direction.

"Right direction to get killed," he muttered. "Jeez, I can't believe I'm doin' this."

For out there, somewhere, were Indians.

The Indians were not at war, Ernest Kichener had said.

Oh, hell, no, they weren't at war. Not a bit. That arrow they had stuck in his leg the year before was all in fun, wasn't it? And even more fun, when they had been jumped by Indians and cavalry both, and nobody knew who was fighting whom . . . fun, sure, except that people were getting killed out here.

"Why didn't I just keep on goin' when I started out?" he demanded, talking to the roan or himself or the wind. It still bothered him there were no echoes. It was like being a ghost to speak and hear no sound come back. "He said he wouldn't have followed me any farther if I hadn't turned around. By now I could have been . . . who knows . . . someplace, prob'ly. That damn Curtis. Who cares if they string his hide on a teepee pole? Him and his damn mules. An' that nigger, who cares about him, either? An' that crazy Spaniard, an' . . . an' that old fool Poole. He should'a known better than to latch up with a loser like me. Who cares about any of 'em, anyway? Cheez, I got no stake in this."

Still, he continued southward, looking for a trace. "Tell 'em to come back, he says! Just like that. Ride right into a bunch of savages an' tell 'em to come back an' see what's happenin'? How can I tell 'em anything? They can't even talk English!"

The roan horse plodded after him, ignoring him, content to be with a person.

"You ain't got any better sense than me," he told it.

Again he swung aboard to stand in the stirrups and look all around. There was no sign of a trail, no sign of anything. And yet . . . to the west of him, not very far, the land seemed strange. It seemed to go on endlessly, yet there was an oddity of proportion there. The grass expanses gave no perspective. But here there were occasional yucca plants and thorn clumps, and these added a dimension that was above the grass. He squinted and looked again. It seemed the continuum was interrupted to the west, as though the land ran out to there and then quit, and then began again a long way off.

He settled into the saddle and reined toward it. "Might as well go look," he muttered. "Nothin' else out here to look at."

He was almost on top of the great canyon breaks before he saw them, and when he did he whistled. Trees grew down there in distant purple shadows, green-gold tops hidden in secret bottoms twisting among spires and steeples that rose to the level of the land where he sat, their caps flat and grass-grown to blend with the elusive prairies.

He sat the roan on a sheer rim, and below him, a long way down, was a different world. He removed his battered hat and stared in awe at the spectacle of the canyons. Prairie winds tumbling across miles of maze twisted and fretted among the spires and sang an eerie song.

"My God," Billy Sipe whispered, and could think of nothing more to say.

There was a spreading meadow out there, fanning around the bases of standing rock monoliths, and on it was a glint of water. Then he saw movement. A line of horsemen, tiny at this range, rode beside a rocky stream that curved toward his vantage. He watched as they came closer, and saw shades of blue and tan, here and there a hint of bright yellow. He rubbed his eyes and squinted. The lowering sun shot spears of brilliance across the scene. The line of riders approached a high shoulder where the stream disappeared, and one by one they were gone from sight, hidden by the canyon where they rode.

Far beyond, down-canyon, was a far larger meadow where the grass was green and animals grazed on it, and beyond that . . . the shadows deceived him. Beyond was something, and he couldn't make it out. Maybe, he thought, that was where the Indians had gone.

"I must be crazy," he told himself again. Then he turned the roan and went in search of a way down into the breaks.

Angling across a stream, through a grove of cottonwood and up a cedar-dotted gully, Hildegarde and her followers found themselves in a broad, grassy meadow sweet with clumps of wild clover. There were animals here, many of them. Hundreds of horses grazed randomly, watched over by people like those who had frightened her. Across the meadow she could see mules, apart and sedate, staying to their own turf as they grazed. She trotted toward them, winding among clusters of strange-scented horses, noticing here and there one whose scent she recognized.

Two of the smoke-smelling men stood tall, noticing her, and one ran to intercept her. Before he could close though, Lucifer charged forward, switched ends and launched a powerful kick in his direction, barely missing him. The person backed away.

Hildegarde continued across to the other mules. One of them wore a bell, and she went to her and nuzzled her, recognizing her as one familiar. She went from one to another, sniffing them, rubbing against them, happy to be rejoined with her herd.

Beyond the meadow on a high shelf of sloping ground stood great numbers of tall, conical things with people moving among them. There was smoke there from many fires, and she drifted that way curiously, stopping only when some of the strange men guarding the herds moved to drive her back. Where she went now Bernice followed happily, her bell clanking a soft, reassuring sound, and the rest stayed close around them.

Hildegarde turned away from the village, then turned back at the sound of people shouting, high-pitched yipping sounds that startled her. Men came, running down the meadow, spreading among the herds, catching and driving horses. They swarmed around and past the mules, but left them alone, choosing horses instead. Within minutes the meadow was cleared of most of its horses and the slope beyond was alive with riders, taking up weapons, painting themselves and the animals they rode. More shouts, more chattering and then a long file of bright-painted horsemen angled westward across the meadow toward the gully at its lower end. Behind them another group of warriors trotted eastward past the village, turned there and began a slow march up the bank of the creek.

The activity of these strange people was of only vague interest to Hildegarde, yet she found that as they moved out, converging away into the higher canyons, there was no one paying any attention to her and the other mules. So she looked again toward the village, curious at scents there which were familiar to her. When no one came to interfere, she tossed her head and trotted up the sloping shelf.

Entering the great cluster of lodges, she began encountering some of the smoke-smell people, but these were mostly very small ones who turned and ran as the twelve tall mules approached them. Moving on, she followed her nose, pausing now and then at teepees to sniff around their skirts. The intriguing scent increased, and she stood tall, sniffing with a velvet nose as perceptive as a hound's. Her ears turned to various sounds, but her dark eyes fixed on a smoke-blackened lodge set back from the center of the village. A man stood just beyond it—one of the strange ones—holding a long stick with bright things on it. He was facing the other way.

Hildegarde walked to the lodge, lowered her head and sniffed, and a gladness filled her equine heart. Inside were friends. As she pulled at the thong that held the lodge to a peg in the ground, most of the other mules stood and watched. Lucifer and Madison, though, elected to look at the other side of the thing and ambled off around it.

Darby Curtis lay on a buffalo robe and rolled his shoulders methodically, one way and then the other, trying to relieve the ache in his bound arms. All the previous night and most of this day they had been held prisoner in this lodge, guarded always by at least one Blackleg warrior near the entrance, released and fed at dawn and noon but then trussed up again with wide, soft leather strapping that their best efforts, working back to back, had failed to untie. Now the others dozed around him on their robes and he wished he also could sleep.

The Indians had been courteous enough to them. So far, no one had been hurt, although he knew from some overheard comments that at least a couple of the younger Blacklegs had some nasty things in mind for Trini Salazar.

Darby shook his head. Not only had the Spaniard tried repeatedly to attack his captors during their trip to these hidden breaks—that wasn't so bad in the eyes of the Kiowa, that was something they could admire, even if they killed him for it.

No, the real trouble had come this morning. They had been released under heavy guard, given food and water and a chance to refresh themselves. And the damned Spaniard, right there in front of God and half the Kiowa nation, had made a play for one of their women.

Darby still couldn't believe it.

They had been beside the creek. Eight Blacklegs had

been with them, guarding them. Some women had gone by, a little way downstream, and they had turned to watch, as had their guards. Some of the Kiowa women were very pretty. One of these in particular—later he heard the name Cas-ca-dee, or Red Sky—was a real beauty and probably worth at least fifty horses to her proud father.

They had watched the women pass, then had turned back to what they were doing. It was a minute or more before any of them, including the guards, realized that Trini was no longer with them. Then a sturdy young warrior named Lizard had noticed their attrition, counted noses and turned to look again. They had all looked.

Little Red Sky, separated from the other women, was strolling toward the village, carrying a load of washed materials. And strutting along beside her, chest thrown out and bootheels tapping a faint *Tarantella* as he pranced, was Trinidad Salazar. He held his hat in one hand, patted her delicious bottom with the other and was doing his best to keep her enthralled with a continuous, intimate discourse in his best imitation of Castilian Spanish.

The girl obviously didn't understand a word of it, but her cheeks were a fine pink and she flashed white teeth at him in a dazzling smile.

Darby had thought the Blackleg guards were going to come unglued. When they dragged Trini back to where the other prisoners stood, Darby had talked long and hard to keep them from removing various parts of him to add to their collections.

Trini sported bruises now that he hadn't had before. And yet, in his sleep, he was smiling.

"God," Darby whispered. He shook his head again and sat up. His wrists ached from their bindings, lashed behind him. The ache had spread until he ached all over.

Through the partially-pulled flap of the teepee he saw the legs of the warrior on guard there.

Suddenly there were distant shouts, then more voices and the soft padding of moccasined feet running. He tried to hear what was being said outside. Something about enemies approaching. He tried to imagine what enemies could be here, in this hidden place. The Comanche to the south would have no trouble finding a place like this. This was more their kind of country than it was the Kiowas'. But the Comanche were not enemies to the Kiowa . . . not lately, at any rate. There were Cheyenne to the west, of course. The Kiowa and Cheyenne had not been on good terms for a long time, not since the days when the Cheyenne had made alliances with the Dakotas, Lakotas and Brules. But he couldn't imagine the Cheyenne being here. Not now.

Who, then? He had no idea. Yet he heard the sounds of horses being driven in, heard the snap of weapons taken up, smelled the raw odors of paint being applied from open pots, smelled the sharp scent of fresh cedar smoking on fires, the medicine-bough of the Kana'tenee. Something was going on, for certain.

Vince Copple was beside him then, a darker shadow in the gloom of the lodge. "What's goin' on, Mister Darby? Can you make it out?"

They heard horses going away, in two directions.

"Somebody's come into the breaks. I don't know who. But I'd hate to be whoever it is. They got a surprise coming in just a little bit."

From one side he heard Edwin Poole's muttered comment, "That make 'em any worse off than us?"

No, Darby thought, the 'enemy' were no worse off than the four of them. He didn't expect to leave this village alive. Old Hawk That Hunts Walking had some notion of a medicine, and he would wait a day or so to see if it happened. But when it didn't, the Kiowa would have no more use for them. He was fairly sure they wouldn't be tortured—unless some of the young bucks decided to trim Trini's ardor with a knife. No, he didn't expect ceremonial treatment. That was reserved for hated criminals or enemies taken in battle. As far as he knew, the Kiowa had nothing against them. So they would just be knocked in the head and dumped someplace for the buzzards to dispose of. It would all be simple and businesslike. No hard feelings.

The guard had disappeared from in front of the lodge. But now he returned again, stopped to peer inside, then resumed his position.

Long moments passed, then Darby's head came up and he turned. At the rear of the lodge he heard small crackling noises, like thongs being torn. The teepee seemed to quiver slightly, as though a silent wind were nudging it. He heard other soft sounds that he couldn't make out, and somewhere, softly, the unmistakable clank of a bell, almost lost among the sounds of the village.

"Mr. Poole?" he whispered. "You awake? Listen."

He looked toward the flap again, trying to see outside. The guard had stepped from direct view. Then suddenly he heard a gasp from there, a quick drumming of hooves, a distinct thud and a trailing, high-pitched howl of pain and surprise. Almost instantly the lodge went darker as the huge dark head of Lucifer was thrust through the little opening, virtually filling it.

The teepee shook again, and this time some of its poles tilted, creaking against each other. Thongs snapped, hides strained and the standing lodge tipped further. Lucifer withdrew from the hole, and now there was light from both front and back. The skirt of hides there lifted, filtering in sunlight, then lifted higher and the teepee seemed to collapse inward upon itself. A mule head, and then another and another, pushed in through the enlarging opening at the back, and lodge-cover hides rode up and up toward tall shoulders. Bare poles cracked and splintered, pushed aside. All of a sudden the teepee was a standing shambles of buckling poles and torn hides, and it was full of mules. With a lurch Darby got to his feet, shouting at the others, "Stand up! Get up, quick!"

A velvet nose nudged him from behind, nuzzling his shoulder, his neck, nibbling delicately at his ear. Hildegarde's tender welcome almost bowled him over. Then he stood amazed as strong teeth toyed with the straps on his wrists, pulling them, rolling and clipping at the knot. In a moment his hands were free. Beyond the tattered remnants of the teepee, its frame somehow still standing, he saw Madison holding a warrior pinned to the ground, chewing on his hair. The mules crowded around him then and all he

212

could see was mules. Somehow it seemed all but two or three of them . . . he knew Lucifer and Madison were outside . . . had packed themselves into the devastated lodge. It was all he could do to get through the crunch, to retrieve a knife from the yowling, struggling guard Madison had pinned to the ground, and to get back in to cut the thongs that bound Copple, Poole and the Spaniard. It was only a little way to the hut where he had seen the Blacklegs pile their equipment. Indian women and children scurried and disappeared before them as a solid phalanx of men and tall mules made their way toward it.

Only a few warriors remained in the village. These came at a run now, attracted by the sounds of chaos. Darby dived into the packs and tarps piled in the lean-to and came up with one of his rifles. Poole and Copple were right behind him, rummaging, screened by mules. When they emerged they were armed, and the warriors backed off, retreating ahead of them step by step toward the center of the village.

Rounding a teepee, Darby saw three old men in robes, standing solemnly before a tall teepee painted with symbols of sun, bison, lightning and a large, black caricature of a crow.

The one in the center was Hawk That Hunts Walking.

For some reason, none of the warriors flanking them had yet cast a lance or loosed an arrow. Now Darby saw the old chief raise his hand, saw the warriors fall back, and he stepped forward, Poole and Copple at his back, twelve big mules clustering about them, heads up and ears twitching in huge curiosity.

The old chief gazed at him. "Hawk That Hunts Walking has seen the medicine of O'gatedota and his ugly horses," he said. Then he turned to the wizened old medicine man beside him. "You see, Keeps His Horses? Sometimes the visions of the Blackleg men are not as crazy as they seem. Stalking Horse said a wild white man with ugly horses would lead the Kana'tenee on their mission."

Darby fought for comprehension. He was missing something here.

The old chief addressed him again. "O'gatedota, I have

213

decided. You will be friend to the Kana'tenee. You will take Hawk That Hunts Walking on a journey. You will show me the way, because I do not know it, and you will be my eyes and my tongue. The Great Father of the whites has sent men to talk peace with the Kiowa, but the Great Father did not come himself. It may be he was too busy. Some chiefs say it is enough to talk with medicine men. Hawk That Hunts Walking does not feel good about that. So you will take me to the Great Father so that I can hear his words from his own mouth. If he is too busy to come to Hawk That Hunts Walking, then Hawk That Hunts Walking is not too busy to go to him."

The old medicine man scowled at Darby, muttered an incantation and shook his rattle at him. "It is as Hawk That Hunts Walking says," he proclaimed in a voice like wind through prairie grass. "Here is the wild one, O'gatedota, and here are his ugly horses. Yet, how does Hawk That Hunts Walking know that this man can be trusted? How can the Kana'tenee know the heart of any white man?"

The old chief smiled, faintly. "The wild one thought he might escape," he said. "And then he stopped to save the children."

XIX

Above rocks and cedar growth where a shoulder of sandstone buttressed the flowing stream, the First Platoon found what cover it could. Here a jutting bastion of striated rock thrust outward from the eastern wall of the canyon breaks, forming a cove that rose up and back, brush-strangled slopes of tumbled stone at the foot of a sheer cliff rearing upward to caprock and the prairies above.

Into this vee Lieutenant Thomas Spradley led his men, pounding upward until their mounts could climb no further, blocked by the head of the cove. Here he had them dismount and spread downward, forming a fan of defense down among the rocks. Four men climbed with Sergeant Hanlon to the thorn-choked ridge of the jutting shoulder to cover their right flank. Arrows whispered among them and a bullet whined off limestone scree, showering Rusty Anderson with burning sand.

Sergeant Ben Foley dragged the trooper back, wiping blood from his face. Stone shards had cut him, but the damage was slight.

"Only a few have guns, Lieutenant," Foley called. "Maybe three or four."

"Hold your fire unless they cross the creek," Spradley ordered. He cupped his hands, turning. "Sergeant Hanlon! If you can, try to pick off the ones carrying rifles!"

Atop the shoulder a carbine barked and a hundred and fifty yards away, on the rising flats beyond the creek, a warrior pitched backward off his pony. The Indians milled, uncertain now, and drew back into the screen of willows that marked a seep where the meadow began. A moment passed, then a feathered Kiowa drummed heels into his mount and came at a belly-down run, sighting a rifle to fire into the rocks. Shards flew and Private Louie Gifford cursed and rolled behind a boulder. The carbine atop the shoulder spoke again and the warrior's horse went down, flailing. The Indian hit the ground rolling, losing his weapon. For a moment he lay sprawled, then was up and running, crouching, making for the rifle. Another shot exploded gravel almost under him and he veered away, running for the willows.

A ragged flight of arrows arced from the screen, upward to rattle among the thin front line of the soldiers. Corporal Tiny Simms yelled, tried to get to his feet and yelled again. A bright arrow shaft stood firmly in the calf of his leg and he writhed on the ground, trying to pull it free.

"Let it alone, Tiny!" Foley snapped. "Hold still, don't pull at it!" Holding the big corporal down, he grasped the shaft and broke it off an inch from the flowing blood on Simms' leg. "Lose that point in there, we'll never get it out."

In the distance, beyond the willows, Indians broke from cover and rode for the meadow, each rider leading several extra horses. The Blacklegs were horsemen, and had hoped to sweep through these intruders with a headlong charge, arrow and lance. Yet now the soldiers were secure, beyond the reach of mounted attack. So now the Blackleg men dismounted to fight on foot.

Screened by willows, Bird crouched behind his shield and spoke to those around him. Then he drew a small pot from his pouch and dipped fingers in it to paint two horizontal black lines across his face, from cheek to cheek.

"It is a good day to fight," he said, "and a good day to die." He passed the little pot to Young Bull, next to him, who drew similar war marks on his face and passed it on.

Yet when the paint came to Stalking Horse, the young chief refused it. "It is a medicine day," he told Bird. "It is not a good day for Blackleg men to die."

216

The older warrior turned slowly toward him, dark eyes fierce above the rim of his black shield. "Is Stalking Horse afraid to die today?"

"Read the wind, Bird," the younger man said softly. "The blue soldiers cannot escape. Leave them to the Real Dog men. This is their work. Today's wind says the Blackleg men must paint for medicine, not for war."

Bird hesitated. "Today the wind says nothing to me. Three times now the wind has chosen Stalking Horse and not Bird. Does Stalking Horse speak now for the Blackleg men?"

"Only the medicine wind says who leads the Blackleg men, respected one," Stalking Horse said. He lowered his eyes and shifted to point behind them. Far across the valley meadow, where the new village lay, smokes rose between wide canyon walls . . . threads of white smoke from village fires, momentarily released by a lull in the shifting canyon winds to stand tall and arrow-straight above the caprock where they bent in unison to stream eastward, signals pointing a way.

Bird gazed at the telling smokes, then lowered his shield. Stalking Horse had not even looked to see what the smokes said of today. He had only pointed. The wind had told him what was there.

Young Bull and Three Moons, their faces already painted in horizontal stripes, looked at each other then lifted veed fingers to their eyes, drawing them downward, breaking the lines. That simply, war paint became medicine paint.

"The wind speaks to Stalking Horse now," Bird said finally. "Stalking Horse must lead the Blackleg men. He will lead well."

"Break your paint, then, respected one," Stalking Horse spoke almost sadly, knowing that a thing had changed and would not change back. "Let the Blackleg men return to our village. For today, leave war to the Real Dog men. It is their purpose to guard the people. Let the Blackleg men read the wind and tell what must come next."

Bird stood, stepped forward and dropped to his knees.

Holding the hooked lance before him with both hands, he presented it to Stalking Horse. When the young chief had accepted it Bird stood again, took up his black shield and his war club and looked at those around him.

"Once before, in the time of grass cutting, I broke the paint of war. It was a good thing to do. But it is not a thing that should be done twice."

Far across the meadow now, out of range of the soldiers' guns, a long line of mounted warriors sat their horses silently, waiting to see what the Blackleg men would do. In the center of the line were the Real Dog men, their paint and feathers brilliant in the sun. They knew where the soldiers were and knew they could not escape. The most honored and most respected of the warrior societies of the Kana'tenee, the Real Dog men were essentially pragmatists. Even in their rituals and ceremonies, the secret traditions that held their society apart from others of the tribe, they practiced little of the mysticism of the Blackleg men. For their purposes, erratic behavior was seldom good. Responsible for protecting the tribe, leading all its warriors who had no society, and guarding the village wherever it located, these senior warriors viewed most things from the practical aspect and left the mysteries of life to the far-ranging, unpredictable Blacklegs.

Even Keeps His Horses, the most senior of medicine men, was at a loss most of the time to predict what the Blacklegs might do next.

Now Twenty Buffalo sat his horse at the head of the Real Dog men and waited for a sign. Three hundred yards away, in a screen of willows, he saw the Blackleg men deploying for battle on foot. Two hundred yards beyond them, in a cove below the canyon's east wall, were the soldiers who had invaded his people's secret place. There were not many of them, and he knew where they were. They had guns that could outreach the arrows of his warriors, but their guns would serve little purpose with the coming of night. If the soldiers were still there when the shadows came, their scalps would adorn lodges tomorrow.

Blackleg horse handlers had drawn back from the willows, holding the mounts prepared but out of range. But now, at some signal, the handlers moved the horses again into the willows and a moment later the Blackleg Society rode out, headed back toward the village.

Twenty Buffalo nodded. It was better this way. The Blackleg men were superb riders and awesome to see at war or in the hunt. Yet, they were not practical. They tended to act impulsively, to charge recklessly . . . and they tended to die a lot. This would be no great battle, only the methodical elimination of a few invaders. It was better left to the Real Dog men.

Twenty Buffalo squinted, watching the Blackleg men leave the field, and noticed then that it was not Bird who carried the hooked lance. The one who led them was Stalking Horse. Peering toward the willows again, he saw Bird standing alone, holding his club and shield, turning toward the cove across the stream, where the soldiers were. As he watched, Bird moved slightly, blending with the willows, and disappeared from sight.

Leadership of the mystic society had passed. And Bird had decided it was a good day to die. Twenty Buffalo sat his horse in silence, wondering how many soldiers the Blackleg warrior would take with him in death, how many would remain for the Real Dog men to eliminate at nightfall.

Distant shouts from the Blacklegs came to him and he turned. Riding out from the village was a strange, unlikely assembly of riders. In the lead, holding his feather fan high, was Hawk That Hunts Walking, the ancient Keeps His Horses riding slumped beside him, brandishing his rattle. Behind came three of the prisoners, all mounted on the big, ugly horses, with others of those trotting after them. Senior warriors and shamans rode at the flanks, fully armed. Further back, just emerging from the village, came the little white man—the crazy one—galloping full tilt atop a yellow pony, dodging as a thrown club flipped past his head. And behind him, gesturing and waving, ran Broken Bow, followed by his daughter Red Sky.

It was more than Twenty Buffalo could comprehend. He

sat upright in his saddle, amazed, and for the moment his expression was other than stolid.

Far up the meadow the two groups met, mingled for a moment and then came on, Hawk That Hunts Walking leading the prisoners—who, Twenty Buffalo could see now, were armed—Stalking Horse and the Blackleg men following along behind.

In the far distance old Broken Bow, afoot, had stopped, panting. He stood there in the field, his posture one of fatigue and fury. The girl, Red Sky, hopped about him, gesturing and shouting at him.

From the cover of the cove, Spradley and his troopers could see nothing of what occurred beyond the willows. They lay hidden among rock and shrub, waiting for attack. But up on the shoulder, crouching behind a cedar stump, Private Mulcahey had a good view and relayed what he saw to Sergeant Hanlon, who lay belly down on the ridge overlooking the creek."

"I can make 'em out in the trees there," Mulcahey said. "They're all gathered around in sort of a circle, passing somethin' . . . it looks like they're having their supper."

A few minutes later he reported, "All those other Indians, the big bunch, they're strung out clear across the pasture out there, but they aren't doin' anything. They're just out there, is all."

"Those ones in the willows, that sent their horses away," he said after a time, "it looks like they're bringin' them back now. I hope this makes sense to you, Sergeant, because it sure doesn't to me."

Hanlon shrugged and passed the word along, down to the lieutenant in the cove. He wondered what it was that had looked to Mulcahey like Indians having their supper.

Time and stillness dragged by. Hanlon raised himself for a look, but everything beyond the willows was screened from him.

"They're movin' out," Mulcahey said. "The ones in the willows, they're ridin' off, out the other side. But them out there in the pasture, they're still just sittin' there."

Hanlon relayed the word. Then he waited.

"Sergeant . . ." Mulcahey's voice was hesitant.

"What do you see, Private?"

"Well, it's . . . way off over there where the smoke is, where the Indians in the trees went to, you know? Well, there's another bunch comin' from there, and it's kind of funny . . ."

"What's kind of funny about it, Mulcahey?" Hanlon suddenly found himself very irritated.

"Well, I can make 'em out, an' most of 'em is those big mules that look kind of like camels except I never saw a camel so I'm just guessin' what a camel looks like . . . but the two in front are ridin' regular horses and they're both Indians and one is shakin' a feather duster an' the other one is sowin' corn or somethin' out of a hand spreader . . . and there's people ridin' on three of those mules and they're all three white except one is black, an' there's some more Indians alongside of 'em . . . an' there's a fellow on a yellow dog chasin' after 'em, really movin' along and it looks like there's an Indian chasin' him afoot and throwing' a boot-jack at him, an' . . . my Lord, Sergeant, I believe that's one of the best-lookin' women I ever seen in my life!"

Hanlon sagged behind his rock, his mouth open. Behind and below him Private Tom Pedigo rolled his eyes skyward. "Mulcahey," he muttered, "I believe you've done set a new record."

"Shut up about him," Jakey Bloom snapped. "He's all right, in my book."

There was motion in the willows then and suddenly an arrow flew from there, its arc hard and shallow. On the tallus below where the mounts were held a soldier screamed and toppled from a stone to lie writhing in the brush below it. Before the troopers could respond another arrow came from the screen, hard across the creek to pierce the exposed arm of Private Frost, just above the elbow. It went all the way through and stood quivering in a clay bank beside him.

"Direct your fire!" Spradley said. "When he moves!" Another arrow sang across and the cove erupted with gunfire, a volley of slugs tearing into the willows in a space of five feet, but the warrior was no longer there. A fourth

221

arrow sang from hiding just to the right of where he had been, narrowly missing Spradley's cheek as he dropped behind a clump of cedar.

Again they volleyed. Heavy slugs snarled through the willows, leaves and bark erupting where they passed.

Nothing moved there. For a moment there was silence, then the screen of boughs exploded and a tall warrior was running toward them. Carrying a black bullhide shield, brandishing a warclub, he dodged and pivoted and came on while bullets shattered gravel behind and around him. His hair stood in a tall roach, feathers bobbing behind it, and his face was a mask of savage pigments with black lines across the cheeks and nose. Troopers in the cove raised and fired, raised and fired again, and still he ran, closing toward the bank of the shallow creek. His cry was a high, piercing yip-yip-yip, nerve-tingling and deadly as wolves at the chase.

A bullet tore his shield, knocking it around, exposing bright quill armor from neck to waist, strings of ornaments at his throat. He dodged again, dropped and rolled and bullets tore the ground behind him.

"My God," Ben Foley whispered. "We can't stop him." He raised, sighted and fired, saw his bullet shatter gravel on the bank, behind where the warrior should have been.

Without breaking stride the warrior whirled, drew back and hurled the heavy club in his hand. Foley saw it coming but the throw was too fast, too hard. It took him in the shoulder and sent him rolling, his arm flopping limply.

Even as Foley fell the tall warrior had changed direction again, almost at the creek now. He dove, rolled and dropped his shield to come up with the discarded rifle that had been dropped there in the first assault. Twenty yards from the cove now he raised, fired and a bullet sang off packed rubble beside Private Dolan.

A dozen carbines answered but he was up again, diagonally into the stream, long strides throwing spray as he came, swinging the rifle like a club. Soldiers in the front line scurried backward, horrified. Blood flew from the warrior's back, and a gout of red erupted through the quillwork on his chest. Guns crashed. A hole appeared in his side, blood spurting from it. He was across the creek and climbing the near bank.

"Jesus!" Hanlon gasped. He stood, leveled his carbine and squeezed the trigger. The warrior seemed to pause in mid-stride. Hanlon levered and fire again. Frozen in place, the Kiowa shuddered as the bullet smashed into him. Then he straightened, turned his head upward to stare directly at Hanlon, and toppled backward into the stream.

Beyond the creek the willow screen exploded outward and riders surged through. In the cove Spradley raised his revolver, then shouted "Hold your fire!"

Some of the riders racing toward them now were white men, and some of them rode huge mules. The first one stood tall in stirrups that barely encased the barrel of his mount and waved a rifle above his head. "Hold your fire!" he shouted. "Stop shooting! Stop shooting!"

Then the far bank was alive with riders, mostly Indians but with white men and a black man at their head.

"Just hold your fire!" the first one shouted again, across the stream. "It's over!"

Shadows like those of evening encompassed the canyon breaks. Smokes lifted from the distant village and there were fires on the creek bank where the troopers of the First Platoon tended their casualties and clustered wide-eyed, watching the somber forms of Indians who came and went about them.

On the gravel slope, away from all the others, an honor guard of Blackleg men stood watch over the battered body of a brave warrior whose time had come.

Lieutenant Thomas Spradley stood in quiet conversation with Darby Curtis, trying to sort out all he was being told. Some of it, he decided, would take a little time. He gazed downstream at the little band of warriors clustered around the body of Bird.

"Who was he?" he asked. "What was he?"

"One of the Blackleg men," Darby said. "One of the

reasons we don't want to fight these people if we can help it."

"I never saw anything like it," Spradley said. "My God . . ."

Darby nodded. "His name was Bird. He decided this was a good day to die."

As lost as he had been up on the plains, Billy Sipe was even more lost now, down in the maze of canyons that told him nothing. He had searched for a trail as long as the light held, and finally had found himself at a dead end with no place to go except back. He made a little fire, ate most of the jerky and hardtack remaining in his pack, and fell asleep muttering. At least, he thought, down here he had echoes.

Pink light was on the rims above when he opened his eyes, started to yawn and then choked and scrambled to his feet, grabbing for his carbine. All around him were Indians, all on horseback, just sitting in a circle around him, looking at him. He blinked, goggled at them and half turned, seeking an escape. He raised his gun.

The voice behind him stunned him. "I sure am glad to see you, Billy. Kind of restores my faith in humanity. Where you been, anyway?"

Poole? Billy spun around. Edwin Poole sat high on a saddled mule, lighting his pipe. Behind him were Darby Curtis, the black man, the Spaniard . . . and soldiers—a battered and bandaged bunch of soldiers flanked by Indians.

One of the Indians, a very old one wrapped in a blanket and carrying a feather fan, walked his horse across to Darby Curtis and said something. Curtis answered him, then turned to Billy Sipe.

"The chief says you can come along if you want to, Billy. He says one more damned white man won't make that much difference."

Billy stared at them, trying to regain his composure. "I . . . I'm not supposed to go with them," he said, realizing how thin his voice must sound. "They're supposed to go with me. Mr. Kichener said to come get them and bring them back."

Darby Curtis frowned, regarding him. He pursed his lips, started to speak, glanced around, and then started over.

"You were sent to get them. These people. The Kana'tenee. To get them and bring them back."

Billy nodded.

"And just how were you supposed to do that, Billy?"

"I don't know," he admitted. "Mr. Kichener said I'd come up with somethin'. But I guess we better be goin', if it's all right with everybody. Mr. Kichener said don't waste too much time."

XX

Once beyond day-patrol distance from Camp Jacob, the First Squadron was deployed by troops, the troops by platoons and the platoons by patrols, providing a broad front of nine small units sweeping westward a mile to two miles apart, always in signal relay contact and covering a surveillance width of nearly twenty miles.

Thus it was that Whiskey Joe and the Spider, riding out on morning scout from the valley of the winding stream, saw exactly what they had been expecting to see for nearly a week—a cavalry patrol coming their way.

"It's just like th' pilgrim said," Whiskey Joe pointed. "They ain't more'n ten of them bluecoats that I can see. Couple minutes of shootin' an' they won't be any. You think we better go tell Cully?"

Spider gazed across the morning prairie. The sun in his eyes was dazzling, but Whiskey Joe was right. The distant band of soldiers couldn't be more than nine or ten men in all. "Cold meat," he said. "Why don't we just lead 'em on in, get it over with. They out here lookin' for redskins, le's show 'em a couple."

Both of them wore buckskins, their leggings smeared with red clay and circles and stripes of soot. Spider pulled off his hat and thrust it into his saddle pouch, then pulled other things from there. "Le's dress us up," he said. Tying a wide strip of leather around his head he thrust turkey feathers into it until Whiskey Joe nodded at the effect. Then he smeared buffalo fat into his long hair until it hung stiff below the headband, spreading like two thick braids.

He daubed his nose and forehead with yellow wax boiled from the kidneys of a buffalo calf, then smeared a mixture of soot and grease on chin and cheeks, pushing lines upward to obscure his short beard.

"If I didn' know better," Whiskey Joe observed, "I'd shoot ye right this minute an' sell your scalp to some Colorado trader an' hang yer balls on my saddle horn for good luck."

"Get painted," Spider said, digging in his pouch. "I got some beads here someplace, ought to look about right."

"Cully an' them will want some notice so's they can get purtied up too."

"Won't take 'em but a minute. We'll still be half a mile ahead of them bluecoats when we ride in. No, don't put them feathers in front like that, damn it! We're Kioways, not Pawnees."

When they were satisfied with their appearance, the two spurred eastward, closing toward the approaching patrol. They knew when they had been seen, saw distant figures pointing to them, raising their hands to peer. Still they closed on them.

"Not too close, Spider," Whiskey Joe warned. "These getups ain't gonna fool anybody right up close."

"You want 'em to foller us, don't you?" Spider growled.

They were not much more than a quarter-mile from the soldiers when Spider drew rein. "This'll do it. Le's give 'em a volley now. But aim wide an' don't hit nobody. No sense them knowin' what these rifles'll do . . . not just yet."

"They fixin' to find out pretty quick, though." Whiskey Joe grinned and raised his buffalo gun. "We gonna lift all their scalps, Spider? Injuns would."

"Sure, An' we gonna cut off some spare parts whilst we're at it, too. An' take ever'thing a redskin would take. Worse we cut 'em up, th' happier DeWitt an' them ought to be. Ready? Le's bring 'em home."

As one, the two men fired their rifles, careful not to expose the range the big guns had, then wheeled their mounts and headed west at a hard run. Cresting a broad rise, Spider looked back. The patrol seemed to have spread, but they were in pursuit. Lashing his horse, he headed for the distant valley where Cully and the rest were camped. Whiskey Joe stayed with him, drumming his mount with cruel heels, laughing as they rode.

A mile passed, and he could see the pursuers again, a bit further back but still in pursuit, spread now to a wide, thin line. "There's not even ten of 'em," he shouted to Whiskey Joe as they swept over a rise and downward, toward the valley, losing sight. "There's only eight. I counted."

Behind them on the prairie, Sergeant Amos Green slowed his patrol to a canter and looked right and left where signalmen were galloping away toward higher ground, tying flags to the muzzles of their carbines as they rode.

"Those two were just out for a lark," he told his men. "Now they're on the way to alert their village. It won't matter, though. There ain't a one of those savages goin' anyplace today but to the devil."

A mile to the south Major Alfred Grimes returned the salute of Lieutenant Chesney Barnes, heard his report and his eyes twinkled happily. One of the units had been fired upon.

Grimes had wondered how the hostiles would react, whether they would play innocent or fight. He had hoped for the latter. "Signalmen out," he told Barnes. "Deploy all units, ends at the gallop, centers at a trot. Captain Sinclair is to cross that creek out there with A Troop, circle and approach from the north. C Troop swing in from the south. We will cut across to join B Troop. I want to see it when our first rank charges them. Close them up now, Lieutenant. Smartly. I want to see a pincers charge right out of the book."

Not far away, now, the land dropped away toward a narrow valley, and in that valley rose the smoke of cooking fires. Like a well-oiled machine, the First Squadron curled itself around that smoke and closed in, a halfmoon of blue horsemen armed and ready, a crescent of firepower at first eight miles from tip to tip, then four miles, then two . . .

Cully did not wait for the soldiers at the old Indian village site. He and his hunters had set up some wagon-tops and hung a few hides on poles, to attract the eye, but he knew nothing they could do would make this look like an Indian village less than a half-mile away.

So when his men were painted and feathered he led them out along the little valley's slopes and spread them in hiding, five hundred yards each way from the path the patrol would follow coming in. Hidden under the crests— exposed caprock in some places, bellied down in thickets or tall grass at others—they could not see the approach of the soldiers. But on the other hand, the soldiers would never see them until they started shooting. It wouldn't take long to put eight soldiers on the ground. Then they would butcher their bodies the way he had heard the Indians sometimes did, take their scalps and collect the rest of their money from DeWitt. After that . . . well, this country didn't have anything Cully wanted. There were other, better places to be.

"Just like a drive on a small herd," he told Fisher and Silk. "Let 'em get in the slot, then cut 'em down. Just remember, we don't want anybody comin' out of this alive. Not a one of 'em."

"They'll go to cover," Fisher pointed out. "Ones we don't get right off, may take a little while."

"So?" he grinned. "You got anything better to do today?"

They waited then, and after a time Silk crawled to where Cully lay. "They should have been here by now," he said. "The Spider, he said they was just a half-mile behind."

"They'll be here directly," Cully scowled. "Little bunch like that, they won't come chargin' in. They'll have to talk it over for a while, then come up cautious-like for a look. I figure they'll have their best look from right down there," he pointed.

Silk grinned. "Right down there is where we'll leave 'em, too."

Feathered and painted the hunters waited. And waited. Nearly an hour had passed before Cully saw the signal from the Spider, highest on the slope. The soldiers were coming. Then distantly, cresting the rise that began the wide slope toward the valley, he saw them. They came at a trot . . . four, six, eight . . . Cully swore. He counted fourteen soldiers out there. Somehow Spider had miscounted. But it made no difference. Let 'em get in the pocket, he thought, and it didn't matter whether there were eight or fourteen. Hell, it wouldn't matter if there were twenty. Below him was a flat from where the soldiers would be able to see the "village." And that flat provided an open field of fire for the hide-hunters—a comfortable range for their buffalo rifles, yet extreme range for the carbines the soldiers would carry. "Cold meat," he muttered.

The group came on, ten men in columns of two with four others riding points and wings. "Rule-book soldiers," Cully told himself. He squinted. At least two of them, he decided, were officers. So much the better. DeWitt would get his money's worth this day.

From his vantage point the Spider watched them pass, and he sighted on the chest of a bright-uniformed officer. A captain, he decided. Maybe even a major. A real popinjay, the way he rode. He was tempted to fire, but he waited. Let them pass. Let them get into the pocket. He'd have his share. Once in, nobody would get out. He knew what buffalo guns could do.

They passed on.

Fisher and Whiskey Joe raised cautious heads to glance at each other as the little column came abreast, a bare five hundreds yards away. Fisher wet his finger with his tongue, then wet his front sight to cool it. Heat-dance could throw a shot off if a man wasn't careful about things like that.

Where the grasslands shelved away toward the valley the lead trooper hauled rein and raised his arm. The others came up to him. They had seen the "village." Cully eased his rifle forward, resting on his elbows to sight it. He took a bead on one who was obviously an officer, then changed his mind. One of the troopers, the one who had been riding drag, had held back. He remained out behind the rest.

"No sense anybody havin' a chance to run," Cully

230

muttered. He shifted to cover that one, took a fine bead and fired.

Out on the flat a soldier pitched sideways from his saddle, then another as big guns opened up on both sides of them. Horses milled in panic and another soldier went down. They were dismounting then, blindly, guns up and firing toward the smokes of the buffalo guns. The carbines were hopelessly outranged. On the slope near him Cully saw Spider leap to his feet, hop around in a parody of an Indian dance, hand flapping at his mouth to produce an undulating war cry, then raise his rifle and fire. "Son of a bitch looks just like a damn Injun," Cully muttered.

Horses were down in the flat, and surviving soldiers hugged the ground, hidden by tall grass, some shielded by their fallen mounts. Carbines spoke and the hide-hunters grinned as ineffectual bullets ripped sod a hundred yards short of them.

Cully saw motion in the grass and raised his rifle to fire, then froze as thunders sounded somewhere and he heard a weird whistling sound above him. An instant later great clouds of earth erupted in the fake village. The buffalo rifles went silent, hunters staring around in shock.

Spider was still on his feet, staring stupidly toward the exploding camp. As hooves pounded behind and above them, he was slow to turn. Turkey feathers drooping in his headband, he bent low and came around, directly in front of charging cavalry. He tried to bring his rifle up and carbine bullets riddled him. He was thrown backward, dead before he hit the ground. Cully dropped his rifle and sprawled in the grass, arms over his head. In the instant of Spider's death Cully had seen long lines of soldiers, all around them, charging down on them.

Fisher tried to fight and went down, his head opened by a saber cut. Silk jumped and ran, away from the field of fire, directly into the tearing fire of two carbines and a revolver. Cavalry hooves trampled him where he lay.

For a moment Whiskey Joe had been hidden, the first wave of A Troop going over and around him. But then there were others behind him and he jumped up, tearing the feathered band from his head. "Don't shoot!" he screamed. "Look, I'm white! I ain't no . . ." The .36 slug that entered his mouth angled downward, severing his spine. As he fell a young trooper reined in his horse, turning back, and leaned from his saddle to look at the tumbled body on the ground. The soldier's revolver still smoked from its shot. He stared and blinked. "That ain't a injun," he breathed, and felt the blood draining from his face.

In the distance, mountain howitzer charges continued to pound the empty village site.

B Troop had five dead. The buffalo guns had left no injured. Those who had been in the advance party had taken all their fire. Major Alfred Grimes scrubbed vainly at a blood-spattered sleeve, then gave up. Then he looked around, wondering which of the dead had bled on him.

It had only taken a few minutes to round up the surviving assassins, and when they were brought down onto the flat he stared at them in disbelief. White men, made up to look like Indians. Stinking, cowering men with grease in their hair and soot in their beards and red clay smeared on their faces. He looked at their collected rifles. There were several varieties, all with one thing in common. All were at least 50 caliber, chambered for great charges to drive a round far and fast. Buffalo guns . . . effective at half-mile range, deadly at anything less. The hide hunters' stock in trade.

Grimes had his tent pitched on the ridge above the shooting flats, and the First Squadron bivouac spread around it.

It was there, in the evening, that Major Grimes and his staff, along with troop leaders, interrogated the prisoners. It was difficult. Most of them remained stubbornly silent, and the two or three that would talk feigned ignorance of everything except to identify their leader, the one named Cully.

"These are the same men," Captain Sinclair advised,

"who were about to be attacked in Sector C-9 when we drove the Indians away."

"Is that true, Mr. Cully?" Grimes asked the sullen prisoner. "It strikes me as odd, then, that thirty or forty Indians could have been considered a threat. I have looked at your rifles. I can't see how a small band of primitives armed mostly with bows and arrows could ever have been a problem to you."

Cully stared sullenly at his feet.

"Sector C-9 is within the patrol perimeters of Camp Jacob," Sinclair said. "It has been a real puzzle to me how—and why—a band of Indians would have come all the way from out here . . . or more likely south of here . . . directly to where you were camped, with the intent of attacking you."

"We was told to kill them buffs down there," one of the hunters piped up. "And we was told where to go after that, to wait for Indians."

Cully turned to stare at his accomplice, murder in his eyes. Sinclair and the major glanced at each other. "That could have started a war," the captain pointed out. "If anybody happened to want one."

Grimes frowned and shook his head. A hard thought was taking shape in his mind. Was it . . . barely . . . possible that he had been used? He didn't want to think about it.

He glared at Cully. "To the point, then. How is it that you men were waiting out here, made up as Indians, when we approached? Two of your men fired on one of my patrols, then when a unit of B Troop came up on you, you were deployed for killing. Not defense, Mr. Cully. Don't shake your head like that. You were defending nothing. You had established a . . . a killing field and I have five dead soldiers to attest to your effectiveness."

The talkative hunter stepped forward, staring directly at his leader. "We're done for, Cully. We're gonna hang. You know that. Maybe if you'd tell him, maybe we could cut a deal . . ."

Abruptly Cully turned, lashed out with a hard fist and the man fell backward, his face a mass of blood and exposed bone. Guards grabbed Cully, imprisoned his arms, hauled him around.

A sergeant stepped to where Grimes sat, bent to whisper to him. "Civilians just rode in, sir. Two of 'em. One of 'em is the sutler. The other one is that gentleman from Washington."

Grimes blinked in surprise. Then he nodded. A moment later DeWitt stepped forward, white-faced, pushed by the man Grimes knew only as Kichener.

DeWitt looked at the officers, then at the prisoners before them. "Oh, God," he breathed.

It was too much for Cully. He twisted and writhed in the grip of the guards. "DeWitt, you son of a bitch! You did this! A thousand dollars! Just for a stinkin' patrol! You set us up an' by God you're goin' with us!" He turned to Grimes. "It was him . . . him an' some partner of his. They said we could kill some injuns an' they'd pay, then th' soldiers come an' that didn't work out. Then he said kill some soldiers instead, make it look like redskins done it. Five hundred dollars he paid, an' another five hundred when we showed the scalps . . ." Once Cully started talking, it seemed there was no stopping him.

DeWitt stood ashen-faced. He seemed to be having trouble breathing.

Aside, Kichener told Sinclair, "Suggest the major look at his sutler's records and cash on hand. I think he will find amounts unaccounted that will match what this man is saying. It appears some people have gone to extreme lengths to be agents for these new lands."

The captain tipped his head, trying to read past the serene countenance, the cold gray eyes of the man. He saw only certainty and a faint amusement there. "But why, sir?"

Kichener shrugged. "Blood breaks treaties," he said.

Scouts entered the perimeter from the south and a moment later Lieutenant Barnes reported to the major. "Indians, sir. A band of forty or fifty, coming this way. They are painted, and armed, but there are white men with them and they have a cavalry escort."

"An escort?" Grimes turned to Sinclair.

"That would be Lieutenant Spradley and his detail, sir. I . . . ah . . . may have given him some discretion in his orders."

Kichener was at Grimes' side. The major was suddenly aware of the credentials the man carried. "The Kiowa are not at war, major," the gray man said. "There certainly is no reason now," he nodded toward the hide hunters and DeWitt, "to presume otherwise."

In the cool of evening Hawk That Hunts Walking and his party, escorted by the Blackleg men and the First Platoon, made camp on the prairie a mile from the squadron bivouac. From there the soldiers continued across to rejoin their command, and they brought emissaries with them. One was a young war leader named Stalking Horse, who carried a hooked lance. The others were two white men riding tall, saddled mules.

"My name is Curtis, Major," the younger one said. This here is Mr. Edwin Poole. We're partners in the High Plains Freight Company. Stalking Horse there comes from Chief Hawk That Hunts Walking. He's the main chief of the Kana'tenee Kiowa. Stalking Horse says to tell you we brought back your soldiers in the best shape we could, and we'd like to ride along with you to Camp Jacob to make sure there's no trouble about anything. He says he's proud you cleaned up those hide hunters that was tryin' to make war, and he's just as . . . what's a good word . . . he's just as . . . ah . . . pissed about the whole thing as you are. So if it's all right with you we'll ride along, and maybe you can get Mr. Chrisman to set up things in Washington, because that's where Hawk That Hunts Walking plans to go."

Grimes blinked at him, trying to absorb it all. "You keep saying *we*," he said finally.

"Yes, sir. The High Plains Freight Company cut a pretty good deal with the Far Grass People. I'm supposed to be their Indian guide while they're back east, and they're going to trade us hides and tallow for blankets and sugar candy, and let us get the best of the deal most times."

Nearby Ernest Kichener stood in shadows, listening.

235

Interesting, he thought, how coincidence could build upon coincidence when properly manipulated. The old chief wanted to go east. Mercer Poling was in the east. Poling would, of course, go to ground now. Yet, what better stage for a hunt than a visit by a Kiowa chief to the white man's home ground. There were, he decided, many fascinating possibilities.

He would need to send some wires, get some things moving back there. And there must be no obstacles to the old chief's plan. If Hawk That Hunts Walking wanted to go to Washington, then that was what he should do. It could be arranged.

Cold eyes glinted in the dusk. Go to ground, Mercer Poling, he thought. Hide well, because your familiar haunts are about to be invaded. These people are westerners, Poling. The red ones and the white, they are a breed apart . . . a sundown breed, possibly. Still, you've used them in your schemes. Now let's see if you are ready for them.

Or for me, he thought. I'll be there too, Poling.

XXI

Working from can to can't as the long prairie days unfolded, they had floored in the buffalo wallow and laid up a stout foundation of curing magnesia rock on which to build a sturdy house. Now each day the old man worked at his well. With Emmett and Jim to spell him he had managed five feet a day while the woman and the girls hauled up soil in buckets and used it to shore up the foundation of their house.

It was slower now. He had hit rock at twenty feet, and the breaking-out was hard. But the slowness gave the others time to tend to other things.

Emmett had been gone nine days now, off to take the lost soldiers home to Camp Jacob if he could find the place. The woman dried meat in the sun and carried water from the stream, hitching an ox to the found cart to haul the barrels.

Jim and the boy Frank had hunted twice and brought in meat. They had found a bank of good clay not far away, and now they broke sod and gathered the hay while the girls made brick in a sun-pit.

The well should make water. His willow fork had told him. But he would take no chances. When the hole was dug and lined he would rig a spout, then when the house was done he would use its roof to capture such rains as fell.

A man made do with what he had, and the years had taught the old man to waste nothing. The Lord made the land for man to use, the book said, and it seemed to him a good idea to use it frugally and tend it well.

Distantly, from the cool bottom of his hard-dug shaft, he heard running steps. Then Emily's face was at the rim, and she was pointing. "Emmett's yonder, Pa," she said. "Be here after a bit."

Straightening in the hole he rubbed sore back muscles and stabbed the spade into a mound of hammered rubble. It seemed to him the work was going better. The limestone now stood shoulder-high to him, and he was finding a bit of sand where he bored. Stooping, he scrabbled away the refuse at the place he had been working, then got down on his knees to press his mouth against the cool stone right at its base. Bracing himself there he sucked at it, and believed he felt a bit of draw. His tongue told him the stone was moist. He got to his feet. "God's world is a wonder," he said.

Using the pulleyed ropes of the hoist he climbed the sheer side and let himself out of the hole. A brisk breeze whispered across the pale miles of grass and cooled the soaked shirt on his back. He sat for a moment at the edge of his well and pulled a blade of stiff grass to chew on its tender shoot.

Often he thought of the land they had left, those high up hills with their greens and grays of vesture and their little winding flats of bottom land. Those had been good lands for a man who could work their soil. And yet, with the passing of the days, he had come to feel a thing about this prairie. Its sameness might fool a man, he thought, because the sameness that it seemed was never real. Now he had seen its pink mornings and heard its larks in flight. He had tasted of the wind and seen how the sod took water when it rained. He had sunk his spade below the sod and known the scent of richness. He had watched thunderheads walk across it and seen the skirts of sweeping rain that were a world away. He had stood in sunset with the woman, and seen its colors in her eyes.

He had paced off what he needed and set cairns there, then helped the children pace a bit more for when they needed homes. What was beyond the cairns he did not want. But he did enjoy seeing of it all, the miles and endless miles unbounded, and with each day he didn't miss the hills so much.

The wagon still was just a speck, a little east of north. Now he went and got his gun and called Jim in. "I heard turkeys yonder, when the sun came up. Take this and fetch us just a pair. We'll eat while Emmett tells us what he's found."

When he heard the first shot, distant on the wind, the carried fuel for the fire and the woman went to get a sack to use for plucking. She had found greens along the creek and these went into a pot to boil.

The sun was low when Emmett rolled in. They unloaded supplies and there was horehound for the children.

"I found who owns the high-sides and the cart," Emmett said. "They're at Camp Jacob now, and they'll come get them directly. They have mules. They said they'll haul us possibles time to time. Those boomers that moved us on, they're out of business now, and I heard we could go back and take up our claim."

The old man thought about it. "I guess our claim is where we stand," he said. "The soil is good and there'll be water in the well."

Emmett nodded. "There's others. I saw wagons movin' west. I told 'em where we are and there's others that might come. There's land a'plenty."

"Wouldn't mind having neighbors," the woman said.

They sat to supper, and Emmett said the grace. Then they talked.

"There's Indians camped up there," Emmett told them. "Somebody coming from Washington to meet them, then they're going east. A man with the Indians said he'd take word to Willow Ford about us, and if we get neighbors they might make a trade route. He said there'll be trade with the Indians yonder," he pointed southwest, "an' we might want to make a way-stop here. We're most midway between. He was one of them with the high-sides and the cart, but he won't be comin' for 'em. He'll be goin' east for a spell, with the Indians."

"Where did you tell 'em this place was?" the old man

asked. "How'll they know to get here."

"I spanned the way, and marked it on a map. Then I told them about God puttin' stone and poles here to be had and a couple of them laughed but they thought that was fittin'. They wrote the name to the place where I marked the map. I said they should call it Buffalo Wallow, but they done it better." He looked at his father and his eyes were bright with affection. "I told 'em our name, so they called the place Todd's Fort."

Dawn was in the sky when the old man crawled from his blankets and picked up his spade and his hammer and single jack. In the hole the rock had seeped and there was a little pool. He dipped his hands and drank. It was sweet and cold. He cleared away the rubble of his dig and when there was light enough in the hole he set to with hammer and jack and started a deeper cut, leaving a ledge of stone where the seep began. Later they would wall the well with brick.

A pair of horsemen rode the endless plains, hard men with guns at their belts and pack horses in tow. As the days crept by they held to west of south and on the third day they came upon a place where old wagons stood beside a nearly-finished house of white stone and a sod barn was going up.

There was no one in sight as they rode in. Pasco pointed at the oxen grazing loose not far away. "They're the ones," he said. "This is them squatters' place."

Tram glanced at him, his eyes hooded. "This has cost us a week. Was Blue worth it?"

"Blue wasn't worth shootin', you know that. It's just I hate to go off an' leave a thing not done. Blue's gun was fired. The one we saw bleedin' is the one we want."

The walked their horses toward the sod barn, then turned when Tram saw movement at the house. For a moment a girl stood there, staring at them, then she disappeared inside.

"That's the same one Blue was sniffin' after," Tram said.

"The one at Willow Ford."

Jim came from the barn then, and they turned to him. Tram heeled his horse, brought it around so his right side was toward the young squatter. "Look him over, Pasco. Is that the one?"

Pasco nodded. "The very one. I saw him bleedin'."

"Then let's get done. I'm tired of this place." With a movement Jim barely saw he drew his gun and fired. Jim was thrown backward to sprawl beside the barn. Tram raised his gun to fire again, then jerked half-around in his saddle as thunder crashed from the house. Bright blood welled from his shoulder and his gun went flying away.

"There's more here!" Pasco shouted, grabbing Tram's reins. "They got guns!" Dragging the hit gunman with him, hauling reins on the pack horses, he wheeled and spurred his mount to a run.

"I'm hit!" Tram screamed as they headed into the bright grass, away from the place. "Damn you, Pasco! You said they didn't have anything!"

Pasco glanced back at him. "You'll live. It's a scratch. We're done here, anyway."

Behind them Emily ran from the house, dropping the shotgun Emmett had brought from Camp Jacob. As the old man came from the well she ran past him, across the scythed clearing to where Jim lay. His hound dog was there, sniffing at the blood on him, licking his still face. Far off there were shouts and she saw her mother and the children coming from the clay pit. The long rifle stood just inside the barn and she grabbed it up, turned and leveled it at the men now far away, out on the prairie. She sighted through fresh tears, set the trigger and fired. The distant men ducked low and spurred their horses, going away.

Her father was there then, kneeling beside his son, and she went to him. Jim was unconscious, but he was still breathing.

"They were the same men," she told the old man. "Two of them that ran us off before. Like the one that tried to . . . to . . ."

The old man picked up Jim, very gently, and carried him

241

to the house. He laid him on soft bedding and Emily went to get the medicine box.

"The bullet is still in him," the old man said. "We'll need a fire, and that long paring knife."

The woman came in then, and the rest.

"Get down the book," the old man told the woman. "Sit here and hold his head, and you can read to me while I work."

When Emmett came later, up from the creek, Jim was still alive and they were fussing around him. Emmett heard it all from Emily, and he looked and found the gun the man had lost. He put it in his pocket. He saddled a fresh horse and led it to the house. "I'll be gone for a time," he told them. "There's fresh meat hanging on the rack out by the barn, and all the sod out there's been cut for lifting. When neighbors come, tell them of this. Tell them to build strong and watch the prairie."

He swung into his saddle, a big man on a fresh horse, a man with a thing that needed done.

"When you come back we'll be right here," the old man said. "This place is Todd's Fort, and you can tell folks if they need the Todds this is where we'll be."

Emmett turned the horse's head and flicked his reins. Once past the sod field he eased the animal to a steady trot. Even across the endless plains, the two men were long since gone from sight. But he knew their direction. They were going east.

A day out of Camp Jacob tall mules trotted easily, carrying light packs and enjoying the travel. Vince Copple rode the high frame of John Adams, leading Hildegarde who wore a new bell. Madison and Lucifer came next, followed by Bernice, with Edwin T. Poole astride her saddle. Beelzebub and Hamilton wore packs filled with tack and rigging for the wagons. Fanny May, Monroe and Washington carried trail supplies, and Sam and Longhandle carried things the people at the new settlement might need. Behind them were a few horses, tended by Billy Sipe on his roan.

It was in Edwin Poole's mind to take the wagons down to Shade's Well for another load of magnesia rock and cedar posts. Then the High Plains Freight Company once more would head for Sly.

PART IV
The Sundown Breed

XXII

At the little railyard outside Emporia on the Neosho River crowds gathered for each arrival. Most people knew that something unusual was about to happen and wanted to be there when it did. Some drove out from the town, some came in from the farms and ranches of the area, and some just seemed to materialize there as people do when idle curiosity reaches its zenith.

Rumors had been floating for weeks—rumors of a new Indian treaty, rumors of an impending Indian war, rumors of troop movements and of visiting dignitaries, rumors without focus. First there had been the assembling of a special prison train in the yards, five passenger cars and three cars for animals. The windows had been barred, the security tight and the guards—a special unit assigned from Leavenworth—tight-lipped. For a day the train had sat on a siding, then from the west had come a string of enclosed military ambulance wagons rigged with cross-bar caging and bolted gates. The wagons had cavalry escort, hard-faced troopers who rode close and never took their eyes off the wagons, and who cleared the way of onlookers with a hundred-yard perimeter of patrol. The wagons had avoided the cluster of buildings that was the Emporia station. Instead they had driven directly to the prison train where they were emptied one at a time. And there and then, a murder had been committed.

For the first time in more than a year, Randolph Yeats for a time did not regret the choice he had made when he volunteered for a tour in the border lands as a "roving

247

correspondent" for the Chicago *Statesman*. The problem had been, no sooner had he embarked for the western lands where all the big postwar news seemed to be happening, than the news shifted. The West had grown quiet, at least as seen from the civilized peripheries where a man had access to telegraph wires and regular baths.

The furor of Indian troubles that had followed the incident at Sand Creek had trailed off into an indiscernible series of minor confrontations at isolated places, and the anticipated explosion of hostilities in the central plains, the Kiowa heartlands, had been averted by a treaty—a treaty almost a year old now, and which might not last, but still a treaty.

Randolph Yeats had contented himself through the season of his discontent by filing minor reports ranging from the mildly interesting—a train robbery in Missouri, for instance, only the second time in history someone had robbed a railroad train, but still second and not first (that had occurred in Ohio months before)—to absolute trivia like the public readings in Westport of a new English book called *Alice's Adventures in Wonderland*, which had captured the fancies of some of the western folk . . . or like the erratic doings of a handful of refugees from the old Quantrill bunch who now where helping themselves to the contents of banks and stagecoaches.

The focus had shifted back to news on the national scene. The United States had completed the purchase of Alaska from the Tzar. Seven million dollars plus for two seal harbors and an ice pack. Yet it was news and he saw other bylines than his on the stories. President Johnson was besieged by his political enemies, pushing him into a corner over his views on reconstruction. And others were covering it, not Randolph Yeats. The biggest thing Yeats had filed in a year was a series of documentaries on the admittance of Nebraska as a state. He had, at least, managed to be on the scene in Omaha for that event.

Yet now the rumors were floating. Something had occurred to the west. Something was occuring. He had word that James Chrisman, the architect of the temporary treaty with the Kiowa tribes, had left Washington and was on his way west. He had word of a realignment of command out of Leavenworth—something involving a detached squadron of cavalry—and traders coming in from the remote places like Chase Crossing and Willow Ford brought stories of claim disputes and vigilance committees . . . and of Indians traveling with what seemed to be cavalry escort.

He held himself suspicious of the rumors. Strange stories were always coming out of the great plains, and most of them were not to be believed. Yet, when that prison train made up outside Emporia he had been there, and he had heard the shot that killed one of the prisoners being transferred from prison ambulance to armored rail car. From the top of a hill he had watched through a telescope and had seen the man fall, and had caught a glimpse of the man who killed him. He had seen a dark-clad man with a rifle, galloping away on a powerful horse. They had never found the shooter, but a cavalry trooper had let it slip that the dead man's name was Cain DeWitt, and that he was linked with a treason of some kind.

It had been Randolph Yeats' first good story in months.

And now, only a few days later, there was activity again at the Emporia railyard. First a train from the east had arrived, pulling four closed passenger cars in addition to its regular complement, and had departed leaving those four cars locked and silent on a guarded siding. Then another train had brought a cadre of official-looking gentlemen who cloistered themselves in a suite of rooms at the Palace Hotel and avoided conversation, never leaving their rooms except to visit the restaurant, use the telegraph several times each day and—Yeats was pleased to have discovered this—send one of their number twice each day out to the railyards to inspect the four locked coaches waiting there. He began a vigil of both the Palace Hotel and the railyards.

One good story had come from those yards, he told himself. Maybe lightning would strike twice.

It struck at the hotel dining room first. Hovering around the mysterious visitors while they had their supper the second day, he overheard a name. One of them addressed another as "Mr. Chrisman."

Filled now with keen anticipation Yeats waited at the foot of the main stairs, and as they filed past him he asked, "Mr. Chrisman?"

The man turned toward him. He was a distinguished-looking man of early middle years, with mild eyes and an air of worried intensity that belied them. "Yes?"

"Mr. Chrisman, my name is Yeats. Randolph Yeats. Chicago *Statesman*. Sir, are you the James Chrisman who . . . ?"

"I'm sorry, Mr. Yeats." The man shook his head. "I have no statement to make at this time." Then he was gone, up the stairs, his companions glancing at Yeats with expressions ranging from concern to irritation.

"Aha!" Yeats told himself. Then he frowned. What did he have? James Chrisman was in Emporia. That in itself was worth ten lines on the wire and maybe a follow-up society feature by mail. Chrisman was a mildly notable figure in Washington. So now he was out here in the wilderness. Maybe he was sight-seeing. News for the little local paper in Emporia. Trivia for the Chicago paper, and less than that for those big periodicals in the east where Yeats hoped to make a name for himself. Hardly the sort of thing the *Post* or the *Sun* or *Harpers* would even look at. Washington notables were turning up all over the country these days. After all, the war was over. It was time for them to make some points.

Deflated, Randolph Yeats went to his box for his mail and his newspaper. The newspaper had its headlines with their bylines: Napoleon III had withdrawn his support and his troops from Maximilian in Mexico; Garibaldi was threatening to march on Rome; fire had gutted buildings in a six-block section of New York City; somebody named Livingstone was setting out to explore the Dark Continent; there was controversy over a book written by a German Englishman named Marx; Canada had been declared a dominion.

All the headlines came from other places. All the bylines belonged to other reporters. There were no stories at

Emporia.

Maybe, he decided, he should pack it in and go back to Chicago. They were building a meat-packing factory there. Maybe somebody at *Harpers* was just sitting there waiting for a first-rate exposé on how many bricks it took to build a meat-packing factory.

Still, his curiosity nagged at him. Why were four first order passenger cars sitting locked and guarded on a siding out at the railyards? And why did one of the Chrisman party keep going out there to look at them? *Why* was Chrisman at Emporia? What was going on with the Indians?

Indians. Tom McNair had made his niche by reporting on the Cheyennes at Sand Creek. Howard Freeman was doing well with the stories about the Sioux. It had been Yeats' dream to be in at the beginning of the Kiowa story. But there hadn't been a story. Still, when one thought Kiowa these days, one thought Chrisman. And Chrisman most assuredly was right here in Emporia.

It was nearly seven o'clock when the Thursday express, scheduled to arrive between noon and four, chugged and smouldered its way to the plank docks at the railyard. Yeats was there, along with about half the town, to see the arrival.

At first it was a typical arrival. The train, a sturdy engine and six cars, shuddered and screeched to a halt beside the docks. Passengers disgorged from each end of the two passenger cars, and porters and dockmen slid open the doors of the boxcars to begin extraction of their contents. An hour later the boxcars were nearly empty and all the passengers had been taken away to town. Yeats sat on the porch of the little station house, watching blue dusk replace the red of evening in the sky. Almost all of the spectators had gone. Yeats yawned, stood and started to leave, to begin the walk back to town. Then he glanced at a group of men standing nearby and he stopped. Chrisman was there, with his entire party. Quietly they stood and watched as trainmen went about their chores.

Yeats noticed then that the engine had not been steamed

down. In fact, rather than being cooled, he saw firemen stoking its boiler. And as he watched, men came to uncouple the train behind the tender. The engineer vented steam and the engine and tender began to roll. Switches were thrown and the engine entered the loop siding that would bring it around to the switching tracks. Once there, it stopped, was shunted onto a siding and backed up. Yeats squinted. It was almost dark. But then he saw where it was going and heard the clank of contact when it arrived. They had coupled the locked cars on the siding and were bringing them off. Other men came now with tow rigs and began shunting and shifting the regular cars of the Thursday express. Yeats watched, puzzled. This was not regular procedure. They should be waiting until morning to make up the eastbound.

The boxcars—all but one—were shoved onto a holding track, and several livestock cars were pulled into place ahead of—now behind, for eastbound travel—the two regular passenger cars at the docks. Across the yard the engine had pulled far out eastward with its tender and the four mysterious guarded cars. Now with a blast of its whistle it reversed itself and was switched back onto the station rail. Within minutes it had coupled with the regular cars there and the livestock cars behind them, and a guard walked across to speak to the party of men with Chrisman. Yeats stood in deepening shadow and watched as they spoke, then as a group started across the dock toward the train.

His curiosity blazed within him. Rounding the corner of the station house he hurried along to its other end, ran around that corner and peeked out from the east side of the building. All the locks were being opened, lamps were being lit and the secret cars stood open and lighted. As he watched the Chrisman party and several other men climbed aboard the nearest one. Railroad guards stood at careful attention along the dock. Far back, a caboose was being towed into place for coupling.

What was happening? Randolph Yeats raised his hat to scratch his unkempt head. What were they doing? Steam vented then in huge clouds, obscuring the docks, and far back he saw a lamp swinging and heard the distant voice of a trainman. Steam vented again and the engine's wheels shrilled on their rails as they began to turn . . . backward.

Hidden by clouds of steam, wondering what he thought he was doing and doing it all at once, Randolph Yeats dashed across the dock, crouched there and then sprinted to the front of the engine where he swung aboard its wide cow-catcher, huddling atop it in shadows under the engine's dull headlamp. The train picked up speed, and Yeats clung wide-eyed to the heavy steel mesh of the cow-catcher, afraid to move. The track they were on only went two miles, out to a cattle siding on Cottonwood Creek, but he felt he was riding off into the unknown. In near-darkness he watched the ties race by three feet below him and conjured up horrible thoughts of what it would do to him if he should fall, if he should lose his grip . . . if his foot should slip through the mesh and be caught between tie and lip of cow-catcher . . . He closed his eyes tightly and clung for dear life.

The ride seemed to last for hours, but it was only a few minutes. Steam flowed around him, hot and wet, and he felt the lurch as brakes were set and the wheels skidded on the rails, slowing. In a billowing cloud of steam the train shuddered to a stop.

Randolph Yeats climbed from the cowcatcher and stood on rubber legs, waiting for vision to clear. People were debarking from the cars, hurrying toward the rear of the train. He heard the sound of cattle cars opening, chutes being set and ramps dropped, and he heard the sound of many horses milling, hooves a drum-rattle on loading ramps.

It was nearly full dark. Away from the lighted cars the only illumination was hand-carried lamps. Forgetting his caution, wide-eyed with curiosity, Randolph Yeats set his hat and ran to fall in with the last group of men off the coaches, hurrying along behind them toward the rear.

By the light of many lanterns, intense activity was underway back there. He saw trainmen and soldiers loading horses aboard the cattle cars. Soldiers were climbing the cars to walk along their tops, inspecting. There were men of the Chrisman party, mingling with them, and others as well, back from the light . . . he edged toward them, peering in the darkness. Strange silhouettes flowed toward him, and he thought momentarily of images he had seen of Roman centurions, crested helmets on their heads and staffs carried high. And among them were robed men. Senators? What, he asked himself numbly, was going on?

He took another step and jostled against someone, and there was an odor of old leather, woodsmoke and earth. "Pardon me," he said, putting out a hand to steady whomever he had bumped. His hand encountered cool, bare skin on an arm that was hard with whipcord muscle. He raised his head, startled. Wavering lamplight revealed a face right out of nightmare, a painted face with a tall crest of waving dark hair atop it, feathers dangling from the crest.

"*A'asta-oye?*" the face said, and Yeats stumbled backward, then tripped and fell.

A tall man appeared, silhouetted against the sky, and leaned to help him up. "Watch yourself," he said. "Tall Wolf isn't fond of bein' touched."

"Mr. Curtis?" someone called. "Can you get them aboard those four front cars? We need to move out."

"Right away," the tall man responded, then he turned and spoke in a loud, clear voice, in a language Randolph Yeats had never heard, and the phalanx of painted Romans moved forward, striding around and past them, toward the front of the train. Soldiers waited there by the front cars, and stood back to let them board, but the Romans hesitated, stopping a few feet away. To Yeats' right trainmen were loading great pouches and long, unwieldy bundles aboard an open boxcar. The tall man walked away, carrying on a running discourse in the strange, sibilant tongue that somehow sounded distinctly unlike Latin to the reporter. Men in dark coats brushed past him and he tried to stay close to them, going toward the passenger cars.

Ahead a robed figure with long gray hair danced along the line of cars, singing wildly and shaking a rattle. Then he straightened, waved his arms at the railcars and said something threatening to them. With a nod, then, he climbed sedately aboard the third car, followed by the other Roman Senators, then by Centurions.

Yeats' mouth was hanging so far open his jaw began to cramp. He closed it with a snap. The dark-suited men were boarding a car beside him and he turned to follow, but was swept up in a hurrying mass of earth-smelling Centurions and bustled forward. He had no choice in the matter. They were all around him and he found himself climbing steps, being pressed into the interior of a dimly-lighted passenger car, being pushed forward until there was nowhere else to go. To escape he scuttled sideways and fell into a seat. Only then did he look at those around him. The car was packed with dark, painted men who wore feathers and bright quills. Some of them carried feathered spears, some bright-painted shields and most bows and arrows. He gawked, tried to speak and could not. They were Indians! Those near him looked at him solemnly, looked at the seat he sat on, looked at the other seats and obediently sat down, one or two to a seat, their long lances standing at steep angles between floor and ceiling of the car.

With the seats all full there were still Indians standing. The connector gate between cars opened and the tall young man who had helped Yeats to his feet came through. He spoke to the Indians and a number of them went into the next car.

He heard clicks and thuds as trainmen inspected coupler safeties and shot grease into carriages.

A soldier stepped into the car at the far end, spotted Yeats and said, "Tell them to put their lances and bows and things up in the luggage rack. They'll be more comfortable." Then the soldier was gone. Yeats looked at the Indians and the Indians looked at Yeats. Unsteadily he got to his feet, and all the Indians stood with him. He sat again, and they sat. Behind the fierce paint on nearby faces he saw puzzled frowns.

Trying to oblige he reached across and gripped the lance held by a warrior with black lightning bolts on his cheeks.

The warrior abruptly drew a knife and pointed it at him. Yeats released the lance. He pointed upward at the luggage racks. "You can put that up there if you want to," he said. The warrior frowned at him, stood, climbed onto the seat and vaulted from there into the luggage rack, still holding his lance. There was barely room for him. He glared at Yeats.

"No, no!" Yeats corrected, gesturing. "Not you. Just your spear."

With a lithe twist and roll the warrior swung to the floor. Yeats pointed at lance, then at luggage rack, and saw the fierce eyes light. The Indian turned his lance, raised it and laid it gently in the rack. Along the line of seats others thought it over, then did likewise.

Yeats heard the boarding gates close, and a pair of soldiers stepped into the car, counted Indians, then walked through to the next car. A moment later the train began to move. Indians sprang from their seats and crowded along the sides of the car, tapping at the glass windows, muttering among themselves, peering out into the darkness.

Seeing his chance to escape Yeats eased from his seat and started along the aisle. Almost immediately hard hands grabbed him and he was lifted bodily and thrust among braves inspecting a window. A warrior tapped the glass, frowned at him and said, *"Ini 'i-shanis."*

"What?"

"Ini'i-shanis!" the warrior repeated, speaking louder.

"Oh," Yeats gulped. "That's glass. Glass."

"Nglatz," the warrior brightened. Then he tapped the window again and told those around him, "Nglatz."

"Nglatz," Yeats assured them.

For several minutes then as the train picked up speed he was very busy giving them names for the interesting things around them. Suddenly he saw the dim lights of the Emporia railyard sliding by outside and he went pale. "Wait," he tried to shout. "That's my stop. I have to get off!" All the warriors stared at him.

"All my things are at the hotel," he tried to explain. "I can't go anywhere . . . I have to get off."

The train continued to gain speed, and now there was nothing beyond the windows except moonlit countryside. Yeats tried to make a break down the aisle again, and was caught and pulled to one side where a pair of braves with large knives were trying to dismantle an oil lamp in its sconce. Again, he was very busy for a time.

The platform door opened and the tall young man appeared there. He thrust another, smaller man through the opening and nodded at Yeats. "Keep him in here, will you? And keep an eye on him. I don't want him scalped." He closed the door.

The man who had been entrusted to him was small, agile looking and had quick dark eyes in a pale, sharp-featured face. He nodded at Yeats.

Yeats sighed, returned to his seat and indicated the empty seat beside him. "At least," he told the newcomer, "I'll have someone I can talk to."

The newcomer glared at the Indians, then shouldered through them to take the seat by Yeats. He removed his hat and extended a hand. *"Buenas tardes, Señor,"* he said. *"Trinidad Salazar. Como se llama usted?"*

XXIII

The special train thundered through the night, its thick braid of dark smoke silvery under a riding moon, a writhing, dissipating snake with showers of twinkling cinders at its head. Through scattered woodlands and broad fields it rolled, big wheels whining, drive-arms a blur of sustained motion. The Kiowa Special had a clear track, a full head of steam and a schedule to make. James Chrisman wanted to be clear of Kansas and into Missouri where troop garrisons could provide security before anyone knew that the chief of the Kana'tenee was on his way east.

Though intrigued with the situation, Chrisman knew as well as anyone how volatile and sensitive it was. For the duration of the trip fifty-six respected members of the Kiowa nation were his responsibility and his alone. One mishap, one slightest incident, and all the treaties with all the Kiowa tribes could collapse. He shuddered as he recalled the elegant, formidable mounted warriors who had displayed their skills at the treaty conference at Willow Ford. To invite war with such people would be insane.

And yet, there were those who wanted just that. Even some of official Washington's eminent denizens had been heard to repeat the old Texas adage, "the only good Indian is a dead Indian," and he had seen their hard eyes glow with greed.

Regarding the Great Plains there was a recognizable "clear land" faction in Washington, and it did not lack in power. Quite a few members of Congress were Manifest Destiny men, who believed that the purpose of their constituents was to spread ever westward, to conquer the continent, and there was simply no place in such a plan for the Indians.

They had support, those Congressmen, Chrisman had seen the web of power woven by men like Mercer Poling, Thomas Gathett and others, and while he recognized their private motives he was powerless to do more than argue reason. Gathett wanted rail claims for his backers, huge spreads of land that could be surveyed and sold to enhance the spread of progress. Poling, less controversial than Gathett but always behind the scenes in every Washington circle—always whispering, always manipulating—wanted nothing less than to be named commissioner and agent for all the unsettled lands from the Smoky Hill and Neosho to the foothills of the Rockies. To get that, though, he would have to clear the land of both treaties and hostiles. In short, Chrisman felt, an Indian war was a priority item on Poling's agenda. An all-out war which the Indians ultimately must lose, no matter what the cost.

"I am still surprised that the president agreed to this," he told those in the car with him as wooded hills flew past outside his window. "I was certain he would not. But someone apparently has done some arranging. Then again, the president is under a great deal of fire at the moment—from some pretty strong enemies—and he may see a state visit by a Kiowa chief as a means of diverting media attention. Whatever the reason, though, Hawk That Hunts Walking at this moment is a foreign head of state in transit on United States soil, and it is our task to see that nothing goes wrong."

L. W. Holmes chewed on his cold cigar and blinked tired, near-sighted eyes. "I share your hope for a long-term solution that doesn't involve bloodshed," he told the Commissioner. "But I don't understand why the old chief had to be declared a head of state of a foreign government. As I see it, that makes for a precarious situation. Wouldn't it have been better simply to dress a few of them in civilized clothing and bring them east quietly? They could have their chat with the president and then we could take them back home. This way, well, it's risky, James."

"Highest visibility for the event," Chrisman said, quoting. "Those are our instructions. Granted, the whole thing could come off as a farce. Or, far worse, something could happen . . . one of the Indians could be hurt, for instance. Or worse, one of them could hurt someone. Disaster. Instant disaster! But the other side of it is Hawk That Hunts Walking and what he wants. He says he doesn't care what kind of clothes he wears, and the other chiefs don't either. But he insists on his . . . ah . . . Blackleg men as a sort of honor guard and there's no way under the sun we can get them to comb their hair down and put on business suits. It's against their religion, or something."

"It would humiliate them," the man sitting in the corner said. "It would be like not wearing the appropriate paint or not carrying their weapons. Take my word for it. I know." Unlike the other men in the rear passenger car, John Miles—Sha'ata'ee to his adopted people, the Three Rivers Kiowa—did not wear a broadcloth suit. Instead, he was dressed in comfortable buckskins and high moccasins with brilliant beadwork. His gray hair was shoulder-length and he wore a beaded headband. He had a devoted Kiowa wife whose name meant Blue Flower and, at last count, four sturdy bronze children with blue eyes.

"A lifetime ago," he said, "I knew everything there was to know about the plains tribes. I even served as guest lecturer on the subject at the United States Military Academy and at a half-dozen universities. It was all so simple. They were interesting primitives best viewed from a distance. Then I got to know them and learned that I had never known about them at all."

He glanced aside at Darby Curtis, and Darby saw the old pain in his eyes. A long time ago, John Miles had turned up at the Curtis place, a desolate young widower wandering the plains looking for a decent way to die. Chance Curtis had taken him in, brow-beat him into taking stock of himself, then had set him up as a consignee to trade with the Kiowa. A few years after that Miles had vanished, only to turn up a long time later as a member of

Chief Cloud's tribe.

"Mr. Miles is right," Darby said. "A lot of Kiowa wouldn't mind, but there is no way a Blackleg warrior would ever show up in public wearing a business suit. He'd rather show up naked."

"Showing up naked wouldn't bother them very much," Miles added, "as long as their hair was done up and they had the proper paint for the occasion. And their ceremonial weapons."

"Which ones are the ceremonial weapons?" Holmes inquired.

Darby shrugged. "All of them."

"The Blackleg men are mystics," Miles explained. "Everything they do, every move they make, has significance to them. All of the tribes have warrior societies, of course, but most of the societies are pretty pragmatic about their ceremonies and their rituals. I'd say the average Horse Clan member, for instance, is about as strong in his beliefs as the average Anglican. . . . forgive me, Mr. Holmes, but . . ."

"Point taken," Holmes said, "Devout is a state of mind, not a natural condition."

"Thank you. At any rate, the Blackleg men of the Far Grass People are one of the most respected groups among the Kiowa. But they aren't like the other groups."

"They're spooky," Darby said, frowning as he glanced toward the far end of the car. Three feathered warriors were back there. Two of them gazed out a window. The third, though, squatted in the middle of the aisle between seats, staring at the floor. Somehow, he had pried the cover off a swamping drain. Now he was watching the rail ties flit past beneath the car.

Distantly, the wail of the engine's whistle drifted back, then the song of the rails changed pitch and there was a staccato vibration in the car. With a cry Stalking Horse jumped up from beside the swamping drain and grabbed his hook lance. John Miles looked out the window. "We're crossing a gorge," he said. "If these people have never seen a railroad train before, it's a safe bet they've never seen a trestle."

In Kiowa Darby told the Indians, "The iron horse is not flying. The rails go over the top of a canyon. Tree trunks hold them up."

Stalking Horse glared at him, responded in clipped, angry tones and returned to his crouch. Darby grinned and John Miles smiled and shook his head. "Stalking Horse feels," he explained to the others, "that this is a stupid way to run a railroad."

Chrisman looked at Darby. "I have noticed, from the time we assembled at Cottonwood Creek, that these three warriors have stayed very close to you."

Darby nodded, frowning. "They're my escort. I made a deal with Hawk That Hunts Walking, and they're keeping tabs on me to make sure I don't back out."

"Mr. Curtis is their medicine," Miles added. "Oh, believe me, gentlemen, they are quite serious. Mr. Curtis told me on the way from Camp Jacob how that one, Stalking Horse, had a vision, and Mr. Curtis is part of it. He is extremely valuable to them, at least until Hawk That Hunts Walking meets with the Great Father."

"They're my bodyguard," Darby said. "Stalking Horse told me himself, they'll kill me before they'll let anything happen to me."

The boarding door banged open and a soldier stuck his head in. He nodded at Chrisman. "Excuse me, sir, but we need an interpreter. Fast."

They were on their feet. "What happened?"

"I'm not sure, sir. One of the redskins got out of his car and climbed up on top. I guess the cinders from the engine set his feathers on fire. Now a bunch of 'em have three of our men prisoner in the second car. Hurry, sir. Please!"

Darby was already on the platform, striding across to the car ahead, Stalking Horse and his assistants right behind him.

Most of Lieutenant Spradley's platoon members were in the next car. They crowded aside as Curtis and his Indians raced through, followed by the commission party. The car beyond was occupied by railroad security men, trainmen and Spradley and his sergeants, Hanlon and the injured Foley. "Two cars ahead," Spradley said.

In the next car Hawk That Hunts Walking, his subchiefs Broken Bow and Dog That Runs With Horses and the old medicine man Keeps His Horses sat stolidly, accompanied by a half dozen select members of the Real Dog Society and three soldiers. The car beyond contained pandemonium.

Spradley was just behind Darby Curtis as they jumped to the platform. The door there hung open and a solid mass of savages had three troopers backed against the left wall, threatening them with lances and clubs.

"You men!" Spradley shouted. "What is this all about?"

Jakey Bloom turned, came away from the wall and then sagged against it again as a needle-pointed lance prodded his belt buckle. "It's nothing, sir. Not really. One of these redskins came whoopin' in here with his head on fire and Mulcahey here . . . well, sir, he extinguished him. That's all."

In Kiowa Darby asked, raising his voice to be heard, "Why do the Blackleg men threaten these blue soldiers who only tried to help one of your own?"

Behind him Stalking Horse pulled a burly warrior aside to ask, "What has Gall Stick done to his hair?"

"The Blue Soldier attacked Gall Stick with a blanket," a warrior snapped at Darby.

"Just how did you extinguish him, Mulcahey?" Spradley demanded.

"The Iron Horse breathed fire on Gall Stick," the warrior told Stalking Horse. "Then a soldier made smoke with him."

"I dropped a blanket over him, sir," Mulcahey admitted.

"Blackleg men!" Stalking Horse thundered. "Stand back and do not hurt the soldiers!"

Darby pushed forward toward the soldiers and a turning lance point caught in his coat. He reached up to wrest it free. More Indians had rushed in from the car ahead, and now several of them were jostled aside as Trinidad Salazar burst through, drawing his revolver. *"Viva Aragon!"* he shouted. His first shot thundered in the car and punched a hole in the roof. A soldier grabbed his gun, wrested it away from him.

The shock of the gunshot in the enclosed car brought a moment of stunned silence. It was reinforced when Private Mulcahey, lowering Salazar's recocked Colt, touched the trigger and shot out a window across the car.

Cool air rushed in and some of the warriors turned to the window in admiration. One of the new arrivals pointed. "Nglatz," he said proudly.

Behind Darby L. W. Holmes muttered, "Merciful God!" and James Chrisman shook his head. "I don't know if this is going to work."

Slowly, with many growls and mutterings, the combatants drew apart. Trini Salazar scowled at the soldier, retrieved his gun, dropped it into his holster and strutted back and forth glaring at the Indians. *"Moros,"* he proclaimed. *"Indios Moros! No son razonables. No tienen discreción."*

A small, rumped man with a battered hat caught Darby's eye. "I'm sorry, sir. I tried to contain your friend, but I don't speak his language."

Chrisman and Holmes stared at the newcomer. "Don't I know you?" Chrisman asked.

"Isn't he with you?" Darby asked Chrisman.

The man removed his hat. "Randolph Yeats, gentlemen. Chicago *Statesman.* I suppose you'll want me to continue with you now."

For the most part, James Chrisman's connections had paid off well. The Kiowa Special passed station after station, into the night hours, without note or interruption. All along the line schedules were altered, signals reset and the special train had clear track. Even entering the valley of the Marais des Cygnes, with its heavy wartime rail networks, the train sped on uninterrupted. The first stop was at nearly eleven o'clock at a siding three miles from Osawatomie, to restack the tender with fuel and take on water for the boilers. From Cedar Ridge to the Fairview trestle, lamps waved at intervals and the big, grim man called Shoaf turned each time to Chrisman and nodded. The train eased in to the Osawatomie siding and dim lanterns revealed lines of infantry along both sides of the roadbed, rifles ready. Darby Curtis and John Miles had instructed all the Kiowa about this, and the lamps aboard the cars were extinguished.

If any trooper or train tender at the Osawatomie yards saw anything unusual about the special train that stopped for water and fuel that night, they could never be sure what they saw.

The stop went without incident, and within thirty minutes the train was rolling again, running through the shadowed hill lands of eastern Kansas, angled north toward the main lines connecting these lands to Westport and the east.

Yet behind, a bespectacled man rode a tired horse up the silent, moonlit street of Osawatomie. He dismounted in shadows beside the telegraph office and used a crowbar to break the padlock there. Inside he flipped two switches, then sat in darkness before the telegraph key and clicked a code. Several minutes passed. Then the bug clicked back at him. He listened until it stopped, then began sending his message.

At an unnamed place where the rail curved around the base of a bluff nine large, rough-clothed men labored by moonlight, piling a barricade of logs across the rails, wedging others endwise just above the ties where they could dismantle a cow catcher and derail an undercarriage.

Another man with a broad slouch hat and the hard, intense eyes of a marmot watched them as they worked, then signaled them in. "Good enough," he told them. "They'll stop for that. Oh, yes, they'll stop. Five of you up there by the bluff, now. Three down there in the draw. Oh, yes, yes, that will be so good. And you, you go along now, yes, and you wait back there where the bend starts, and when you see their lamp you set your flare. Yes. Oh, yes. The rest of you . . . once they stop I need a little time. Just a very little time, indeed. You will provide me that, won't you? Yes. Ah, indeed, yes."

Watching them move away he smiled . . . a cold, simpering smile, a smile that was not sane. But then, no one in these hills had ever claimed that Willy Tomm was sane. Most wanted no part of him, ever. But there were one or two—had always been one or two—who recognized a value to Willy Tomm and were willing to pay for that value. It was said that Willy Tomm was unnatural. It was said he could see in the dark, and could find a target any time, any place in the dark, and use his knife and be gone before anyone knew what had happened.

What they did not know, because Willy Tomm did not choose to tell them, was how much he knew about those who knew of him and sometimes paid him. He was a methodical man, a very thorough man, and it was his pleasure to know exactly who had hired him, and at whose orders, and who was connected with whom. It pleased him to know a great deal more about those who paid him than they would ever have believed a sane man might suspect. But then, no one ever claimed that Willy Tomm was sane.

Far away down a winding valley where moonlight glistened on intermittent fields among the shadowed woodlands there was a speck of light, moving. He smiled, visualizing the train. Engine, tender, six passenger coaches, a boxcar, two or three stock trucks and a caboose. The redskin chief would not be in the first passenger car, nor in the last one. And he would be forward of the soldiers . . . one car? Two? It wouldn't matter. It wouldn't take Willy Tomm very long to find him.

XXIV

From his tender the fireman saw the flare ahead and shouted to the engineer. The engineer leaned from his cab, then jammed his valve throttle to vent the head of steam in the big boilers ahead of him. "Hang on!" he shouted, and thrust the brake lever home.

At his shout the burly railroad guard riding deadhead in the cab grasped a handrail, braced his feet and drew his gun. Drive pistons slammed down, braking lugs locked and the big drive-wheels crashed and groaned. Driven by the dead weight of its haul, the engine shrilled as it skidded along the polished rails. In an instant it was past the flare and curving around a bend below a bluff, losing speed but still moving.

It took nearly a quarter of a mile of track to bring the train to a creep, and the guard hung from the cab's right side portal, his gun high and ready. "Go on," he told the engineer. "Ease her forward, but stay in your beam." Ahead there was a dark mass on the tracks. Light from the feeble headlamp found it. It was a barricade of logs. The engineer lit his lever again and the train shuddered to a stop, ten yards short of the engine-killer.

Below the bluff a gun roared, and the train guard ducked as a bullet whined through the open cab. He dodged behind sheet-iron cowl and the engineer hit the deck behind him. Another shot, and lead whanged and whined from the cowl. The guard snapped a shot at the flash and ducked again. Along the bluff and from brush to the left other guns opened up.

Glass shattered in the first car where Randolph Yeats lay spreadeagled on the floor, covered by a tangle of sprawled and chattering Indians. The halt had been abrupt, and most of them had been on their feet at the time, threatening him because of something the Spaniard had done. Now by dim lamplight he saw some of them crouching, standing, peering out into darkness. He heard shots and saw a warrior stagger, his hands going to his face. "Get down!" he shouted, struggling to get up. "You stupid Indians! Get down!"

Most of them had dropped to the shelter of the walls, but one—the one with blood running from his face, still stood, wavering. There was a scuffle and Trinidad Salazar shouted, *"Moro! Cuidado!"* Then with a long, flying tackle he drove the Indian to the floor and held him there. He drew his gun, chattering in his excitement, trying to see all the windows at once. He saw a flash beyond a shattered window and raised to pump three quick shots toward it, the revolver thundering in the enclosed car.

In the second car John Miles unwrapped himself from a standing bar and waved an eloquent hand in a quick double arc and a slash to the side. "Blackleg men! Stay low! The fight belongs to the soldiers!" Obediently, they crouched low and Miles scurried through the car, rising only to extinguish the sconced lamps.

Rail security men had already darkened the third car where Real Dog men crouched in a ring around the chiefs, lances and clubs at ready, listening to the return fire from cars behind, the slamming of platform gates, the drumming of boots along the gravel bed outside as soldiers ran to flank the train, railroad guards to defend the doors.

They were well-drilled, James Chrisman noted, crouching behind a seat in the darkened sixth car. Lieutenant Spradley's commands were quick, crisp and unnecessary. The railroad men were at their stations almost before the train had stopped.

And then there was silence outside . . . here and there a voice raised in query, and silence.

"They've gone," someone said. "Whoever they were,

they've gone."

"Spread and inspect!" Lieutenant Spradley barked. "You men, stand guard at each platform. You two, forward to the engine. Sergeant, take four and check the stock cars."

Following a flurry of inspection in the dark sixth car Darby Curtis found his rifle. He ran out to the platform and jumped from there to the ground. Soldiers there glanced at him, then turned back to the darkness beyond. Crouching, glancing toward the too-near brush that had held gunmen moments before, he ran forward, skirting around soldiers and train guards. At each of the three forward cars he stopped, found an open sash and called urgently, "People of the Kana'tenee! Stay out of sight! Stay inside!"

At the tender he stopped, scanning the moon-shadowed brush beside the roadbed, then turned and cursed. He had forgotten his bodyguards. Stalking Horse, White Hand and the dour Sunshine were right behind him, a half-circle of lethal Kiowa Blacklegs guarding him with drawn bows.

"Stalking Horse," he snapped in Kiowa, "Let the Blackleg men put down their arrows. The enemy have gone." And what the hell, he muttered to himself in English, are you doing out here anyway? It was a silly question.

Pushing past them he stalked back toward the rearward cars. Men were lighting lamps now ahead and behind, preparing to inspect the train. What was that all about? he wondered. He felt he was missing something. Whatever had happened, it didn't seem to make sense.

A bulk in the darkness, coming toward him, became the head of security, Hank Shoaf. The man paused, squinting in the darkness. "What did you see, Curtis?"

"Nothing," he admitted.

"Get those Indians back on the train." Shoaf moved on, forward.

Darby passed the third car, glanced that way, then stopped again. The platform was dark and silent, the guard there still, and something was not right. Darby motioned his escort to stand where they were, then he stepped to the

269

platform and swung aboard. The guard's head hung at an angle, and the darkness down his coat front was shiny and wet. He was not standing. His throat had been cut, and he was hanging by his collar from a lamp stanchion. Even as Darby recognized what he was seeing a shadow appeared in the car's platform gate. Beyond the gate, in the interior of the car, was a faint rustling and muttering of Kiowa.

Darby glanced at the man in the door. "Give me a hand here," he began, then whirled aside as instincts quicker than sight told him there was something wrong. The shadow flowed into sudden motion and Darby saw a glint as a blade whisked past his face. He reached to catch the arm but there was no arm there. The man somehow was almost impossible to see in the shadows, the faint moonlight. He had ducked, and now came upright and Darby turned, feeling hot pain as a razor edge sliced through his coatsleeve, finding the flesh below. He kicked, felt his boot glance from turning muscle, and his foot slipped in the blood on the platform. He went down, grabbing a handrail as he fell. Again he saw the knife, stabbing past his ear, slitting the brim of his hat. He rolled, tried to kick again, but the shadow had turned in a swirl of dark coattails and was gone, off the platform. He heard catlike steps in the gravel, then an instant of silence followed by a thud and the clatter of a knife dropped against a rail.

He got to his feet, slipped again, then swung down from the platform. Though it was dark, he knew he was covered with blood and a little of it, at least, was his. Past the shadow of the canopy dark, feather-crested shapes waited. Moonlight glinted on the muffled mule bell decorating the shield of Stalking Horse. The other two dangled a silent, long-coated man between them.

"Sunshine hit this man," Stalking Horse explained casually.

There were voices inside the darkened third car now, angry Kiowa voices that rose in pitch as faint light appeared in windows. A lamp had been hit.

Carrying a lantern dimmed to no more than a blue glow, John Miles appeared at the car door and paused for a moment to look at the dead guard hanging there, the blood on the flooring. Then he swung down and crouched to study the face of the moaning, sagging man Sunshine and White Hand held.

"An assassin," he told Darby. Then he rose and spoke softly in Kiowa. Two of the Real Dog men appeared on the platform. Miles looked thoughtfully toward the rear of the train. There were soldiers back there, inspecting the horses in their stock cars. "Give the man to us," he told Darby's three Blacklegs. "You can see if O'gatedota is wounded."

Darby realized when he said it that he was sagging, cradling his arm, and that he had lost his rifle somewhere. Sounds were returning, and here and there dim light. Fifty yards forward, men had begun clearing away the barricade. As his Blacklegs gathered around him, inspecting him as they would a piece of meat, he saw John Miles and a pair of the Real Dog men walking away toward the rear of the train, the warriors carrying a sagging man between them.

In the third car, in a pool of blood, the sub-chief Dog That Runs With Horses lay dead, still wrapped in his favorite blanket. His throat had been cut the entire span of his jawline and he had died in silence, the spasmed hissing of his lungs lost in the turmoil of gunfire in that moment when men had fired upon the train.

Dim lamps were lit again, and Chrisman and Holmes went with Lieutenant Spradley to look at the dead Kiowa. With Hank Shoaf and two of his men they had gone through the car methodically, much aware of the inscrutable eyes of armed Real Dog men following them, of the cold silence of Hawk That Hunts Walking and Broken Bow ignoring them, of the venom in the ancient eyes of Keeps His Horses as he muttered and shook his rattle over the dead chief.

"In the dark," Shoaf told Chrisman, nodding at the Indians, "a man might have mistaken that one for the chief there. They both have white hair."

The Kiowa tolerated them for a few minutes, then Hawk That Hunts Walking said something and the four warriors around him lifted their lances and made it very clear that

271

the white men were to leave the car.

Now, assembled in the open-sashed sixth coach, they could hear distantly the eerie, crying song of the Real Dog men in the closed third car, and the more subdued chanting of Blackleg men in the first and second cars. A chief had begun his journey to the great hunting ground, and the men of the Far Grass People huddled in railroad cars ten miles west of the reconstructed state of Missouri to congratulate him and sing him on his way.

Most of the blood now drying on the cast-off clothes of Darby Curtis had come from the throat-cut train guard. Darby had a shallow knife cut on his temple and a deeper one in his left forearm. That one had bled freely, but the cut was clean. He gritted his teeth and tears flowed down his crusted cheeks as Sergeant Ben Foley poured rum into the cut then methodically stitched it shut with a needle and gut from the platoon's supplies.

"I seen a lot worse than this," Foley remarked as he tied off the gut and snipped it. He measured sacking for a bandage. " 'Course, if you wind up losin' that arm, then you can say I underestimated the situation."

"There isn't any doubt this was a planned assassination," L. W. Holmes told James Chrisman. "The whole thing was staged to put that murderer on the train."

"I think Shoaf is right," Chrisman agreed. "He was after Hawk That Hunts Walking. He made a mistake."

"Well, mistake or not, we have real trouble now. We promised those people a safe passage. Now one of them is dead, and at least one of those Blacklegs up there is injured. They won't even let us in to see how bad he is."

"That reporter locked in there with them said the Spaniard was patching him up. He should be all right. He said the Spaniard saved the Indian's life."

Darby looked up, blinking. It was the first he had heard of that. "You mean Trini?"

"What the man said. They haven't let us in to see."

"I'm keeping my guard posted along those cars," Spradley said. "Mr. Shoaf said we should be able to roll again in less than an hour."

Holmes rubbed the stubble of beard beneath his sideburns. "James, you don't think those Indians will blame us, do you? I mean, surely they can see we're doing all we can to protect them."

"Don't ever expect Kiowas to think the way you think, Mr. Holmes," Darby Curtis offered. "I don't know what they'll make of this. Like these three here . . ." he turned toward the rear of the car. Sunshine and White Hand regarded him solemnly. ". . . these three . . ." he turned back, squinted at Spradley. "Where is Stalking Horse? I thought he was here."

"Why, I don't know." They all turned to look. There were only two Indians in the car with them.

"If only we could have shown them the enemy," Holmes went on, undaunted. "If we could have captured a few . . . even killed one or two, we could show them we are trying to protect them. As it is . . ."

Darby cocked an eyebrow. "But we did. Where is the man we caught? He can probably tell you all about it."

They looked at him, blankly.

"The one who cut me," Darby explained. "The Blacklegs got him. Sunshine there whopped him, but he was alive. Mr. Miles and a pair of the Real Dogs took him to give him to the . . ." he glanced sharply at Spradley then. "Don't your men have him, Lieutenant?"

Spradley shook his head. Darby stared at him, suddenly going pale. Then he stood, pulled on his fresh shirt and said, "Come on!"

On the gravel roadbed, as they piled out of the car behind him, he paused, listening. From forward, the wailing of the Real Dog men and the chanting of Blacklegs continued. He turned toward the rear. "Hush," he told those with him. "Listen."

Somewhere there was a discordant sound, like a sheep bleating in terror. As they listened the bleating rose suddenly to a muted scream, quickly cut off. As one, they ran.

The car behind the sixth coach was a closed boxcar. Its lock hung open. Darby skidded to a stop beside it and pressed his ear to the door. Then, cradling his rifle in his injured arm he reached up and rolled the door open. Light from lamps flooded the trackside, and curious faces looked out at him. Beside him Chrisman gasped and L. W. Holmes began to gag, turning quickly away.

The baggage had been pushed back to either end of the car, packed teepees and parfleches, traveling gear of the Kana'tenee piled high at one end, trunks and bales of army gear at the other. In the clear center, spatters of bright blood flecked the far wall, red echoes of the welter of blood on the floor.

What lay there had once been a man. Now it was nothing more than shreds of bleeding flesh and exposed pink bone. Parts of it were missing. A pair of Real Dog warriors squatted there holding honed knives that dripped red. Beyond them John Miles and the painted Stalking Horse stood solemnly, side by side.

"We have learned quite a lot," John Miles told those who stared horrified through the open door. "I think he told me everything he knew. His name, to begin, was Willy Tomm. He was employed to kill Hawk That Hunts Walking."

Holmes had staggered away in the brush and was being sick. Chrisman tried to speak and made only gagging sounds. Spradley shook his head. "My God," he muttered. Darby glanced at Hank Shoaf. The big security boss had his mouth open, and his face was gray with shock.

"I should have known," Darby shook his head. "Lordy, but those Real Dogs are thorough."

The disassembled thing lying on the bloody floor twitched and made a sound. John Miles glanced at Stalking Horse. "We have finished," he said in Kiowa.

Stalking Horse raised his crooked lance. Its point, descending, was bright in the lamplight. When he raised it again it was brilliant red.

James Chrisman tore his eyes from the sight to stare at John Miles. In a voice like paper crumpling he said, "Mr. Miles, how could you . . . how could . . ."

Miles shrugged, his blue eyes mild above his gray beard. "Remember, Mr. Chrisman, I am one of these people. I have been for ten years."

274

XXV

Morning sun stood on Missouri Hills. The Kiowa Special shunted slowly back and forth on double sidings at a garrison compound outside Cutter's Haven, dropping cars, coupling others, reassembling itself for the long trip eastward. In a dew-covered field a quarter mile from the tracks Indian ponies grazed alongside cavalry remounts, and nearly a hundred men gathered around a little cluster of tents where army chuckwagons grouped and army cooks tended their fires.

From here eastward, the journey of the Kana'tenee would be no secret. Even now at Cutter's Haven, a few miles away, L. W. Holmes was monopolizing the telegraph while Randolph Yeats of the Chicago *Statesman* impatiently waited his turn and bided his time by sharing tidbits of news with a pair of rival reporters who would have to await their turn to file, after him.

In the guarded field outside of town red men and white men had their breakfast and watched their train reassembling itself in the distance.

"Who is Poling?" Hawk That Hunts Walking sipped bemusedly at hot coffee and watched old Keeps His Horses trying to use a fork to eat a fried egg. The medicine man was making it clear that he approved of neither the implement nor the egg.

"He is the man who tried to make the soldiers break their treaty with Cloud and the other chiefs," John Miles told him. "He is a man who would like to see the Kiowa go to war."

"He is the same man who pulled Stalking Horse's hair at Willow Ford," Darby Curtis added, then was sorry he had.

He glanced around at Stalking Horse and saw sudden recognition in the warrior's eyes—recognition and a flat, hard hatred that made him shiver.

"He is the one who sent the ghost man to kill Dog That Runs With Horses?"

Miles shrugged. "Before he died the ghost man said a man named Fenley sent him. He also said that man Fenley is as a brother to another man named Winter who . . ." he paused. There was no Kiowa equivalent of "works for." ". . . who does what Mercer Poling says for him to do."

"Why did the ghost man kill Dog That Runs With Horses?" The old chief's expression revealed nothing, but Darby thought his eyes were moist.

"The ghost man thought Dog That Runs With Horses was Hawk That Hunts Walking," Miles told him. "He never knew he had made a mistake."

Hawk That Hunts Walking sipped his coffee. He understood very well. In war it was normal for warriors to try to kill the chiefs of their enemies. What he did not quite understand was who his enemies were.

"If all the tribes of the white men live together as brothers," he asked, "then how can one tribe be at war with the Kana'tenee and the others not? If the Kana'tenee paint for war against another people and the Three Rivers People do not, then the Kana'tenee do not go among the Three Rivers people until the war is done because it is not their war. Among the white people, how can we tell which are at war with us and which are not?"

John Miles thought about the question, then translated it for James Chrisman. Chrisman thought for a time in silence. "Tell Hawk That Hunts Walking," he said finally, "that the white men have many different kinds of war. Some are fought by our soldiers—our warriors—others by men like Poling who wear no paint and go like weasels in the night to hurt their enemies, and then send others to fight for them when their enemies strike back. Tell him the Great Father knows there are such men among his children, but they are very hard to stop because some of them stay hidden and others are in very high places."

Miles nodded, liking the answer. He repeated it to the old chief and Chrisman wondered how a statement like that would fare for him in Washington. Probably end his career, he thought, bleakly. And yet, he found it difficult not to be totally candid with these Indians. Not for the first time, he wondered whose side he was really on.

"The iron horse grows longer," Stalking Horse observed, watching the train taking on cars in the distance.

"More cars for soldiers," Darby told him. "From here the chief will have many soldiers to escort him." He stood, stretching long legs, and winced as he tried to straighten his left arm. The assassin's cut had gone deep into the muscle, and Ben Foley's stitching had been merciless. Stalking Horse stood beside him, eyeing him curiously. White Hand and Sunshine were close by. Since the day they had left the hidden canyon he had not been out of the sight of these three Blacklegs. He was becoming very tired of it.

"O'gatedota's heart is sad," Stalking Horse said. "Yet he is among brothers."

Darby looked to the west. Two hundred miles away, and becoming farther by the day, was Willow Ford and Melissa Muldoon. And somewhere beyond, maybe another hundred miles, a dozen tall mules were by now hauling trade goods toward some distant settlement.

"I don't want to go east," he told the Indian. "You don't need me any more. The soldiers and Chrisman will take good care of Hawk That Hunts Walking. You have John Miles—Sha'ata'ee—to speak for you. There is nothing I can do. Let me go, now, Stalking Horse. I do not like the east."

For the first time, there was something like sympathy in the dark eyes of the warrior. "I have never seen the east, O'gatedota. Is it so bad? This place here," he waved his lance, indicating the quiet Missouri hills, "has too many trees and too many shadows. The sky is small here. The land stands on edge and is not friendly. Yet men live here. Is the east so much worse than this?"

Vaguely Darby realized the others had stopped talking and were listening. John Miles murmured translations to

277

Chrisman and he heard him add, ". . . young fellow is more Kiowa than me, I think."

"I saw the east at war," Darby looked to the west, sadly. "I saw Antietam and . . . and other places Stalking Horse has never heard about. I saw Richmond. I do not want to see those places again. I think the east is always at war."

Stalking Horse considered it. "O'gatedota has seen ghosts," he decided.

Trini Salazar came from the chuckwagons, followed by a large warrior named Lizard who had a plaster on his face. Lizard was of the opinion that Trini had saved his life, and he had adopted the Spaniard. Both of them carried portions of cooked meat and beans. Trini chose a place to sit, near Darby. He pointed at the ground and glanced at Lizard. *"Sientate, Moro!"* Lizard obediently squatted on his heels and Trini sat beside him.

"Where there are too many men with bad hearts there are too many ghosts," Darby told Stalking Horse. "I have seen the Great Father's city of Washington. I do not want to see it again."

Hawk That Hunts Walking gazed at him over the rim of his coffee mug and John Miles whispered a translation to Chrisman.

"This man speaks as though he were a prisoner," Chrisman said. "I don't see why they insist he go with them, if he doesn't want to."

Miles translated for Hawk That Hunts Walking. The old chief set down his coffee, got to his feet and pulled his blanket around him against a chill that he alone felt. He moved to stand in front of Darby Curtis, and the three Blacklegs stepped back, respectfully.

"O'gatedota has made a bargain with Hawk That Hunts Walking." The old man's voice was reeds in the wind, but his eyes were clear and steady. "The Blackleg men have had a vision. In that vision the hope of the Kana'tenee—of all the Kiowa people—lies in the east where Hawk That Hunts Walking may find the Great Father. I think it is a small hope. I think the Great Father is only a man, as we are only men. Yet, I think the children of the Kana'tenee may live at peace a few more seasons by this hope."

Darby lowered his head and shrugged. "I have made a bargain, Respected One. Yet you have others who can help you more." He indicated Chrisman and Miles, and winced again. He kept forgetting about his sore arm. "Chrisman's home is in the east. He knows the land. Sha'ata'ee came from the east. He knows the pathways there. I only know the ghosts."

The old face tipped, and webwork lines deepened around the clear, dark eyes. "You will see better than they, O'gatedota, as one sees better among the enemy than in his own village. Your eyes will be sharp because you will not be at home. Keep your bargain, Wild One who was named by Bird, and the Kana'tenee will keep theirs."

James Chrisman sipped his army coffee and found himself wondering about the tall, explosive-seeming young man the Kiowa had chosen as their escort. Antietam, he had said. And Richmond. He had seen war. Idly, the commissioner wondered which side of it Darby Curtis had been on. He decided not to ask.

There was activity at the compound gate nearby, and a corporal of infantry came at a trot, carrying a packet. Stepping warily around the savages, his eyes wide, he delivered it to Chrisman then beat a hasty retreat.

Hawk That Hunts Walking had returned to his seat on a field stool, and to his coffee. It was his fourth cup, by Chrisman's count, and the commissioner made a mental note to have someone instruct the Indians in the proper use of latrine facilities on the train.

"O'gatedota—Curtis—does not like Washington," Hawk That Hunts Walking told John Miles. "He will be my eyes when we are there."

Miles began to translate for Chrisman, but Chrisman stopped him. He was reading his messages.

"We won't be going to Washington, it seems, Mr. Miles." He tapped a paper. "The president is on tour. Things are going rather badly for him since he pardoned those southerners. He is trying to mend his fences. We will reroute, to meet him in New York City."

With a crash of tin implements Trinidad Salazar surged to his feet, his eyes blazing. Lizard whipped his warclub from its thong and whirled upright to defend the Spaniard's back.

"New York Ceety!" Trini shouted. *"Miguel Jesus Montoya ya vive en New York Ceety. Ai, qué esplendor! Qué magnificencia! Caminar en New York Ceety para matar a Miguel Jesus Montoya!* Sonamabitch!"

At the shouted outburst nervous troopers and armed warriors came running from all sides, all of them ready to defend someone against someone. In his excitement the little Spaniard had drawn his revolver and Darby leaped to knock it from his hand, then howled and ducked as pain shot through his injured arm and Lizard's warclub whisked past his head. John Miles was on his feet, a skinning knife in his hand, and James Chrisman had gone over backward, his feet tangled in his camp stool. Before Lizard's club completed its arc White Hand and Sunshine had his arms pinned and were shouting at him in rapid Kiowa.

Hawk That Hunts Walking sipped his coffee and observed.

Darby grimaced, trying to ease his injured arm. He stooped and picked up Trini's gun, let the hammer down and dropped it back in the Spaniard's holster. "Damn it, Trini," he hissed. "Can't you behave yourself for a solid minute?"

Trini gazed at him, wide-eyed, then shrugged and lowered his head. *"Perdoneme,"* he whispered.

Darby turned to Chrisman, who was just getting to his feet. "I'm sorry, sir. He gets like that sometimes. If there was a horse tank here I'd throw him in it."

The commissioner stared at the Spaniard. "Is he dangerous, Mr. Curtis?"

Darby glanced at Stalking Horse, still crouched and ready to wield his hooked lance . . . at the mild, bearded John Miles who held a skinning knife in his hand and a few hours before had presided at the butchery of an assassin . . . at Lizard who a few seconds before had tried to brain him . . . at the four Real Dogs in guard position around the old chief and the medicine man . . . at the gathering crowd of mingled savages and soldiers, the bristling lances and the drawn weapons . . . at big Hank Shoaf who held a heavy revolver in his hand and at old Broken Bow who had an arrow nocked and aimed at the heart of the little foreigner who had tried to steal his best daughter. He looked at them and something broke loose inside him. He chuckled, and the chuckle became a torrent. He roared, danced, tried to hold his aching sides and gasped as pain shot through his arm.

Stalking Horse stared at him, then grinned and lowered his lance, infected by it. John Miles turned away, his shoulders twitching.

When Darby could control himself again he turned to Chrisman. At sight of the man's worried face he went into another spasm. "Dangerous?" he managed, sobbing. "Is he . . . dangerous . . ." He couldn't finish the answer.

In the distance a whistle sounded. The Kiowa Special was made up and ready to roll.

John Miles was gasping, trying to translate for Hawk That Hunts Walking and the other Indians. In waves, the laughter spread around the compound.

Chrisman shook his head. "I don't know if this is going to work," he told himself. "Lord, I just don't know."

At an austere house a mile from the telegraph office at Clyden Cross Ernest Kichener stood in shadows and watched as a surrey cab stopped at the gate. The man who stepped down was of medium height, heavy shouldered and wore tailored clothing of muted shades. He paid the driver, watched as he turned and rolled away toward Clyden Cross, then pulled a watch from his vest and stared at it as though it should tell him something other than the time.

The house was empty. Kichener had investigated that in the hour he had waited in this secluded place. Watching the man by the gate, he read again in his mind the note that had come this morning by wire from Baltimore: "Hawk hunt failed. Hunter field dressed. Fenley is yours. Good hunting." It was signed, "Bliss."

Volumes of meaning were in the few words, and Kichener smiled as the man turned toward his house. The smile was serene, a faint smile of contentment. But the eyes above it were crackling ice. For a number of years the man whose name in some small circles meant retribution had suspected that Joe Fenley had been involved in the killing of Merritt Fields, a decent man whose only sin was to run afoul of a powerful man. He had suspected Fenley was involved. He had not known for sure. Now he knew.

Because Poling had been involved. Poling had been the key. Now the fox had gone to ground and Kichener's hunters' instincts told him the moves. When the fox goes to ground it takes the old paths, the tested and trusted paths where it has been before.

For a fox like Poling, paths were people. And the old paths would be the people who killed Merritt Fields.

He waited until the man was at his door, then he stepped out of the shadows and came up behind him.

"Good morning, Mr. Fenley," he said. "I take it there has been no news from Kansas today."

For an instant the man stood frozen, his door half open, then he turned abruptly, his hand going to his coat. With a grip that was sheathed steel Kichener caught his arm, twisted it down and back, reached under his coat and drew out the gun there. He tossed it into shrubbery beside the porch. Then with a smile that was almost gracious he pushed the man backward, through the door, to fall on the flagstones inside. Kichener followed him in and bolted the door.

"Who are you?" Fenley gasped, trying to get his feet under him.

"We have never met," the gray man said. "I must tell you, though, there will be no message from your assassin. He failed in his mission. He is dead. I gather he died quite painfully, and in the process he mentioned your name."

Fenley crouched, backing away. His face was white with fear and rage. "I don't know what you're talking about. You can't come into my house and . . ."

282

"But I'm already in, Mr. Fenley. You see, I wanted to ask you about another incident, some years ago. I believe you recall the name, Merritt Fields. Besides you and Mercer Poling, I'd like the names of the others who were involved in his death."

"I don't know what you're . . ." the man charged him, strong shoulders rolling, heavy arms reaching to grasp and kill. Kichener stepped aside. Fenley flailed at air, and then a fist like driven timber doubled him over and he fell.

"You're wasting time, Mr. Fenley. I think you had better just tell me the names."

For a minute or more, Fenley lay gasping on the flagstones. Then he struggled upright, now between Kichener and the door. He jostled a spindly table and a pewter vase tipped, rolled and clattered on the tiles. "You're mad," he panted. "Get out of my house."

Kichener smiled a serene smile at him and turned away, looking at the house and its fixtures. "You live well," he said. "What share of Merritt Fields' holdings did you acquire?" He heard the scuff of boots on tile and crouched, turning. A fist holding a pewter vase blurred past his head and he drove an elbow into the man's midsection, doubling him over again. Fenley staggered toward the door and Kichener watched him curiously, waiting. He knew what he would do. For an instant Fenley rested against the frame of a tiny coat pantry, catching his breath. Then he whirled, reached inside and came out with a double barrelled shotgun. He grinned, cocking the hammers.

"You are a fool," Fenley said. "Whoever you are, you have made your last mistake. We're alone in this house and I am about to kill an intruder."

"The way you killed Merritt Fields?" Kichener's eyes were pond ice. "The way you tried to have an old Indian killed last night? But no, you simply hired that done, didn't you, Mr. Fenley? Maybe you have always hired your work done. Maybe you have never done it yourself. Am I right?"

"Damn you!" Fenley's face went dark. "If you know about Fields you know there was no hiring. I . . . we took

283

care of that ourselves . . ."

"We?" Kichener asked, casually.

But Fenley's eyes changed then. He was through playing games. He was through talking. The shotgun came level.

"The gun is empty," Kichener told him, quietly. "I had hoped it might help you tell me more, if you thought you had a weapon in your hands."

Fenley's eyes went wild. He squeezed the triggers and the hammers fell with a double click.

"You still might like to . . ." Kichener began. But Fenley heard no more. Raising the shotgun, swinging it like a club, he lunged, and his heel slid on wet tile where the vase had spilled. Off balance with the gun raised, he fell flat, backward, and the sound of his head striking the flagstone tiles was the sound of a melon dropped on stone. The shotgun clattered to the floor beyond him.

Ernest Kichener crouched beside him, touched a finger to one staring, glazing eye, then stood and shook his head. "A pity," he said. "You might have been more help."

Stepping around the dead man, Kichener retrieved the shotgun, pulled two shells from his pocket and reloaded it. Then he replaced it in its pantry, picked up the pewter vase and lay it where it had first fallen.

He let himself out of the house. He had hoped to add names to his list, but he was not disappointed. One by one, the fox at bay would show his teeth. One by one, he would pull them. Then he would pull the fox itself, from ground.

XXVI

"Was ever a president so vilified?" the secretary of state paced to the edge of the deep-hued carpet, his hands clasped behind him, then turned sharply to fix his level gaze on the solid old man sitting in the maroon-velvet chair. "To those from the northern states—and damn us all sometimes for the lot of unforgiving fire-eaters that we are—he is a turncoat because of his amnesty for the Confederates. To those from the south he is a traitor because he opposed their secession at the outset. To the radicals in the Congress he is a threat because he stands in the way of Secretary Stanton's ambitions. To the conservatives even of his own party he is an embarrassment because he stands four-square for those same principles they pretend to serve.

"He refuses clemency to President Lincoln's assassins and is labeled a bloodthirsty beast. He grants clemency to those whose only crime was to be on the losing side in a dispute no one ever wanted except a few radicals, and for that they label him impotent. He attends an inauguration still suffering from a bout of fever, and they label him a drunkard. He expands our nation's holdings to the Aleutian Straits and they revile him for buying a 'worthless chunk of ice' . . ." The secretary flushed with anger. The old man in the chair held his tongue. The president was not alone in reaping scurrility as a result of the purchase of Russian America. Many were calling it "Seward's Folly," as well.

"Forgive me, General," the secretary said. "Politics can

make a man turn bitter, as I am sure you know."

"No apology is necessary," the old man said. "It is rare enough to hear a man defend another for his honor instead of for his money. I agree with you, President Johnson is a most maligned man. It may, though, be only the times, don't you think? We have been through agonies these past seven years . . . the war, the hatreds, the shock of Mr. Lincoln's death . . . and we as a people are only human. The easiest way to clear the air has always been a sacrificial lamb."

Secretary Seward nodded, shrugging to relieve the tensions that beset him. "Of course. Please realize that I know little about you, General . . . and not much more about your successor. Very few outside the president—possibly not even the other members of the cabinet—have even heard of the, ah, executive function you and your people perform. Or that you did perform before your retirement. . . ."

"My successor permits me to keep my hand in now and then," the old man said. "A few loose ends, a minor project here and there, things that are of a personal interest."

"Like the matter of the Kiowa lands." Seward studied the old man—his bulldog face, deeply lined, the thin white hair and snowy sideburns, the modest cut of his brown suit— and felt a chill. He was looking at a legend. A legend every president since Jefferson had furthered because for the house of democracy to stand firm there must be a few quiet, efficient craftsmen like this one to repair its flaws now and then. He glanced from the general to the only other person in the room, a large, graying man introduced only as Mr. Bliss. The secretary wondered how many of these men there had been—how many there were now—who operated so discreetly and yet, according to a whisper he had heard once or twice, so lethally.

He wondered about the private inquiry he had received from Commissioner Chrisman, for information about a man named Kichener. No connection was evident, but there was something about the information he had been able to obtain, or the lack of it . . . "General," he asked, "is one of your associates by any chance named Kichener?"

Seward didn't know whether he saw or only imagined a flicker of mirth in the old man's eyes.

"I have associated with many men," the general said. "But you do deserve a response, Mr. Secretary. It is a fair question. Yes, I have known Mr. Kichener for a long time. We have exchanged services at times. I gather you have received a query about his credentials. They are quite valid. I arranged they be supplied to him. But only for the duration of a project."

"He is one of your men, then?"

"Oh, no," the general smiled. "Mr. Kichener's projects are his own. At the moment, he is interested in some people who committed a murder a few years ago. It happens that the same people are involved now in a matter of interest to me."

"And that is . . ."

"There are men who specialize in the creation of private empires out of chaos. To a great extent this has been the pattern of history, and as such it is not necessarily an evil thing. The evil comes when such men scheme first to create a chaos within which to operate. That sort of behavior is not tolerable in a nation such as ours. Through encounters with the old Boston Combine, and later with the Mississippi cabal which so disrupted our nation's economy . . . and other such schemes of more recent years . . . a few of us have become somewhat expert at recognizing the symptoms of these movements. My present concern is that the central plains do not become a battleground. Or at least, not to serve the purposes of men like Mercer Poling."

The secretary was pacing again. "Poling has powerful friends. Men like Secretary Stanton, possibly General Sheridan . . . I would not want to add issues to the president's problems with Secretary Stanton, sir."

"Nor would I. My concern is Poling, not Stanton. The secretary of war is the president's problem. Mine is to allow Mr. Poling the opportunity to act on his own behalf, separately from his influential associates, and thus expose himself."

"Expose himself to your Mr. Kichener?"

"Given the circumstance, I believe Ernest can arrange that. He is a unique man, Mr. Secretary. Quite awesome, in fact."

"Apparently. Yet I have learned very little about him."

For the first time, the large man sitting aside from them spoke. His voice was deep, polite and respectful. "Mr. Secretary, have you ever seen a hawk in stoop?"

Puzzled, Seward cocked a heavy eyebrow at him. "Yes, I believe I have, Mr. Bliss. It was an awesome sight."

"When you think of Ernest Kichener, think of that."

"I certainly could not condone action outside of the law," the secretary told the general.

"Of course not. Nor would we. The only laws that I ask you to manipulate are the laws of circumstance."

"I think that has already been done," Seward frowned. "Secretary Stanton is having a field day with this visit to the east by an Indian chief. Absurd, he says, to recognize a savage as a head of state. Where, he asks, are the sovereign lands of this head of state? Our own territories, he points out. The man is ruthless in his politics."

The general nodded. "And the president's response is excellent. The Indians are part of this land. Better to treat them as neighbors than to force them to be enemies. But you see, enmity is exactly what Mr. Poling wants. In the event of a Kiowa war at this moment, who would wind up controlling the plains?"

"Well, obviously the army."

"Yes, eventually. But who would head the civilian authority?"

"I suppose Mercer Poling. He is in line for it, should that happen."

"Exactly. The fox is in the chicken coop. Now all he needs is elimination of the fighting cocks."

"The Kiowa."

"Precisely."

"But what you are asking me to do . . ."

"Is to take a hand in the security of Hawk That Hunts Walking while he is in the east. Establish a pattern of security that is tight and sure."

"But the pattern you outline would have a hole in it."

"And the fox is sure to recognize that hole and take advantage of it. My hawk is not after your chickens, Mr. Secretary. He is after the fox."

Secretary of State William Seward glanced again at the quiet Mr. Bliss, wondering what the man had seen that so reminded him of a hawk in stoop. Something like a chill crept up his spine as he recognized a world beyond his own realms of civilized, cultivated politics. Somewhere out there, a man who was only a name to him was making plans. The man's name was Kichener.

"Where is he now?" the secretary asked.

The general turned to Mr. Bliss.

"A place called Clyden Cross," the large man said. "Or possibly, by now, eastbound."

Seward felt the chill again. The hawk was homing on its prey.

The general stood then, drawing a gold watch from his vest. "We must hurry if I am to make my appointment with Secretary Stanton."

Seward glanced at him, startled. "Stanton?"

"Why, yes. It strikes me, Mr. Secretary, that the secretary of war is a man who would be most unhappy to find himself in a compromising position. I thought I might suggest to him a means for avoiding embarrassment."

At Georgetown, in the parlor of a rented house, Mercer Poling sipped at good brandy and frowned at the telegraph message lying on a spindly table by his chair. Winter had waited at Kansas City, for word from Fenley regarding the train. But no word came and Winter had started east. He was vague about his reasons. Poling assumed he would be at Bonneset.

Late sunlight slanted across Poling's rough, sharp features as a servant adjusted the blinds in a parlor window, then went to answer a knock at the hall door. The man was back in a minute or two, with a sealed paper for his master. Poling took it, dismissed him, then opened it and read it. He read it twice, and when he set down the brandy snifter his hand trembled slightly. Dark rage burned in his eyes. The special railroad train was still moving eastward, and the old Kiowa was still alive. But the train was not coming toward Washington. It had been diverted in Missouri and now was rolling on clear track eastward, heading for New York City. Elaborate security had been established along the entire route—not the security plan set up by the War Department, containing a few suggestions from Poling, but a new plan which he did not recognize. The letter suggested the State Department had intervened.

Poling's mind raced. Chrisman? No, the commissioner could not have pulled such strings. For a moment he had a suspicion that someone had gotten to Secretary Seward himself. And yet, that idea was preposterous. No, it had to be coincidence. The president had decided to meet with the Kiowa in New York. Possibly he felt the political value would be greater there.

But whatever the reason, Poling knew it was time for a change of plan. He studied the security arrangements as spelled out by his contact in Stanton's office. They were airtight, all the way to the Hudson River. But then . . . he read them again and an idea began to form.

Ten minutes later the Commissioner of Central Territories—not yet appointed but approved—pulled a bell cord to summon the servant.

"Pack my trunk and two bags," he told the man, "and make arrangement for me on tomorrow's express to New York City.

When the man had gone Poling crossed to a little writing desk and got out paper and pen. Carefully, couching the words in a manner to go without notice, he drafted telegraph messages to three people.

The message to Winter at Bonneset and the one to Pasco to be delivered when he and Tram changed trains at Republic Junction were essentially the same message. They were to meet him in New York. He specified the place.

The message to New York was different. It was detailed and lengthy. The man who would receive it was expert at arranging things in New York City. Poling gave him instructions on what he wanted arranged.

As he stepped aboard a liveried coach for an afternoon of hurried business in Washington, he puzzled over the change of plans for the Kiowa train, and over the mysterious alterations in security procedure. He kept coming back to James Chrisman, but it was somehow not a thing Chrisman seemed likely to have done.

He puzzled also over what could have gone wrong in Kansas. Fenley's people usually were competent and reliable. Yet the old chief was still alive. And he wondered what had delayed Fenley in reporting to Winter. Where was the man?

There were few people that Mercer Poling felt he could trust. Fenley was one, because of what Poling knew and could prove about him. He and Fenley went back a number of years, as did he and Pasco. The three of them had taken care of a problem one time, jointly. And while Poling could prove murder against them, they could prove nothing against him. The only person who could have done that was the fourth man, and he was dead—mysteriously, of course, but Poling was satisfied that he was. Therefore he trusted Fenley and Pasco.

Winter was a cypher, a border gunman Poling had found useful enough that he had kept him on for odd jobs.

In Washington City he picked up a newspaper.

He knew then what had gone wrong in Kansas. Headlines told of the band of wild Indians on their way east to meet with the president of the United States, escorted by Commissioner James Chrisman and a cavalry unit. Separate headlines, much smaller, told of the death of a lunatic who had tried to board the special train and apparently had fallen under its wheels. The reporter, someone named Randolph Yeats, claimed to have seen the body and wrote with horror of what iron wheels on iron rails could do to a human body.

In a third story, a sidebar to the first, the same reporter

noted the death of an old Indian with the commission party. The aging savage, an associate of the Indians' chief, had died in his sleep.

Poling read the elaborate prose of the reporter and tried to find meanings in the lines. A chill of premonition crept up his spine, a feeling as though a shadow had passed across him, the shadow of something soaring high above, something he could neither see nor understand.

He folded the newspaper and placed it in his valise. There would be time to read it again tomorrow, on the way to New York.

XXVII

Except for isolated incidents, the passage of the Kiowa Express through the United States midlands was uneventful . . . at least to the outside world. At each daytime stop crowds of people gathered to see the Indians, and cordons of soldiers worked to keep them back.

Chrisman and Holmes decided at Springfield, in Illinois, to keep a ledger of accounts payable. The first entry was for the price of a camera, flash stick and minor injuries to a photographer. No one had thought to explain to Hawk That Hunts Walking's party about flash powder. The man had made his picture—a solemn pose of seated chiefs, standing warriors and the commissioner—then had been mauled by four Real Dog men alarmed by the flash and protecting their chief. At Indianapolis, in Indiana, city officials had prevailed upon Washington to approve a parade and Chrisman found he had no choice in the matter. To the Indians and their cavalry escorts, tired of the monotony of long days of travel, it was an outing. Emerging from the guarded depot into an open park where long rows of carriages awaited them, the Real Dog men were painted all in red and the Blackleg men wore their gaudiest colors and finest beads and feathers, their hair standing tall in feathered roaches. To them, it was an occasion for formal dress. To the crowds gathered beyond the infantry cordon and along the streets around the town square, it was the most blood-chilling, savage sight most had ever seen.

Chrisman put his ledger in his pocket and took it along. It was as well that he did. The first to break ranks was

Trinidad Salazar.

For the first twenty minutes of the festive parade the Spaniard sat tall and proud atop the front rail of an elegant open carriage which contained Darby Curtis and several brilliantly-painted Blacklegs. The Indians were not comfortable sitting in the presence of so many strange white people, so several of them chose to stand. Stalking Horse leaned on his hooked lance ablaze with bright feathers and kept an eye on the crowds, the soldiers lining the way, the innumerable strange buildings . . . and on Curtis.

Trini grinned his toothiest grin for a time, waving and doffing his hat whenever he caught the eye of ladies. He wore his red shirt and silver-trimmed jacket, and his boots were polished to a high gloss. And yet, he began to feel lonely. The people lining the streets were not watching him. They were looking at the *Indios*.

Finally, growing tired of the parade, the Spaniard spotted an opening in the crowd where soldiers were manning barricades to keep a cross-street open, and he decided to have a look around and stretch his legs.

He glanced back toward Darby, wanting approval, but the standing Indians were in the way. Trini shrugged, stepped to the side and dropped from the rolling carriage. Without hesitation he strolled between soldiers, their backs to him as they watched the crowds, and along the open path to where a walkway began. He heard gasps of astonishment in his wake, noticed some people at the back of the crowd had turned his way and were pushing back to give him room, and he grinned and bowed, then strutted along the walk, looking at storefronts.

Arriving at a haberdashery that had a single-pane window at least four feet square, he paused to admire the elegant attire inside, wishing he had brought his money with him. His savings, though, were still in his pack aboard the train.

It pleased him to be receiving so much attention from the people thronging at the edge of the walk. Eyes were wide, mouths open and there was a babble of astounded talk. He started to turn, then noticed the reflection in the window.

There was his own handsome self reflected there, and another. A tall, brilliantly-painted Blackleg warrior stood at his shoulder, studying the window with him.

"Nglatz," Lizard said, tapping the window with his club. The window dissolved in a shower of bright shards. Women screamed and men shouted. Beyond the window a man with a measuring tape draped over his shoulder stood open-mouthed, making strangling sounds.

Soldiers descended upon them then. Armed men in uniform shouted at them, gestured and cleared a path for them, back to the street. The parade had stopped and Darby Curtis stood tall on the seat of a carriage, surrounded by Blacklegs and soldiers, arguing with both groups. As he caught sight of Trini he shouted at him and waved an exasperated fist. Trini ducked his head in shame and climbed aboard another carriage, not wanting a confrontation in front of so many people. Lizard padded after Trini to board the same carriage. When it started moving again he sat on the floor of it, pulled a leather thong from his pouch and went to work affixing a bright maroon cravatte to the center of his shield. Two carriages back Chrisman received reports and made entries in his ledger.

At a review stand in front of a large building tall-hatted men with pale faces awaited them and the parade stopped again. John Miles spoke to Hawk That Hunts Walking, and the old chief stepped from the carriage and climbed the steps to the review stand, followed by Broken Bow and the Real Dog men. Keeps His Horses shuffled and danced below the stand, shaking his rattle and muttering incantations.

In a short, solemn ceremony which John Miles interpreted, the men on the stand presented Hawk That Hunts Walking with a bright red velvet sash from which was suspended a large brass key.

The man who had presented the sash spoke then to the assembled crowds, and there was laughter at some of his words. John Miles scowled as he whispered to Hawk That Hunts Walking, "He says it is very funny that Indians are being welcomed to the City of Indians. He tells his people

295

not to worry. The key will not open anything, and their families are safe. He speaks to make himself seem very wise and to make the Kana'tenee seem very foolish. He wonders now whether the chief of the Indians would like to say anything."

"The white men are very strange," Hawk That Hunts Walking told Sha'ata'ee. "They welcome us to their village, then they make fun of us. We would not do so to them. It would be bad manners."

"He asks again whether the chief would like to speak," Miles said.

Hawk That Hunts Walking looked across the crowded square, and at his own people waiting in the carriages below the stand. He caught the eye of Darby Curtis, noticed the scowl on his face and was glad O'gatedota was offended at the white chief's words. It spoke well of the wild one.

He handed the folded sash and its key ceremoniously to Broken Bow, then turned to stand beside the grinning tall hat. "We of the Kana'tenee," he said in a dry old voice that yet carried to the crowd, "are pleased to cross the white men's lands as quickly as we can on our journey to see the Great Father."

He paused to let John Miles repeat his words in English, then continued, "We have seen things of wonder in your lands. There are so many of you it is hard to understand how you do not all starve, but we have learned even in our own lands that white men will eat almost anything." He paused again, noticing the odd, thoughtful hesitations in Sha'ata'ee's translation. He decided Sha'ata'ee was not telling them exactly what he had said, and he shrugged. Hawk That Hunts Walking knew about diplomacy. No man could be a chief and not know the paths of the forked tongue.

"It is difficult to know," he continued, gesturing about at the city, the many buildings, "how so many people who smell so bad can live together for so long in the same place and not all go away to find better places. But it is fortunate that you are content to live in this manner, because otherwise there would be more of you for us to contend with."

In the street James Chrisman stepped from his carriage and walked back to where Darby Curtis sat, grinning. "They aren't saying the same things, are they?"

"Not hardly," Curtis chuckled. "Probably just as well. The chief is saying exactly what he thinks. Miles is making an acceptance speech."

His words finished, Hawk That Hunts Walking stepped solemnly to the nearest of the Real Dog men and took his lance. Then with great dignity the old chief raised the lance and touched the first tall hat on the shoulder with its point. That done he proceeded to touch the next, and the one after that, performing the ritual with solemn dignity as the Kiowa in their carriages cheered, laughed and stamped their feet.

Darby Curtis laughed and applauded, and the crowd of white people took up the applause, not certain what was happening but enjoying the spectacle.

Hawk That Hunts Walking handed the lance back to the beaming warrior, who grinned and pulled bright feathers from a pouch, adding them to the lance's decorations, tying them in place with lengths of fine gut.

"What was that all about?" Chrisman asked, puzzled. "Did he give them titles or something?"

"I'll tell you about it later," Curtis laughed, still applauding.

The ceremonies over, the Indians and John Miles descended from the platform to get back in their carriages. Darby looked back to make sure Trini was still where he was supposed to be, then he settled into the padded cushions of the elegant vehicle and felt very good about the world in general. Most of the people crowding the parade route would never realize that they had watched and applauded while the old chief of the Far Grass Kiowa counted coup on their entire city council.

By the time they changed trains for the third time at Wooster, Ohio, the Kiowa had become relatively blasé about the marvelous sights to be seen in white man territory. They had seen farms and villages, mills and boats, towns and cities, and the new had mostly worn off. They still ogled the upended countryside they passed through now and then and marveled at the varieties of plants, the tiny fields of grain, the dense forests, the rivers that were wide and deep and full of water.

But the attitude of the savages toward the lands of the white men became more and more a mixture of contempt and pity as the days passed.

"This is all very bad," Keeps His Horses lectured as he gazed from an open window at the rolling lands outside the bustling town of Pittsburgh at the convergence of rivers. "The people here do not live on the land. They live in it. They tear up the land and change it and it traps their feet so they cannot get away. This is not good land. This is land that has been hurt too much and now it makes war upon its people. There are too many ghosts here. It is very bad."

John Miles heard the words of the old medicine man and looked thoughtfully across at Darby Curtis, wondering what the westerner saw when he looked at the land. He knew Darby saw ghosts here, and it puzzled him that he himself, who had been Kiowa for ten years—who was in some ways more Kiowa than the Kiowa—yet could not see the ghosts they saw . . . and that Darby Curtis saw.

That one was born where they were born, he told himself. The western lands were in their blood.

When the train raced through a rainstorm driving off the Appalachians Kiowa warriors crowded onto the open platforms and climbed atop the cars to feel the rain and bathe in it, and people gawked from windows at Carrolton Station then talked for a long time in hushed tones about what they thought they had seen.

At a water stop outside the town of Dreiting a burly station worker drove a supply wagon alongside the train, pulled his reins and then stood atop his wagon bench to look into the first car, marveling at the fierce adornments of the naked savages who gathered around the window to look back at him.

From the shadowy interior Randolph Yeats, again consigned to lonely vigil with a band of jabbering Indians and a Spaniard, called to him, "Welcome, sir, welcome! Yours is the first good American face I have seen since two days hence. Come and have a few words with me."

The stationman rose to tiptoes, peering around in the car. His eyes had not adjusted to the gloom. "*Ich nicht sehen sie, Meinherr. Wo sind sie?*"

With a sigh, Yeats sank lower on the padded seat and turned away.

Flooding on the upper Susquehanna halted the train at Pittston, and queries were wired ahead. On a gray afternoon two companies of infantry were placed in cordon around the West Pittston yards and the train was unloaded. While James Chrisman paced and worried saddle stock was let into a fenced pasture with a corral at its north end, baggage and gear was loaded aboard army wagons, and men of the First Platoon and the Blackleg Society began carrying saddles and gear to the corral.

"From here we must ride," Chrisman told Hawk That Hunts Walking. Miles translated for him. "When we reach the river there will be a barge to carry us across, then we will travel to Scranton where another train will be ready for us. It is dangerous here because the people of the valley will not expect to see red people mounted. It would be a good thing if the men of the Kana'tenee would let the blue soldiers ride escort around them."

Hawk That Hunts Walking had no objection, although there was grumbling among some of the Blackleg men. They did not like the impression that would be given to people who saw them surrounded by soldiers. Yet Stalking Horse demanded it and the warriors complied.

There was little traffic on the road downward into the valley. Hawk That Hunts Walking, Broken Bow and Keeps His Horses rode an eight-seat army coach with John Miles, Holmes and Chrisman, while the Real Dog men pranced their horses in close-order guard around them. A surrey was provided for Hank Shoaf and a pair of dignitaries from the State of Pennsylvania who had met them at Pittsburgh. Lieutenant Spradley positioned his platoon in three patrols, one leading and flanking the vehicles, the others flanking and trailing the mounted Blacklegs who followed with their guests.

For the first two miles Trinidad Salazar was ecstatic to be once more in the saddle of his beloved mustard pony, and he patted its neck and leaned forward often to croon to it, *"Mi querido caballo amarillo, bienvenido al oriente. Caballo fuerte y mas vigoroso, pronto arribaremos en* New York Ceety."

Darby Curtis, aboard a cavalry remount, turned in his saddle to squint at the Spaniard. It was beyond him why anyone would sing to horses. Mules, maybe, but not horses.

Cresting the valley's eastern slopes late in the evening they saw ahead of them, still some distance, a large railyard and beyond it the lights and smokes of a large town, and a private pointed east and said to one of his comrades, "From here that place looks like it could be New York City."

The Spaniard's eyes opened wide and he squinted into the darkening distance. The soldier had said New York City. A great well of glory opened in his heart and poured forth emotions as raw and hot as the soil of Aragon. In the distant lights he imagined he could see the lovely Doña Lucinda Villanova-Madeiro languishing in foul captivity awaiting her rescuer, and though years had passed he felt he could not waste another minute. He would charge into the city, find Miguel Jesus Montoya, deal violently with him and free the fair Doña Lucinda who would thereafter be his own devoted slave. He would even forgive her of her sins . . . eventually.

As dusk settled on the rolling hills Trini eased back until he rode beside the supply wagons and baggage carts. Stolid Kiowa warriors plodded along on all sides, their faces and their horses painted for travel in strange lands. The soldiers driving the vehicles had long since grown accustomed to the sight.

Finding the wagon he wanted, he looped the pony's reins to its trail standard, jumped down and stepped quietly onto the moving bed. Only a minute of quiet search produced what he wanted, his saddlebags and his pack. He stepped down and trotted alongside his pony, lashing them in place.

Then he gathered his reins, remounted and rode forward to flank Darby Curtis again, intending to thank him for all he had done and to wish him a good journey. But Curtis was embroiled at the moment in a argument with one of the *Moros*—the one with the crooked spear—and would not be interrupted. So the Spaniard waited, plodding along behind.

But then the road turned, southward toward the railyards. Curtis was still arguing with the Moro. Trini shrugged and edged away toward the left flank, ignoring the comings and goings of the Indians around him. From a distance he gazed at the receding back of the big Americano, then raised his hat. "*Vaya con Dios, amigo,*" he whispered.

The flanking cavalrymen went by, and there was a gap. So far as he could tell, no one noticed when Trinidad Salazar, *viajero magnifico* and conquistador-to-be of the heart of a stolen lady, put heels to his mustard pony and headed eastward to the distant city.

In fact, hardly anyone did notice his departure. Of the entire assemblage only one man had seen him go.

It was almost full dark when the waiting cars were loaded in the railyards, all the stock was aboard slat-cars and the baggage had been reloaded. The engine had steam up, lanterns waved in signal and a whistle sounded. Darby Curtis was almost running when he entered the last coach, and he grabbed a seat-brace and clung as the train lurched and began the last leg of the journey.

"Where's Trini?" he asked the men there, and damned their blank faces. "My Spaniard! Has anybody seen him? I can't find him."

Stalking Horse, Sunshine and White Hand had followed him into the coach, and now another Indian entered, followed by Sergeant Hanlon.

In Kiowa tongue, Gall Stick reported to Stalking Horse, "One of the Blackleg men is missing, respected one. We cannot find Lizard."

And almost simultaneously Hanlon saluted Lieutenant Spradley. "Correction on the roll, sir. Four of our men are

301

not aboard. Sergeant Foley says the last he saw of 'em they was gone to bring back one of the Indians that got loose from the rest. We thought they was back, sir. But they're not on the train."

Darby whirled to Chrisman. "Stop the train."

"It's too late, Mr. Curtis." Chrisman looked at the rushing dusk outside, the receding lights of the yard, the lights of the city creeping past in the distance. He turned. "Lieutenant, what will your men do if they've missed the train?"

"Why, then it will be up to them to meet us at our destination. And if there's an Indian out there, I guess they'll just have to bring him along. I don't know how we'd find them now, sir."

Wesley Keeler kept a smithy on the outskirts of the city, and he worked late that evening fashioning a heavy turn-back hasp of unique design. It was an idea he hoped to sell to the mills in the area, and he was anxious to get it done. So it was full dark when he stepped out of his open shed for a breath of fresh air. This far from the residential and commercial areas, the only lights at this time of evening were the lamplight from his smithy and the lanterns hanging from his gateposts. All else in the neighborhood was closed and dark.

Keeler sat on a bench in the evening cool and sipped from a jug of spirits, listening to the quarrel of night birds, the tiny sounds of insects and the distant rumble of stamping mills working around the clock. He heard hooves on the dirt road and looked around as a rider came into the pool of light from his lanterns. The man was small and sleek, with a broad hat and black short-coat trimmed in silver. He wore tall boots and carried a holstered revolver at his hip. His horse carried traveling gear.

The man swept off his hat as he halted, a courtly gesture unlike anything Wesley Keeler had seen outside of plays at the Rialto Theater downtown. *"Buenas noches, Señor. Trinidad Salazar a sus órdenes. Por favor, a donde esta la casa de Miguel Jesus Montoya?"*

Keeler sipped his spirits and stared at the man, wondering what he had said. Before the war, this had been a nice little town. But now everything was different. The mills were running and the roads were open and a man just never knew who might show up next. He shrugged, spread his hands and shook his head. "Try the town," he pointed. "There's some eye-talians around there. Even some Greeks. All kinds of foreign jabber."

The man seemed disappointed, but he smiled as he replaced his hat. *"Gracias,"* he said. Then he flicked a rein and was gone, up the road.

Keeler found the cork and plugged his spirits, ready to go back to work. But again there were hooves, and a rider coming into the light. Keeler's mouth fell open and his breath went ragged. Tall, raven hair full of feathers stood above a face painted in stripes of black and patterns of yellow and white. Muscular naked shoulders glinted dull red in the lantern light. A hideous grin appeared on the painted face.

"A'a sasamqua ko'a-ywa?" the savage's hands moved eloquently as he spoke, but Keeler's attention now was riveted on the feathered lance across his saddle, the vicious toothed club at his thigh, the shield on his arm.

Keeler stared and gasped.

The warrior shrugged, turned up his nose and kicked his horse. "Sona-bish k'ay," he said scornfully, and was gone, up the road.

Wesley Keeler removed the cork from his jug and took a good pull of spirits. He was still standing there, staring up the road, when four mounted troopers in the field uniform of frontier cavalry trotted into his lantern light. The first one touched his hatbrim smartly and asked, "Beg pardon, sir, but did ye see a painted red Indian pass by here recently?"

Of course he had, Keeler thought, and took another pull at his spirits. That was exactly what he had seen. Regular as milkwagons and the Tuesday mail, a man saw painted-faced Indians pass by. Hardly give it a second thought. And

Mexican bandits. He tried to speak and had difficulty, so he took another pull at the spirits and pointed up the road.

"Thank ye, sir," the corporal saluted again. "Have a nice evenin'."

Eventually Wesley Keeler got back to his forge and his anvil, but it was too late then. He couldn't for the life of him remember how to make a turn-back hasp.

XXVIII

In darkness the Kiowa Express snaked across the Lehigh Valley with its patterned farms and its villages every six miles, through forests and breaks and up into the Poconos where the Kana'tenee covered their faces and mourned, and even John Miles did not know what they mourned about.

"There are ghosts here," Darby Curtis muttered. "They don't like the way the shadows move." He said it scornfully, but Miles noticed he turned away from the window and did not look out again.

With first light of morning they were at Bethlehem Cross where the train was uncoupled and the cars shunted two by two onto a rail ferry to cross the Delaware. Soldiers from the garrison at Allentown cordoned the west bank. Soldiers from Fort Hackett met them on the Jersey slopes and two coaches of infantry were added to the train.

Hank Shoaf received his messages and pondered over them, then met with James Chrisman and the others beside the chief's car. "Somebody has changed the agendas," he said. "We have first-rate security all the way from here to New York. But it's a different plan than we started with. Instead of laying over at Newark, with the barracks there, we go right on to the Hudson yards and we'll ferry across there to the old Battery docks. The city has a new park up north of town, a big tract above 57th Street, where the Indians can pitch their lodges. It's far enough out that we can cordon it, but still close enough that we can work with the local police to keep the citizens separated from your Indians. Any time you have three quarters of a million people in one place, there are problems. But between Secretary Seward taking an interest in this, and Tweed making hay out of it, we'll have plenty of help.

"Provided," he added, scowling at Darby Curtis, "you don't let any more of those Blacklegs get loose."

"What are you talking to me for?" Darby bristled. "They aren't my Blacklegs. Tell Stalking Horse."

"You tell him," Shoaf said. "From here to New York we can keep the public away from the Indians. But I sure don't like having an Indian running loose. There's no word so far about that one that got away at Scranton . . ." he turned to Spradley, "or about your soldiers, Lieutenant. I assume they would wire if they caught him?"

"Of course. Don't worry about it. They'll find him. How far can a Kiowa warrior go, alone, in eastern Pennsylvania? He doesn't know the language, he doesn't know how to feed himself. He doesn't know anything. They'll find him."

"Yeah." Shoaf gazed at the lieutenant. "If he's alone. But what if he has that Spaniard with him?"

Darby Curtis caught his breath. Of course Lizard had gone. He had seen Trini Salazar leave, and followed him. "Oh, God," he muttered. He had worried through the night about Trini, wondering where he was, what kind of trouble he could be in. Now he tried to cope with the idea of a Blackleg warrior and a fiery, erratic Spaniard turned loose on the eastern world. Together. "Oh, God," he said again.

And yet, Stalking Horse had shown no real concern over the disappearance of one of his men. "Lizard is a man," he had said, shrugging it off. "He goes where he chooses."

Chrisman had been relieved. The Kiowa would not hold it against the whites if something happened to Lizard. Shoaf was not relieved. "There'll be hell to pay if he decides to take a few scalps," he pointed out.

"At any rate," he said now, "if you gentlemen can

contain your Indians from here to New York City, we can keep them safe."

"The president will be in New York next Tuesday and Wednesday," Chrisman said. "Hawk That Hunts Walking will have an appointment with him Wednesday. I don't have the details yet. But we have an additional problem. Hawk That Hunts Walking wants to see the ocean. Someone has been telling him about it and he wants to see it for himself."

"We'll cross the Passaic and the Hackensack, and we'll ferry to the Battery," Shoaf said. "That's ocean enough for any Indian."

"That won't do. He knows the difference between rivers and bays and the ocean. Somebody told him. We have to take him to Brooklyn."

Shoaf glanced uptrack where John Miles walked with the old chief and his party. He shook his head. "We'll see. By the way, we'll be taking on another passenger at Newark. Do you know someone named Kichener?"

"I've met him. I'm not sure who he is. He was at the Willow Ford conference."

"Is that the same one that pulled a gun on that Poling jasper at Willow Ford?" Curtis asked. "That Kichener?"

"Poling?" Chrisman's eyes went wide. "Mercer Poling? Kichener drew a gun on him?"

"Yeah. He caught Stalking Horse nosing around and humiliated him . . . him and a couple of his gunhands. I stopped them, but Poling went for a gun and that fellow Kichener braced him. I never saw anybody so sudden."

Spradley frowned. "There was a Kichener at Camp Jacob. I think he was the one who diverted our company over to Sector Nine when we headed off the Kiowa from jumping some hunters. Probably the same hunters that we rounded up out at the old village. The ones that were tied up with Cain DeWitt. Kichener was there, too. He brought DeWitt to us."

"Cain DeWitt is dead," Shoaf said, puzzled over the pattern of coincidence. "Somebody shot him when they were transferring him to the prison train at Emporia. I

307

really didn't make any connection, though, to what we're doing. Who is this Kichener, anyway?"

They looked at one another. None of them knew. But the name kept coming up, it seemed.

In a span of three decades the eastern rail system had grown from intermittent lines shuttling between cities to a web of bright iron that lay like a glinting net upon the earth and covered a third of a continent with strands of efficient travel. And more and more as the web grew, its anchor points strengthened at the centers of commerce and the centers of population. Lines of many names from many places came together at the Hudson Yards at the top of New York Bay, and at any hour of any day dozens of engines were running toward this point, from many directions.

No lines yet crossed the Hudson, but they came from the west through Middletown, Paterson, Somerville and Trenton to converge at Hoboken and the Hudson Yards, and they came from the north through White Plains and Yonkers to plunge rail lines down the finger of Manhattan to the Battery.

Between the Hudson Yards and the Battery Docks barges worked in ceaseless scurry across the inlet to the bay.

The man named Winter had not stopped over at Bonnesset, had been long past there when Poling's message came, but he had come to New York anyway. He had business there of his own. A bearer bond with three thousand dollars rested in the pocket of his dark coat, a bond removed from the wallet of a dead man at Kansas City. Winter had expected money. The man had looked like money. But he had not expected a windfall. Still, he needed to be far away from the border states for a time. Since he had killed Cain DeWitt at Emporia station, he had been running. The bearer bond gave him a destination. He had come to New York to find a way to cash it.

Arriving at Manhattan, he had wired Mercer Poling at Georgetown, but there had been no response. He had found a room on Greenwich Street. From there during the days he scouted the banks and the curbstone brokerages of Wall and Exchange Streets, proceeding cautiously. In the evenings, though, he found less need for caution. There were pleasures to be found in the teeming streets and dark back ways of the Battery on summer nights . . . pleasures which came easy to a man bred raw and tempered hard on the Missouri border.

What he wanted, he took—by gun, by knife and by craft—and the denizens of that square mile he made his hunting ground were no match for him. From Delancey Street to Greenwich, from Market Street to the waterfront he prowled, learning the land and living off it. Naked skill and the lessons of Quantrill served him well here. He went unnoticed for more than a week. And when the wilderness sense told him it was time to shift his terrain, he found a hole on Bleeker Street and waited out the hunters. Then he began again.

He wired Poling again and a response came. Poling had gone to New York days earlier. No address had been left.

Winter puzzled over it, then he read again the newspaper about arrangements for a visit to New York by a band of plains Indians who wanted to see the president. Poling would be interested in that, of course. It would be the same bunch Cain DeWitt had tried to set at war in the Kansas plains, the same bunch he had contacted Joe Fenley about, when Fenley said he knew someone who could kill the chief. Fenley had failed. He had heard nothing more from him.

The Kiowa were coming to New York. Poling had come to New York. For a time Winter put away the idea of the bearer note. If he could find Poling, there might be interesting work for him.

Five years of war had brought renewed vigor to the city's economy. The scars of the '57 panic were healed and the city was building and growing. At the hole on Bleeker Street a drab and furtive Winter, the Winter of the river streets, disappeared behind a door. An hour later another Winter came out, tailored and trimmed, dressed in tan

309

morning suit and long dark coat and carrying a trim valise. He closed the door behind him. Inside the room all trace of the Bleeker Street Winter smoldered and burned, and summer breeze through an open window fanned the flames. He walked to Seventh Avenue and found a hansom cab to take him uptown.

Somewhere in the vicinity of Park Avenue and 42nd Street he would begin his search. It was the part of town where a man like Mercer Poling would be. Somewhere behind him bells clanged in the morning streets, and a horse-drawn pumper clattered past on 14th to turn south at Greenwich. There was a fire somewhere. There were always fires somewhere in New York City.

A few miles away across the Hudson a quiet young man stained dark with coal dust climbed down from the tender of the Weehawken Limited and walked to a stock tank beyond the platform where he stripped off his shirt and scrubbed himself thoroughly with cold water. He shook back his hair and toweled his face with rough sacking, then hung his shirt to dry on a deadman cable beside the tower and walked back to the engine.

The engineer grinned at him, shrewd eyes taking in the heavy shoulders, iron-hard arms and calloused hands of a man who had never known ease. "Aye, young feller, you've earned your passage," he said. "I've not found many who'll scoop a tender for the price of a pass these days. Old John has kept his firebox happy and never had to climb the bins for fuel."

"You said you'd ask around here," the young man reminded him.

"Aye, and I have that. The two you're lookin' for were here just yesterday. Ben Hibbs at the station shack noticed them. They took the Weehawken Ferry. Ben says if you'll ask for Shad O'Reilly on the far side, he was workin' it yesterday and he's a man with good eyes. Like enough he can tell you where they went from there."

The young man went back for his shirt, then climbed the

cab ladder to get down his gear, a small parcel wrapped in a burlap bag.

"I set that aside from the ridin' bench," the engineer said, eyeing him curiously. "Felt to me like there was a revolver in there."

"There is," the young man nodded. Then he smiled and extended a hand. "My thanks to you," he said.

The engineer took his hand. "And mine to you, Emmett Todd. The saints be with you . . . and mind yourself on the far side. Benn Hibbs says that's a tough pair you're chasin' after."

A few years earlier, before the war, when the city lay desolated by economic depression, little more than open fields lay above Union Square. The Crystal Palace and its surrounding shops and houses clustered nearly a mile north of even the nearest residential areas of the old city. Yet the war of secession had done its work for New York City. The city had invested and the returns were huge. Even now great tracts of new buildings were going up in places as remote as Fifth Avenue and East 52nd street, multi-story buildings presided over by the spire of St. Patrick's Cathedral. Fine homes had been completed along the extended Madison Avenue, and large sections of burned out tenements south of Canal Street were being rebuilt.

The teeming streets of Greenwich and Columbus Park off the Bowery masked the dark side of the city where criminal elements born of the depression had taken hold, yet within view of the killing alleys now were the bright restored faces of Palmer's Opera House and Astor Place House, and gilded carriages rolled through lamplit streets in the evenings to discharge patrons at Niblo's, Wallack's and the Vauxhall.

More than three-fourths of a million people now were gathered at the tip of Manhattan Island, and as their numbers grew with the profits of war they spread northward and clustered southward. Few buildings had exceeded four stories until these late years. Now there were many that stood eight to ten floors above the street.

Mercer Poling had been busy since his arrival. A political favor had gained him the use of a fine penthouse on new Seventh Avenue whose veranda overlooked Broadway at a distance of two hundred yards. With the house had come the use of a flat south of Astor Place whose windows looked down on Broadway, and an upstairs office on Chambers that looked out on City Hall.

Poling was a wealthy man since the death of Merritt Fields, and had resources to make contacts among the right people in two layers of the city—those who knew the politics of the metropolis and those who knew the ways of the streets. Among these latter in recent days there had been turmoil. A renegade unknown had been operating in their neighborhoods, without their leave, and seemed to come and go as he pleased. Poling was not interested. He had other things on his mind.

Though relegated to small headlines by the latest fire, the sinking of the *Eleutha* off Bedloe's Island and the controversy over construction of a bridge to Brooklyn, the impending presidential visit to New York still was news. And a continuing sidebar to the news was the anticipated arrival of plains Indians who would camp for a time in Central Park.

The details of the proposed meeting of the president with the Indians' chief were secret. Federal officials insisted on that, as a security precaution. Still, it was suspected that the Indians would be entertained in a manner to provide maximum spectacle for the citizens of New York. It was the style of William Tweed and his partners, including Mayor Hall, to entertain the citizens at every opportunity.

But Poling had the plans, in detail. A connection in Washington had arranged that. Now he surveyed the city as a general surveys a battleground, and planned his moves accordingly.

Pasco and his cohort Tram were on their way. There had been no response to his wire to Winter at Bonneset, and that rankled him. Of them all, Winter was his best piece for a quick kill. It was for that reason he had sent Winter to eliminate Cain DeWitt. Winter was quick and sure, although not entirely to be trusted.

Still, he had found plenty of talent right in New York, pools of men to draw from for a price, who would be good backup for what he had in mind.

Poling had no concern about embarrassing Tweed or his henchmen. Tweed's power in New York was awesome, but it did not extend to Washington or to the western lands.

Poling knew that the meeting of the president and the Kiowa chief was to take place at City Hall. From the park where they would camp to City Hall was nearly five miles. Oakley Hall's plan was that the entire five mile route be a festive parade.

Somewhere along that route Hawk That Hunts Walking—and maybe a few more Indians—would die. Even better, if he could arrange it properly, some of the Indians might retaliate and innocent people be hurt or killed. That would be perfect for his purposes. With such impetus, the extermination of Kiowa on the Central Plains would be sealed, and so would his appointment as commissioner.

In two years' administration of the little Smoky Hill Strip, with a staff of a half dozen enforcers, Poling had netted more than $50,000. Administration of the Central Plains with the War Department at his call would be worth a hundred times that, at least.

At a shunt siding on the Passaic, a heavily-guarded train eased onto tiered sidetrack between two other trains awaiting signal from the Jersey yards.

Randolph Yeats peered out his window, into the window of a crowded westbound car on the next track. A family of people in drab clothing, their bundles piled around them, looked back at him. He tried to raise his sash, struggled with it as it stuck, and a burly Blackleg warrior reached over and flicked it up for him. "Op'm nglatz," the Kiowa said. In the opposite car the man opened his sash and stared across at him.

"Is this New York City?" Yeats called. "Where are we

313

now?"

The man shrugged and shook his head. "*Eda ven ene Nea Yorke*," he said, and leaned out to point. *E touti e politea ene to Jersey. E Nea Yorke ene eis tin anatoli.*"

Yeats sagged in his window. Immigrants. The words were Greek to him.

The man pointed at the warrior beside Yeats. "*E toutos o antrhopos ene Indianos*," he told his wife, proud of his knowledge of this new land.

XXIX

"I smell food," Mulcahey said for the forth time in less than an hour. "I smell roast lamb and cabbage, and boiled potatoes, and sort of a plum pudding with cloves, and maybe smothered partridge and hot coffee. I really smell it."

Jakey Bloom looked at him sadly. "Of course you do, Irish. So do the rest of us . . . maybe. But it's all in your head. That's the first sign of starvation, is when you keep thinking you smell food."

"I don't just think I smell it." Mulcahey blinked at him, unsure again. "I . . . well, I do think I smell it. Every time this train slows down, I smell food cooking."

Tom Pedigo just shook his head and huddled into his coat. The wind in these hills was cold, and they had nothing to protect them but the plank rails of an odorous stock car clattering through moonlit mountains shadowed by dark forest. Their corporal, Jamie Finnegan, had talked fast and lied profoundly to get them passage on this market express headed for Albany, but he was beginning to wonder if it had been such a good idea. There were no coaches on this train, no amenities at all. Only a long line of slat-boxed flatcars carrying livestock and a few plain flatcars toward the end, carrying stamped steel members from the mills at Scranton.

The four troopers had searched Scranton, looking for their lost Indian. There had been plenty of clues—wide-eyed witnesses here and there who had seen phantoms, and at least three badly-mauled toughs who had thought to have a bit of sport with a foreigner in a wide hat, then had been attacked by a madman with paint on his face—but they had not found the Indian.

Their train had gone when they returned to the yards, so Finnegan had fast-talked the engineer and the brakeman of this stock train into taking them east. Special orders from the War Department, he had said. Direct orders from General Grant himself, he had implied. Something to do with meeting the president, he had hinted. That, and the three dollars they had put up, had got them and their horses aboard.

It wasn't until the train was moving, eastward into more and more desolate night-shrouded mountains, that they remembered they hadn't eaten since the previous noon. Now the more they thought about it the hungrier they became, and Mulcahey's constant talk about smelling food didn't help any.

Through the long valleys the train clipped along at flank speed, making better time than a passenger train could have because the engineer did not have to consider comfort of travel . . . only the bonus that would be his if he got his payload to Albany ahead of schedule. They could get off outside of Middletown, he assured them, and catch another train south from there.

On the climbs the engine slowed perceptibly, and Pedigo was grateful for the lull in the cold wind. But he was not grateful for Mulcahey. For a long time now, each time the train slowed Mulcahey had started talking about food. First he had smelled turkey baking. Then it had been steamed clams, then roast pork with fresh bread and honey. Now he was smelling full, four-course meals. All Pedigo could smell was the stink of sheep in the forward half of their car and the two cars ahead, and now and then a rankle of goat from the car behind. He was cold and hungry and he wished Mulcahey would shut up.

The engine was climbing again. The rush of wind dwindled to calm and Mulcahey sniffed the air. "Do you know what it is now?" he announced. "Baked beans with pork fat and onions. I can smell it like it was cooking right here beside us."

Pedigo gritted his teeth and Jakey Bloom looked very sad. But now the corporal sat up straight, his nose twitching. Then he got to his knees. "I'll be damned," he said. "I smell it too. But that isn't beans, Mulcahey. It's codfish, fried with pepper and bay. I'd know that smell anywhere."

Pedigo stared at him. "Jesus," he whispered.

Bloom sniffed the cold air. Then he stood, brushing his britches. "Gefiltefish," he corrected. "And hot bagles."

Then they were all standing, their noses high and twitching like hounds'. Pedigo squinted. "Maybe I do smell smoke," he admitted. "But where? We haven't even seen a house for the past two hours, not since we got into these hills."

"Maybe they're cooking dinner up in the engine."

"Naw. If they were we'd smell it when they speed up, not when they slow down. Besides, they don't cook in those engines. They bring their lunch."

Corporal Finnegan walked a few feet forward to check on their horses. They were secure and content, riding in a sort of rope corral the troopers had rigged between themselves and the mass of huddled sheep that occupied the remainder of the stock car.

"I guess we could take a look at those cars back there," Finnegan decided. "If anybody wants to."

Mulcahey climbed to the top rail rear, looking back. All he could see were the carload of goats behind them and the pile of metal forms on the flatcar beyond. "I'll see if I can get back there," he said. "Do you remember whether there's a caboose? There might be something cooking there, if there is."

"If there's a caboose it's empty," Finnegan said. "Only three men runnin' this train, and they're all up there in the engine and tender. Go ahead, Mulcahey. I'm right behind you."

They all went. Mulcahey jumped to the goat car's plank roof, Finnegan followed and Bloom came after them.

"Wienerschnitzel," he said over his shoulder to Pedigo. "That's what it is. Wienerschnitzel and sauerbraten, roasting."

Pedigo's stomach rumbled and he crouched to run along the top of the goat-car, following the rest.

The first flat car was piled with three tall stacks of large metal forms. Trestle joints, for the construction of trusses for a bridge. The second flat had only two stacks, with a clear span of flooring between, and they gathered on the front stack to look down at the two people crouched there, cooking something over an open fire. A large pile of stockcar railing lay beside them, for use as firewood.

The one with tall hair and feathers glanced up, saw them there and grinned. The other squinted up at them from the shadow of his hatbrim. Smears of grease glistened on his chin and his hands. He stood, swept off his hat and bowed. *"Bienvenido, Soldados. Tienen hambre? Tenemos cabrito aqui."*

Speechless, the troopers climbed down the stack of trusscocks and gaped at the Spaniard and the Indian.

"Nuestro cabrito es su cabrito," Trini invited, indicating the dripping cut of meat roasting over the shielded fire.

Lizard stood back, studying the soldiers, glancing from them to the fire. Then he picked up his warclub and went to get another goat.

As the stock train approached Middletown early in the morning four cavalry mounts, a notch-eared paint and a mustard pony were saddled and ready. By the time the train was halted at a watertank and the brakeman walked back to check his couplings, the passengers were gone into the forest. South of Middletown the Nyack line ran down toward the Hudson Yards. Corporal Jamie Finnegan thought as they rode, wondering whether it would be worth the effort to try to find another train, or whether they might just point their Kiowa in the required direction and then pace their mounts to his. Sloatsburg wasn't far away, and from there it was only twenty miles cross-country to the Palisades and the Bronx Passage ferry. To a Kiowa, twenty miles was nothing.

Debarkation at the Hudson Yards was a barely-controlled madhouse. While solid ranks of infantry cordoned the space between the transit shed to the north and the Holland docks to the south, train-bound cavalry troopers and bedecked Kiowa warriors burst from the coaches, pranced along empty sidings and raced toward the stock cars to get their horses. The warriors of Stalking Horse's Blackleg Society and the warriors of Lieutenant Thomas Spradley's First Platoon Detached had one thing in common. They did not like to be afoot.

Darby Curtis was right behind the first rush, flanked by White Hand and Sunshine. Stalking Horse had gone ahead to take charge of the Blackleg men. Darby swung his rifle as he trotted, and rolled his shoulders to relieve the strain of long days of travel under trying circumstances. Looking around him at the sights of the Jersey ways, the masses of wide-eyed people crowding the cordon lines, he thought how easy it might be just to veer aside, slip through those lines and once and for all be done with the whole crazy Kana'tenee tribe and their crazy ideas. Yet, he had given his word to Hawk That Hunts Walking, to bring him to the Great Father, and there still were a few miles to go.

Besides, he knew it was problematical whether he could outrun White Hand or out-wrestle Sunshine, and to get away he would have to do both. The Blacklegs would brain him and scalp him just as readily in the middle of the Jersey Ways as they would on the Kansas prairies.

At the stock cars a clamor of impatience arose in two languages and trainmen hustled to get the gates open and the ramps down. The forward box car was open and Kiowas and soldiers worked side by side, handing down their possessions and gear.

At Camp Jacob, Darby had been provided with a horse saddle, trappings and two good horses to use on the trip. Now he reclaimed his gear and trudged to the railside corral to pick out the best of the horses, a long-legged, deep-bodied bay that reminded him—barely—of Hildegarde.

Stalking Horse met him there. The Indian was tightening cinches on a liver-and-white paint with goose feathers tied into its mane. Saddled up, the warrior slipped his belled shield onto his shoulder, lifted his hooked lance and swung aboard. The horse shivered, then came unglued beneath him, spinning, rearing and kicking, almost somersaulting in its effort to throw him. Stalking Horse clung like a leech, awaited his chance, then brought the hooked lance down in a hard swing, to swat the animal between its ears. "Sona'bish!" he said. The word was neither English or Kiowa. It was an expression most of them had picked up from Trini Salazar. Hearing it brought a renewed bleakness to Darby's spirits. He probably would never see the crazy little Spaniard again. But it dawned on him that he might miss him.

His horse calmed, Stalking Horse sat his saddle and watched as Darby saddled the bay. "You have a sad heart," he said.

Darby looked up at him, then gestured. "Look around you, Stalking Horse. This is a place of the white people. This is where the Great Father will be. It was your vision that brought us all here. Are you content now with your vision?"

The Indian stared out at the sea of white faces beyond the distant ranks of soldiers. Beyond lay transit shed and hoists, cargo docks and mills, and everywhere were buildings. Smoke rose from many of them and the bright air was greasy with it. The sky was clear, but low and brassy, and a smell of dead fish pervaded everything. "It is not a good place," he admitted. "It would not be a good place for the Kana'tenee. But it is as the white men have made it. I think it is not an evil place, O'gatedota. Only a bad place." He peered down at the white man. "Do the spirits talk to O'gatedota? Does the wind speak?"

"The wind speaks," Darby nodded. "There is evil here, somewhere, and it waits for us."

Stalking Horse raised his head, sunlight blazing from the bright colors of his paint, glistening in his feathers. "It must be so," he said finally. "In this place even the Blackleg men do not hear the wind, Darby Curtis. It no longer speaks the language of our people."

Darby had his saddle in place and a foot in the stirrup, but he paused, frowning at the Indian face above him. It was the first time he had heard his real name, his English name, from Stalking Horse. He wondered what it meant. To the Blacklegs, everything meant something.

"Teach your horse his time of laziness is over," the Indian said, and wheeled away.

Darby swung into the saddle. The bay exploded. It arched its back, shot straight up and landed on stiff legs. Then it shied violently, switched ends and went into a series of jolting bucks, rattling its rider's teeth. Darby swore, raised his rifle and thumped the animal's skull. All over the corral, horses were pitching, riders clinging, and here and there a man hit the ground. But all those thrown wore blue uniforms. Soldiers glared at gloating Indians and caught up their horses to try again.

Riding from the corral, Darby found another rider pacing beside him and glanced around, then caught his breath. The man was tall, lithe and gray-haired, dressed in perfectly-tailored urban attire and wore a flat-crowned dark hat. Mild eyes as gray and cold as pond ice gazed at him from a serene, unlined face, and the man extended a hand. "Good morning, Mr. Curtis. Nice to see you again."

Darby hesitated, then took the hand. It was a trim hand, slim and long-fingered, and it felt like iron. "Mr. Kichener. Mr. Chrisman said you'd be here. They all seemed a little puzzled as to why, though."

Kichener smiled then, and his eyes held a deep humor. "I suspect they are," he said. "I really have not bothered to explain to anyone, and they are civilized people. They wouldn't think of asking."

"Well, I would. If you don't want to answer, don't answer. Who are you and what do you want?"

The gray man chuckled with real pleasure. "Ah. The western breed. You already know who I am. My name is Ernest Kichener. We first met when you translated some things for me at the Willow Ford conference, though I have to admit I knew you before that."

"What do you mean?"

"I make it my business to know those I will associate with, young Curtis. I have known your father for quite a long time. And I know a little about you."

"He never told me about you."

"He wouldn't," Kichener chuckled again. "Anyway, you asked what I want, meaning of course why am I here. I am here for the same reason you are, Darby Curtis. To protect Hawk That Hunts Walking."

"You think someone will try kill him again?"

"I know someone will. To the best of my ability I have narrowed it to a slim range of where and when. But I need other eyes than mine now, Darby Curtis. Hawk That Hunts Walking thinks you can see ghosts. He is convinced of it."

"You've been talking to John Miles."

"Of course. And I believe it. I think somehow you will see dangers that others might miss. I want you to watch for those."

"In New York City? How can I watch for anything with three Blacklegs tailing along everywhere I go?"

Kichener glanced across at him, then back. "I see no Blacklegs, Darby Curtis."

Startled, Darby drew rein and turned in his saddle. They had ridden most of the length of the train, and they were alone. In the distance, by the corral, he saw Stalking Horse and the others. They were looking his way, but made no motion to follow.

"They brought you here for a reason," Kichener said. "Now you are here, they'll leave you alone. They trust you to do what you came to do."

Darby's brow came down and his temper flared. "What I came to do? Hell, they've never told me what I came to do. What is this . . . that medicine business again? You sound just like the old chief, do you know that? Do what I came to do. See ghosts. 'Be my eyes.' My God, Mr. Kichener, people keep talking to me and they don't tell my anything. I'm here because I made a deal to come, because I want to do business out there in the plains and I don't want a war getting in the way. But I don't know anything about New York City, and I don't want to. Now just exactly what is it . . ."

Kichener raised a hand, cutting him off. "You just keep your eyes open, Darby. You stay with the Indians if you feel like it, and if you feel like scouting around you do that. Keep your eyes open and remember why you made a deal. Remember Hawk That Hunts Walking."

Darby started to protest again, but the man turned away. "They're bringing in the first barge," he said. "Infantry will cross first, then the cavalry escort, then old Hawk and his party with the commissioner and some of his men. Then the rest of the Indians will go over, with Infantry bringing up the rear. Choose your barge, Darby. You can take any one you like. Good day to you, sir."

Kichener touched his hat, touched his reins and rode away, and Darby sat speechless, in his mind a vivid image of ice-gray eyes straight out of hell and an impression of steel swathed in gray velvet.

Finally he took a deep breath, tapped heels to the bay and rode down to the loading docks. The first barge was just pulling in. He rode aboard, dismounted and waited as an infantry unit marched on with him.

He could have his choice, the man had said. Fine. If he had to go to New York City he would go. And he would cross the Hudson first, ahead of everybody.

XXX

Through the day and into the evening he explored, sometimes riding the bay horse, sometimes leading it. People turned to look at him, curious—not at seeing a horseman, New York was full of horsemen—but at something about the tall young man that set him apart. His clothing was vaguely notable, tough and efficient-seeming, neither street clothes nor workmen's clothes but something in between. That he carried a rifle was notable too. Many people in New York carried guns, but usually these were hidden weapons—derringers in sash pockets or vests, or revolvers under long coats.

The wide western hat he wore was a type uncommon on city streets. Made for shielding glare and turning wind-blown dust, for deflecting rain and for catching up water from a stream, in spoke of far open spaces and was noticeable among the varieties of headgear in the city.

These things were noted as he scouted the streets and ways of lower Manhattan. People by the thousands glanced at him and glanced again, but these trappings were not what held the gaze. He seemed out of place here, a tall man wandering the streets, looking, pausing, turning to look in other directions. It was an attitude that people noticed, a way of seeming to see more than they saw. He looked at the buildings and at the people, yet it seemed he looked through them and beyond them with eyes focused on distances not bounded by the walls and the ways around them.

Still, New York City was full of strange sights and Darby

Curtis was a minor one among them. People had come from the fish docks and the financial district, from the Bowery and East Delancey, from the upper West Side and the huddled tenements of Division and Rutgers and Gouverneur, and they lined the streets to see the Indians arrive. People by the thousands thronged high windows and sat on roof tops from Greenwich to Union Square for a view of the wild, painted savages from the western plains.

Darby sat his saddle in front of an alley a block from Canal Street, looking over the heads of the crowd to watch them pass, and he felt a kinship that surprised him. Here among hundreds of thousands of people of his race, of his native language, he was a foreigner. But when they came into view, proceeding along Broadway flanked by a moving cordon of soldiers, escorted by a platoon of plains cavalry garbed now in dress uniform, he looked at the roached hair of the Blacklegs, the fierce painted faces and bedecked mounts, the shields and lances, and they were people who had names. They were people like him, and the land they found themselves in now was as strange to him as it was to them.

Stalking Horse rode at the head of the Blackleg men, his belled shield bright at his shoulder, hooked lance tall and streaming feathers in the sun. Stalking Horse studied the massed crowds as they passed, then turned and looked directly at Darby Curtis across the interval, holding his eyes.

Behind the Blacklegs Hawk That Hunts Walking shared a carriage with Keeps His Horses, Broken Bow, James Chrisman, L. W. Holmes and John Miles. The carriage driver wore the bright helmet and dress uniform of New York police, and a squad of mounted police followed behind and at the flanks.

At the corners of the carriage, and one ahead and one behind, rode Real Dog men in full ceremonial gear, large dark warriors emblazoned with crimson paint who carried their weapons as seasoned soldiers do and whose eyes missed nothing. Of those in the carriage only Keeps His Horses stood, glaring at the crowds, the buildings, the strange sights of the place, shaking his rattle to ward off evil.

As they passed Hawk That Hunts Walking turned and Darby knew the old man saw him. The expression on the creased old face did not change, but the eyes held a certainty that Darby would not fail him . . . that he would do what they had brought him to do.

He cursed himself and wheeled the bay horse to ride away down the alley. He didn't know what they expected of him. And yet, he felt the need to scout the land—to hunt.

Trotting northward on Mercer he reentered Broadway at Astor Place, now well ahead of the procession, and set a course northward. Everywhere he looked there were buildings—old buildings with tree-lined walks, new buildings going up to overshadow them—and people. He shuddered, his senses alert.

Nearing Union Square he reined in and looked around. A cold tingling spread up his neck and across his shoulders, a feeling he remembered from Antietam. It was an acute uneasiness, and he looked around, trying to focus it. His gaze rested on a building there, not on Broadway but overlooking it, and the feeling intensified. It was as though the building were a place and a time—a place where danger had been and a time when no birds sang. The building looked like its neighbors, yet it captured his attention and he backed the bay to curbside, gripping his rifle.

Minutes passed and the crowds increased, surging northward on Broadway. Where the wide street bent westward the crowds were pushed back and soldiers appeared, then the lances and plumes of the Blacklegs. He noticed a presence beside him and whirled around. Ernest Kichener was there, cool and elegant, astride a dark sorrel gelding with an English saddle.

"Trouble, Darby?" he asked quietly. Darby noticed at a glance that the butt of a sleek Colt revolver peeked from the open waist of his mist-gray coat.

"I don't know. Just a feeling. I guess if I was in the field right now I'd be wondering who holds the high ground. That building over there . . . there's something wrong with it."

Kichener looked, then nodded. "Good eyes, young man.
There are no people at the windows on the fourth floor."

"Maybe the floor is vacant."

"Not likely. Some of the windows are open. How do you
feel about it?"

"Nervous, I guess."

"Nervous now?"

Darby glanced at him. The question was serious. "I
don't know. Maybe not now. Maybe later . . . sometime."

Kichener nodded, then touched heels to the sorrel and
headed downstreet. A few minutes later soldiers hurried
ahead of the procession and took up positions where Darby
waited. They did not openly look at the building across the
way. They ignored it. But he knew they were watching it.
The chill feeling diminished.

Darby watched the approaching procession for a time,
then turned to look northward up Broadway. A half-mile or
so away, the ranks of huddled buildings seemed to spread,
to open out, and on impulse he turned the bay's head that
way and flipped his rein. He was tired of the noise, the
stink, the closeness of city streets. His head hurt from the
constant echoing of sounds off blind walls. He wanted
space around him.

Above Fourteenth Street the packed city became looser,
newer, clusters of structures here and there among small
open fields, and the roads were irregular and erratic
although all the stub ends pointed at other stub ends they
some day would meet.

He passed carriages and surreys coming into town, and
the people looked at him curiously, noticing the hint of far
places about him. Mostly he ignored them, but when a red-
haired girl with a parasol, riding with her family in an open
phaeton, glanced at him and went wide eyed, he doffed is
hat, bowed slightly and grinned. Her face went bright pink,
a shade that matched her dress.

She reminded him of Melissa Muldoon, and he was
lonely then. He missed his mules, and he missed the vast
open lands with the high sun on the grasses, and he missed

the clean distances where a man could shout and not be plagued by echoes. But even more than all of those, he missed Melissa Muldoon. "Melly Bright-eyes," he whispered, "take care of yourself. I'm farther away than I've been before and hard put from here to keep you out of trouble."

Even out here there was a smell of the sea, and he shaded his eyes to look east and west. Stands of forest beyond the fields and building clusters blocked the view, but in both directions there were occasional glimpses of water.

Stub roads led off to east and west and a sign on a painted stone post said "34th Street." Even though there were planted fields here, beyond them on all sides were clusters of buildings, standing villages of stone and wood lath. He sighed, understanding the horror he had seen in the old eyes of Keeps His Horses when he first looked at the eastern lands. People obviously could live this way. Huge numbers of them did. But why? Yet he agreed with Hawk That Hunts Walking that it was a good thing they did. Otherwise the prairies would be swarming with them.

Tall new buildings stood close and defensive in five distinct groups at a paved intersection. At least two of them sported marble facades, and several of them climbed to dizzy heights, as tall as the walls of the hidden canyon of the Kana'tenee. He counted ten floors in one of them and wondered what the people would do if there were a fire. No ladder could reach them, and stairwells would roar like furnace flues. There was something about these people out here on the edge of the world that made them crowd together and climb atop one another . . . a craving to live on other people's roofs. They were cliff dwellers, taking apart a little island and rearranging its bones so they would have cliffs.

Darby shook his head, deeply disturbed. Then, again, he felt the tingle of a chill unfocused and reined in. He was among the buildings, and people stood at picket fences to gawk at him. Children ran from skinny houses to wonder who he was.

He dismounted, trying to focus on the source of the chill.

To appearances, it was a little town, separated by a mile from the city to the south, yet it seemed all one with the place, the distance bridged by the tall buildings ahead where street markers proclaimed "Broadway," "Seventh Avenue" and "42nd Street."

A man with grizzled whiskers stood beside a rail fence and as Darby glanced at him he nodded. "Ay-yuh. Like as not ye'll be one ah them."

"Them?"

"Them as brings th' painted savages t' camp yondah in th' meadow. Seen a few of ye already today. I reckon ye're another."

"What are those buildings over there?" Darby asked him.

"Them?" The man stuck a stub of pipe between his teeth and struck a sulphur match to light it. "Abominations is what they be. Wicksville ain't Wicksville any moah. Now it's all in N'yawk City, if ye please. Next plantin' place of th' high society, so they say. No use arguin' with City Hall, an' ye cehtain can't fight Tammany. So th' tycoons they come an' put up edifices like yondah."

"That one there," Darby pointed. "What building is that?" He didn't like the building. It felt ominous to him.

"Butlah Buildin'," the man said. "Lawyahs an' govah-'ment folk, mostly. Some high-falutin' Publican magnate has a penthouse up on top, but he's let it out f' th' season. Wheah you from, Mistah?"

"West," Darby said, still studying the Butler Building. It made him uneasy. He began to wonder if Hawk That Hunts Walking was right . . . if he did see ghosts.

"That bunch I seen this noon, th' soldiahs with th' painted Injun an' the furrinah, was them some of yoah'n?"

Darby stared at the man. He could't have seen soldiers and Indians earlier today. Not unless . . . "Where were they?"

"Yondah." The man pointed north. "I net th' shoals up theah mahnin's. They come by, all ridin' like th' ol' Scratch was aftah theyah souls, but th' furrinah he stopped, wanted to know 'bout Miguel Jesus Montoya."

329

"Do you know where they went?"

"T' see Miguel Jesus Montoya, I reckon. That's wheah I sent 'em."

"You know him?"

"I reckon. He's a shippin' agent. Got hisself a place at Peel House, Bleekah an' Eighth, on th' squaah. Buys my catch most Thuhsdays. Top dollah, too."

Trini. The crazy Spaniard had made it. Darby sighed, not quite certain how glad he was. At any rate, what he had to do now was to round him up before he got himself into any more trouble.

He gazed again at the Butler Building, in the distance, and the uneasiness returned. Touching his hatbrim to the whiskered man he mounted, turned the bay's head south again headed back down the road called Broadway. Behind him, beyond the gate where the whiskered man stood, a man stepped from the shadows and looked after him. Though the shadows of evening lengthened across Manhattan Island, Winter felt the sun of fortune shining upon him. Long ago, he had set aside the debt Darby Curtis owed him as something to collect at some future time when the opportunity was right. He would never have dreamed that Curtis would be here in New York, fifteen hundred miles from his own stomping grounds, but here he was, and it was as the fates decreed.

For years, Winter had intended to track down Darby Curtis one day and kill him. And now here he was, and here Darby was. There was no time like the present.

Methodically, Winter drew the revolver from its oiled holster beneath his long coat and checked its loads. Then he walked west on the paved stub of 42nd Street until he found a riding stable catering to the gentry of the new uptown.

He had not yet found Poling, but he would look for him tomorrow. Right now he had better things to do.

The wagon road now designated as Eighth Avenue was an unpaved track, separated from Broadway by fields and woodlots and occasional truck farms. From the edge of a woodlot Winter watched Darby rein in to speak to another rider, pointing back to the north. Then they separated, Darby going south at a mile-eating lope. Just beyond was the Kiowa procession, coming northward toward the park that would be their quarters. Winter saw Curtis veer off on another road leading due south, and he spurred his horse to pace him. In the distance he thought Kiowa faces turned toward him, but the procession continued northward.

As the quick dusk of Atlantic evening purpled in the east, Winter kept his eyes on the rider a half mile away, and those eyes were bright with hatred and revenge.

XXXI

Like a ferret that scents it prey, Trinidad Salazar homed on the abode of Miguel Jesus Montoya, and the four troopers of the First Platoon, A Troop, First Squadron, Fifth Cavalry Regiment of the Ninth Division, United States Army, had little recourse but to follow.

Where the Spaniard went, there went the Indian called Lizard. And where the Indian went—until they could return him safely to their command—there must they go also. Corporal Finnegan had no more precise description of their destination than "New York City," and as Jakey Bloom was quick to point out, New York City was several miles in any direction. So through the afternoon hours six riders on six very tired horses crisscrossed upper New York City from Washington Avenue to Avenue B and from East 13th to Grand while Trini Salazar searched for an address he had barely understood and had not been able to explain to the others at all. It was only when they rode past a street brawl and Trini heard the lyric tones of rapid-fire Spanish that he stopped his relentless quest and proceeded thoughtfully.

Approximately twenty men were involved in the mayhem taking place. Trini kicked the mustard pony and waded right in, followed by Lizard. That was almost enough to break up the hostilities. A four-man cavalry charge finished the job and Trini knelt by the pummeled man who had shouted in Spanish. He helped him to his feet, supporting his weight, and snapped questions at him. Where is Bleeker Street? Where is Eighth Avenue? Where is Miguel Jesus

Montoya?

In slurred and shaken Spanish, the man responded, grateful to have found a friend. He was bleeding freely from several cuts, and seemed to have a broken shoulder. Trini listened, taking in the directions, focusing on distances and vectors, intersections and turns.

"*Gracias*," he said then, and ran for his pony. By the time the beaten man had sagged again to the street, Trinidad Salazar was at full gallop along Delancey Street, scattering afternoon crowds before him, a yipping Kiowa warrior and four cavalrymen pounding in his wake.

A squad of harness bulls running from the Bowery to break up the street fight scattered like quail before the six, and the police whistles that shrilled through the streets were far behind them.

Blue of evening was descending as the six led exhausted horses up Bleeker Street, Trini following the map in his mind.

"Doesn't that Spaniard ever slow down?" Tom Pedigo complained. "If I thought this horse's feet were half as sore as mine are, I'd shoot him out of mercy."

"I'm hungry," Mulcahey announced. "Everywhere we turn around here I smell food. We ought to at least stop someplace and see if we could get a meal."

"If you decide to shoot your horse," Jakey Bloom told Pedigo, "I want the tenderloin."

"I'm hungry enough to eat a horse, too," Finnegan told them. "But we don't have any money, remember? What we need to do is find our outfit."

Pedigo glanced dubiously at a hash-house where people were pouring out the door to watch them pass. He noticed Lizard was sniffing the air and staring at the eatery. "I wonder if any of these places here serve Indians."

"If they do," Bloom told him, "I'll take mine medium rare."

"Listen, Trinidad," Finnegan hurried to catch the stalking Spaniard, "If you could stop for a little bit maybe we could get a restaurant to take Army scrip. Aren't you hungry?"

Trini looked at him blankly. *"No comprendo,"* he shrugged and went back to his study of signs and numbers. Rounding a protruding corner he peered at a building, deciphered the sooted numbers and nodded. His dark eyes glistened in the light of gas lamps. *"Aqui es el sitio,"* he said, *"y ahora la hora."* He turned to his followers, handed his reins to Mulcahey and glared at Lizard. *"Quedate aqui, Moro,"* he said. Then he strode across the walkway and through the entrance door of the building.

"Where's he going?" Mulcahey asked the corporal. "What is he going to do?"

"Best I can figure it out, I think he's going in there to kill somebody."

"Well, when he gets done, then can we get something to eat?"

Crowds gathered on the street corners, staring at them.

Inside the building Trini puzzled over a paper directory pinned to a wall, running his eyes along its lines. He brightened then. Miguel Jesus Montoya. Suite 22.

Fingering the revolver at his belt the Spaniard pounded up a flight of steps, paused at the landing, found the number he sought and went to the door. Holding the butt of his gun with his right hand he knocked with his left.

There were sounds from inside, then the door was pulled open by a plump and exhausted young woman clutching a baby to her breast while three small children clung to her skirts and stared up at the intruder.

Trini started to speak, then recognition came and his mouth hung open. It was Doña Lucinda. The radiant, the lovely, the comely Doña Lucinda Villanova-Madeiro, daughter to a minister of Portugal, the captor of the heart of Trinidad Salazar and the purpose of his life, stood surrounded by her children and stared suspiciously at him with no sign of recognition. The scent of cooking cabbage wafted from the suite behind her.

"Yes?" she prompted.

Trini released his gun and swept off his hat. *"Por favor, Señora, viven aqui el Señor Miquel Jesus Montoya?"*

She nodded, still suspicious, then turned her head to

call, *"Miguelito? Un visitante!"*

Trini looked from one to another of the children. They seemed clean and well-fed, and they stared at him with dark button eyes. He smiled at them. The two oldest smiled back, hesitantly, while the youngest sucked his thumb. At Doña Lucinda's breast the baby suckled contentedly. He looked at her, at them, and a warmth grew around his heart.

Then a man came to the door. He was in shirtsleeves and was drying his hands with a towel. He was thin, almost frail, and he peered through thick glasses. But the quick smile he gave his wife as she stepped aside was a golden thing.

"En Español," she whispered to him.

He looked at Trini. In Spanish he said, "I am Miguel Jesus Montoya. May I be of service to you, Señor?"

Trini backed away a half-step, studying the man. He had had so many images of Miguel Jesus Montoya. How had none of them been like this man? He tried to speak and found no words. His hands trembled and he gripped his hat brim with them both. The man waited, beginning to seem concerned. As the silence continued the woman stepped into the doorway again, beside her husband, and looked at Trini.

"Señor," she asked, "Are you ill? May I get you something?"

Trini shook his head. "No, thank you. No. I am well, thank you. I . . . I should not be here, Señora . . . Señor. I have come to the wrong place. I am very sorry. Ah, you are all so beautiful. I wish you well." His voice shook and a tear rolled down his cheek, unheeded. Turning abruptly, he crammed his hat back on his head and stumbled down the stairs. Behind him the man and woman looked at each other blankly.

Trini Salazar had been gone a few minutes when Darby Curtis rounded the corner on a snorting bay horse and pulled to a stop, recognizing the Indian and the soldiers. He dismounted and hurried across the street. "Lizard," he told the warrior in Kiowa, "Your brothers have missed

335

you." To the soldiers he said, "I'm glad you made it. Is Trini with you?"

"He'll be along in a minute," Finnegan said. "You know where our outfit is, Mr. Curtis? They didn't tell us, except that we were going to New York City."

"Sure. They're up past the north edge of the city. They have a big meadow to camp in, with the Kiowa. They're probably putting up their teepees for them by now."

"Why don't the redskins put up their own teepees?" Bloom asked.

"Oh, they don't do that. That's women's work. The men just sit around and watch."

"I'll be damned . . ." Finnegan erupted, then grinned. "Well, it's not us four that's doin' it."

"All we're doin' is starvin'," Mulcahey agreed. "Mr. Curtis, you don't happen to have a bit of cheese with you, I suppose? Or a bit of bread or a lemon or . . ."

Jakey Bloom stared at him, horrified. "A lemon?"

"Well, yeah. I may be on the verge of scurvy."

Darby looked around, at the gathering crowds. Lizard was attracting a lot of attention. "Where did you say Trini went?"

"In there," Finnegan pointed. "He was looking for somebody."

"Who?"

"I don't know. Jesus Montoya, something like that . . ."

Darby was already racing toward the steps. He stopped when the door opened and Trini Salazar came out, head down and shoulders slumped. For a moment the Spaniard stood at the top of the steps, then he pulled off his hat and turned to look upward at the face of the building.

"Mi Corazon," he proclaimed, *"mi estrellita Lucinda, vaya con Dios."*

With that he put on his hat and started down the stairs. In the light of gas lamps, Darby had seen that his cheeks were wet.

He started toward him, and there was a sudden scuffling in the crowd at the corner, then a dark-coated figure strode through and stopped, his face shadowed. White teeth glinted as he grinned.

"Darby Curtis!" he said. "You can go straight to hell!"

With a motion that was a blur, he swept back his coat, drew a gun, pointed and fired . . . just as Trinidad Salazar stepped from the porch.

The roar of the gun drummed in the echoing street, its tongue of flame brilliant, and the Spaniard stopped in mid-stride, his head going back, arms flailing, rising to tiptoes. Then he fell, face down. People in the crowd screamed and surged, panicked and fled. Darby swung his rifle to his shoulder but there were people everywhere. The gunman hesitated for an instant and a Kiowa war-cry split the air. A feathered lance whistled across open space and opened a gash in the man's cheek, splitting his ear to stand quivering in a lamp post behind him. The gunman turned, ducked into the jostling crowd and disappeared.

Darby shouted, "Winter!" and ran after him, gripping his rifle. Through fleeing crowds of onlookers he zigzagged a block, and then another, and realized he had lost the man. From a distance came the diminishing staccato of galloping hooves on paved streets.

Pale and shaken, Darby ran back the way he had come. Most of the people were gone now, except those staring from upstairs windows. In the street four soldiers struggled to hold a thrashing Kiowa warrior, and horses shied away in fright.

On the walkway, almost directly under a gas lamp, a mustard pony nuzzled the hand of Trini Salazar, a hand that was still and cold.

Darby knelt by the Spaniard, listening to police whistles in the distance, to the shouts of excited people, to the echoes of the crowded street. When the police came he told them what he could, and the troopers and other witnesses filled in bits and pieces. They covered Trinidad Salazar with a sheet, and a wagon came and took the body away.

It was nearly dark when Darby Curtis and a softly chanting Lizard rode north through city streets followed by four silent cavalrymen grimly armed and alert.

"You knew that man, Mr. Curtis?" the corporal asked

when they has passed Union Square and the city began to open out around them.

"I know him. His name is Winter."

"Well, I hope they catch the son of a bitch. I liked that little Spaniard. I hope they find that man."

"I'll find him," Darby said.

Jakey Bloom shook his head. "This is an awful big city."

Darby turned toward him and the trooper could see the glint of steel in hat-shadowed eyes. "It isn't that big, Trooper. I'll find him."

Lizard paused in his chanting. He turned to look back at the city behind them. "Sona'bish," he muttered. "Win-ter. Sona'bish *k'etaya. Ata ko'aywa.*"

"Like hell he does," Darby muttered. "The son of a bitch belongs to me."

XXXII

From the tenth floor penthouse of the Butler Building they watched the Kana'tenee and their escort turn onto Seventh Avenue and ride the remaining mile to the new park where they would camp. With a glass, Poling could see soldiers erecting teepees, canvas sheds and tents beyond the screening forest where a businesslike infantry cordon was placed. Supply wagons came from the city, and water was brought from a small lake nearby. Soon he could see cooking fires.

"Why don't you just let it go?" Pasco mused. "Too many soldiers out there. Too many guards."

Poling turned. "If you want out, Pasco, you take your shadow there and walk out the door and don't come back."

Pasco glanced at the gunman, Tram, then shook his head. "I don't mean anything like that, Mr. Poling. It's just that this ain't like takin' on a few squatters out on the plains in Kansas. Or pickin' off a stray Indian here and here. This thing you're planning . . . well, it's *serious*. Those Indians, they're here to see the president. If we kill that old chief . . ."

"*When* we kill the chief," Poling interrupted, "I'll tell you exactly what will happen. First, there will be a dust-up in this city with every badge and harness bull in town looking for somebody to blame, but we won't be here. I'll be on my way back to Washington and you'll be on your way west with money enough to keep you happy for a long

339

time. Second, the president will be embarrassed. His political coup will turn into a joke and the papers will skin him alive . . . and I have associates in Washington who will pay well to see that happen. They *will* pay well. Third, the old man's tribe will go to war on the plains, and when they go to war five other tribes of Kiowa will join them. The treaty will be broken, the army will move in and clear out the Kiowa and I will have control of two hundred and forty thousand square miles of empty land that the settlers want, the railroads want, the mining companies want and several big cattle interests want. And fourth, Mr. Stanton will have the president and Secretary Seward in a box . . . in gratitude for which he will arrange for my controls to supersede those of state and territorial governments.

"That, Mr. Pasco, is what will happen when Hawk That Hunts Walking dies."

"But the soldiers," Pasco sputtered, aghast at the magnitude of Poling's plans. "The police, the guards . . ."

"Of course they have tight security on this meeting," Poling nodded. "But I have their plan and I assure you, there is a hole in it. The hole is right here, in this city, tomorrow when the chief goes to City Hall to meet the president. They'll make a parade of it. All the way from the park over there down to City Hall. President Johnson arrived today, and he'll be there waiting for them. The mayor wants some ceremony or another outside, in City Hall Park, then they'll meet inside."

"Is that where we shoot the chief?"

"If it comes to that," Poling nodded. "But we have three chances. The first will be right here, when they pass on the street out there." He glanced at Tram, at his injured hand. They had never told him how that happened. "Can you still use a rifle?"

"I can use a rifle," the gunman snapped, then turned back to the window, studying the range, the open space, the juncture of streets.

Poling opened an ornate wardrobe and removed a case. He laid it on the bed beside the nearest window and opened it. "Can you use this?"

Tram turned to study the weapon. It was a modified Long Henry, heavy and bull-barrelled, with adjustable sights. A buffalo rifle. He lifted it, felt its weight and balance, put it to his shoulder, then squatted by the open window and sighted on the gas lights, the carriages rolling by, the evening crowds strolling." I can use it," he said.

"I don't want to use local talent unless I have to," Poling said. "The more we keep this among ourselves the better we all will get along . . . and the bigger cut you two and Winter stand to make."

"Where is Winter?" Pasco asked. "He should have been here by now."

"He'll show up. I'm sure he's in town by now. I have people looking for him. They'll take him to the flat on Astor Place when they find him."

"You said three chances," Pasco said. "That Astor Place location, is that one of them?"

"That's the second. Tram will be here. You will be there. If Tram misses for any reason, then it's up to you. You'll be even closer to the street there, looking directly across an open lot. Eighty yards at the most, and a back stairs that leads to an alley where a hansom will be waiting. Tram has the same arrangements here."

"I won't miss," Tram said. "You can forget about the rest of it."

"We shall take no chances," Poling said coldly. "There is too much at stake here for us to fail."

"If they put a flag on that pole out there it could spoil my aim," Tram said, frowning at the horizontal pole that jutted from the penthouse wall between the windows, its heavy lanyard looped to cleats at its base.

"They'd have to come in here to get to it," Poling said. "And you'll lock yourself in here. As far as anyone knows, this penthouse is vacant and there are no spare keys."

"Where's the third place?" Pasco asked.

"Right at City Hall. I'll be there, as a guest for the ceremonies, and I have a place arranged for Winter. If necessary, he is last resort. But gentlemen," he eyed them coldly, "I sincerely hope the chief does not live to reach

City Hall. I am counting on you . . . one or the other of you."

"I won't miss," Tram repeated, still playing with the big rifle. He paused then, peering into the streets beyond. "I think there's somebody down there watching this building."

Poling went to the window. The evening streets were busy, traffic up Broadway merging with that from Seventh Avenue. Entertainment centers were opening now in this new area, and people came from the city each evening to throng the streets.

"I don't see anyone," Poling said. "Just people. We shall be leaving now, Tram. You have everything you need here. When you have finished tomorrow—or if you miss—you know where to wait for the rest of us."

"I know," Tram said. "I won't miss."

Poling and Pasco had been gone for more than an hour when Tram heard a knock at the door. He had been dozing, lying on the bed. He sat up, blinking, and the knock came again. He started for the door, then remembered that no one was supposed to be here. The penthouse was supposed to be vacant. He stopped and turned away. The knock came again, then there was silence.

Curious, Tram crouched by the door, trying to look through the keyhole. The hall outside was dark and silent. Whoever it was had gone away. Still, he lowered his head to look again.

The door exploded inward, the crystal knob stunning him with its force, the weight of the door and the man behind it throwing him into the center of the room. He lay for a moment, dazed, then he groaned and got to his hands and knees, looking up. A man stood over him, hands at his hips. As Tram's vision cleared he saw a face that was somehow familiar, a hard young face, windhoned and sunhardened, a square, open, plain face with eyes that were flat and determined.

The man drew a revolver from his belt and dropped it on the floor between Tram's hands. "This is yours," he said.

Tram shifted his weight, grabbed for the gun and a heavy boot took him in the chest, flipping him backward. He rolled, gasping, and came to his feet, backstepping as the man crowded him. He swung a fist and a large, muscular arm deflected it casually. He retreated again, and was at the open window. Suddenly the intruder was on him, forcing him backward, bending him across the sill. Tram fought desperately, scratching and flailing, but the man was bull strong. A large, calloused hand covered Tram's face and bent him backward. Below him people strolled along a walk, ten floors down where gas lamps lit the street. The man was holding him with one arm. He saw the other reach for the flagpole and unwrap the halyard rope.

"This is for Jim," the intruder said, winding rope around Tram's neck.

"Who are you?" Tram gasped.

"Nobody much," the man said. "Just a squatter." He tied the rope then and pushed the gunman out the window into darkness. It would be morning before anyone noticed him there, hanging from the flagpole on the Butler Building.

It was past midnight when Poling heard a knock at the door of the flat on Centre Street, just off Astor Place, and sent Pasco to answer it. Pasco returned to the back room followed by Winter, dirty and disheveled, holding a bloody cloth to his face.

"What happened to you?" Poling demanded.

"Nothing. It's all right."

"What have you been doing, Winter?"

"Nothing, I said. I was jumped in the street. Thugs. Got my face cut. That's all."

"I paid the man who brought him," Pasco said. "Told him to get rid of his horse and then get lost."

"Winter, if you've done anything to compromise my arrangements . . ." Poling's hand snaked toward the gun in his coat and suddenly Winter's gun was pointing at him. "Ah. I must admit, Winter. You are very good. There's water in the basin over there, and cloth in the cabinet. Take care of that and then we'll talk. You'll need fresh clothing,

343

I suppose. You have bled all over that suit."

Winter put the gun away. "You have something for me to do. Tell me about it."

"Oh, it's your kind of work, Winter. The very thing you are best at. You see, if for any reason Tram or Pasco should fail to kill that old Kiowa chief tomorrow, then it will be up to you."

"Fine. How about if I kill more than one?"

Poling turned away, then glanced back at the gunman, puzzled. Blood was still seeping from the matted cut on his cheek and from a deep gash in his ear. Thugs, he had said. Hoodlums in the street. Vaguely, Poling felt disturbed. There was something he should know but didn't. He shrugged it off.

"Kill as many as you want to," he said coldly. "But do it my way, Winter. Only my way."

Randolph Yeats felt a bit dizzy as the open surrey clattered through dim streets and drew to a halt before a narrow-looking three-story building with lamplight in its lower windows. He was not quite sure what was happening. First James Chrisman had sent for him and turned him over to the man named Kichener. Then Kichener had boosted him aboard a saddled horse for a wild ride along dusk-veiled roads and into the city, where he had again been turned over, this time to the large, untalkative man who waited with the surrey. Then there had been a surrey ride through nameless streets until Yeats was totally lost, and now the large man was helping him down from the surrey with a seeming gentleness that was pure steel beneath its polite surface.

Yeats steadied himself, trying to find his land legs again, and the large man pulled a sheaf of papers from his coat and handed it to him. At a glance, there seemed to be a letter, a document of some sort and some pages of careful notes. But the large man didn't give him time to read. "Put it in your pocket," he said. "You'll need it in a few minutes."

With that he hustled Yeats up a short flight of stairs and knocked on the door of the building.

The man who opened the door was middle-aged, heavy-browed and impatient. He wore garters on his shirtsleeves and had a vest pocket full of pens and crayons.

"Good evening, Mr. Ives," the large man said. "My name is Bliss. This young gentleman is Randolph Yeats."

"I got your message, Mr. Bliss," the gartered one frowned. "I hope this is good, because we're an hour from lockup right now." He looked at Yeats, still blocking the door, not ready to let anyone in. From behind him came sounds of metal on metal and the heady reek of ink. "What do you have for me, Mr. Yeats?"

Yeats' mouth opened in protest, but Mr. Bliss interrupted. "Mr. Yeats has hurried to come here, Mr. Ives. He has his notes and is ready to write, but you will need to give him a place to work. He should have an excellent article for you in a very short time. He has experience with the Chicago *Statesman*."

"I've heard of it," Ives admitted grudgingly. He pierced Yeats with a hostile gaze. "If you can write, why are you working for a sheet like that?"

"It's . . . it's the only job I have," Yeats gulped.

"Well, if you can write, we might be able to correct that situation. But if you've wasted my time, Heaven help you. Come in, then. I'll give you a desk and paper, and you've got an hour to give me reason for having waited for you. Well, come on! Come on!"

Bliss leaned to whisper in his ear, "It's all in the notes, Mr. Yeats. Good luck, and good writing." Then he propelled him through the door and Ives closed it.

"Take the far desk on the right," Ives said. "I'll have a devil stand by to take your copy stick by stick. I don't know if they bother with deadlines in Chicago, but in New York we worry about things like that and you might as well get used to it if you want to work for me."

Yeats goggled at him. "Oh, I will. Yes, sir. Ah, if you don't mind . . . who are you?"

It was the man's turn to be startled. "What do you mean,

who am I? I'm Ives. Phillip Ives. And this is the *New York Times*, and the clock is ticking."

At the 800-plus-acre rectangle of woodland, lake and meadow north of New York City that was being called Central Manhattan Park for lack of a better name, uniformed police officers gaped at the standing teepees of the Kiowa and at the Kiowa themselves while Police Captain J. Ellis Maxey checked some last-minute notes with Chrisman, Holmes, Miles and Lieutenant Spradley.

"I'll tell you just how it is, gentlemen," Maxey said tiredly. "We have a president to guard, a governor to guard, a mayor to guard and keep happy, we have your visiting Indians to guard—despite the fact that His Honor has ordered them paraded the length of Broadway in full view of God and everybody—and we have a few odd jobs to do on the side. There are people running around killing people, people having riots, people setting fires, people selling horsemeat for the price of beef, people committing burglary, assault and battery, malicious mischief and common scold, people drowning, people racing through the streets, people stealing watches, wallets and wives—you name it, we have people here doing it every day of the week. Every uniform, reserve and volunteer I have is assigned tomorrow, and even with these footsoldiers on the route it isn't enough.

"We're going to do our level best to keep every Indian you have alive and well, and we maintain a hope that the scalping of citizens will be held to a minimum. But don't ask miracles of us. If you believe someone is planning to kill chief what's-his-hunts-ever, give us something to go on. Those names you have don't mean anything. Even if they're here, they're tourists. Who knows where tourists go?"

"What about those two buildings Mr. Curtis told us about?" Chrisman asked. "Can you put some men there or something?"

Maxey looked at the addresses again. "We can make a run past. That's about all. I don't understand, though.

What's special about these buildings? They're just build-ings."

Chrisman flushed and glanced at Darby Curtis.

"They don't feel good," Darby said, staring into his hands in the light of lanterns, lost in his own thoughts.

"They what?"

John Miles raised a hand. "Take his word for it, please, Captain. Hawk That Hunts Walking brought Mr. Curtis fifteen hundred miles to read the wind for him. Usually the Blackleg men do that, but the wind here doesn't speak their language. There are too many ghosts."

The policemen stared at those around them, then at one another. Finally Maxey shrugged. "Whatever you say," he said.

Lieutenant Spradley stood, stretched and strolled away across the grass to where Sergeant Foley sat beside a lighted campaign tent. "Get the men up early, Sergeant," he said. "We may need to give the police a little help."

Wrapped in blankets, Hawk That Hunts Walking and Keeps His Horses sat before a tiny fire, watching its embers glow and wane as breezes touched it.

For a long time Keeps His Horses had talked, trying to persuade his chief either to avoid tomorrow's ceremonies in the white man's city or at least to go there in stealth. But Hawk That Hunts Walking would consider neither. He had come a vast distance to meet with the Great Father. He would not back away now, even though they knew there were men who would kill him if they could.

Now for a time they sat in silence. Then Keeps His Horses quivered his rattle, taking courage from its dry rasp that was familiar here where all things were strange. "It is bad here, Respected One," he said. "The white people kill their land. They rend it and smother it and make it bad. It is not like our land at all."

Hawk That Hunts Walking stared into the embers. "We have traveled a long way from our land. We have seen much of the white man's land. But where have we seen a place

347

where a man could stand, where the land is bad on one side and good on the other? There is no place where one land begins and the other ends. These people look toward our land and they see only one land, all the same."

The medicine man shook his head. "These people are like the prairie dog. Where they burrow the land is no good anymore. Snakes and owls might live among them but the buffalo will not go there. Yet who can stop them from burrowing? They are too many."

"We will make treaty with the Great Father," Hawk That Hunts Walking said. "Then maybe for a time the people who come to our land will leave us alone to live as we live. I look around me and I think that is a very good thing to wish for now, in the last days of our people."

The medicine man looked at him. "Why does Hawk That Hunts Walking speak of last days? The Kana'tenee are strong, and all the Ko'a-ywa are brothers. If we must fight all the tribes will stand with us."

"To stand would be to die," the chief breathed. "For those who came before us it was different. Always there were the Ko'a-ywa and among them the Kana'tenee. And always there was the land and the sky. And these things had no end. Now only the sky has no end. The children of the Kana'tenee will see the land change and will have to change with it. I think to make treaty with the Great Father is a good thing now. Maybe it will give the children a few more seasons in which to find other ways."

"What do we know of other ways?" Keeps His Horses shook his rattle again. "The way of the Kana'tenee is as it has always been. How can it be otherwise? Does Hawk That Hunts Walking see new paths?"

The old chief pulled his blanket more tightly about him. "There is Twenty Buffalo. And there is Bull Hump, and Two Knife and Man Far Away. Maybe they can show new paths to the people. Maybe Stalking Horse and the Black-leg men can read the wind and tell them where to look. Our seasons are ending, Keeps His Horses. We are old men now. We have seen one path too long to know how to find others."

"The ways of young men are uncertain," the medicine man said. "They have no answers. They have only questions. Sometimes they are not wise. Would Hawk That Hunts Walking leave the council fire to others?"

"My heart is heavy," the chief said. "I think of the children and I do not know what to do for them except give them a few more seasons. I have no answers either. There have been chiefs before me. There will be others. When this is done here in this place I will move aside. Let the young men look at the people and the land. Their hearts are stronger. They will decide."

For a time the medicine man stared at embers. Then he shrugged. "Then what do you wish, Respected One?"

The old chief's voice was wind through far grass. "I am far away and my heart is heavy. I want to go home. We are old now, you and I. It is our time to move aside and look at the sky."

He straightened and raised his head, then his frail shoulders sagged and he looked again into the embers. A mist had moved in from the sea. Hawk That Hunts Walking could no longer see the sky.

XXXIII

In the dark of morning Darby Curtis opened his eyes, then rolled from his blankets and crawled out of the campaign tent, careful not to disturb the others sleeping there. He pulled on his boots, put on his hat and walked down to the pond where he washed the sleep from his eyes.

Beside a sentries' fire he squatted and helped himself to coffee. Then he found a lantern and left the campsite.

In the meadow beyond the pond, he searched until he found the bay horse. When it shied from his lantern he set the lantern down and approached it from another direction, crooning to the animal as an Indian would, wooing it, getting a hand on its muzzle, blowing in its nostrils. When it was calmed he picked up the lantern and led the bay around the pond to where the gear was stored in wagons.

In minutes he was saddled and ready.

He checked the loads in his rifle and thrust it into a scabbard behind his saddle, then swung aboard and looked around at the sleeping encampment. Sentries tending fires glanced at him and he ignored them. He walked the horse through brush to the south gate, leaned to push its swinging bar aside and went through. A pair of infantrymen approached and he nodded at them in the gloom, then tapped heels to the bay and headed south along the faint, pale roadway as first gray light touched the cold mists of morning.

In shadows behind him a horseman moved, watching, then trotted into the open and pulled up, tall in his saddle, head high to catch the wind. High-roached hair stood in a tall crest on his head, and the feathers of owl and eagle rippled there. Quill vest covered his chest and back, leaving dark arms free to carry lance and shield, free to find and wield toothed warclub. The patterns of paint on his face and shoulders and on the neck and haunches of his mount were intricate, and subtly different from the paints worn by the Blackleg men for ceremony or for travel. Few white men had ever seen the colors he wore now, black lines drawn from temple to temple across cheeks and nose, scarlets and yellows on forehead and lips, white of chalk and oil at eyelids and chin.

Today the Blackleg men would paint for ceremony, for a time of counsel, for fulfillment of mission, for the meeting of their chief with the Great Father.

But Lizard would go his own way today, as a man was free to do. And the paint he wore was not the paint of ceremony. It was the paint of war.

He saw where O'gatedota had gone, and he followed.

Southward on Sixth Avenue Darby rode, letting the bay have its head the first mile or more. He angled across Broadway and continued southward, nostrils twitching at first scent of the spreading city ahead. Another mile and he was into its sprawl, a mile more and he was deep into the old city, trotting paved ways, turning one way and another in his saddle, testing the air, seeing everything, letting instinct guide him. To the northwest, just a short way, was the streetcorner where Trinidad Salazar had died. He looked back that way then continued southward. Another half mile and he bore left past a great, charred area where whole blocks of buildings had burned to leave black skeletons against the pale gray of dawn.

At Broadway he turned south again and lamp-tenders turned to glance at him as he passed, then turned away. At an intersection ahead a milkwagon rolled past. Here and there workmen appeared at doorways and descended to the streets.

At Chambers Street he paused to study the rear facade of the City Hall building, then rode a block further to look along its front. Wide steps led up from a graveled walk to a landing lined with free-standing ionic columns. Above, a portico fronted a taller second story and the columns there were attached and corinthian. Above it stood an attic clock tower and cupola, framed and patched over where a one-time dome had burned. Exterior walls of the first floor were heavy red granite. The walls above were a smoother, lighter stone. Long rows of windows, round-topped and noble, dressed the place in a sense of solid timelessness, of wisdom and age.

Before the building graveled paths wound through a tree-lined park where in a few hours the men of the Kana'tenee would face the leaders of this city and the president of the United States.

Across the park a tree-lined street angled toward Broadway, and beyond it were buildings, some as tall as City Hall. He started that way, then stopped as a premonition tightened his scalp. The wind, he thought. Damned savages have me reading the wind. Yet he hesitated, then wheeled to ride across the park, past the wide center steps of City Hall, and enter the next street above and out of sight of the buildings across the way. A wide car barn sat in a tiny meadow two streets away, its hansoms, surreys and transit carriages already out for the day. He left his horse there, took his rifle and went into the streets on foot.

Behind him a mounted warrior ghosted from a shadowed alley way, unshod hooves of a painted horse soft on city streets. Lizard dismounted in the car barn, turned his horse in to a stall and followed after Darby, staying out of sight. His eyes were black and hard, his senses keen to all around him and his mocassins made no sound. Lance and shield he left tied to his saddle. He carried a stout bow of honeyed bois d'arc and a quiver of fletched arrows with small flint points bound with gut.

With dawn Spradley and half his platoon were at Fifth Avenue and 42nd Street where foundations were being set for a long row of new buildings which would link those clustered at Broadway between Sixth and Eighth with the modest skyline arising at Park Avenue where a second rail terminal was planned. A new city was spreading here, the distant but connected spawn of the city to the south.

The policeman riding with them pointed west. "That's the Butler Building over there. The tallest one. That's the one you're looking for."

They turned west.

"Ten years ago there wasn't a thing up this way but farms," the policeman said. "Now the money's come and more people, and here we go again."

"What do people livin' up that high do if there's a fire?" Tom Pedigo asked him.

He shrugged. "Generally they jump."

Another new building, not as tall but ornate with columns and chiseled stonework, blocked their view as they approached and Mulcahey rode on ahead to see around it. He stared, then he turned his mount and hurried back to them.

"Do these buildings have captains?" he asked the policeman. "Like ships, I mean?"

The policeman frowned at him.

Mulcahey turned to the lieutenant. "Sir, it's like maybe there was a mutiny aboard because I can see a man hanging from a yardarm up there near the top."

In the penthouse, where the remains of Tram hung suspended ten feet away, they found a broken door, a Colt revolver, a buffalo rifle and a clear view of Broadway where the treaty party would pass in less than an hour.

"He was right," Spradley said. "He said this place didn't feel good. Where is that other place he told us about?"

"In town, below 14th." The policeman was staring in disgust at the body hanging from the flagpole. Hauling it in would be a risk of life and limb. It would be better just to cut the rope and then collect what was left below.

In the flat off Astor Place Pasco saw the cavalry coming, saw them looking toward his window, saw them divide to approach from two directions. "Crap," he muttered. Poling had said the place was secure. Poling had been wrong. He wondered how many things Poling had been wrong about.

Quickly he wrapped his rifle in a blanket, picked up his satchel and left, hurrying through hallways and down dark stairs to exit from the rear. A block away he watched from a cartage gate as soldiers and police entered the building he had left. Somewhere downtown Poling and Winter were waiting. Or were they? It occurred to him then that Poling had been acting oddly toward him for a long time. Once he had thought they were partners, after the Merritt Fields thing. But then Poling had changed. Pasco had never known how much money Poling made from the death of Merritt Fields, but he knew what his cut had been and it hadn't lasted very long. Now Poling was wealthy and influential, with strong ties in high politics, and Pasco worked for him.

Then Winter had joined them. Now when Poling chose a man to back him it was Winter. Winter wasn't out here on sniper duty. Winter was downtown with Poling.

A thought struck him. Winter knew nothing about the Merritt Fields business. Winter had come along later. But Pasco knew about Fields, and he knew things about Poling. Suddenly he felt he had been set up. It was just too convenient. Poling had left him here, secure. Then Poling had taken Winter and gone. Now soldiers and police swarmed the flat where he had been.

Poling. Poling was getting rid of him. Getting rid of evidence. Why had there been two sniper points? Tram wouldn't miss. The old Indian probably was already dead, or would be shortly. So why was he here, Pasco thought. To be disposed of? As a diversion? A decoy? More police had come from the street to the building a block away. Pasco felt cold. Poling had decided he was expendable. He was supposed to be dying now, in that building.

Poling had said a hansom would be waiting out back. There was no hansom. Only police and soldiers.

Poling had set him up. Poling was through with him. Now he was supposed to die.

He heard no sound in the cartage way, but when he turned there was a man there in the shadows, a man in a tailored suit and flat-crowned hat, a man whose eyes were

354

cold gray fire.

"Good morning, Mr. Pasco," the man said. "Joseph Fenley would have sent his regards. Unfortunately, Joseph Fenley is dead."

Pasco gaped at him. "Poling . . ." he gasped, then backed away, trying to free the buffalo rifle of its blanket.

"Thank you," the stranger said. "I hoped you might confirm that name."

Pasco dropped satchel and blanket, raised the heavy rifle, and heard shouts from his right. He turned in confusion. Policemen were pointing at him, running toward him. He looked back into the cartage way and there was no one there. He realized he had backed into the middle of the street. They were coming for him. They had guns drawn . . . he raised the rifle and fired. Its roar pounded among the buildings. A policeman somersaulted backward, gore exploding from his spine.

"Damn you, Poling!" Pasco screamed as bullets tore into him, through him, shredding him. The heavy rifle clattered to the pavement. Pasco staggered a step forward, then a step back, and fell across it.

From various parts of the city carriages arrived at City Hall, stately carriages discharging stately people, each wave arriving precisely in accordance with the prescribed choreography that ruled events social and political in New York City. First to arrive were hordes of functionaries to open doors, light lamps and stand at attention. Following them came the minor officeholders, notable tradesmen, the ward workers of Tammany Hall and the Republican Party, journalists and civic personages. In their wake came chief officers of the various city administrations, prominent businessmen and developers, brokers, shippers and bankers. Mayor Oakley Hall and dignitaries from the governor's office in Albany arrived then, followed by Republican notaries in defensive clusters and the Grand Sachem of Tammany Hall, William Tweed.

After moments of waiting interspersed with a spate of

late arrivals, the grand carriages of the Astors rolled into the drive. William Astor himself opened the door for Secretary Seward and President Andrew Johnson.

A few catcalls sounded from the streets, but in the cordoned confines of City Hall Park decorum was better kept. Very few here were fond of Andrew Johnson. But he was the president.

Solidly-built, of medium height and quiet-mannered, Johnson looked around him at the delegation and nodded to one or two. Black hair above a high forehead fell thick to curl around his ears. Deep-set dark eyes and a wide mouth with lines of grim determination gave him an almost Indian appearance, emphasized by the harsh battles he had fought since the death of Lincoln.

"Welcome, Mr. President . . . Mr. Secretary," the mayor bowed slightly. "Your, ah, guests should be here very soon. Would you care to wait inside?"

Beside the path, standing among those other guests who had received special invitation, Mercer Poling smiled to himself. If the guests arrived at all it would be without their chief. He wondered sometimes about Pasco in situations like this, but he had been impressed by the gunman Tram. Tram said he would not miss. Poling felt certain he would not.

The president passed, trailed by a half-dozen party faithful and several traveling companions from Washington.

For an instant Poling caught the eye of Mason McDowell, an assistant undersecretary with the War Department, and nodded. McDowell turned away abruptly and Poling frowned. Something was wrong here. Glancing around he saw Secretary Seward looking at him, a faint smile on his face.

Someone jostled Poling and he turned to look up at a large, somber man standing next to him. The man touched his hat brim and lifted a folded newspaper to hand it to him. It was the latest *New York Times*. "I think you might want to see this, sir," the man said deferentially, then edged away in the crowd.

Poling pursed his lips, scowling. He opened the paper. A

column was marked. Under the byline of one Randolph Yeats, it was reported that the Secretary of War, Edwin Stanton, had withdrawn his support for the creation of a Commission of Public Lands for areas presently beyond the platted and settled areas of the western states and territories. In view of the fact that treaties existed with a number of the plains tribes, and with respect for the attempts of federal authorities to expand such treaties, the secretary said he had reconsidered his position and must, in this one particular, agree with Secretaries Seward and Long. Creation of an agency for settlement of lands bound by treaty might be viewed as a breach of treaty condoned by the government.

Poling read further, and a pallor crept into his face. Stanton! At this moment, now after all his trouble, the bastard was trying to pull the rug from under him. Well, he would not succeed. By now the chief was dead and the Kiowas were as good as at war. Still, it haunted him. Something had happened in Washington—something he could not understand but did not like.

Cheers and applause from up Broadway imposed upon his thoughts, and he turned with everyone else to see what was happening. For a time nothing could be seen from the Park Drive. Then soldiers appeared at the entrance, hustling the crowds back, a unit of uniformed police aligning behind them to open a wide path from the street.

Mounted police rode in, followed by nearly a dozen cavalrymen in dress uniform, column of twos, erect and precise as on a parade ground.

Two carriages came through the gate, the first carrying dark-suited men who moved quickly into prescribed security positions, the second carrying James Chrisman and his party.

Poling's breath caught in his throat. He paled again, grasping the significance of the arrival just as brilliantly-feathered and painted Indians appeared at the gate, red-painted warriors on red-painted mounts, two abreast, stately and grim. They parted, three to a side, and a liveried coach entered the grounds. Poling gasped. In the coach were elderly Indians and a bearded white man in buckskin clothing.

Hawk That Hunts Walking was alive!

The carriage came on, and a long file of multi-colored warriors with tall lances and bright shields followed it, marching their horses with a fine precision more graceful even than the cavalry had shown. Throughout the grounds, people applauded.

Poling felt sick. How could the old man be alive? Even if Tram had missed him, there was still Pasco. Where were they? What had happened? Drawing back in panic, he looked across at the windows of the building across from the park. The windows were closed, and one was broken. His eyes gone wild, gasping in his panic, Poling stood watching his world dissolve.

Distantly, almost drowned by the applause in the park, there was a sound of shooting—several shots in rapid succession, then a pause, then another shot.

XXXIV

Darby had done all he could do for the Kana'tenee. He had never known what they wanted of him, exactly. He didn't know if he had done anything, for sure. But he had "read the wind" for them and done what he could. He had done what he could for everyone. There was one thing more to do before he could go home.

Armed with eyes attuned to the distances of the prairies—to complexities that disguised themselves as sameness—armed with ears that could hear beyond the rustle of grass underfoot—that could hear what was significant above what was constant—armed with senses bred to the western lands and a lore as deep and old as the sod, Darby Curtis went hunting. Somewhere in this tumultuous city blithering at the edge of a continent there was a snake with a gun and he set out to find the snake.

Logic brought him to the heart of the city to begin. Winter did not just happen to be in New York City. Coincidence was not a factor in Darby's experience. If Winter was here it was because Poling was here and because the Indians were here. If Poling was here he would be at City Hall. If he intended to have Hawk That Hunts Walking dead he would set others to do it because that was his way, and he would be at the place where the results could be seen. And where Poling was, Winter would not be far away. Poling the easterner had selected Winter the hillman to be his dark shadow—his constant ace in the hole. He would keep him close at hand when the cards were dealt.

Logic pointed the hunt to City Hall. Instinct told him where to start. Given the terrain, where would a coyote lie in wait for prey? In this precipitous tangle of stone, man-made yet so much like the redland breaks where Darby had hunted sometimes with his father, where would a snake lie in wait. Eyes that knew the prairies looked at and through the city, and saw the likely places.

Across from the park there were buildings. One of those in particular offered a view of the city building, its drives and its park, unobstructed. Poling the city man would have selected it, and Winter the hillman would have approved of it. Uninterrupted view, and easy shooting distance. Winter favored a handgun, but Darby knew he could use a rifle. Any man who had spent time on the prairies could use a rifle.

From a doorway in the dawn Darby studied the terrain and selected routes and paths. For now he saw no build-ings—only mazes of porous stone that formed patterns not unlike the patterns of the breaks. And the stone had eyes like the caves and snake-holes of wind-honed canyons where countless creatures lived. Countless creatures lived in these holes here, as well, and like those out there they lived in a confusion proportional to their number. Snakes and rabbits, prairie dogs and ground squirrles, burrow owls and sage hens and sparrow hawks and quail, all lived a life of eliptical dance determined by the movement of all the other things around them, all fearing the carnivore, the ferret, and all unaware that the ferret was only among them when it came from elsewhere. The ferret did not live in the warrens and the burrows. It came there only to feed.

Bleak humor twitched at his cheeks as he thought of Winter here in this city, Winter rampant in a huge warren that had no defense against his kind. He suspected Winter had found good sport here. Yet in his turn Winter was only a hillman, only a ferret among twitching prey. No ferret was a match for a prairie wolf.

As quickly as the thought came he dismissed it. The ferret was quick, and it had sharp eyes and sharper teeth. To stalk the ferret often was to bleed.

Trini had bled. Poor, crazy little Spaniard, he had bled his life out in a city street a world away from anywhere he had ever called home. He had bled because the ferret had seen Darby—had gone for Darby—and had bit Trini instead.

From the doorway he slipped across to where short trees lined the park, and moved beneath the trees until there was a break above and he could see directly into the pair of windows he had been watching. They were closed, and their glass reflected the light of the morning sky. He studied terrain again, the moved back to where an alley entered from across the street. When a baker's wagon turned from the alley into the street its driver glanced at him, completed his turn and glanced again. There was no one there. Darby was into the alley and running. Halfway along he found a gutterspout that was braced with iron to the stone. With his rifle thrust through the back of his belt he leaped and climbed to emerge on a second-story roof, ran across it to a narrow chasm and jumped to another building, scuttling up its sloping tiles to slide down the other side and swing from its eave to the top of a closed hearse standing there. It was untended.

He hesitated an instant, his eye catching a shadow on the wall opposite, a shadow like a crested head moving above him on the roof he had left. Yet he glanced again and there was nothing.

Across the narrow way he climbed again, to reach the level of the suspect windows. There was a ledge here two feet wide, and he edged along it until he clung beside the first of the uncurtained windows. If his prey was inside, the thing to do was to flush him, get him into the open. He leaned out to risk a glance through the glass. The man inside was standing, turned partly away, but there was white on the right side of his head. Bandage and plasters. Lizard had marked him, and Darby saw the mark.

Returning to the cornice he climbed again, finding handholds in the elaborately carved stone. At the roof's edge he swung over and found himself on tarred timbers directly above Winter's lair.

The question now was, how to get him out, how to bring him into the open. He saw movement again at his level and turned. Thirty yards away on the next roof a Blackleg warrior in full adornment squatted on sloping tiles, watching him. His breath caught in his chest as he saw the patterns of paint on the Indian's face. It was war paint.

Lizard squatted there, gazing at him, waiting. Across the street, beyond the tip of the park, carriages were rolling into the wing drives in front of City Hall and people were gathering. There were crowds, and he looked among them. He saw no one he knew.

What was Lizard doing here . . . what was he doing here with war paint? The answer was obvious. He was doing what Darby was doing. He was hunting a ferret.

Darby pulled the rifle from his belt and stooped at the fasciaed edge of the roof. Clinging with his left hand and knee he eased himself over, his belly against the face of the building. Holding his rifle by its muzzle he swung it downward. Below him, glass shattered. With a heave that left him winded he pulled himself back onto the roof and rolled away from its edge. Below the edge he heard the falling of shards, a quick intake of breath and the muffled clatter of broken glass swept aside. Winter would be leaning out now, looking.

Darby rolled to the edge, bringing his rifle up to shoot downward. In an instant glance he saw the gunman's startled, upturned face below him, and then it was gone from sight. He pressed his ear to the tarred roof planking and thought he heard boots on flooring beneath, as a man running. He listened for boots on stairs, heard nothing and rolled again, coming to his feet. There would be back stairs, and a back entrance.

Across the park was movement and hints of bright color, and he saw six Real Dog warriors in ceremonial paint round the corner from Broadway. In the carriage behind them were Hawk That Hunts Walking, Broken Bow, Keeps His Horses and John Miles. Beyond were Blacklegs.

Darby let out a deep breath. He realized he had worried about the old chief. With a start, he realized he cared.

362

Crouching then, he ran toward the back of the roof.

From near the front, the roof was shed-sloped and the tar was moist from the morning's mist. Darby ran, and at the edge he saw a door opening below him, a dark-coated man coming out. He saw that and he saw that he couldn't stop. His feet slid off into space and he flailed for balance.

He landed on his feet, buckled and rolled, and his rifle flew from his hand. Winter stood just outside the door, and as Darby hit the ground he drew his gun and fired. Brick dust stung Darby's face as he flipped and rolled again, two more shots following him, throwing yellow shards that stung and cut him. Stupid! he raved at himself, a frenzy of violent motion. Flush the ferret and fall in front of him. Stupid! He glimpsed his rifle and flung himself toward it. Solid agony pounded at his thigh and drove him into another roll. Another bullet sang past his ear. He reached for his rifle and lost his momentum. As his hand grasped the cold action he looked around and saw Winter's grin. The target was still now. He lowered his gun, made a mock bow and then methodically began to raise it for the final shot. The gun started upward, then stopped and Winter's eyes and mouth opened wide as a fletched arrow pinned his arm to his side, piercing his body until only bright feathers showed at his sleeve. He arched his body, raised up on tiptoes and his gun discharged into the brick at his feet. The scream that came from him was not human, but it went on and on. Darby brought up his rifle and fired dead center, just to put an end to the scream.

On the wide-stepped portico of City Hall tall columns stood in rows, and the two flanking the double front doors were set with oak wood uprights displaying the carved seal of the Governor of New York on the left and of the President of the United States on the right. The doors were open and as Hawk That Hunts Walking alighted from his coach and walked to the steps followed by his advisors, men came from the interior to line up outward on the portico. Then the Great Father stepped out, hands clasped behind

him, and bent his head in welcome to the chief of the Fa
Grass People.

"Welcome, Hawk That Hunts Walking, to my people'
land," the president said in labored Kiowa that bore th
marks of hard practice.

The old chief looked up at him, gazed at the eyes of a
man whose ghosts were real and whose enemies were too
close and too many, and knew him as a brother. "We ar
honored, Respected One," he said for John Miles to trans
late, "that you turn from the attacks of your enemies t
counsel with your children. It is a difficult thing to do."

As Miles translated, the president's face twitched an
there was a hint of bleak humor there. He nodded. "Tel
the chief," he said, "that I think we know each other ver
well."

Just a few feet to one side now, behind the first rank o
dignitaries and guests, Mercer Poling's face was white, hi
eyes wild. It was too much to accept. Frantically he looke
around, searching the crowd for a sign of Winter. Winte
was his last hope. This must not proceed. The old Indian'
profile burned into his mind, his presence an affront, hi
very existence now unthinkable, unacceptable . . . unten
able.

Someone was at his elbow. He turned and saw a face h
had seen before, a face that somehow haunted him. Gra
hair lay smooth below a flat-crowned hat, framing a fac
that was serene, almost smiling . . . except that the eye
flamed cold like fire through gray ice and drove his tenuou
soul to its knees inside him.

"It has all collapsed, hasn't it, Poling?" Kichener mu
mured for only him to hear. "Everything. You have faile
in everything. You might never have existed at all, Merce
Poling. In fact, maybe you never did."

Poling stared at him, his chin quivering. "No! No, it a
works out . . . only there can be no treaty. They are onl
Indians. Only a few Indians in the way. They can't be i
my way, you see . . ." Blinking furiously, his hands twitc
ing, Poling turned back toward the steps. The old chief wa
climbing them now, reaching to take the hand of th

president.

"No," Poling whispered, now seeing only the old Indian. There was no one else there. Just the old Indian, his profile burning at him like a taunt, an unacceptable affront.

"No!" Poling screamed. From his vest he drew a short revolver and pushed through the crowd, throwing shadows of people aside. "No! Damn you! You have to die!"

Somewhere a woman screamed. Men shouted and clawed at him, but he dodged them, gaining the top of the steps, seeing Indian faces turn toward him. He couldn't tell now which was which, yet there was only one. One Indian in his way. He levelled the pistol at the affronting face . . .

A blur of motion. A whispering ripple of bright color in sunlight. A hollow, echoing thud and a bubbling gasp . . . Mercer Poling, wild-eyed and hollow, hung sagging from an oakwood brace beside a white ionic column. His pistol slipped from nerveless fingers to clatter on the portico. His head drooped slowly to the side as blood frothed from his lips, and still his gazing eyes were fixed on Hawk That Hunts Walking. "No," he tried to whisper. The sound that came from him was a tiny, liquid rattle. He drooped and was still, suspended on the stout shank of a feathered lance planted firmly in the wood frame behind him. The lance was almost eight feet long, festooned with beaver fur, beads and bright feathers, and its end was curved like a shepherd's crook.

In stunned silence people looked at him, some shocked and staring, some turning suddenly away.

"That Indian saved the president's life," someone said, and others echoed the words. "Assassin," they muttered, ". . . tried to assassinate the president . . ." and slowly the eyes turned toward the warrior who was sliding from his horse, handing its reins to another Kiowa.

"That man tried to kill the president. The Indian saved his life . . ."

Stalking Horse spoke then to Hawk That Hunts Walking, and Hawk That Hunts Walking turned to John Miles. "He says that is the man who pulled his hair."

John Miles—Sha'ata'ee of the Kiowa People—stroked

365

his beard and looked at the stunned faces thronging the drive and the park beyond. From the steps he could see the crowd reanimating itself at its edges, beginning to swirl and move, a great beast stunned and beginning to recover. In the street beyond an Indian was coming, moving slowly, supporting the weight of a tall young man who limped on a bloody leg.

James Chrisman stood open-mouthed in the drive, still holding a carriage door. Around him Blackleg warriors, still mounted, sat their ponies and watched the crowd with eyes that missed nothing while Real Dog men moved up to flank their chief.

A moment before, Miles had seen the man named Kichener. He had been just at the foot of the broad steps. Now he was not there . . . or anywhere to be seen.

Sha'ata'ee stroked his beard and whispered to the chief of the Kana'tenee, "I think the white men are happier if they see what they want to see here, Respected One. I think it is better if we do not bother them with private matters now."

TALES OF THE OLD WEST

SPIRIT WARRIOR (1795, $2.50)
by G. Clifton Wisler
The only settler to survive the savage indian attack was a little boy. Although raised as a red man, every man was his enemy when the two worlds clashed — but he vowed no man would be his equal.

IRON HEART (1736, $2.25)
by Walt Denver
Orphaned by an indian raid, Ben vowed he'd never rest until he'd brought death to the Arapahoes. And it wasn't long before they came to fear the rider of vengeance they called . . . Iron Heart.

WEST OF THE CIMARRON (1681, $2.50)
by G. Clifton Wisler
Eric didn't have a chance revenging his father's death against the Dunstan gang until a stranger with a fast draw and a dark past arrived from West of the Cimarron.

HIGH LINE RIDER (1615, $2.50)
by William A. Lucky
In Guffey Creek, you either lived by the rules made by Judge Breen and his hired guns — or you didn't live at all. So when Holly took sides against the Judge, it looked like there would be just one more body for the buzzards. But this time they were wrong.

GUNSIGHT LODE (1497, $2.25)
by Virgil Hart
When Ned Coffee cornered Glass and Corey in a mine shaft, the last thing Glass expected was for the kid to make a play for the gold. And in a blazing three-way shootout, both Corey and Coffee would discover how lightening quick Glass was with a gun.

BOLT

An Adult Western Series by Cort Martin

#10: BAWDY HOUSE SHOWDOWN	(1176, $2.25)
#11: THE LAST BORDELLO	(1224, $2.25)
#12: THE HANGTOWN HARLOTS	(1274, $2.25)
#13: MONTANA MISTRESS	(1316, $2.25)
#14: VIRGINIA CITY VIRGIN	(1360, $2.25)
#15: BORDELLO BACKSHOOTER	(1411, $2.25)
#16: HARDCASE HUSSY	(1513, $2.25)
#17: LONE-STAR STUD	(1632, $2.25)
#18: QUEEN OF HEARTS	(1726, $2.25)
#19: PALOMINO STUD	(1815, $2.25)
#20: SIX-GUNS AND SILK	(1866, $2.25)

Available wherever paperbacks are sold, or order direct from the Publisher. Send cover price plus 50¢ per copy for mailing and handling to Zebra Books, Dept. 1860, 475 Park Avenue South, New York, N.Y. 10016. DO NOT SEND CASH.